THE
FACE

ALSO BY DEAN KOONTZ

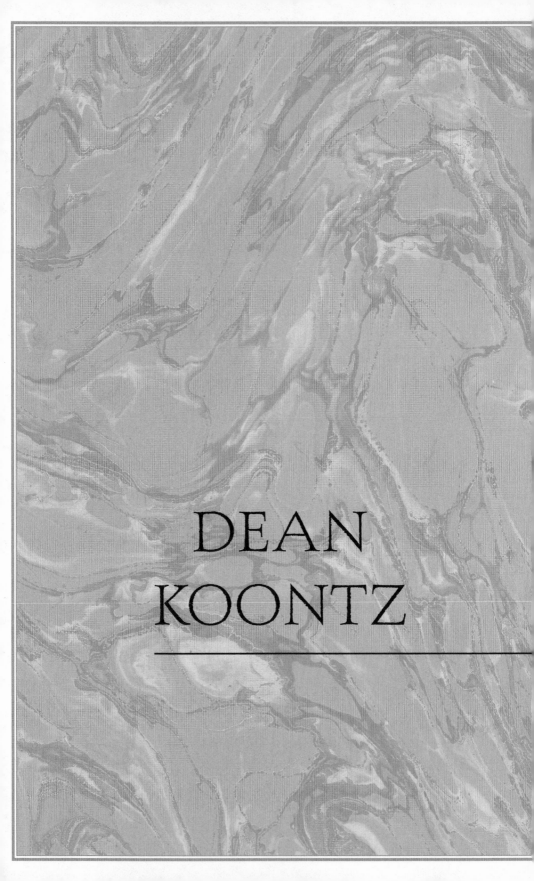

DEAN
KOONTZ

THE
FACE

DOUBLEDAY LARGE PRINT HOME LIBRARY EDITION

Bantam Books

This Large Print Edition, prepared especially
for Doubleday Large Print Home Library,
contains the complete, unabridged text
of the original Publisher's Edition.

THE FACE
A Bantam Book

Published by Bantam Dell
A Division of Random House, Inc.
New York, New York

ISBN 0-7394-3462-4

Manufactured in the United States of America
Published simultaneously in Canada

This Large Print Book carries the
Seal of Approval of N.A.V.H.

This book is dedicated to three exceptional men—and to their wives, who have worked so very hard to sculpt them from such rough clay. From the ground up: To Leason and Marlene Pomeroy, to Mike and Edie Martin, and to Jose and Rachel Perez. After The Project, I will not be able to get up in the morning, spend a moment at home during the day, or go to bed at night without thinking of you. I guess I'll just have to live with that.

The civilized human spirit . . . cannot get rid of a feeling of the uncanny.

—*Doctor Faustus,* Thomas Mann

THE
FACE

CHAPTER 1

After the apple had been cut in half, the halves had been sewn together with coarse black thread.

Ten bold stitches were uniformly spaced. Each knot had been tied with a surgeon's precision.

The variety of apple, a red delicious, might have significance. Considering that these messages had been delivered in the form of objects and images, never in words, every detail might refine the sender's meaning, as adjectives and punctuation refined prose.

More likely, however, this apple had been selected because it wasn't ripe. Softer flesh would have crumbled even if the needle had been used with care and if each stitch had been gently cinched.

Awaiting further examination, the apple stood on the desk in Ethan Truman's study. The black box in which the apple had been packed also stood on the desk, bristling with shredded black tissue paper. The box had already yielded what clues it contained: none.

Here in the west wing of the mansion, Ethan's ground-floor apartment was comprised of this study, a bedroom, a bathroom, and a kitchen. Tall French windows provided a clear view of nothing real.

The previous occupant would have called the study a living room and would have furnished the space accordingly. Ethan did too little living to devote an entire room to it.

With a digital camera, he had photographed the black box before opening it. He had also taken shots of the red delicious from three angles.

He assumed that the apple had been sliced open in order to allow for the insertion of an object into the core. He was reluctant to snip the stitches and to take a look at what might lie within.

Years as a homicide detective had hardened him in some respects. In other ways, too much experience of extreme violence had made him vulnerable.

He was only thirty-seven, but his police career was over. His instincts remained sharp, however, and his darkest expectations were undiminished.

A sough of wind insisted at the French panes. A soft tapping of blown rain.

The languid storm gave him excuse enough to leave the apple waiting and to step to the nearest window.

Frames, jambs, rails, muntins—every feature of every window in the great house had been crafted in bronze. Exposure to the elements promoted a handsome mottled-green patina on exterior surfaces. Inside, diligent maintenance kept the bronze a dark ruby-brown.

The glass in each pane was beveled at every edge. Even in the humblest of service rooms—the scullery, the ground-floor laundry—beveling had been specified.

Although the residence had been built for a film mogul during the last years of the Great Depression, no evidence of a construction budget could be seen anywhere from the entrance foyer to the farthest corner of the last back hall.

When steel sagged, when clothes grew moth-eaten on haberdashery racks, when cars rusted on showroom floors for want of customers, the film industry nevertheless flourished. In bad times as in good, the only two absolute necessities were food and illusions.

From the tall study windows, the view appeared to be a painting of the kind employed in motion-picture matte shots: an exquisitely rendered dimensional scene that, through the deceiving eye of the camera, could serve convincingly as a landscape on an alien planet or as a place on this world perfected as reality never allowed.

Greener than Eden's fields, acres of lawn rolled away from the house, without one weed or blade of blight. The majestic crowns of immense California live oaks and the drooping boughs of melancholy deodar cedars, each a classic specimen, were silvered and diamonded by the December drizzle.

Through skeins of rain as fine as angel hair,

Ethan could see, in the distance, the final curve of the driveway. The gray-green quartzite cobblestones, polished to a sterling standard by the rain, led to the ornamental bronze gate in the estate wall.

During the night, the unwanted visitor had approached the gate on foot. Perhaps suspecting that this barrier had been retrofitted with modern security equipment and that the weight of a climber would trigger an alarm in a monitoring station, he'd slung the package over the high scrolled crest of the gate, onto the driveway.

The box containing the apple had been cushioned by bubble wrap and then sealed in a white plastic bag to protect it further from foul weather. A red gift bow, stapled to the bag, ensured that the contents would not be mistaken for garbage.

Dave Ladman, one of two guards on the graveyard shift, retrieved the delivery at 3:56 A.M. Handling the bag with care, he had carried it to the security office in the groundskeeper's building at the back of the estate.

Dave and his shift partner, Tom Mack, x-rayed the package with a fluoroscope. They were looking for wires and other metal components of an explosive device or a spring-loaded killing machine.

These days, some bombs could be constructed with no metal parts. Consequently, following fluoroscopy, Dave and Tom employed a trace-scent analyzer capable of recognizing thirty-two explosive compounds from as few as three signature molecules per cubic centimeter of air.

When the package proved clean, the guards unwrapped it. Upon discovering the black gift box, they had left a message on Ethan's voice mail and had set the delivery aside for his attention.

At 8:35 this morning, one of the two guards on the early shift, Benny Nguyen, had brought the box to Ethan's apartment in the main house. Benny also arrived with a videocassette containing pertinent segments of tape from perimeter cameras that captured the delivery.

In addition, he offered a traditional Vietnamese clay cooking pot full of his mother's *com tay cam,* a chicken-and-rice dish of which Ethan was fond.

"Mom's been reading candle drippings again," Benny said. "She lit a candle in your name, read it, says you need to be fortified."

"For what? The most strenuous thing I do these days is get up in the morning."

"She didn't say for what. But not just for Christmas shopping. She had that temple-dragon look when she talked about it."

"The one that makes pit bulls bare their bellies?"

"That one. She said you need to eat well, say prayers without fail each morning and night, and avoid drinking strong spirits."

"One problem. Drinking strong spirits is how I pray."

"I'll just tell Mom you poured your whiskey down the drain, and when I left, you were on your knees thanking God for making chickens so she could cook *com tay cam.*"

"Never knew your mom to take no for an answer," Ethan said.

Benny smiled. "She won't take yes for an answer, either. She doesn't expect an answer at all. Only dutiful obedience."

Now, an hour later, Ethan stood at a window, gazing at the thin rain, like threads of seed pearls, accessorizing the hills of Bel Air.

Watching weather clarified his thinking.

Sometimes only nature felt real, while all human monuments and actions seemed to be the settings and the plots of dreams.

From his uniform days through his plainclothes career, friends on the force had said that he did *too much* thinking. Some of them were dead.

The apple had come in the sixth black box received in ten days. The contents of the previous five had been disturbing.

Courses in criminal psychology, combined with years of street experience, made Ethan hard to impress in matters regarding the human capacity for evil. Yet these gifts provoked his deep concern.

In recent years, influenced by the operatically flamboyant villains in films, every common gangbanger and every would-be serial killer, starring in his own mind movie, could not simply do his dirty work and move along. Most seemed to be obsessed with developing a dramatic persona, colorful crime-scene signatures, and ingenious taunts either to torment their victims beforehand or, after a murder, to scoff at the claimed competence of law-enforcement agencies.

Their sources of inspiration, however, were all hackneyed. They succeeded only in making fearsome acts of cruelty seem as tiresome as the antics of an unfunny clown.

The sender of the black boxes succeeded where others failed. For one thing, his wordless threats were inventive.

When his intentions were at last known and the threats could be better understood in light of whatever actions he took, they might also prove to be clever. Even fiendishly so.

In addition, he conferred on himself no silly or clumsy name to delight the tabloid press when eventually they became aware of his game. He signed no name at all, which indicated self-assurance and no desperate desire for celebrity.

For another thing, his target was the biggest movie star in the world, perhaps the most guarded man in the nation after the President of the United States. Yet instead of stalking in secret, he revealed his intentions in wordless riddles full of menace, ensuring that his quarry would be made even more difficult to reach than usual.

Having turned the apple over and over in his mind, examining the details of its packaging and presentation, Ethan fetched a pair of cuticle scissors from the bathroom. At last he returned to the desk.

He pulled the chair from the knee space. He sat, pushed aside the empty gift box, and placed the repaired apple at the center of the blotter.

The first five black boxes, each a different size,

and their contents had been examined for finger-prints. He had dusted three of the deliveries him-self, without success.

Because the black boxes came without a word of explanation, the authorities would not consider them to be death threats. As long as the sender's intention remained open to debate, this failed to be a matter for the police.

Deliveries 4 and 5 had been trusted to an old friend in the print lab of the Scientific Investigation Division of the Los Angeles Police Department, who processed them off the record. They were placed in a glass tank and subjected to a cloud of cyanoacrylate fumes, which readily condensed as a resin on the oils that formed latent prints.

In fluorescent light, no friction-ridge patterns of white resin had been visible. Likewise, in a dark-ened lab, with a cone-shaded halogen lamp fo-cused at oblique angles, the boxes and their con-tents continued to appear clean.

Black magnetic powder, applied with a Magna-Brush, had revealed nothing. Even bathed in a methanol solution of rhodamine 6G, scanned in a dark lab with the eerie beam from a water-cooled argon ion laser generator, the objects had revealed no telltale luminous whorls.

The nameless stalker was too careful to leave such evidence.

Nevertheless, Ethan handled this sixth delivery with the care he'd exhibited while examining the five previous items. Surely no prints existed to be spoiled, but he might want to check later.

With the cuticle scissors, he snipped seven stitches, leaving the final three to serve as hinges.

The sender must have treated the apple with lemon juice or with another common culinary preservative to ensure a proper presentation. The meat was mostly white, with only minor browning near the peel.

The core remained. The seed pocket had been scooped clean of pits, however, to provide a setting for the inserted item.

Ethan had expected a worm: earthworm, corn earworm, cutworm, leech, caterpillar, trematode, one type of worm or another.

Instead, nestled in the apple flesh, he found an eye.

For an ugly instant, he thought the eye might be real. Then he saw that it was only a plastic orb with convincing details.

Not an orb, actually, but a hemisphere. The back of the eye proved to be flat, with a button loop.

Somewhere a half-blinded doll still smiled.

When the stalker looked at the doll, perhaps he saw the famous object of his obsession likewise mutilated.

Ethan was nearly as disturbed by this discovery as he might have been if he'd found a real eye in the red delicious.

Under the eye, in the hollowed-out seed pocket, was a tightly folded slip of paper, slightly damp with absorbed juice. When he unfolded it, he saw typing, the first direct message in the six packages:

THE EYE IN THE APPLE? THE WATCHFUL WORM? THE WORM OF ORIGINAL SIN? DO WORDS HAVE ANY PURPOSE OTHER THAN CONFUSION?

Ethan was confused, all right. Whatever it meant, this threat—the eye in the apple—struck him as particularly vicious. Here the sender had made an angry if enigmatic statement, the symbolism of which must be correctly interpreted, and urgently.

CHAPTER 2

Beyond the beveled glass, the iron-black clouds that had masked the sky now hid themselves behind gray veils of trailing mist. The wind went elsewhere with its lamentations, and the sodden trees stood as still and solemn as witnesses to a funeral cortege.

The gray day drifted into the eye of the storm, and from each of his three study windows, Ethan observed the mourning weather while meditating on the meaning of the apple in the context of the five bizarre items that had preceded it. Nature peered back at him through a milky cataract and, in sympathy with his inner vision, remained clouded.

He supposed the shiny apple might represent fame and wealth, the enviable life of his employer. Then the doll's eye might be a worm of sorts, a symbol of a particular corruption at the core of fame, and therefore an accusation, indictment, and condemnation of the Face.

For twelve years, the actor had been the biggest

box-office draw in the world. Since his first hit, the celebrity-mad media referred to him as the Face.

This flattering sobriquet supposedly had arisen simultaneously from the pens of numerous entertainment reporters in a shared swoon of admiration for his charismatic good looks. In truth, no doubt a clever and perpetually sleepless publicist had called in favors and paid out cold cash to engineer this spontaneous acclamation and then to sustain it for more than a decade.

In a black-and-white Hollywood so distant in time and quality that contemporary moviegoers had only a little more knowledge of it than they had of the Spanish-American War, a fine actress named Greta Garbo had in her day been known as the Face. That flattery had been the work of a studio flack, but Garbo had proved to be more than mere flackery.

For ten months, Ethan had been chief of security for Channing Manheim, the Face of the new millennium. As yet he hadn't glimpsed even the suggestion of Garboesque depths. The face of the Face seemed to be nearly all there was of Channing.

Ethan didn't despise the actor. The Face was affable, as relaxed as might be a genuine demigod living with the sureness that life and youth were for him eternal.

The star's indifference to any circumstances other than his own arose neither from self-absorption nor from a willful lack of compassion. Intellectual limitations denied him an awareness that other people had more than a single script page of backstory, and that their character arcs were too complex to be portrayed in ninety-eight minutes.

His occasional cruelties were never conscious.

If he hadn't been who he was, however, and if he hadn't been so striking in appearance, nothing that Channing said or did would have left an impression. In a Hollywood deli that named sandwiches after stars, Clark Gable might have been roast beef and Liederkranz on rye with horseradish; Cary Grant might have been peppered chicken breast with Swiss cheese on whole wheat with mustard; and Channing Manheim would have been watercress on lightly buttered toast.

Ethan didn't actively dislike his employer, and he didn't need to like him in order to want to protect him and keep him alive.

If the eye in the apple was a symbol of corruption, it might represent the star's ego inside the beautiful fruit.

Perhaps the doll's eye didn't stand for corruption, but for the downside of fame. A celebrity of Channing's magnitude enjoyed little privacy and was always under scrutiny. The eye in the apple might be symbolic of the stalker's eye—always watching, judging.

Crap. Cheap analysis. For all his somber brooding, in weather conducive to contemplation and to dark speculation, Ethan's every observation seemed obvious and useless.

He ruminated on the apple-damp words: THE EYE IN THE APPLE? THE WATCHFUL WORM? THE WORM OF

ORIGINAL SIN? DO WORDS HAVE ANY PURPOSE OTHER
THAN CONFUSION?

Stumped, he was grateful when the phone rang
at a few minutes past ten o'clock, drawing him
away from the windows and to the desk.

Laura Moonves, an old friend from the LAPD,
had been tracking down a license-plate number
for him. She worked out of the Detective Support
Division. Only once before in the past year had he
presumed upon their friendship in this way.

"Got your pervert," Laura said.

"Suspected pervert," he corrected.

"The three-year-old Honda is registered to Rolf
Herman Reynerd in West Hollywood." She spelled
each name and gave him an address.

"What kind of parents *Rolf* a kid?"

Laura knew all about names. "It's not so bad.
Nicely masculine, in fact. In Old German, it means
'famous wolf.' Ethan, of course, means 'permanent, assured.' "

Two years ago, they'd dated. For Laura, Ethan had
been anything but permanent, assured. She'd have
liked permanence, some assurance. He had been
too wounded to provide what she wanted. Or too
stupid.

"Looked him up for a rap sheet," Laura said, "but
he's clean. DMV says 'hair brown, eyes blue.' Says
'sex male.' I like sex male. I don't get enough sex
male. Height six-one, weight one-eighty. DOB—
June sixth, nineteen seventy-two, which makes
him thirty-one."

Ethan had it all on a notepad. "Thanks, Laura. I owe you one."

"So then tell me—how big's his charlie?"

"Isn't that in the DMV file?"

"I don't mean Rolf's charlie. I mean Manheim's. Does it hang to his ankles or just to his knees?"

"I've never seen his charlie, but he doesn't seem to have any trouble walking."

"Cookie, maybe you can introduce us sometime."

Ethan had never known why she called him Cookie. "The man would bore your ass off, Laura, and that's the truth."

"Pretty as he is, I wouldn't need conversation. I'd just shove a rag in his mouth, tape his lips shut, and off we'd go to paradise."

"Basically it's my job to keep people like you away from him."

"Truman derives from two Old English words," she said. "It means 'steadfast, loyal, trustworthy, constant.' "

"You can't get a date with the Face by making me feel guilty. Besides, when wasn't I loyal and trustworthy?"

"Cookie, two out of four doesn't mean you deserve your name."

"You were too good for me anyway, Laura. You've got more to give than a shlump like me can appreciate."

"I'd like to see your old Ten Card," she said, referring to his record of service on the force. "Must be more brown stars for ass kissing on that baby than any hundred other cards in the history of the job."

"If you're done dissing me, I've been wondering. . . . Rolf. Famous wolf. Does that make sense? What's a wolf have to do to get famous?"

"Kill a lot of sheep, I guess."

By the time Ethan said good-bye to Laura, a thin rain had begun to fall again. Without the ardor of a wind, the droplets barely kissed the study windows.

Using the remote control, he switched on the TV and then the VCR. The tape was already loaded. He'd watched it six times before.

Exterior security cameras throughout the estate numbered eighty-six. Every house door and window and all the approaches across the grounds were monitored.

Only the north wall of the estate abutted public property. This long rampart, including the gate, was under surveillance by cameras mounted in the trees on the land directly across the street, a parcel also owned by Channing Manheim.

Anyone reconnoitering the front-wall security, the operation of the gate, and the protocols of visitor identification would detect no cameras on the public side or in the estate trees that overhung the wall. They would assume that surveillance could be conducted solely from within the property.

Meanwhile, they would be watched by the cameras on the farther side of the narrow Bel Air byway, barely two lanes wide, which lacked side-walks and streetlamps. A zoom shot would pro-vide a clear ID to help ensure a conviction if the subject proceeded from reconnoitering to any act of criminal intent.

The cameras operated 24/7. From the security of-fice in the groundskeeper's building and from sev-eral points in the house, any videocam in the sys-tem could be accessed if you knew the command.

Several televisions in the house and a bank of six in the security office could receive the video feed from any camera. One TV could display as many as four views simultaneously in quarter-screen for-mat. Therefore, the security team was able to study images from as many as twenty-four cam-eras at any one time.

Mostly, the guards drank coffee and bullshitted each other. If an alarm was triggered, however, they could have an immediate, close look at what-ever corner of the estate had been violated. Cam-era by camera, they would be able to track an in-truder as he moved from one field of view into another.

From the security-office keyboard, a guard could direct the video feed from any of the eighty-six sources to a VCR. The system included twelve VCRs capable of simultaneously recording forty-eight feeds in quarter-screen format.

Even if a guard were not paying attention, motion detectors associated with each camera would in-stigate automatic recording of that field of vision when any living thing larger than a dog passed through its area of responsibility.

At 3:32 A.M. the previous night, motion detectors related to Camera 01, which ceaselessly panned the western end of the north perimeter, picked up a three-year-old Honda. Instead of passing by as the infrequent other traffic had done throughout the night, the car pulled off the pavement and parked a hundred yards short of the entrance gate.

The previous five black boxes had come by Federal Express with fake return addresses. Here Ethan had been presented with the first opportunity to identify the sender.

Now, less than seven hours later, he stood in his study and watched the Honda in full-screen format. The narrow shoulder of the road prevented the driver from parking the car entirely out of the eastbound lane.

In daylight, the exclusive streets of Bel Air didn't carry a heavy load of traffic. At that late hour, they were hardly traveled.

Nevertheless concerned about safety, the driver of the Honda didn't kill his headlights when he parked. He left the engine running and switched on his emergency blinkers.

The camera, featuring advanced night-vision technology, provided a high-resolution picture in spite of the darkness and foul weather.

For a moment, Camera 01 continued panning away from the Honda—then halted its programmed sweep and returned to the car. Dave Ladman had been on a routine foot patrol of the estate grounds at that time. Tom Mack, manning the security office, had recognized the presence of a suspicious vehicle and had overridden 01's automatic function.

Rain had been falling heavily. Ceaseless barrages of raindrops shattered against the blacktop with force, creating such a froth and dancing spray that the street appeared to be aboil.

The driver's door opened, and Camera 01 zoomed in for a close-up as a tall, solidly built man got out of the car. He wore a black waterproof windbreaker. His face was hidden in the shadow of a hood.

Unless Rolf Reynerd had loaned his car to a friend, this was the famous wolf. He fit the physical profile on Reynerd's license.

He closed the driver's door, opened the rear door, and took a large white ball from the backseat. This appeared to be the garbage bag containing the gift of the sutured apple.

Reynerd closed the door and started toward the front of the car, toward the driveway gate a hundred yards away. Abruptly he halted and turned to peer along the dark rain-swept lane, poised for flight.

Perhaps he thought that he'd heard an approaching engine above the rushing rustle of the rain racing down through the trees. The security tape provided no sound.

At that lonely hour, if another vehicle *had* arrived on the scene, chances were good that it would have been a cruiser belonging to the Bel Air Patrol, the private-security force that assisted in the policing of this extremely wealthy community.

When neither a cruiser nor a less-official vehicle appeared, the hooded man regained his confidence. He hurried eastward to the gate.

Camera 02 followed him as he stepped beyond the panning arc of Camera 01. As he neared the gate, Camera 03 watched him from across the street, zooming in for an intimate appraisal.

Immediately upon arrival at the entrance gate, Reynerd threw the white bag toward the top of that bronze barrier. Failing to clear the highest scrollwork, the package bounced back at him.

On his second attempt, he succeeded. When he turned away from the gate, his hood slipped half off, and Camera 03 captured a clear image of his face in the glow of the flanking gate lamps.

He had the chiseled features needed to be a successful waiter in the trendiest of L.A. restaurants, where both the service staff and the customers enjoyed the fantasy that any guy or gal ferrying plates of overpriced swordfish from kitchen to table during the Tuesday dinner shift might be offered, on Wednesday, a coveted role in Tom Cruise's next hundred-fifty-million-dollar picture.

Turning from the gate, having delivered the apple, Rolf Reynerd was grinning.

Perhaps if Ethan hadn't known the meaning of the man's first name, the grin wouldn't have seemed wolfish. Then he might have been reminded instead of a crocodile or a hyena.

In any case, this was not the merry expression of

a prankster. Captured on videotape, this curve of lips and bared teeth suggested a lunatic glee that required a full moon and medication.

Splashing through black puddles filigreed with silver by the headlights, Reynerd returned to the car.

As the Honda pulled off the shoulder and onto the eastbound lane once more, Camera 01 executed a swivel and zoom, then Camera 02. Both delivered readable shots of the rear license plate.

Dwindling into the night, the car conjured briefly lingering ghosts from its tailpipe.

Then the narrow street lay deserted, in wet gloom except for the lamps at the Manheim gate. Black rain, as if from a dissolving night sky, poured down, poured down, driving the darkness of the universe into the universally coveted Bel Air real estate.

Before leaving his quarters in the west wing, Ethan called the housekeeper, Mrs. McBee, to report that he'd be out most of the day.

More efficient than any machine, more dependable than the laws of physics, as trustworthy as any archangel, Mrs. McBee would within minutes dispatch one of the six maids under her command to Ethan's apartment. Seven days a week, a maid collected the trash and provided fresh towels. Twice weekly, his rooms were dusted, vacuumed, and left immaculate. Windows were washed twice a month.

agreed with it in such a charming fashion that he seemed both erudite and every bit a kindred spirit.

As Ethan slid *Lord Jim* onto a shelf between two other Conrad titles, a small reedy voice behind him said, "Is there magic in it?"

Turning, he discovered ten-year-old Aelfric Manheim all but swallowed alive by one of the larger armchairs.

According to Laura Moonves, Aelfric (pronounced *elf-rick*) was an Old English word meaning "elf-ruled" or "ruled by elves," which had first been used to describe wise and clever actions, but had in time come to refer to those who acted wisely and cleverly.

Aelfric.

The boy's mother—Fredericka "Freddie" Nielander—a supermodel who had married and divorced the Face all in one year, had read at least three books in her life. *The Lord of the Rings* trilogy. In fact she had read them repeatedly.

She had been prepared to name the boy Frodo. Fortunately, or not, one month before Freddie's due date, her best girlfriend, an actress, had discovered the name Aelfric in the script for a cheesy fantasy film in which she had agreed to play a three-breasted Amazon alchemist.

If Freddie's friend had landed a supporting role in *The Silence of the Lambs,* Aelfric would probably now be Hannibal Manheim.

The boy preferred to be called Fric, and no one but his mother insisted on using his full name. Fortunately, or not, she wasn't around much to torture him with it.

Reliable scuttlebutt had it that Freddie had not seen Fric in over seventeen months. Even the career of an aging supermodel could be demanding.

"Is there magic in what?" Ethan asked.

"That book you just put away."

"Magic of a sort, but probably not the kind of magic you mean."

"This one has a shitload of magic in it," Fric said, displaying a paperback with dragons and wizards on the cover.

"Is that advisable language for a wise and clever person?" Ethan asked.

"Heck, all my old man's friends in the biz talk worse stuff than *shitload*. So does my old man."

"Not when he knows you're around."

Fric cocked his head. "Are you calling my dad a hypocrite?"

"If I ever call your dad such a thing, I'll cut my tongue out."

"The evil wizard in this book would use it in a potion. One of his most difficult tasks is to find the tongue of an honest man."

"What makes you think I'm honest?"

"Get real. You've got a triple shitload of honesty."

"What're you going to do if Mrs. McBee hears you using words like that?"

"She's somewhere else."

"Oh, she is?" Ethan asked, suggesting that he knew something regarding Mrs. McBee's current whereabouts that would make the boy wish he'd been more discreet.

Unable to repress a guilty expression, Fric sat up straight and surveyed the library.

The boy was small for his age, and thin. At times, glimpsed from a distance as he walked along one of the vast halls or across a room scaled for kings and their entourages, he seemed almost wispy.

"I think she has secret passages," Fric whispered. "You know, pathways in the walls."

"Mrs. McBee?"

The boy nodded. "We've lived here six years, but she's been here *forever*."

Mrs. McBee and Mr. McBee—both in their middle fifties—had been employed by the previous owner of the property and had stayed on at the request of the Face.

"It's hard to picture Mrs. McBee skulking about in the walls," said Ethan. "She's not exactly a dastardly sort."

"But if she *was* dastardly," Fric said hopefully, "things would be more interesting around here."

Unlike his father's golden locks, which with a shake of the head always fell perfectly into place, Fric's brown mop achieved perpetual disarray. Here was hair that foiled brushes and broke good combs.

Fric might grow into his looks and prove equal to his pedigree, but currently he appeared to be an average ten-year-old boy.

"Why aren't you in class?" Ethan wondered.

"You an atheist or something? Don't you know

it's the week before Christmas? Even home-schooled Hollywood brats get a break."

A cadre of tutors visited five days a week. The private school that Fric attended for a while had not proved to be a suitable environment for him.

With the famous Channing Manheim for a father, with the famous and *notorious* Freddie Nielander for a mother, Fric became an object of envy and ridicule even among the children of other celebrities. Being the skinny son of a buffed star adored for heroic roles also made him a figure of fun to crueler kids. The severity of his asthma further argued for schooling at home, in a controlled environment.

"Have any idea what you'll get Christmas morning?" Ethan asked.

"Yeah. I had to submit my list to Mrs. McBee by December fifth. I told her not to bother wrapping the stuff, but she will. She always does. She says it's not Christmas morning without *some* mystery."

"I'd have to agree with that."

The boy shrugged, and slumped in his chair again.

Although the Face was currently on location for a film, he would return from Florida the day before Christmas.

"It'll be good to have your dad home for the holidays. You guys have any special plans once he gets back?"

The boy shrugged again, attempting to convey lack of knowledge or indifference, but instead—

almost certainly would be alerted by someone. Thereafter, he would grow too wary to be approached directly.

Ethan preferred to start with the man himself and work outward from that initial contact.

He closed his eyes, tipped his head back against the headrest, and brooded about how to proceed.

The engine roar of an approaching car grew so loud that Ethan opened his eyes, half expecting to hear a sudden siren and to see a police chase in progress. Traveling far too fast for a residential street, a cherry-red Ferrari Testarossa exploded past, as though the driver were in fact hoping to run down a darting child or an old lady slowed by orthopedic shoes and a cane.

A tire-thrown plume spewed up from the puddled street, drenching the Expedition. The glass in the driver's door briefly clouded with ripples of dirty water.

Across the street, the apartment house appeared to shimmer as if it were a place in a dream. Some aspect of that transient distortion seemed to trigger a vague memory of a long-forgotten nightmare, and the sight of the building in this warped condition caused the hairs to rise inexplicably on the back of Ethan's neck.

Then the last gouts of the plume drained off the window. Falling rain quickly cleared the murky residue from the glass. The apartment house was nothing more than what it had been when he'd first seen it: a nice place to live.

After judging that the rain was falling only hard

enough to make an umbrella more trouble than it was worth, he got out of the SUV and dashed across the street.

In southern California during the late autumn and early winter, Mother Nature suffered unpredictable mood swings. From one year to the next, and even from day to day in the same year, the week before Christmas could vary from balmy to bone-chilling. This air was cool, the rain colder than the air, and the sky as dead gray as it might have been in any truly wintry clime much farther north.

The main door of the building featured no buzz-through security lock. The neighborhood remained safe enough that apartment lobbies did not ab-solutely require fortification.

Dripping, he entered a small space, less a lobby than a foyer, with a Mexican-tile floor. An elevator and a set of stairs served the upper stories.

The foyer air curdled with the lingering meaty scent of Canadian bacon, cooked hours ago, and the musty smell of stale pot smoke. Weed had a singular aroma. Someone had stood here this morning, finishing a joint, before stepping out to meet the dreary day.

From the bank of mailboxes, Ethan counted four apartments on the ground floor, six on the second, and six on the third. Reynerd lived in the middle of the building, in 2B.

Only the last names of the current tenants were printed on the mailboxes. Ethan needed more in-formation than these stick-on labels provided.

An open communal receptacle, recessed in the

wall, had been provided for magazines and other publications on those occasions when the volume of other mail didn't permit the postman to put all items in the boxes.

Two magazines lay in the tray. Both were for George Keesner in Apartment 2E.

Ethan rapped a knuckle against the aluminum doors on several of the mailboxes for the apartments in which he had no interest. The hollow sound suggested they were empty. Most likely the daily mail had not yet been delivered.

When he rapped on Keesner's box, it sounded as though it was packed full of mail. Evidently the man had been away from home for at least a couple days.

Ethan climbed the stairs to the second floor. One long hall, three doors on each side. At 2E, he rang the bell and waited.

Reynerd's unit, 2B, lay directly across from 2E.

When no one answered the bell at Keesner's apartment, Ethan rang it again, twice. After a pause, he knocked loudly.

Each door had been fitted with a fisheye lens to allow the resident to examine a caller before deciding whether or not to admit him. Perhaps from across the hall, Reynerd was watching the back of Ethan's head right now.

Receiving no response to his knock, Ethan turned away from Keesner's door and made a show of frustration. He wiped his rain-wet face with one hand. He pushed that hand through his damp hair. He shook his head. He looked up and down the hall.

When Ethan rang the bell at 2B, the apple man answered almost at once, without the protection of a security chain.

Although an unmistakable match for the image captured by the security camera, he proved to be more handsome than he'd been in the rain the previous night. He resembled Ben Affleck, the actor.

In addition to the Affleck aspect, however, he had a welcome-to-the-Bates-Motel edge to him that any fan of Anthony Perkins would have recognized. The tightness at the corners of his mouth, the rapid pulse visible in his right temple, and especially the hard shine in his eyes suggested that he might be on methamphetamine, not fully amped but clipping along at high altitude.

"Sir," Ethan said even as the door was still opening, "I'm sorry to bother you, but I'm sort of desperate to get in touch with George Keesner over there in 2E. Do you know George?"

Reynerd shook his head. He had a bull's neck. Lots of time spent on weight machines at the gym.

"I know him to say hello in the hall," Reynerd said, "and how's the weather. That's all."

If that was true, Ethan felt secure enough to say, "I'm his brother. Name's Ricky Keesner."

That scam ought to work as long as Keesner was somewhere between twenty and fifty years old.

"Our Uncle Harry's on his deathbed in the ICU," Ethan lied. "Not going to hold on much longer. Since yesterday morning, I been calling George at every number I've got for him. He doesn't get back to me. Doesn't answer the door now."

"I think he's away," said Reynerd.

"Away? He didn't say anything about it to me. You know where he might've gone?"

Reynerd shook his head. "He was going out with a little suitcase the night before last, as I was coming in."

"He tell you when he'd be back?"

"We just said how it looked like rain coming, and then he went out," Reynerd replied.

"Man, he's so close to Uncle Harry—we both are—he's going to be upset he didn't get a chance to say good-bye. Maybe I could leave him a note, so he sees it first thing he gets back."

Reynerd just stared at Ethan. An artery began throbbing in his neck. His speed-cycled brain was racing, but although meth ensured frenetically fast thinking, it didn't assist *clear* thinking.

"The thing is," Ethan said, "I don't have any paper. Or a pen, for that matter."

"Oh. Sure, I got those," said Reynerd.

"I really hate to bother you—"

"No bother," Reynerd assured him, turning away from the open door, going off to find a notepad, a pen.

Left at the threshold, Ethan chafed to get into the apartment. He wanted a better look at Reynerd's nest than he could obtain from the doorway.

Just as Ethan decided to risk being rude and to enter without an invitation, Reynerd halted, turned, and said, "Come on in. Sit down."

Now that the invitation had been extended, Ethan could afford to inject a little authenticity into this charade by demurring. "Thanks, but I just came in from the rain—"

"Can't hurt this furniture," Reynerd assured him.

Leaving the door open behind himself, Ethan went inside.

The living room and dining area comprised one large space. The kitchen was open to this front room, but separated from it by a bar with two stools.

Reynerd proceeded into the kitchen, to a counter under a wall phone, while Ethan perched on the edge of an armchair in the living room.

The apartment was sparsely furnished. One sofa, one armchair, a coffee table, and a television set. The dining area contained a small table and two chairs.

On the television, the MGM lion roared. The sound was low, the roar soft.

On the walls were several framed photographs: large sixteen-by-twenty-inch, black-and-white art prints. Birds were the subject of every photo.

Reynerd returned with a notepad and a pencil. "This do?"

"Perfect," Ethan said, accepting the items.

Reynerd had a dispenser of Scotch tape, as well. "To fix the note on George's door." He put the tape on the coffee table.

"Thanks," Ethan said. "I like the photographs."

"Birds are all about being free," Reynerd said.

CHAPTER 3

Ethan opened his eyes.

Traveling far too fast for a residential street, a cherry-red Ferrari Testarossa exploded past, casting up a plume of dirty water from the puddled pavement.

Through the side window of the Expedition, the apartment house blurred and tweaked into strange geometry, like a place in a nightmare.

As if he'd sustained an electrical shock, he twitched violently, and inhaled with the desperation of a drowning man. The air tasted sweet, fresh and sweet and clean. He exhaled explosively.

No gut wound. No chest wound. His hair wasn't wet with rain.

His heart knocked, knocked like a lunatic fist on the padded door of a padded room.

Never in his life had Ethan Truman experienced a dream of such clarity, such intensity, nor any nightmare so crisply detailed as the experience in Reynerd's apartment.

He consulted his wristwatch. If he'd been asleep, he had been dreaming for no more than a minute.

He couldn't have explored the convolutions of such an elaborate dream in a mere minute. Impossible.

Rain washed the last of the murky residue off the glass. Beyond the dripping fronds of the phoenix palms, the apartment house waited, no longer distorted, but now forever strange.

When he'd leaned back against the headrest and closed his eyes, the better to formulate his approach to Rolf Reynerd, Ethan had not been in the least sleepy. Or even tired.

He was certain that he had not taken a one-minute nap. He had not taken a five-second nap, for that matter.

If the first Ferrari had been a figment of a dream, the second sports car suggested that reality now followed precisely in the path of the nightmare.

Although his explosive breathing had quieted, his heart clumped with undiminished speed, galloping after reason, which set an even faster pace, steadily receding beyond reach.

Intuition told him to leave now, to find a Starbucks and have a large cup of coffee. Order a blend strong enough to dissolve the swizzle stick.

Given time and distance from the event, he would discover the key that unlocked the mystery and allowed understanding. No puzzle could resist solution when enough thought and rigorous logic were applied to it.

Even though years of police work had taught him

to trust his intuition as a baby trusts its mother, he switched off the engine and got out of the Expedition.

No argument: Intuition was an essential survival tool. Honesty with himself, however, was more important than heeding intuition. In a spirit of honesty, he had to admit that he wanted to drive away not to find a place and time for quiet reflection, not to engage in Sherlockian deduction, but because fear had him in a pincer grip.

Fear must never be allowed to win. Surrender to it once, and you were finished as a cop.

Of course he wasn't a cop anymore. He had left the force more than a year ago. The work that had given his life meaning while Hannah was alive had meant steadily less to him in the years after her death. He had ceased to believe that he could make a difference in the world. He had wanted to withdraw, to turn his back on the ugly reality of the human condition so evident in the daily work of a homicide detective. Channing Manheim's world was as far as he could get from reality and still earn a living.

Although he didn't carry a badge, although he might not be a cop in any official sense, he remained a cop in essence. We are what we are, no matter what we might wish to be, or pretend to be.

Hands shoved in the pockets of his leather jacket, shoulders hunched as if the rain were a burden, he dashed across the street to the apartment house.

Dripping, he entered the foyer. Mexican-tile floor. Elevator. Stairs. As it should be. As it had been.

Stale with the greasy scent of cooked breakfast meat and pot smoke, the air felt thick, seemed to cloy like mucus in his throat.

Two magazines lay in the tray. On each mailing label was the name George Keesner.

Ethan climbed the stairs. His legs felt weak, and his hands trembled. At the landing, he paused to take a few deep breaths, to knit the raveled fabric of his nerve.

The apartment house lay quiet. No voices muffled by the walls, no music for a melancholy Monday.

He imagined that he heard the faint tick and scrape of crow claws on an iron fence, the flap and rustle of pigeons taking flight, the *tick-tick-tick* of insistently pecking beaks. In truth, he knew that these were only the many voices of the rain.

Although he could feel the weight of the pistol in his shoulder holster, he reached under his coat and placed his right hand on the weapon to be certain that he had brought it. With one fingertip, he traced the checking on the grip.

He withdrew his hand from under his jacket, leaving the pistol in the holster.

Having collected hair by hair along the back of his head, rain reached a trickling finger down the nape of his neck, teasing a shudder from him.

When Ethan reached the second-floor hallway, he barely glanced at Apartment 2E, where George Keesner would fail to respond to either the bell or a fingernails of his right hand. A dark substance, reddish-black.

He stared at this material for a long time, reluctant to take steps to determine if it was real or hallucinated.

Finally he used the thumbnail of his left hand to scrape out a small portion of the matter that was trapped under the nail of his right thumb. The stuff proved slightly moist, gummy.

Hesitantly, he brought the smear to his nose. He sniffed it once, twice, and though the scent was faint, he didn't need to smell it again.

Ethan had blood under all five nails of his right hand. With a certainty seldom given to any man who understood the world to be a most uncertain place, he knew that this would prove to be his own blood.

CHAPTER 4

Palomar Laboratories in North Hollywood occupied a sprawling single-story concrete-slab building with such small and widely spaced windows and with such a low and slightly pitched sheet-metal roof that it resembled a bunker in the storm.

The medical-lab division of Palomar analyzed blood samples, Pap smears, biopsies, and other organic materials. In their industrial division, they performed chemical analyses of every variety for both private-sector and government clients.

Each year, fans of the Face sent over a quarter of a million pieces of mail to him, mostly in care of his studio, which forwarded weekly batches of this correspondence to the publicity firm that responded to it in the star's name. Among those letters were gifts, including more than a few home-made foods: cookies, cakes, fudge. Fewer than one in a thousand fans might be sufficiently deranged to send poisoned brownies, but Ethan nevertheless operated on the better-safe-than-sorry principle: All foodstuffs must be disposed of without sampling by anyone.

Occasionally, when a homemade treat from a fan arrived with a particularly suspicious letter, the edible goodie would not be at once destroyed but would be passed along to Ethan for a closer look. If he suspected contamination, he brought the item here to Palomar to be analyzed.

When a total stranger could work up sufficient hatred to attempt to poison the Face, Ethan wanted to know that the bastard existed. He subsequently cooperated with authorities in the poisoner's hometown to bring whatever criminal charges might be sustained in court.

Now, proceeding first to the public reception lounge, he signed a form authorizing them to draw his blood. Lacking a doctor's order for tests, he paid cash for the analyses he required.

He requested a basic DNA profile. "And I want to know if any drugs are present in my body."

"What drugs are you taking?" the receptionist asked.

"Nothing but aspirin. But I want you to test for every possible substance, in case I've been drugged without my knowledge."

Perhaps in North Hollywood they were accustomed to encounters with full-blown paranoids. The receptionist didn't roll her eyes, raise an eyebrow, or in any other way appear to be surprised to hear him suggest that he might be the victim of a wicked conspiracy.

The medical technician who drew his sample

was a petite and lovely Vietnamese woman with an angel's touch. He never felt the needle pierce the vein.

In another reception lounge provided for the delivery of samples unrelated to standard medical tests, he filled out a second form and paid another fee. This receptionist did give him an odd look when he explained what he wanted to have analyzed.

At a lab table, under harsh fluorescent lights, a technician who resembled Britney Spears used a thin but blunt steel blade to scrape the blood from under the fingernails of his right hand, onto a square of acid-free white paper. Ethan hadn't trimmed his nails in over a week, so she retrieved a significant number of shavings, some of which still appeared to be gummy.

His hand trembled throughout the process. She probably thought her beauty made him nervous.

The material from under his fingernails would first be tested to determine if it was indeed blood. Thereafter it would be conveyed to the medical-lab division to be typed and to have the DNA profile compared to the blood sample that the Vietnamese technician had drawn. Full toxicological results wouldn't be ready until Wednesday afternoon.

Ethan didn't understand how he could have his own blood under his fingernails when he had not, after all, been shot in the gut and the chest. Yet as migrating geese know south from north without the aid of a compass, he knew this blood was his.

CHAPTER 5

In the Palomar parking lot, as the rain and the wind painted a procession of colorless spirit shapes on the windshield of the Expedition, Ethan placed a call to Hazard Yancy's cell phone.

Hazard had been born Lester, but he loathed his given name. He didn't like Les any better. He thought the shortened version sounded like an insult.

"I'm not *less* of anything than you are," he'd once said to Ethan, but affably.

Indeed, at six feet four and 240 pounds, with a shaved head that appeared to be as big as a basketball and a neck only slightly narrower than the span of his ears, Hazard Yancy was nobody's idea of a poster child for minimalism.

"Fact is, I'm *more* of a lot of things than some people. Like more determined, more fun, more colorful, more likely to make stupid choices in women, more likely to be shot in the ass. My folks should have named me More Yancy. I could've lived with that."

When he had been a teenager and a young man, his friends had called him Brick, a reference to the fact that he was built like a brick wall.

Nobody in Robbery/Homicide had called him Brick in twenty years. On the force, he was known as Hazard because working a case in tandem with him could be as hazardous as driving a dynamite truck.

Gumshoe duty in Robbery/Homicide might be more dangerous than a career as a greengrocer, but detectives were less likely to die on the job than were night clerks in convenience stores. If you wanted the thrill of being shot at on a regular basis, the Gang Activities Section, the Narcotics Division, and certainly the Strategic Weapons and Tactics teams were better bets than cleaning up after murderers.

Even just staying in uniform promised more violence than hitting the streets in a suit.

Hazard's career was an exception to the rule. People shot at him with regularity.

He professed surprise not at the frequency with which bullets were directed at him, but at the fact that the shooters were people who didn't know him personally. "Being a friend of mine," he once said, "you'd think it would be the other way around, wouldn't you?"

Hazard's uncanny attraction for high-velocity projectiles wasn't a consequence of either recklessness or poor investigative technique. He was a careful, first-rate detective.

In Ethan's experience, the universe didn't always

Much hot water and much rubbing left his skin a boiled red. He could see no slightest stain remaining. Nevertheless Ethan felt that his hands were still unclean.

He was troubled by the disturbing notion that as long as even a few molecules of that stigmatic residue of his foretold death clung to his hands, the Reaper would track him down by smell and cancel the reprieve that had been granted to him.

Studying his reflection in the mirror, he half expected to see through his body, as through a sheer curtain, but he was solid.

Sensing in himself the potential for obsession, concerned that he might wash his hands without surcease, until they were scrubbed raw, he quickly dried them on paper towels and left the men's room.

He shared an elevator with a solemn young couple holding hands for mutual strength. "She'll be all right," the man murmured, and the woman nodded, eyes bright with repressed tears.

When Ethan got off at the seventh floor, the young couple rode farther up to higher misery.

Duncan "Dunny" Whistler had been abed here on the seventh floor for three months. Between confinements to the intensive care unit—also on this floor—he was assigned to different rooms. During the five weeks since his most recent crisis, he'd been in Room 742.

A nun with a kind Irish face made eye contact with Ethan, smiled, and passed by with nary a swish of her voluminous habit.

The order of sisters that operated Our Lady of Angels rejected the modern garb of many nuns, which resembled the uniforms of airline flight attendants. They favored instead the traditional floor-length habits with commodious sleeves, guimpes, and winged wimples.

Their habits were radiant white, rather than white and black. When Ethan saw them gliding ethereally along these halls, seeming less to walk than to drift like spirits, he could almost believe that the hospital did not occupy only Los Angeles real estate, but bridged this world and the next.

Dunny had existed in a limbo of sorts, between worlds, ever since four angry men shoved his head in a toilet bowl once too often and held him under too long. The paramedics had pumped the water out of his lungs, but the doctors hadn't been able to stir him from his coma.

When Ethan arrived at Room 742, he found it in deep shadow. An old man rested in the bed nearest the door: unconscious, hooked to a ventilator that pumped air into him with a rhythmic wheeze.

The bed nearest the window, where Dunny had spent the past five weeks, stood unoccupied. The sheets were crisp, fresh, luminous in the gloom.

Drowned daylight projected vague gray images of ameboid rain tracks from the window glass onto the bed. The sheets appeared to be acrawl with transparent spiders.

When he saw that the patient's chart was missing, Ethan figured that Dunny had been moved to another room or transferred to the ICU yet again.

At the seventh-floor nurses' station, when he inquired as to where he might find Duncan Whistler, a young nurse asked him to wait for the shift supervisor, whom she paged.

Ethan knew the supervisor, Nurse Jordan, from previous visits. A black woman with a drill sergeant's purposeful carriage and the soft smoky voice of a chanteuse, she arrived at the nurses' station with the news that Dunny had passed away that morning.

"I'm so sorry, Mr. Truman, but I called both numbers you gave us and left voice-mail messages."

"When would this have been?" he asked.

"He passed away at ten-twenty this morning. I phoned you about fifteen or twenty minutes later."

At approximately ten-forty, Ethan had been at Rolf Reynerd's apartment door, trembling with the memory of his foreseen death, pretending to be looking for the nonexistent Jim Briscoe. He'd left his cell phone in the Expedition.

"I know you weren't that close to Mr. Whistler," said Nurse Jordan, "but it's still something of a shock, I'm sure. Sorry you had to learn this way—the empty bed."

"Was the body taken down to the hospital garden room?" Ethan asked.

Nurse Jordan regarded him with new respect. "I didn't realize you were a police officer, Mr. Truman."

Garden room was cop lingo for *morgue*. All those corpses waiting to be planted.

"Robbery/Homicide," he replied, not bothering to explain that he had left the force, or why.

"My husband's worn out enough uniforms to retire in March. I'm workin' overtime so I don't go crazy."

Ethan understood. Cops often went through long law-enforcement careers without worrying much about the dust-to-dust-ashes-to-ashes business, only to tighten with tension so much in the last months before retirement that they needed to eat Metamucil by the pound to stop retaining. The worry could be even worse for spouses.

"The doctor signed a certification of death," Nurse Jordan said, "and Mr. Whistler went down to cold holding pending mortuary pickup. Oh . . . actually, it won't be a mortuary, will it?"

"It's a murder now," Ethan said. "The medical examiner's office will want him for an autopsy."

"Then they'll have been called. We've got a foolproof system." Checking her watch, she said, "But they probably haven't had time to take custody of the body yet, if that's what you're wondering."

Ethan rode the elevator all the way down to the dead. The garden room was in the third and lowest level of the basement, adjacent to the ambulance garage.

Descending, he was serenaded by an orchestrated version of an old Sheryl Crow tune with all the sex squeezed out of it and with a perkiness squeezed in, retaining only the skin of the melody them, so he moves in. All three come on to him, say let's go back to our place, and he figures he's so Brad Pitt they want to three-on-one him."

"But it's a robbery setup," Ethan guessed.

"Worse. He leaves his car, rides in theirs. Two girls get him hot in the backseat, half undress him—then push him out for fun."

"So the hotties were hopped on something."

"Maybe so, maybe not," said Toledano. "Turns out they'd done it twice before. This time they got caught."

Ethan said, "I came across this old movie on TV the other night. Frankie Avalon, Annette Funicello. One of those beach-party flicks. Women sure were different back then."

"So was everybody. Nobody's got better or nicer since the mid-sixties. Wish I'd been born thirty years sooner. So how'd yours die?"

"Four guys thought he'd cheated them out of some money, so they thumped him a little, taped his wrists behind his back, and submerged his head in a toilet long enough to cause brain damage."

"Man, that's ugly."

"It's not Agatha Christie," Ethan agreed.

"But you're dealing with all this, it proves there must've been something left between you and your buddy. Nobody has to be executor of an estate, they don't want to be."

Two meat haulers from the medical examiner's office pushed open the double doors and entered the garden-room reception area.

The first guy was tall, in his fifties, and obviously proud about having kept all his hair. He wore it in a pompadour elaborate enough that it should have been finished with bows.

Ethan knew Pomp's partner. Jose Ramirez was a stocky Mexican-American with myopic eyes and with the sweet dreamy smile of a koala bear.

Jose lived for his wife and four children. While Pomp dealt with the paperwork supplied by the attendant, Ethan asked Jose to see the latest wallet photographs of Maria and the kids.

Once formalities were completed, Toledano led them through an inner door, into the garden room. Instead of a vinyl-tile floor as in the reception area, this chamber featured white ceramic tile with only sixteenth-inch grout joints: an easy surface to sterilize in the event that it became contaminated with bodily fluids.

Although continually cycled through sophisticated filters, the cold air carried a faint but unpleasant scent. Most people didn't die smelling of shampoo, soap, and cologne.

Four standard stainless-steel morgue drawers might have held bodies, but two cadavers on gurneys made an immediate impression. Both were draped with sheets.

A third gurney stood empty, trailing a tangled shroud, and to this one Toledano proceeded with a stupefied expression. "This was him. Right here."

Frowning with confusion, Toledano peeled the sheets back from the heads of the other two cadavers. Neither was Dunny Whistler.

One at a time, he pulled open the four stainless-steel drawers. They were empty.

Because the hospital sent the vast majority of its patients home rather than to funeral services, this garden room was small by the standards of the city morgue. All possible hiding places had already been explored.

CHAPTER 7

In this windowless chamber three stories underground, the four living and the two dead were for a moment so silent that Ethan imagined he could hear rain falling in the streets far above.

Then the meat hauler with the pompadour said, "You mean you released Whistler to the wrong people?"

The attendant, Toledano, shook his head adamantly. "No way. Never did in fourteen years, not startin' today."

A wide door allowed bodies on gurneys to be conveyed directly from the garden room into the ambulance garage. Two deadbolts should have secured it. Both were disengaged.

"I left them locked," Toledano insisted. "They're always locked, *always,* 'cept when I'm overseeing a dispatch, and then I'm always here, right here, watching."

"Who'd want to steal a stiff?" Pomp asked.

"Even some perv wanted to steal one, he couldn't," Vin Toledano said, pulling open the door

CHAPTER 8

The Armenian restaurant on Pico Boulevard had the atmosphere of a Jewish delicatessen, a menu featuring food so delicious that it would inspire a condemned man to smile through his last meal, and more plainclothes cops and film-industry types together in one place than you would find anywhere outside of the courtroom devoted to the trial of the latest spouse-murdering celebrity.

When Ethan arrived, Hazard Yancy waited in a booth by a window. Even seated, he loomed so large that he would have been well advised to audition for the title role in *The Incredible Hulk* if Hollywood ever made a black version.

Hazard had already been served a double order of the kibby appetizer with cucumbers, tomatoes, and pickled turnip on the side.

As Ethan sat across the table from the big detective, Hazard said, "Somebody told me they saw in the news your boss got twenty-seven million bucks for his last two movies."

"Twenty-seven million *each.* He's the first to break through the twenty-five-million ceiling."

"Up from poverty," Hazard said.

"Plus he's got a piece of the back end."

"That kind of money, he can get a piece of anybody's back end he wants."

"It's an industry phrase. Means if the picture is a big hit, he gets a share of the profits, sometimes even a percentage of gross."

"How much might that amount to?"

"According to *Daily Variety,* he's had worldwide hits so big he sometimes walks away with fifty million, thereabouts."

"You read the show-biz press now?" Hazard asked.

"Helps me stay aware of how big a target he's making himself."

"You got your work cut out for you, all right. How many movies does the man do a year?"

"Never fewer than two. Sometimes three."

"I was planning to chow down so much on his dime, Mr. Channing Manheim himself would notice, and you'd get fired for abusing your credit-card privileges."

"Even you can't eat a hundred thousand bucks' worth of kibby."

Hazard shook his head. "Chan the Man. Maybe I'm not hip anymore, but I don't see him being fifty million cool."

"He also owns a TV-production company with three shows currently on major networks, four on cable. He pulls in a few million a year from Japan, doing TV commercials for their top-selling beer. He has a line of sports clothes. Lots more. His agents call the nonacting income 'additional revenue streams.' "

"People just pissing money on him, huh?"

"He'll never need to shop for bargains."

When the waitress came to the table, Ethan ordered Moroccan salmon with couscous, and iced tea.

Taking Hazard's order, she wore the point off her pencil: lebne with string cheese and extra cucumbers, hummus, stuffed grape leaves, lahmajoon flatbread, seafood tagine. . . . "Plus give me two of those little bottles of Orangina."

"Only person I ever saw eat that much," Ethan said, "was this bulimic ballerina. She went to the john to puke after every course."

"I'm just sampling, and I never wear a tutu." Hazard cut his last kibby in two. "So how big an asshole is Chan the Man?"

The masking roar of other lunchtime conversations provided Ethan and Hazard with privacy nearly equal to that on a remote Mojave hill.

"It's impossible to hate him," Ethan said.

"That's your best compliment?"

"It's just that in person he doesn't have the impact he does on the screen. He doesn't stir your emotions one way or the other."

Hazard forked half a kibby into his mouth and made a small sound of pleasure. "So he's all image, no substance."

"That's not quite it. He's so . . . bland. Generous

to employees. Not arrogant. But there's this . . . this weightlessness about him. He's sort of careless how he treats people, even his own son, but it's a *benign* indifference. He's not an actively bad guy."

"That money, that much adoration, you expect a monster."

"With him, you don't get it. You get . . ."

Ethan paused to think. In the months he'd worked for Manheim, he had not spoken this much or this frankly about the man to anyone.

He and Hazard had been shot at together, and each had trusted his life to the other. He could speak his mind and know that nothing he said would be repeated.

With such a confidential sounding board, he wanted to describe the Face not only as honestly as possible but as perceptively. In explaining Manheim to Hazard, he also might be able more fully to explain the actor to himself.

After the waitress brought iced tea and the Oranginas, Ethan at last said, "He's self-absorbed but not in the usual movie-star way, not in any way that makes him appear egotistical. He cares about the money, I guess, but I don't think he cares what anyone thinks of him or that he's famous. He's self-absorbed, all right, totally self-absorbed, but it's like this . . . this Zen state of self-absorption."

"Zen state?"

"Yeah. Like life is about him and nature, him and the cosmos, not him and other people. He always seems to be half in a meditative state, not entirely her screwing around, so he considers her filthy, a worthless piece of crap."

"Plus maybe he had knowledge of the treatment plant, knew an easy way to get the body in there. Is that a cashmere sweater?"

"Cotton. So your perp works at the plant?"

Hazard shook his head. "He's a member of the city council."

At once losing his appetite altogether, Ethan put down his fork. "A politician? Why don't you just find a cliff and jump?"

Shoving a stuffed grape leaf in his maw, Hazard managed to grin while he chewed, without once opening his mouth. After swallowing, he said, "I've already got a cliff, and I'm pushing *him* off."

"Anybody winds up broken on the rocks, it'll be you."

"You've just taken the cliff metaphor one step too far," said Hazard, spooning hummus into a pita wedge.

After a half-century of squeaky-clean public officials and honest administration, California itself had lately become a deep sewage slough not seen since the 1930s and '40s when Raymond Chandler had written about its dark side. Here in the early years of the new millennium, on a state level and in too many local jurisdictions, corruption had attained a degree of rot seldom seen outside a banana republic, though in this case a banana republic without bananas and with pretensions to glamour.

A significant percentage of the politicians here

operated like thugs. If the thugs saw you going after one of their own, they would assume you'd
come after them next, and they would use their
power to ruin you one way or another.

In another gangster-ridden era, in a crusade
against corruption, Eliot Ness had led a force of
law-enforcement agents so beyond reach by
bribery and so undeterred by bullets that they became known as the Untouchables. In contemporary California, even Ness and his exemplary crew
would be destroyed not by bribes or bullets, but by
bureaucracy wielded as ruthlessly as an ax and by
slander eagerly converted to libel by a feeding-
frenzy media with a sentimental affection for the
thugs, both the elected and unelected varieties,
upon whom they daily reported.

"If you were still doing real work like me," Hazard
said, "you'd handle this no different than I'm handling it."

"Yeah. But I sure wouldn't sit there grinning
about it."

Indicating Ethan's sweater, Hazard said, "Cotton—like Rodeo Drive cotton?"

"Cotton like Macy's on-sale cotton."

"How much you pay for a pair of socks these
days?"

Ethan said, "Ten thousand dollars."

He'd been hesitant to bring up the Rolf Reynerd
situation. Now he figured he could do nothing better for Hazard than distract him from this suicidal
mission to nail a city councilman for murder.

"Take a look at these." He opened a nine-by-twelve manila envelope, withdrew the contents, and passed them across the table.

As Hazard reviewed what he'd been given, Ethan told him about the five black boxes delivered by Federal Express and the sixth thrown over the gate.

"They came by Federal Express, so you know who sent them."

"No. The return addresses were fake. They were dropped off at different mom-and-pop mailbox shops that collect for FedEx and UPS. The sender paid cash."

"How much mail does Channing get a week?"

"Maybe five thousand pieces. But almost all of it is sent to the studio where it's known he has offices. A publicity firm reviews it and responds. His home address isn't a secret, but it's not widely known, either."

In the envelope were high-resolution computer printouts of six digital photographs taken in Ethan's study, the first of which showed a small jar standing on a white cloth. Beside the jar lay the lid. Spread across the cloth were what had been the contents of the jar: twenty-two beetles with black-spotted orange shells.

"Ladybugs?" Hazard asked.

"The entomological name is *Hippodamia convergens*, of the family Coccinellidae. Not that I think it matters, but I looked it up."

Hazard's shrewd expression spoke clearly enough without words, but he said, "You're stumped worse than a quadruple amputee."

"This guy thinks I'm Batman, he's the Riddler."

"Why twenty-two bugs? Is the number significant?"

"I don't know."

"They alive when you received them?" Hazard asked.

"All dead. Whether they were alive when he sent them, I don't know, but they looked like they'd been dead for a while. The shells were intact, but the more delicate bug parts were withered, crumbly."

In the second photo, a collection of different, spirally coiled, light brown shells were canted at angles in a gray pile of sludge that had been emptied from a black box onto a sheet of waxed paper.

"Ten dead snails," Ethan said. "Well, actually, two were alive but feeble when I opened the box."

"That's a fragrance Chanel won't be bottling."

Hazard paused to fork up some seafood tagine.

The third photo was of a small, clear-glass, screw-top jar. The label had been removed, but the lid indicated that the container had once held pickle relish.

Because the photograph wasn't clear enough to reveal the murky contents of the jar, Ethan said, "Floating in formaldehyde were these ten pieces of translucent tissue with a pale pinkish tint. Tubelike structures. Hard to describe. Like tiny exotic jellyfish."

"You took 'em to a lab?"

"Yeah. When they gave me the analysis, they

also gave me a weird look. What I had in the jar were foreskins."

Hazard's jaws locked in midchew, as if the seafood tagine had hardened like a dental mold.

"Ten foreskins from grown men, not infants," Ethan amplified.

After chewing mechanically, not with his former relish, and after swallowing with a grimace, Hazard said, "Ouch. How many grown men get themselves circumcised?"

"They're not standing in line for it," Ethan agreed.

CHAPTER 9

Corky Laputa thrived in the rain.

He wore a long shiny yellow slicker and a droopy yellow rain hat. He was as bright as a dandelion.

The slicker had many inside pockets, deep and weatherproof.

In his tall black rubber boots, two layers of socks kept his feet pleasantly warm.

He yearned for thunder.

He ached for lightning.

Storms in southern California, usually lacking crash and flash, were too quiet for his taste.

He liked the wind, however. Hissing, hooting, a champion of disorder, it lent a sting to the rain and promised chaos.

Ficus and pine trees shivered, shuddered. Palm fronds clicked and clattered.

Stripped leaves whirled in ragged green conjurations, short-lived demons that blew down into gutters.

Eventually, clogging drain grills, the leaves would be the cause of flooded streets, stalled cars, delayed ambulances, and many small but welcome miseries.

Here in the blustery, dripping midday, Corky walked a charming residential neighborhood in Studio City. Sowing disorder.

He didn't live here. He never would.

This was a working-class neighborhood, managerial-class at best. Intellectual stimulation in such a place would be hard to find.

He had driven here to take a walk.

Emergency-yellow, blazing canary, he nevertheless passed along these streets with complete anonymity, drawing as little notice as might a ghost whose substance was but a twist of ectoplasmic mist.

He had yet to encounter anyone on foot. Few cars traveled the quiet streets.

The weather kept most people snug indoors.

The glorious rotten weather was Corky's fine conspirator.

At this hour, of course, most residents of these houses were away at work. Toiling, toiling, with stupid purpose.

Because this was a holiday week, children had not gone to school. Today: Monday. Christmas: Friday. Deck the halls.

Some children would be in the company of siblings. A lesser number would be under the protection of a nonworking mother.

Others were home alone.

In this instance, however, children were not

Corky's avenue of expression. Here, they were safe from the yellow ghost passing among them.

Anyway, Corky was forty-two. Kids these days were too savvy to open their doors to strange men.

Welcome disorder and lovely decadence had deeply infected the world in recent years. Now the lambs of all ages were growing wary.

He contented himself with lesser outrages, just happy to be out in the storm and doing a little damage.

In one of his capacious inner pockets, he carried a plastic bag of glittering blue crystals. A wickedly powerful chemical defoliant.

The Chinese military had developed it. Prior to a war, their agents would sow this stuff in their enemy's farms.

The blue crystals withered crops through a twelve-month growing cycle. An enemy unable to feed itself cannot fight.

One of Corky's colleagues at the university had accepted a grant to study the crystals for the Department of Defense. They felt an urgent need to find a way to protect against the chemical in advance of its use.

In his lab, the colleague had a fifty-pound drum of the stuff. Corky had stolen one pound.

He wore thin protective latex gloves, which he could easily hide in the great winglike sleeves of his slicker.

The slicker was as much a serape as a coat. The sleeves were so voluminous that he could withdraw his arms from them, search his interior pockets, and slip into the sleeves again with fistfuls of one poison or another.

He scattered blue crystals over primrose and liriope, over star jasmine and bougainvillea. Azaleas and ferns. Carpet roses, lantana.

The rain swiftly dissolved the crystals. The chemical seeped into the roots.

In a week, the plants would yellow, drop leaves. In two weeks, they would collapse in a muck of reeking rot.

Large trees would not be affected by the quantities that Corky could scatter. Lawns, flowers, shrubs, vines, and smaller trees would succumb, however, in satisfying numbers.

He didn't sow death in the landscaping of every house. One out of three, in no apparent pattern.

If an entire block of homes were blighted, neighbors might be drawn closer by the shared catastrophe. If some were untouched, they would become the envy of the afflicted. And might arouse suspicion.

Corky's mission was not merely to cause destruction. Any fool could wreck things. He intended also to spread dissension, distrust, discord, and despair.

Occasionally a dog barked or growled from the shelter of a porch where it was tethered or from within a doghouse behind a board fence or a stone wall.

Corky liked dogs. They were man's best friend, though why they would want to fill that role remained a mystery, considering the vile nature of humanity.

Now and then, when he heard a dog, he fished tasty biscuits from an inner pocket. He tossed them onto porches, over fences.

In the interest of societal deconstruction, he could put aside his love of dogs and do what must be done. Sacrifices must be made.

You can't make an omelet without breaking eggs, and all that.

The dog biscuits were treated with cyanide. The animals would die far faster than the plants.

Few things would spread despair so effectively as the untimely death of a beloved pet.

Corky was sad. Sad for the luckless dogs.

He was happy, too. Happy that in a thousand little ways he daily contributed to the fall of a corrupt order—and therefore to the rise of a better world.

For the same reason that he didn't damage the landscaping at every house, he didn't kill every dog. Let neighbor suspect neighbor.

He wasn't concerned that he would be caught in these poisonings. Entropy, the most powerful force in the universe, was his ally and his protecting god.

Besides, the at-home parents would be watching sleazy daytime talk shows on which daughters revealed to their mothers that they were whores, on which wives revealed to their husbands that they were having affairs with their brothers-in-law.

With school out, the kids would be busy learning homicidal skills from video games. Better yet, the pubescent boys would be surfing the Net for pornography, sharing it with innocent younger brothers, and scheming to rape the little girl next door.

Because he approved of those activities, Corky went about his work as discreetly as possible, so as not to distract these people from their self-destruction.

Corky Laputa was not merely a dreary poisoner. He was a man of many talents and weapons.

From time to time, as he plodded along the puddled walkways, under the drizzling trees, he indulged in melody. He sang "Singin' in the Rain," of course, which might be trite, but which amused him.

He did not dance.

Not that he *couldn't* dance. Although not as limber and as right with rhythm as Gene Kelly, he could dazzle on any dance floor.

Capering along a street in a yellow slicker as roomy as any nun's habit was, however, not wise behavior for an anarchist who preferred anonymity.

The streetside mailbox in front of each house always sported a number. Some boxes featured family names, as well.

Sometimes a name appeared to be Jewish. Stein. Levy. Glickman.

At each of these boxes, Corky paused briefly. He inserted one of the letter-size white envelopes that he carried by the score in another slicker pocket.

On each envelope, a black swastika. In each,

two sheets of folded paper certain to instill fear and stoke anger.

On the first page, in bold block letters, were printed the words DEATH TO ALL DIRTY JEWS.

The photo on the second page showed bodies stacked ten deep in the furnace yard of a Nazi concentration camp. Under it in red block letters blazed the message YOU'RE NEXT.

Corky had no prejudice against the Jewish people. He held all races, religions, and ethnic groups in equal contempt.

At other special venues, he had distributed DEATH TO ALL DIRTY CATHOLICS notices, DEATH TO ALL BLACKS, and IMPRISON ALL GUN OWNERS.

For decades, politicians had been controlling the people by dividing them into groups and turning them against one another. All a good anarchist could do was try to intensify the existing hatreds and pour gasoline on the fires that the politicians had built.

Currently, hatred of Israel—and, by extension, all Jews—was the fashionable intellectual position among the most glamorous of media figures, including many nonreligious Jews. Corky was simply giving the people what they wanted.

Azalea to lantana to jasmine vine, dog to dog to mailbox, he journeyed through the rain-swept day. Seeding chaos.

Determined conspirators might be able to blow up skyscrapers and cause breathtaking destruction. Their work was helpful.

Ten thousand Corky Laputas—inventive, diligent—would in their quiet persistent way do more, however, to undermine the foundations of this society than all the suicide pilots and bombers combined.

For every thousand gunmen, Corky thought, *I'd rather have one hate-filled teacher subtly propagandizing in a schoolroom, one day-care worker with an unslakable thirst for cruelty, one atheist priest hiding in cassock and alb and chasuble.*

By a circuitous route, he came within sight of the BMW where he had parked it an hour and a half earlier. Right on schedule.

Spending too much time in a single neighborhood could be risky. The wise anarchist keeps moving because entropy favors the rambler, and motion foils the law.

The dirty-milk clouds had churned lower during his stroll, coagulating into sooty curds. In the storm gloom, in the wet shade of the oak tree, his silver sedan waited as dark as iron.

Trailers of bougainvillea lashed the air, casting off scarlet petals, raking thorny nails against the stucco wall of a house, making sgraffito sounds: *scratch-scratch, screek-screek.*

Wind threw sheets, lashed whips, spun funnels of rain. Rain hissed, sizzled, chuckled, splashed.

Corky's phone rang.

He was still half a block from his car. He would miss the call if he waited to answer it in the BMW.

He slipped his right arm out of its sleeve, under his slicker, and unclipped the phone from his belt.

Arm in sleeve again, phone to ear, toddling along as buttercup-yellow and as smile-evoking as any character in any TV program for children, Corky Laputa was in such a good mood that he answered the call by saying, "Brighten the corner where you are."

The caller was Rolf Reynerd. As thick as Corky was yellow, Rolf thought he'd gotten a wrong number.

"It's me," Corky said quickly, before Reynerd could hang up.

By the time he reached the BMW, he wished he had never answered the phone. Reynerd had done something stupid.

CHAPTER 10

Beyond the restaurant window, falling rain as clear as a baby's conscience met the city pavement and flooded the gutters with filthy churning currents.

Studying the photo of the jar full of foreskins, Hazard said, "Ten little hats from ten little proud heads? You think they could be trophies?"

"From men he's murdered? Possible but unlikely. Anybody with that many kills isn't the kind to taunt his victims first with freaky gifts in black boxes. He just *does the job*."

"And if they were trophies, he wouldn't give them away so easy."

"Yeah. They'd be the central theme of his home decor. What I think is he works with stiffs. Maybe in a funeral home or a morgue."

"Postmortem circumcisions." Hazard twisted some string cheese onto his fork as he might have spun up a bite of spaghetti. "Kinky, but it's got to be the answer, 'cause I haven't heard about ten unsolved homicides where it looks like the perp might be a lunatic rabbi." He dunked the string cheese in lebne and continued with lunch.

Ethan said, "I think he harvested these from cadavers for the sole purpose of sending them to Channing Manheim."

"To convey what—that Chan the Man is a prick?"

"I doubt the message is that simple."

"Fame doesn't seem so appealing anymore."

The fourth black box had been larger than the others. Two photos were required to document the contents.

In the first picture stood a honey-colored ceramic cat. The cat stood on its hind paws and held a ceramic cookie in each forepaw. Red letters on its chest and tummy spelled COOKIE KITTEN.

"It's a cookie jar," Ethan said.

"I'm such a good detective, I figured that out all by myself."

"It was filled with Scrabble tiles."

The second photo showed a pile of tiles. In front of the pile, Ethan had used six pieces to spell OWE and WOE.

"The jar contained ninety of each letter: *O, W, E.* Either word could be spelled ninety times, or both words forty-five times side by side. I don't know which he intended."

"So the nutball is saying, 'I owe you woe.' He thinks somehow Manheim has done him wrong, and now it's payback time."

"Maybe. But why in a cookie jar?"

"You could also spell *wow*," Hazard noted.

"Yeah, but then you're left with half the Os and all

the *E*s not used, and they don't make anything together. Only *owe* or *woe* uses all the letters."

"What about two-word combinations?"

"The first one is *wee woo*. Which could mean 'little love,' I guess, but I don't get the message in that one. The second is *E-W-E,* and *woo* again."

"Sheep love, huh?"

"Seems like a dead end to me. I think *owe woe* is what he intended, one or the other, or both."

Smearing lebne on a slice of lahmajoon flatbread, Hazard said, "Maybe after this we can play Monopoly."

The fifth black box had contained a hardcover book titled *Paws for Reflection*. The cover featured a photo of an adorable golden retriever puppy.

"It's a memoir," Ethan said. "The guy who wrote it—Donald Gainsworth—spent thirty years training guide dogs for the blind and service dogs for people confined to wheelchairs."

"No bugs or foreskins pressed between the pages?"

"Nope. And I checked every page for underlining, but nothing was highlighted."

"It's out of character with the rest. An innocuous little book, even sweet."

"Box number six was thrown over the gate a little after three-thirty this morning."

Hazard studied the last two photos. First, the sutured apple. Then the eye inside. "Is the peeper real?"

"He pried it out of a doll."

"Nevertheless, this one disturbs me most of all."

"Me too. Why you?"

"The apple's the most crafted of the six. It took a lot of care, so it's probably the one he finds most meaningful."

"So far it doesn't mean much to me," Ethan lamented.

Stapled to the last photograph was a Xerox of the typewritten message that had been folded in the seed pocket, under the eye. After reading it twice, Hazard said, "He didn't send anything like this with the first five packages?"

"No."

"Then this is probably the last thing he's sending. He's said everything he wants to say, in symbols and now in words. Now he moves from threats to action."

"I think you're right. But the words are as much of a riddle as the symbols, the objects."

With silvery insistence, headlights cleaved the afternoon gloom. Radiant wings of water flew up from the puddled pavement, obscuring the tires and lending an aura of supernatural mission to the vehicles that plied the currents of Pico Boulevard.

After a brooding silence, Hazard said, "An apple might symbolize dangerous or forbidden knowledge. The original sin he mentions."

Ethan tried his salmon and couscous again. He might as well have been eating paste. He put down his fork.

"The *seeds* of knowledge have been replaced by the eye," Hazard said, almost more to himself than to Ethan.

A flock of pedestrians hurried past the restaurant windows, bent forward as if resisting a wind greater than the one that the December day exhaled, under the inadequate protection of black umbrellas, like mourners quickening to a grave.

"Maybe he's saying, 'I see your secrets, the source—the seeds—of your evil.' "

"I had a similar thought. But it doesn't feel entirely right, and it doesn't lead me anywhere useful."

"Whatever he means by it," Hazard said, "it bothers me that you have this eye in the apple come just after this book about a guy who raised guide dogs for the blind."

"If he's threatening to blind Manheim, that's bad enough," said Ethan, "but I think he intends worse."

After shuffling through the photos once more, Hazard returned them to Ethan and again addressed the seafood tagine with gusto. "I assume you've got your man well covered."

"He's filming in Florida. Five bodyguards travel with him."

"You don't?"

"Not usually. I oversee all security operations from Bel Air. I talk to the head road warrior at least once a day."

"Road warrior?"

"That's Manheim's little joke. It's what he calls the bodyguards who travel with him."

"That's a joke? I fart funnier than he talks."

"I never claimed he was the king of comedy."

"When somebody tossed the sixth box over the gate last night," Hazard asked, "who was the somebody? Any security tape?"

"Plenty. Including a clear shot of his license plate."

Ethan told him about Rolf Reynerd—though he didn't mention his encounters with the man, neither the one that he knew to be real nor the one that he seemed to have dreamed.

"And what do you want from me?" Hazard asked.

"Maybe you could check him out."

"Check him out? How far? You want me to hold his privates while he turns his head and coughs?"

"Maybe not that far."

"You want I should look for polyps in his lower colon?"

"I already know he doesn't have any criminal priors—"

"So I'm not the first one you're calling in a favor from."

Ethan shrugged. "You know me, I'm a user. No one's safe. It'd be useful to know, does Reynerd have any legally registered firearms."

"You been talking to Laura Moonves over in Support Division?"

"She was helpful," Ethan admitted.

"You should marry her."

"She didn't give me *that* much on Reynerd."

"Even all us morons can see you and her would be as right as bread and butter."

places like that, where he can reach for it, and you don't realize what he's doing."

Hazard stared at him, saying nothing.

"Maybe it's a nine-millimeter Glock," Ethan added.

"He have a nuclear weapon, too?"

"Not that I know of."

"Probably keeps the nuke in a box of Cheez-Its."

"Just take a bagful of mamouls, and you can handle anything."

"Hell, yeah. Throw one of these, you'd crack a guy's skull."

"Then eat the evidence."

The waitress returned with his credit card and the voucher.

As Ethan added the gratuity and signed the form, Hazard seemed almost oblivious of the woman and did not once look at her.

With needles of rain, the blustering wind tattooed ephemeral patterns on the window, and Hazard said, "Looks cold out there."

That was exactly what Ethan had been thinking.

CHAPTER 11

Slickered and booted, wearing the same jeans and wool sweater as before, sitting behind the wheel of his silver BMW, Corky Laputa felt stifled by a frustration as heavy and suffocating as a fur coat.

Although his shirt wasn't buttoned to the top, anger pinched his throat as tight as if he'd squeezed his sixteen-inch neck into a fifteen-inch collar.

He wanted to drive to West Hollywood and kill Reynerd.

Such impulses must be resisted, of course, for though he dreamed of a societal collapse into complete lawlessness, from which a new order would arise, the laws against murder remained in effect. They were still enforced.

Corky was a revolutionary, but not a martyr.

He understood the need to balance radical action with patience.

He recognized the effective limits of anarchic rage.

To calm himself, he ate a candy bar.

Contrary to the claims of organized medicine, both the greed-corrupted Western variety and the spiritually smug Eastern brand, refined sugar did not make Corky hyperkinetic. Sucrose soothed him.

Very old people, nerves rubbed to an excruciating sensitivity by life and its disappointments, had long known about the mollifying effect of excess sugar. The farther their hopes and dreams receded from their grasp, the more their diets sweetened to include ice cream by the quart, rich cookies in giant economy-size boxes, and chocolate in every form from nonpareils to Hershey's Kisses, even to Easter-basket bunnies that they could brutally dismember and consume for a double enjoyment.

In her later years, his mother had been an ice-cream junkie. Ice cream for breakfast, lunch, dinner. Ice cream in parfait glasses, in huge bowls, eaten directly from the carton.

She hogged down enough ice cream to clog a network of arteries stretching from California to the moon and back. For a while Corky had assumed that she was committing suicide by cholesterol.

Instead of spooning herself into heart failure, she appeared to grow healthier. She acquired a glow in the face and a brightness in the eyes that she'd never had before, not even in her youth.

Gallons, barrels, troughs of Chocolate Mint Madness, Peanut-Butter-and-Chocolate Fantasy, Maple Walnut Delight, and a double dozen other flavors seemed to turn back her biological clock as the waters of a thousand fountains had failed to turn back that of Ponce de Leon.

Corky had begun to think that in the case of his mother's unique metabolism, the key to immortality might be butterfat. So he killed her.

If she had been willing to share some of her money while still alive, he would have allowed her to live. He wasn't greedy.

She had not been a believer in generosity or even in parental responsibility, however, and she cared not at all about his comfort or his needs. He'd been concerned that eventually she would change her will and stiff him forever, sheerly for the pleasure of doing so.

In her working years, his mother had been a university professor of economics, specializing in Marxist economic models and the vicious departmental politics of academia.

She had believed in nothing more than the righteousness of envy and the power of hatred. When both beliefs proved hollow, she had not abandoned either, but had supplemented them with ice cream.

Corky didn't hate his mother. He didn't hate anyone.

He didn't envy anyone, either.

Having seen those gods fail his mother, he had rejected both. He did not wish to grow old with no comfort but his favorite premium brand of coconut fudge.

Four years ago, paying her a secret visit with the intention of quickly and mercifully smothering her in her sleep, he had instead beaten her to death with a fireplace poker, as if he were acting out a story begun by Anne Tyler in an ironic mood and roughly finished by a furious Norman Mailer.

Though unplanned, the exercise with the poker proved cathartic. Not that he'd taken pleasure in the violence. He had not.

The decision to murder her had really been as unemotional as any decision to purchase the stock of a blue-chip corporation, and the killing itself had been conducted with the same cool efficiency with which he would have executed any stock-market investment.

Being an economist, his mother surely had understood.

His alibi had been unassailable. He inherited her estate. Life went on. His life, anyway.

Now, as he finished the candy bar, he felt sugar-soothed and chocolate-coddled.

He still wanted to kill Reynerd, but the unwise urgency of the compulsion had passed. He would take time to plan the hit.

When he acted, he would follow his scheme faithfully. This time, pillow would not become poker.

Noticing that the yellow slicker had shed a lot of water on the seat, he sighed but did nothing. Corky was too committed an anarchist to care about the upholstery.

Besides, he had Reynerd to brood about. A perpetual adolescent inside a dour exterior, Rolf had been unable to resist the temptation to deliver the sixth box in person. Looking for a thrill.

The fool had thought that perimeter security cameras did not exist solely because he himself could not spot them.

Are there no other planets in the solar system, Corky had asked him, *just because you can't locate them in the sky?*

When Ethan Truman, Manheim's security chief, came calling, Reynerd had been stunned. By his admission, he behaved suspiciously.

As Corky wadded up the candy wrapper and stuffed it into the trash bag, he wished that he could dispose of Reynerd as easily.

Suddenly rain fell more heavily than at any previous moment of the storm. The deluge knocked stubborn acorns from the oak under which he had parked, and cast them across the BMW. They rattled off the paint work and surely marred it, snapped off the windshield but did not crack it.

He didn't have to sit here, in a danger of acorns, plotting Reynerd's demise, until a rotting thousand-pound limb broke free, fell on the car, and crushed him for his trouble. He could get on with his day and mentally draw up blueprints for the murder while he attended to other business.

Corky drove a few miles to a popular upscale shopping mall and parked in the underground garage.

He got out of the BMW, stripped off his slicker and his droopy rain hat, which he tossed onto the

Past the foyer, the secure lobby was small but cozy, with an area rug to soften the marble, two Art Deco armchairs, and a table with a faux Tiffany lamp in red, amber, and green stained glass.

Although stairs served the five-story building, Ethan took the slow-moving elevator. Dunny Whistler lived—had lived—on the fifth floor.

Each of the first four floors held four large apartments, but the highest was divided into only two penthouse units.

A faint unpleasant odor lingered in the elevator from a recent passenger. Complex and subtle, the scent teased memory, but Ethan could not quite identify it.

As he ascended past the second floor, the elevator cab suddenly impressed him as being smaller than he remembered from previous visits. The ceiling loomed low, like a lid on a cook pot.

Passing the third floor, he realized that he was breathing faster than he should be, as though he were a man on a brisk walk. The air seemed to have grown thin, inadequate.

By the time he reached the fourth floor, he became convinced that he detected a *wrongness* in the sound of the elevator motor, in the hum of cables drawn through guide wheels. This creak, that tick, this squeak might be the sound of a linchpin pulling loose in the heart of the machinery.

The air grew thinner still, the walls closer, the ceiling lower, the machinery more suspect.

Perhaps the doors wouldn't open. The emergency phone might be out of order. His cell phone might not work in here.

In an earthquake, the shaft might collapse, crushing the cab to the dimensions of a coffin.

Nearing the fifth floor, he realized that these symptoms of claustrophobia, which he had never previously experienced, were a mask that concealed another fear, to which he, being a rational man, was loath to admit.

He half expected Rolf Reynerd to be waiting on the fifth floor.

How Reynerd would have known about Dunny or where Dunny lived, how he would have known when Ethan intended to come here—these were questions unanswerable without extensive investigation and perhaps without the abandonment of logic.

Nevertheless, Ethan stepped to the side of the cab, to make a smaller target of himself. He drew his pistol.

The elevator doors opened on a ten-by-twelve foyer paneled in honey-toned, figured anigre. Deserted.

Ethan didn't holster his weapon. Identical doors served two penthouse units, and he went directly to the Whistler apartment.

With the key provided by Dunny's attorney, he unlocked the door, eased it open, and entered cautiously.

The security alarm was not engaged. On his most recent visit, eight days ago, Ethan had set the alarm when he'd left.

The housekeeper, Mrs. Hernandez, had visited in the interim. Before Dunny landed in a hospital, in a coma, she had worked here three days a week; but now she came only on Wednesday.

In all likelihood, Mrs. Hernandez had forgotten to enter the alarm code when she'd departed last week. Yet as likely as this explanation might be, Ethan didn't believe it. Juanita Hernandez was a responsible woman, methodically attentive to detail.

Just inside the threshold, he stood listening. He left the door open at his back.

Rain drummed on the roof, a distant rumble like the marching feet of legions gone to war in some far, hollow kingdom.

Otherwise, only silence rewarded his keen attention. Maybe instinct warned him or maybe imagination misled him, but he sensed that this was not a slack silence, that it was instead a coiled quiet as full of potential energy as a cobra, rattler, or black mamba.

Because he preferred not to draw the attention of a neighbor and didn't want to facilitate any exit but his own, he closed the door. Locked it.

From scams, from drugs, from worse, Duncan Whistler had made himself rich. Criminals routinely grab big money, but few keep it or keep the freedom to spend it. Dunny had been clever enough to avoid arrest, to launder his money, and to pay his taxes.

Consequently, his apartment was enormous, with two connecting hallways, rooms leading into rooms, rooms that ordinarily did not spiral as they seemed to spiral now like nautilus shell into nautilus shell.

Searching in a hostile situation of the usual kind, Ethan would have proceeded with both hands on the gun, with arms out straight, maintaining a measured pressure on the trigger. He would have cleared doorways quick and low.

Instead, he gripped the pistol in his right hand, aimed at the ceiling. He proceeded cautiously but not with the full drama inherent in police-academy style.

To keep his back always to a wall, to avoid turning his back to a doorway, to move fast while scanning left-right-left, to be ever aware of his footing, of the need to stay sufficiently well balanced to assume, in an instant, a shooting stance: Doing all that, he would have had to admit that he was afraid of a dead man.

And there was the truth. Evaded, now acknowledged.

The claustrophobia in the elevator and the expectation that he would find Rolf Reynerd on the fifth floor had been nothing but attempts to deflect himself from consideration of his true fear, from the even less rational conviction that dead Dunny had risen from the morgue gurney and had wandered home with unknowable intent.

Ethan didn't believe that dead men could walk.

He doubted that Dunny, dead or alive, would harm him.

His anxiety arose from the possibility that Duncan Whistler, if indeed he'd left the hospital garden room under his own power, might be Dunny in name only. Having nearly drowned, having spent three months in a coma, he might be suffering brain damage that made him dangerous.

Although Dunny had his good qualities, not least of all the sense to recognize in Hannah a woman of exceptional virtues, he had been capable of ruthless violence. His success in the criminal life had not resulted from polished people skills and a nice smile.

He could break heads when he needed to break them. And sometimes he'd broken them when skull cracking wasn't necessary.

If Dunny were half the man that he'd once been, and the *wrong* half, Ethan preferred not to come face to face with him. Over the years, their relationship had taken peculiar turns; one final and still darker twist in the road could not be ruled out.

The huge living room featured high-end contemporary sofas and chairs, upholstered in wheat-colored silk. Tables, cabinets, and decorative objects were all Chinese antiques.

Either Dunny had discovered a genie-stuffed lamp and had wished himself exquisite taste, or he'd employed a pricey interior designer.

Here high above the olive trees, the big windows revealed the buildings across the street and a sky that looked like the soggy char and ashes of a vast, extinguished fire.

Outside: a car horn in the distance, the low

somber grumble of traffic up on Wilshire Boulevard.

The June-bug jitter, scarab click, tumblebug tap
of the beetle-voiced rain spoke at the window,
click-click-click.

In the living room, stillness distilled. Only his
breathing. His heart.

Ethan went into the study to seek the source of a
soft light.

On the chinoiserie desk stood a bronze lamp
with an alabaster shade. The buttery-yellow glow
struck iridescent colors from the border of mother-
of-pearl inlays.

Previously a framed photograph of Hannah had
been displayed on the desk. It was missing.

Ethan recalled his surprise on discovering the
photo during his first visit to the apartment, eleven
weeks ago, after he had learned that he held authority over Dunny's affairs.

Surprise had been matched by dismay. Although
Hannah had been gone for five years, the presence of the picture seemed to be an act of emo-
tional aggression, and somehow an insult to her
memory that she should be an object of affection—and once an object of desire—to a man
steeped in a life of crime and violence.

Ethan had left the photograph untouched, for
even with a power of attorney covering all of
Dunny's affairs, he had felt that the picture in the
handsome silver frame hadn't been his property
either to dispose of or to claim.

At the hospital on the night of Hannah's death,

again at the funeral, following twelve years of es-
trangement, Ethan and Dunny had spoken. Their
mutual grief had not, however, brought them together otherwise. They had not exchanged a word
for three years.

On the third anniversary of Hannah's passing,
Dunny had phoned to say that over those thirty-six
months, he had brooded long and hard on her untimely death at thirty-two. Gradually but profoundly, the loss of her—just knowing that she was
no longer out there somewhere in the world—had
affected him, had changed him forever.

Dunny claimed that he was going to go straight,
extract himself from all his criminal enterprises.
Ethan had not believed him, but had wished him
luck. They had never spoken again.

Later, he heard through third parties that Dunny
had gotten out of the life, that old friends and associates never saw him anymore, that he had become something of a hermit, bookish and with-
drawn.

With those rumors, Ethan had taken enough salt
to work up a thirst for truth. He remained certain
that eventually he would learn Duncan Whistler
had fallen back into old habits—or had never truly
forsaken them.

Later still, he heard that Dunny had returned to
the Church, attended Mass each week, and carried himself with a humility that had never before
characterized him.

Whether this was true or not, the fact remained
that Dunny had held fast to the fortune that he

amassed through fraud, theft, and dealing drugs. Living in luxury paid for with such dirty money, any genuinely reformed man might have been racked with guilt until at last he put his riches to a cleansing use.

More than the photograph of Hannah had been taken from the study. An atmosphere of bookish innocence was gone, as well.

A double score of hardcover volumes were stacked on the floor, in a corner. They had been removed from two shelves of the wall-to-wall bookcase.

One of the shelves, which had seemed to be fixed like all the others, had been removed. A section of the bookcase backing, which also had appeared fixed, had been slid aside, revealing a wall safe.

The twelve-inch diameter door of the safe stood open. Ethan felt inside. The spacious box proved empty.

He hadn't known that the study contained a safe. Logic suggested that no one but Dunny—and the installer—would have been aware of its existence.

Brain-damaged man dresses himself. Finds his way home. Remembers the combination to his safe.

Or . . . dead man comes home. In a mood to party, he picks up some spending money.

Dunny dead made nearly as much sense as Dunny with severe brain damage.

CHAPTER 13

Fric in a fracas: two trains clackety-clacking and whistling at key crossroads, Nazis in the villages, American troops fighting their way down from the hills, dead soldiers everywhere, and villainous SS officers in black uniforms herding Jews into the boxcars of a third train stopped at a station, more SS bastards shooting Catholics and burying their bodies in a mass grave here by a pine woods.

Few people knew that the Nazis had killed not only Jews but also millions of Christians. Most of the higher-echelon Nazis had adhered to a strange and informal pagan creed, worshiping land and race and myths of ancient Saxony, worshiping blood and power.

Few people knew, but Fric knew. He liked knowing things that other people didn't. Odd bits of history. Secrets. The mysteries of alchemy. Scientific curiosities.

Like how to power an electric clock with a potato. You needed a copper peg, a zinc nail, and some wire. A potato-powered clock looked stupid, but it worked.

Like the truncated pyramid on the back of the one-dollar bill. It represents the unfinished Temple of Solomon. The eye floating above the pyramid is symbolic of the Grand Architect of the Universe.

Like who built the first elevator. Using alternatively human, animal, and water power, Roman architect Vitruvius constructed the first elevators circa 50 B.C.

Fric knew.

A lot of the weird stuff he knew didn't have much application in daily life, didn't alter the fact that he was short for his age, and thin for his age, or that he had a geeky neck and the huge unreal green eyes that magazine writers slobbered about when describing his mother but that made him look like a cross between a hoot owl and an alien. He liked knowing these weird things anyway, even if they did not lift him out of the mire of Fricdom.

Having exotic knowledge rare in other people made Fric feel like a wizard. Or at least like a wizard's apprentice.

Aside from Mr. Jurgens, who came to the estate two days every month to clean and maintain the large collection of contemporary and antique electric trains, only Fric knew *everything* about the train room and its operation.

The trains belonged to that world-renowned movie star, Channing Manheim, who also happened to be his father. In the private world of Fric, the movie star had long been known as Ghost Dad because he was usually only here in spirit.

Ghost Dad knew very little about the train room. He had spent enough money on the collection to purchase the entire nation of Tuvalu, but he rarely played here.

Most people had never heard of the nation of Tuvalu. On nine islands in the South Pacific Ocean, with a population of just ten thousand, its major exports were copra and coconuts.

Most people had no idea what copra might be. Neither did Fric. He'd been meaning to look it up ever since he'd learned about Tuvalu.

The train room was in the higher of two basements, adjacent to the upper garage. It measured sixty-eight feet by forty-four feet, which amounted to more square footage than in the average home.

The lack of windows ensured that the real world could not intrude. The railroad fantasy ruled.

Along the two short walls, floor-to-ceiling shelves housed the train collection, except for whatever models were currently in use.

On the two long walls hung fabulous paintings of trains. Here, a locomotive exploded through thick luminous masses of fog, headlamp blazing. There, a train traveled a moonlit prairie. Trains of every vintage raced through forests, crossed rivers, climbed mountains in rain and sleet and snow and fog and dark of night, clouds billowing from their smokestacks, sparks flying from their wheels.

At the center of this great space, on a massive

table with many legs, stood a sculptured landscape of green hills, fields, forests, valleys, ravines, rivers, lakes. Seven miniature villages comprised of hundreds of intricately detailed structures were served by country lanes, eighteen bridges, nine tunnels. Convex curves, concave curves, horseshoe curves, straightaways, descending grades, and ascending grades featured more train track than there were coconuts in Tuvalu.

This amazing construction measured fifty feet by thirty-two, and you could either walk around it or, by lifting a gate, enter into it and take a tour on an inner racetrack walkway, as though you were a giant vacationing in the land of Lilliput.

Fric was in the thick of it.

He had distributed armies of toy soldiers across this landscape and had been playing trains and war at the same time. Considering the resources at his command for the game, it should have been more fun than it was.

Telephones were located at both the exterior and the interior control stations. When they rang with his personal tone, the sound startled him. He seldom received calls.

Twenty-four phone lines served the estate. Two of these were dedicated to the security system, another to the off-site monitoring of the hotel-type heating and air-conditioning system. Two were fax lines, and two were dedicated Internet lines.

Sixteen of the remaining seventeen lines were rationed to family and staff. Line 24 had a higher purpose.

Fric's father enjoyed the use of four lines because everyone in the world—once even the President of the United States—wanted to talk to him. Calls for Channing—or Chan or Channi, or even (in the case of one infatuated actress) Chi-Chi—often came in even when he wasn't in residence.

Mrs. McBee had four lines, although this didn't mean, as the Ghost Dad sometimes joked, that Mrs. McBee should start to think that she was as important as her boss.

Ha, ha, ha.

One of those four lines served Mr. and Mrs. McBee's apartment. The other three were her business phones.

On an ordinary day, management of the house didn't require those three lines. When Mrs. McBee had to plan and execute a party for four or five hundred Hollywood nitwits, however, three telephones were not always sufficient to deal with the event designer, the food caterer, the florist, the talent bookers, and the uncountable other mysterious agencies and forces that she had to marshal in order to produce an unforgettable evening.

Fric wondered if all that effort and expense was worthwhile. At the end of the night, half the guests departed so drunk or so drug-fried that in the morning they wouldn't remember where they had been.

If you sat them in lawn chairs, gave them bags of burgers, and provided tanker trucks of wine, they would get wasted as usual. Then they'd go home and puke their guts out as usual, collapse into unconsciousness as usual, and wake up the next day none the wiser.

Because he was chief of security, Mr. Truman had two lines in his apartment, one personal and one business.

Only two of the six maids lived on the estate, and they shared a phone line with the chauffeur.

The groundskeeper had a line of his own, but the totally scary chef, Mr. Hachette, and the happy cook, Mr. Baptiste, shared one of Mrs. McBee's lines.

Ms. Hepplewhite, personal assistant to Ghost Dad, had two lines for her use.

Freddie Nielander, the famous supermodel known in Fricsylvania as Nominal Mom, had a dedicated phone line here, although she had divorced Ghost Dad nearly ten years ago and had stayed overnight less than ten times since then.

Ghost Dad once told Freddie that he called her line every now and then, hoping she would answer and would tell him that she had come back to him at last and was home forever.

Ha, ha, ha. Ha, ha, ha.

Fric had enjoyed his own line since he was six. He never called anyone, except once when he'd used his father's contacts to get the unlisted home number for Mr. Mike Myers, the actor, who had dubbed the voice of the title character in *Shrek,* to tell him that *Shrek* absolutely, no doubt about it, *rocked.*

Mr. Myers had been very nice, had done the Shrek voice for him, and lots of other voices, and had made him laugh until his stomach hurt. This injury to his abdominal muscles resulted partly from the fact that Mr. Myers was wickedly funny and partly because Fric had not recently exercised his laugh-muscle group as much as he would have liked.

Fric's father, a believer in a shitload of paranormal phenomena, had set aside the last telephone line to receive calls from the dead. That was a story in itself.

Now, for the first time in eight days, since the Ghost Dad's most recent call, Fric heard his signature tone coming from the train-room phones.

Everyone on the estate had been assigned a different sound for the line or lines that were dedicated to him or her. Each of Ghost Dad's lines produced a simple *brrrrrrrr*. Mrs. McBee's signature tone was a series of musical chimes. Mr. Truman's lines played the first nine notes from the theme song of an ancient TV cop show, *Dragnet,* which was stupid, and Mr. Truman thought so, too, but he endured it.

This highly sophisticated telephone system could produce up to twelve different signature tones. Eight were standard. Four—like *Dragnet*—could be custom-designed for the client.

Fric had been assigned the dumbest of the standard tones, which the phone manufacturer described as "a cheerful child-pleasing sound suitable for the nursery or the bedrooms of younger children." Why infants in nurseries or toddlers in cribs ought to have their own telephones remained a mystery to Fric.

Were they going to call Babies R Us and order lobster-flavored teething rings? Maybe they would phone their mommies and say, *Yuch. I crapped in my diaper, and it don't feel good.*

Stupid.

Ooodelee-ooodelee-oo, said the train-room phones.

Fric hated the sound. He had hated it when he'd been six, and he hated it even worse now.

Ooodelee-ooodelee-oo.

This was the annoying sound that might be made by some furry, roly-poly, pink, half-bear, half-dog, half-wit character in a video made for preschoolers who thought stupid shows like *Teletubbies* were the pinnacle of humor and sophistication.

Humiliated even though he was alone, Fric pushed two transformer switches to kill power to the trains, and he answered the phone on the fourth ring. "Bob's Burger Barn and Cockroach Farm," he said. "Our special today is salmonella on toast with coleslaw for a buck."

"Hello, Aelfric," a man said.

Fric had expected to hear his father's voice. If instead he had heard the voice of Nominal Mom, he would have suffered cardiac arrest and dropped dead into the train controls.

The entire estate staff, with the possible exception of Chef Hachette, would have mourned for him. They would have been deeply, terribly sad. Deeply, deeply, terribly, terribly. For about forty minutes. Then they would have been busy, busy, busy preparing for the post-funeral gala to which would be invited perhaps a thousand famous and near-famous drunks, druggies, and butt-kissers eager to plant their lips on Ghost Dad's golden ass.

"Who's this?" Fric asked.

"Are you enjoying the trains, Fric?"

Fric had never heard this voice before. No one on the staff. Definitely a stranger.

Most of the people in the house didn't know that Fric was in the train room, and no one outside the estate could possibly know.

"How do you know about the trains?"

The man said, "Oh, I know lots of things other people don't. Just like you, Fric. Just like you."

The talented hairs on the back of Fric's neck did impressions of scurrying spiders.

"Who are you?"

"You don't know me," the man said. "When does your father return from Florida?"

"If you know so much, why don't you tell me?"

"December twenty-fourth. In the early afternoon. Christmas Eve," the stranger said.

Fric wasn't impressed. Millions of people knew his old man's whereabouts and his Christmas plans. Just a week ago, Ghost Dad had done a spot on *Entertainment Tonight,* talking about the film that he was shooting and about how much he looked forward to going home for the holidays.

"Fric, I'd like to be your friend."

"What're you, a pervert?"

Fric had heard about perverts. Heck, he'd probably met hundreds of them. He didn't know all the things they might do to a kid, and he wasn't *exactly* sure what thing they liked most to do, but he knew they were out there with their collections of kids' eyeballs, wearing necklaces made out of their victims' bones.

"I have no desire to hurt you," said the stranger, which was no doubt what any pervert would have said. "Quite the opposite. I want to help you, Fric."

"Help me do what?"

"Survive."

"What's your name?"

"I don't have a name."

"Everyone has to have a name, even if it's just one, like Cher or Godzilla."

"Not me. I'm only one among multitudes, nameless now. There's trouble coming, young Fric, and you need to be ready for it."

"What trouble?"

"Do you know of a place in your house where you could hide and never be found?" the stranger asked.

"That's a weird-ass question."

"You're going to need a place to hide where no one can find you, Fric. A deep and special secret place."

"Hide from who?"

"I can't tell you that. Let's just call him the Beast in Yellow. But you're going to need a secret place real soon."

Fric knew that he should hang up, that it might be dangerous to play along with this nutball. Most likely he was a pathetic pervert loser who got lucky with a phone number and would sooner or later start with the dirty talk. But the guy might also be a sorcerer who could cast a spell long distance, or he might be an evil psychologist who could hypnotize a boy over the telephone and make him rob liquor stores and then make him turn over all the money while clucking like a chicken.

Aware of those risks and many more, Fric nevertheless stayed on the line. This was by far the most interesting phone conversation he'd ever had.

Just in case this guy with no name happened to be the one from whom he might need to hide, Fric said, "Anyway, I've got bodyguards, and they carry submachine guns."

"That's not true, Aelfric. Lying won't get you anything but misery. There's heavy security on the estate, but it won't be good enough when the time comes, when the Beast in Yellow shows up."

"It is true," Fric deceitfully insisted. "My bodyguards are former Delta Force commandos, and one of them was even Mr. Universe before that. They can for sure kick major ass."

The stranger didn't respond.

After a couple seconds, Fric said, "Hello? You there?"

The man spoke in a whisper now. "Seems like I have a visitor, Fric. I'll call you again later." His whisper subsided to a murmur that Fric had to strain to hear. "Meanwhile, you start looking for that deep and special hiding place. There's not much time."

"Wait," Fric said, but the line went dead.

CHAPTER 14

Gun ready, muzzle up, chamber by hall by chamber, through Dunny Whistler's nautilus apartment, Ethan came to the bedroom.

One nightstand lamp had been left on. Against the headboard of the Chinese sleigh bed, decorative silk pillows fashioned from cheongsam fabrics had been artfully arranged by the housekeeper.

Also on the bed, cast off with evident haste, lay articles of men's clothing. Wrinkled, stained, still damp from the rain. Slacks, shirt, socks, underwear.

Tumbled in a corner were a pair of shoes.

Ethan didn't know what Dunny had been wearing when he had left the morgue at Our Lady of Angels Hospital. However, he wouldn't have wagered a penny against the proposition that these were the very clothes.

Moving closer to the bed, he detected the faint malodor that he'd first smelled in the elevator. Some of the components of the scent were more easily identified than they had been earlier: stale perspiration, a whiff of rancid ointment with a sulfate base, thin fumes of sour urine. The smell of illness, of being long abed and bathed only with basin and sponge.

Ethan became aware of a background sizzle, which he initially mistook for a new manifestation of the rain. Then he realized that he was listening to the fall of water in the master-bathroom shower.

The bathroom door stood ajar. Past the jamb and through the gap, with the sizzle came a wedge of light and wisps of steam.

He eased the door all the way open.

Golden marble sheathed the floor, the walls. In the black granite countertop, two black ceramic sinks were served by brushed-gold spouts and faucets.

Above the counter, a long expanse of beveled mirror, hazed with condensation, failed to present a clear reflection. His distorted shape moved under that frosted surface, like a strange pale something glimpsed swimming just beneath the shadow-dappled surface of a pond.

Veils of steam floated in the air.

Within the bathroom was a water closet. The door stood open, the toilet visible. No one in there.

Dunny had nearly been drowned in this toilet.

Neighbors in a fourth-floor apartment had heard him struggling furiously for his life, shouting for help.

Police arrived quickly and caught the assailants in desperate flight. They found Dunny lying on his side in front of the toilet, semiconscious and coughing up water.

By the time the ambulance arrived, he had fallen into a coma.

His attackers—who'd come for money, vengeance, or both—had not been cheated recently by Dunny. They had been in prison for six years and, only recently released, had come to settle a long-overdue account.

Dunny might have hoped to journey far from his life of crime, but old sins had caught up with him that night.

Now on the bathroom floor lay two rumpled, damp black towels. Two dry towels still hung on the rack.

The shower was in the far-right corner from the entrance to the bathroom. Even if the steam-opaqued glass door had been clear, Ethan couldn't have seen into that cubicle from any distance.

Approaching the stall, he had an image in his mind of the Dunny Whistler whom he expected to encounter. Skin sickly pale where not a lifeless gray, impervious to the pinking effect of hot water. Gray eyes, the whites now pure crimson with hemorrhages.

Still holding the gun in his right hand, he gripped the door with his left and, after a hesitation, pulled it open.

The stall was unoccupied. Water beat upon the marble floor and swirled down the drain.

Leaning into the stall, he reached behind the cascade, to the single control, and turned off the flow.

The sudden silence in the wake of the watery sizzle seemed to announce his presence as clearly as if he had triggered an air horn.

Nervously, he turned toward the bathroom entrance, expecting some response, but not sure what that might be.

Even with the water turned off, steam continued to escape the shower, though in thinner veils, pouring over the top of the glass door and around Ethan.

In spite of the moist air, his mouth had gone dry. Pressed together, tongue and palate came apart as reluctantly as two strips of Velcro.

When he started toward the bathroom door, his attention was drawn again to the movement of his vague and distorted reflection in the clouded mirror above the sinks.

Then he saw the impossible shape, which brought him to a halt.

In the mirror, under the skin of condensation, loomed a pale form as blurred as Ethan's veiled image but nonetheless recognizable as a figure, man or woman.

Ethan was alone. A quick survey of the bathroom failed to reveal any object or any fluke of architecture that the misted mirror might trick into a ghostly human shape.

So he closed his eyes. Opened them. Still the shape.

He could hear only his heart now, only his heart, not fast, but faster, sledgehammer heavy, pounding and pounding, slamming blood to his brain to flush out unreason.

Of course his imagination had given meaning to a meaningless blur in a mirror, in the same way that he might have found men and dragons and all kinds of fanciful creatures among the clouds in a summer sky. Imagination. Of course.

But then this man, this dragon, whatever—it moved in the mirror. Not much: a little, enough to make Ethan's sledgehammer heart stutter between blows.

Maybe the movement also was imaginary.

Hesitantly he approached the mirror. He didn't step directly in front of the phantom form, for in spite of the strong rush of blood that ought to have clarified his thinking, Ethan suffered from the superstitious conviction that something terrible would happen to him if his reflection were to overlay the ghostly shape.

Surely the movement of the misted apparition had been imaginary, but if it had been, then he imagined it *again*. The figure seemed to be motioning for him to come forward, closer.

Ethan would not have admitted to Hazard Yancy or to any other cop from the old days, perhaps not even to Hannah if she were alive, that when he put his hand to the mirror, he half expected to feel not wet glass, but the hand of another, making contact from a cold and forbidding Elsewhere.

He swabbed away an arc of mist, leaving a glimmering smear of water.

Even as Ethan's hand moved, so did the phantom in the mirror, sliding away from the cleansing swipe. Cunningly elusive, it remained behind the shielding condensation—and moved directly in front of him.

With the exception of his face, Ethan's vague reflection in the misted glass had been dark because his clothes were dark, his hair. The steam-frosted shape now before him rose as pale as moonlight and moth wings, impossibly supplanting his own image.

Fear knocked on his heart, but he wouldn't let it in, as when he'd been a cop under fire and dared not panic.

Anyway, he felt as though he were half in a trance, accepting the impossible here as he might easily accept it in a dream.

The apparition leaned toward him, as if trying to discern his nature from the far side of the silvered glass, in much the same way that he himself leaned forward to study it.

Raising his hand once more, Ethan tentatively wiped away a narrow swath of mist, fully expecting that when he came eye to eye with his reflection, the eyes would not be his, but gray like Dunny Whistler's eyes.

Again the mystery in the mirror moved, quicker than Ethan's hand, remaining blurred behind the frosting of condensation.

Only when breath exploded from Ethan did he realize that he had been holding it.

On the inhale, he heard a crash in a far room of the apartment, the brittle music of shattering glass.

CHAPTER 15

Ethan had told Palomar Laboratories to analyze his blood for traces of illicit chemicals, in case he'd been drugged without his knowledge. During the events at Reynerd's apartment house, he had almost seemed to be in an altered state of consciousness.

Now, leaving the steamy bathroom, he felt no less disoriented than when, after being gut shot, he had found himself behind the wheel of the Expedition once more, unharmed.

Whatever had happened—or had only seemed to happen—at the mirror, he no longer entirely trusted his senses. As a consequence, he proceeded with greater caution than before, assuming that yet again things might not be as they appeared to be.

He passed through rooms he'd already searched and then into new territory, arriving at last in the kitchen. Shattered glass sparkled on the breakfast table and littered the floor.

Also on the floor lay the silver picture frame missing from the desk in the study. The photo of Hannah had been stripped out of it.

Whoever had taken the picture had been in too great a hurry to release the four fasteners on the back of the frame, and had instead smashed the glass.

The rear door of the apartment stood open.

Beyond lay a wide hall that served the back of both penthouse units. At the nearer end, an exit sign marked a stairwell. Toward the farther end was a freight elevator big enough to carry refrigerators and large pieces of furniture.

If someone had taken the freight route down, he had already completed his descent. No sound issued from the elevator machinery.

Ethan hurried to the stairs. Opened the fire door. Paused on the threshold, listening.

Groan or moan, or melancholy sigh, or clank of chains: Even a ghost ought to make a sound, but only a cold hollow silence rose out of the stairwell.

He went down quickly, ten flights to the ground floor, then another two flights to the garage. He encountered neither a flesh-and-blood resident nor a spirit.

The scent of sickness and fever sweats, first detected in the elevator, didn't linger here. Instead, he smelled a faint soapy odor, as if someone fresh from a bath had passed this way. And a trace of spicy aftershave.

Pushing open the steel fire door, stepping into the garage, he heard an engine, smelled exhaust fumes. Of the forty parking stalls, many were empty at this hour on a work day.

Toward the front of the garage, a car backed out of a stall. Ethan recognized Dunny's midnight-blue Mercedes sedan.

Triggered by remote control, the garage gate was already rising with a steely clack and clatter.

Pistol still in hand, Ethan ran toward the car as it pulled away from him. The gate rose slowly, and the Mercedes had to stop for it. Through the rear window, he could see the silhouette of a man behind the steering wheel, but not clearly enough to make an identification.

Drawing near to the Mercedes, he swung wide of it. He intended to go directly to the driver's door.

The car shot forward while the barrier continued to rise, before it was fully out of the way. The roof of the Mercedes came within a fraction of an inch of leaving a generous paint sample on the bottom rail of the ascending gate, and raced up the steep exit ramp to the street.

The driver thumbed CLOSE on his remote even as he passed under the gate, which was clattering down again when Ethan reached it. Already the Mercedes had turned out of sight into the street above.

He stood there for a moment, peering through the gate into the gray storm light.

Rainwater streamed down the driveway ramp. Foaming, it vanished through the slots of a drain in the pavement immediately outside the garage.

On that concrete incline, a small lizard, back broken by a car tire, but still alive, struggled gamely against the sluicing water. So persistently did it twitch upward inch by inch that it seemed to believe all its needs could be satisfied and all its injuries healed by some power at the summit.

Not wanting to see the little creature inevitably defeated and washed down to die upon the drain grate, Ethan turned away from the sight of it.

He returned the pistol to his shoulder holster.

He studied his hands. They were trembling.

On the back stairs once more, climbing to the fifth floor, he encountered the lingering soapy smell, the trace of aftershave. This time, he also detected another odor less clean than the first two, elusive but disturbing.

Whatever else he might be, Dunny Whistler was surely a living man, not an animated corpse. Why would one of the walking dead come home to shower, shave, and dress in clean clothes? Absurd.

In the apartment kitchen, Ethan used a Dust-Buster to vacuum up the fragments of picture-frame glass.

He found a spoon and an open half-gallon container of ice cream in the sink. Apparently, those who were recently resurrected enjoyed chocolate caramel swirl.

He put the ice cream in the freezer and returned the empty picture frame to the study.

In the master bedroom, he stopped short of the bathroom doorway. He had intended to check the mirror once more, to see if it was still misted and if, in the glass, anything moved that shouldn't be there.

Actively seeking that phantom suddenly seemed to be a bad idea. Instead, he left the apartment, turning off the lights and locking the door behind him.

In the main elevator, as Ethan descended, he thought, *For the same reason that the proverbial wolf put on a sheep's skin to move undetected among the lambs.*

That was why one of the walking dead would shower, shave, and put on a good suit.

As the elevator conveyed Ethan to the ground floor, he knew how Alice must have felt in free fall down the rabbit hole.

CHAPTER 16

After shutting down the railroads, Fric left the dirty Nazis to their evil schemes, departed the unreality of the train room for the unreality of the multi-million-dollar car collection in the garage, and ran for the stairs.

He should have taken the elevator. That cable-less mechanism, which raised and lowered the cab on a powerful hydraulic ram, would be too slow, however, for his current mood.

Fric's engine raced, raced. The telephone conversation with the weird stranger—whom he had dubbed Mysterious Caller—was high-octane fuel for a boy with a boring life, a feverish imagination, and empty hours to fill.

He didn't climb the stairs; he *assaulted* them. Legs pumping, grabbing at the handrail, Fric flung himself up from the basement, conquering two, four, six, eight long flights, to the top of Palazzo Rospo, where he had rooms on the third floor.

Only Fric seemed to know the meaning of the name given to the great house by its first owner:

Palazzo Rospo. Nearly everyone knew that *palazzo* was Italian for "palace," but no one except perhaps a few sneeringly superior European film directors seemed to have any idea what *rospo* meant.

To be fair, most people who visited the estate didn't give a rip what it was called or what its grand name actually meant. They had more important issues on their minds—such as the weekend box-office numbers, the overnight TV ratings, the latest executive shuffles at the studios and networks, who to screw in the new deal that they were putting together, how much to screw them out of, how to bedazzle them so they wouldn't realize they were being screwed, how to find a new source for cocaine, and whether their careers might have been even bigger if they had begun having face-lifts when they were eighteen.

Among the few who had ever given a thought to the name of the estate, there were competing theories.

Some believed the house had been named after a famous Italian statesman or philosopher, or architect. The number of people in the film industry who knew anything about statesmen, philosophers, and architects was almost as small as the number who'd be able to give a lecture regarding the structure of matter on a subatomic level; consequently, this theory was easily embraced and never challenged.

Others were certain that Rospo had been either the maiden name of the original owner's beloved mother or the name of a snow sled that he had ridden with great delight in childhood, when he had been truly happy for the last time in his life.

Still others assumed that it had been named after the original owner's secret love, a young actress named Vera Jean Rospo.

Vera Jean Rospo had actually existed back in the 1930s, though her real name had been Hilda May Glorkal.

The producer, agent, or whoever had renamed her Rospo must have secretly despised poor Hilda. *Rospo* was Italian for "toad."

Only Fric seemed to know that Palazzo Rospo was as close as you could get, in Italian, to naming a house Toad Hall.

Fric had done some research. He liked knowing things.

Evidently, the film mogul who built the estate more than sixty years ago had possessed a sense of humor and had read *The Wind in the Willows.* In that book, a character named Toad lived in a grand house named Toad Hall.

These days, no one in the film business read books.

In Fric's experience, no one in the business had a sense of humor anymore, either.

He climbed the stairs so fast that he was breathing hard by the time that he reached the north hallway on the third floor. This wasn't good. He should have stopped. He should have rested.

Instead, he hurried along the north hall to the east hall, where his private rooms were located.

The antiques that he passed on the top floor were spectacular, although not of the museum quality to be found on the two lower levels.

Fric's rooms had been refurnished a year ago. Ghost Dad's interior designer had taken Fric shopping. To redo the furniture in these quarters, his father had provided him with a budget of thirty-five thousand dollars.

Fric had not asked for fancy new furniture. He never asked for anything—except at Christmas, when he was required to fill out the childish Dear Santa form that his father insisted be provided by Mrs. McBee. The idea of refurnishing was entirely Ghost Dad's.

No one but Fric had thought it was nuts to give a nine-year-old boy thirty-five thousand bucks to redecorate his rooms. The designer and the salespeople acted as if this were the usual drill, that every nine-year-old had an equal amount to spend on a room makeover.

Lunatics.

Fric often suspected that the soft-spoken, seemingly reasonable people surrounding him were in fact all BIG-TIME CRAZY.

Every item in his remade rooms was modern, sleek, and bright.

He had nothing against the furniture and artworks of distant times. He liked all that stuff. But sixty thousand square feet of fine antiques was enough already.

In his own private space, he wanted to feel like a kid, not like an old French dwarf, which sometimes departed the lavatory corridor in the approximate time frame of the vandalism. But they would not be able to obtain a useful image of his face.

He had intentionally worn nondescript clothes, the better to fade into the rabble. On videotapes recorded elsewhere in the mall, he wouldn't be easily identifiable as the same man who had visited the restroom just prior to the flood.

A gorgeous excess of spangled and frosted holiday decorations further compromised the usefulness of the cameras, infringing upon the established angles of view.

The winter-wonderland theme avoided both direct and symbolic references to Christmas: no angels, no mangers, no images of Santa Claus, no busy elves, no reindeer, no traditional ornaments—and no festive lengths of colored lights, only tiny white twinkle bulbs. Festoons of plastic and shiny aluminum-foil icicles, measured in miles, glimmered everywhere. Thousands of large, sequined Styrofoam snowflakes hung on strings from the ceiling. In the central rotunda, ten life-size ice skaters, all mechanical figures moving on tracks, glided around a fake frozen pond in an elaborate re-creation of a winter landscape complete with snowmen, snow forts, robot children threatening one another with plastic snowballs, and animated figures of polar bears in comical poses.

Corky Laputa was enchanted by the pure, blissful vacuousness of it all.

On the first escalator to the ground floor, on the

second to the garage, he brooded over a few details of his scheme to kill Rolf Reynerd. Both as he
had shopped and as he had enjoyed his destructive escapades in the mall, Corky had carefully laid
a bold and simple plan for murder.

He was a natural-born multitasker.

To those who had never studied political strategy
and who also lacked a solid grounding in philosophy, Corky's capers in the men's room might have
seemed at best to be childish larks. A society
could seldom be brought down solely by acts of
violence, however, and every thoughtful anarchist
must be dedicated to his mission every minute of
the day, wreaking havoc by actions both small and
large.

Illiterate punks defacing public property with
spray-painted graffiti, suicide bombers, semico-
herent pop stars selling rage and nihilism set to an
infectious beat, attorneys specializing in tort
law and filing massive class-action suits with the
express intention of destroying major corporations
and age-old institutions, serial killers, drug deal-
ers, crooked cops, corrupted corporate executives cooking the books and stealing from pension
funds, faithless priests molesting children, politicians riding to reelection by the agitation of class
envy: All these and numerous others, working at
different levels, some as destructive as runaway
freight trains hurtling off the tracks, others quietly
chewing like termites at the fabric of civility and
reason, were necessary to cause the current order
to collapse into ruin.

If somehow Corky could have carried the black plague without risking his own life, he would have enthusiastically passed that disease to everyone he met by way of sneezes, coughs, touches, and kisses. If sometimes all he could do was flush a cherry bomb down a public toilet, he would advance chaos by that tiny increment while he awaited opportunities to do greater damage.

In the garage, when he reached his BMW, he shrugged out of his sports coat. Before settling behind the steering wheel, he donned the yellow slicker once more. He put the droopy yellow rain hat on the front passenger's seat, within easy reach.

Besides providing superb protection in even a hard-driving rain, the slicker was the ideal gear in which to commit homicide. Blood could be easily washed off the shiny vinyl surface, leaving no stain.

According to the Bible, to every season there is a purpose, a time to kill and a time to heal.

Not much of a healer, Corky believed there was a time to kill and a time not to kill. The time to kill had arrived.

Corky's death list contained more than one name, and Reynerd was not at the top. Anarchy could be a demanding faith.

CHAPTER 18

Fric in the suffacatorium, anxious and wheezing, and no doubt bluer than a blue moon, dragged himself out of the middle of the room and sat with his back against a steel wall.

The medicinal inhaler in his right hand weighed slightly more than a Mercedes 500 M-Class SUV.

If he'd been his father, he would have been surrounded by an entourage big enough to help him lift the stupid thing. Yet another disadvantage of being a geek loner.

For lack of oxygen, his thoughts grew muddled. For a moment he believed that his right hand was trapped on the floor under a heavy shotgun, that it was a shotgun he wanted to lift, put in his mouth.

Fric almost cast the device away in terror. Then in a moment of clarity, he recognized the inhaler and held fast to it.

He couldn't breathe, couldn't think, could only wheeze and cough and wheeze, and seemed to be spiraling into one of those rare attacks that were severe enough to require hospital emergency-room treatment. Doctors would poke him and prod him, bend him and fold him, babbling about their favorite Manheim movies. The scene with the elephants! The airplane-to-airplane midair jump with no parachute! The sinking ship! The alien snake king! The funny monkeys! Nurses would gush over him, telling him how lucky he was and how exciting it must be to have a father who was a star, a hero, a hunk, a genius.

He might as well die here, die now.

Although he was not Clark Kent or Peter Parker, Fric raised the gazillion-pound device to his face. He slipped the mouthpiece between his lips and administered a dose of medication, sucking in the deepest breath that he could manage, which wasn't deep at all.

In his throat: a hard-boiled egg or a stone, or a huge wad of phlegm worthy of the Guinness book of world records, a plug of some kind, allowing only thin wisps of air to enter, to exit.

He leaned forward. Clenching and relaxing neck muscles, chest and abdominal muscles. Struggling to draw cool medicated air into his lungs, to exhale the hot stale breath pooled like syrup in his chest.

Two puffs. That was the prescribed dosage.

He triggered puff two.

He might have gagged on the faint metallic taste if his inflamed and swollen airways could have executed a gag, but the tissues were able only to contract, not expand, flexing tighter, tighter, tighter.

A yellow-gray soot seemed to sift down through his eyes, the slow fall of an interior twilight.

Dizzy. Sitting here on the floor, back against the wall, legs straight out in front of him, he felt as if he were balanced on one foot on a high wire, teetering, about to take a death plunge.

Two puffs. He'd taken two doses.

Overmedicating was inadvisable. Dangerous.

Two puffs. That ought to be enough. Usually was. Sometimes just one dose allowed him to slip out of this invisible hangman's noose.

Don't overmedicate. Doctor's orders.

Don't panic. Doctor's advice.

Give the medication a chance to work. Doctor's instruction.

Screw the doctor.

He triggered a third puff.

A bone-click sound like dice on a game board rattled out of his throat, and his wheezing became less shrill, less of a whistle, more of a raw windy rasping.

Hot air exploding out. Cool air going down. Fric on the mend.

He dropped the inhaler on his lap.

Fifteen minutes was the average time required to recover from an asthma attack. Nothing could be done but wait it out.

Darkness faded from the edges of his vision. Blur gradually gave way to clarity.

Fric on the floor in an empty steel room, with nothing to distract him but hooks in the ceiling, naturally looked at those peculiar curved forms, and thought about them.

When he'd first discovered the room, he'd been reminded of movie scenes set in meat lockers, cow carcasses hanging from ceiling hooks.

He had wondered if a mad criminal genius had hung the bodies of his human victims in *this* meat locker. Perhaps the room had once been refrigerated.

The hooks weren't set far enough apart to accommodate the bodies of grown men and women. Initially, Fric had sprung to the grim conclusion that the killer had collected dead, refrigerated *children*.

On closer inspection, he had seen that the stainless-steel hooks were not sharp. They were too blunt to pierce either kids or cows.

That's when he'd set the matter of the hooks aside for later contemplation and had come to the determination that the room had been a suffacatorium. The existence of the interior lock release, however, had proved this theory wrong.

As his wheezing quieted, as breath came more easily, as the tightness in his chest loosened, Fric studied the hooks, the brushed-steel walls, trying to arrive at a third theory regarding the purpose of this place. He remained mystified.

He'd told no one about the pivoting section of closet shelving or about the hidden room. What made the hidey-hole so cool was less its exotic nature than the fact that only he knew it existed.

This space could serve as the "deep and special

secret place" that, according to Mysterious Caller, would soon be needed.

Maybe he should stock it with supplies. Two or three six-packs of Pepsi. Several packages of peanut-butter-and-cracker sandwiches. A couple flashlights with spare batteries.

Warm cola would never be his first choice of beverage, but it would be preferable to dying of thirst. And even warm cola was better than being stranded in the Mojave with no source of water, forced to save and drink your own urine.

Peanut-butter-and-cracker sandwiches, tasty under ordinary circumstances, would be unspeakably vile if accompanied by urine.

Maybe he should stock *four* six-packs of cola.

Even though he wouldn't be drinking his urine, he would need something in which to pee, supposing that he would be required to hide out longer than a few hours. A pot with a lid. Better yet, a jar with a screw top.

Mysterious Caller hadn't said how long Fric should expect to be under siege. They would have to discuss that in their next chat.

The stranger had promised that he would be in touch again. If he was a pervert, he would call for sure, drooling all over his phone. If he wasn't a pervert, then he might be a sincere friend, in which case he would still call, but for better reasons.

Time passed, the asthma relented, and Fric got to his feet. He clipped the inhaler to his belt.

A little woozy, he balanced himself with one hand against the cold steel wall as he went to the door.

A minute later, in his bedroom, he sat on the edge of the bed and lifted the handset from the telephone. An indicator light on the keyboard appeared at his private line.

No one had phoned him since he'd answered his *Ooodelee-ooodelee-oo* in the train room. After pressing *69, he listened while his phone automatically entered the number of his most recent caller.

If he'd been a brainiac trained in the skills required to be an enormously dangerous spy, and if he'd had the supernaturally attuned ear of Beethoven before Beethoven went deaf, or if one of his parents had been an extraterrestrial sent to Earth to crossbreed with humans, perhaps Fric could have translated those rapidly sounded telephone tones into numerals. He could have memorized Mysterious Caller's phone number for future use.

He was nothing more, however, than the son of the biggest movie star in the world. That position came with lots of perks, like a free Xbox from Microsoft and a lifetime pass to Disneyland, but it didn't confer upon him either astonishing genius or paranormal powers.

After waiting through twelve rings, he engaged the speakerphone feature. He went to a window while the number continued to ring.

The billiards-table smoothness of the east lawn sloped away through oaks, through cedars, to rose gardens, vanishing into gray rain and silver mist.

Fric wondered if he should tell anyone about

Mysterious Caller and the warning of impending danger.

If he called Ghost Dad's global cell-phone number, it would be answered either by a bodyguard or by his father's personal makeup artist. Or by his personal hair stylist. Or by the masseur who always traveled with him. Or by his spiritual adviser, Ming du Lac, or by any of a dozen other flunkies orbiting the Fourth Most Admired Man in the World.

The phone would be handed from one to another of them, across unknowable vertical and horizontal distances, until after ten minutes or fifteen, Ghost Dad would come on the line. He would say, "Hey, my main man, guess who's here with me and wants to talk to you."

Then before Fric could say a word, Ghost Dad would pass the phone to Julia Roberts or Arnold Schwarzenegger, or to Tobey Maguire, or to Kirsten Dunst, or to Winnie the Wonder Horse, probably to all of them, and they would be sweet to Fric. They would ask him how he was doing in school, whether he wanted to be the biggest movie star in the world when he grew up, what variety of oats he preferred in his feed bag. . . .

By the time that the phone had been passed around to Ghost Dad again, a reporter from *Entertainment Weekly,* using the wrong end of a pencil, would be taking notes for a feature piece about the father-son chat. When the story hit print, every fact would be wrong, and Fric would be made to look like either a whiny moron or a spoiled sissy.

Worse, a giggly young actress with no serious credits but with a little industry buzz—what they used to call a starlet—might answer Ghost Dad's phone, as often one of them did. She would be tickled by the name Fric because these girls were always tickled by everything. He'd talked to scores of them, hundreds, over the years, and they seemed to be as alike as ears of corn picked in the same field, as if some farmer *grew* them out in Iowa and shipped them to Hollywood in railroad cars.

Fric wasn't able to phone his Nominal Mom, Freddie Nielander, because she would be in some far and fabulously glamorous place like Monte Carlo, being gorgeous. He didn't have a reliable phone number for her.

Mrs. McBee, and by extension Mr. McBee, were kind to Fric. They seemed to have his best interests always in mind.

Nevertheless, Fric was reluctant to turn to them in a case like this. Mr. McBee was just a little . . . daffy. And Mrs. McBee was an all-knowing, all-seeing, rule-making, formidable woman whose soft-spoken words and mere looks of disapproval were powerful enough to cause the object of her reprimand to suffer internal bleeding.

Mr. and Mrs. McBee served *in loco parentis.* This was a Latin legal phrase that meant they had been given the authority of Fric's parents when his parents were absent, which was nearly always.

When he'd first heard *in loco parentis,* he'd thought it meant that his parents were loco.

The McBees, however, had come with the house, which they had managed long before Ghost Dad had owned it. To Fric, their deeper allegiance seemed to be to Palazzo Rospo, to place and to tradition, more than to any single employer or his family.

Mr. Baptiste, the happy cook, was a friendly acquaintance, not actually a friend, and certainly not a confidant.

Mr. Hachette, the fearsome and possibly insane chef, was not a person to whom *anyone* would turn in time of need, except perhaps Satan. The Prince of Hell would value the chef's advice.

Fric carefully planned every foray into the kitchen so as to avoid Mr. Hachette. Garlic wouldn't repel the chef, because he loved garlic, but a crucifix pressed to his flesh would surely cause him to burst into flames and, screaming, to take flight like a bat.

The possibility existed that the psychotic chef was the very danger about which Mysterious Caller had been warning Fric.

Indeed, virtually any of the twenty-five staff members might be a scheming homicidal nutjob cunningly concealed behind a smiley mask. An ax murderer. An ice-pick killer. A silk-scarf strangler.

Maybe *all twenty-five* were ax murderers waiting to strike. Maybe the next full moon would stir tides of madness in their heads, and they would explode simultaneously, committing hideous acts of bloody violence, attacking one another with guns, hatchets, and high-speed food processors.

If you couldn't know the full truth of what your father and your mother thought of you, if you couldn't *really* know who they were and what went on inside their heads, then you couldn't expect to know for sure anything about other people who were even less close to you.

Fric pretty much trusted Mr. Truman not to be a psychopath with a chain-saw obsession. Mr. Truman had once been a cop, after all.

Besides, something about Ethan Truman was so *right*. Fric didn't have the words to describe it, but he recognized it. Mr. Truman was solid. When he came into a room, he was *there*. When he talked to you, he was *connected* to you.

Fric had never known anyone quite like him.

Nevertheless, he wouldn't tell even Mr. Truman about Mysterious Caller and the need to find a hiding place.

For one thing, he feared not being believed. Boys his age often made up wild stories. Not Fric. But other boys did. Fric didn't want Mr. Truman to think he was a lying sack of kid crap.

Neither did he want Mr. Truman to think that he was a fraidy-cat, a spineless jellyfish, a chicken-hearted coward.

No one would ever believe that Fric could save the world twenty times over, the way they believed his father had done, but he didn't want anyone to think he was a timid baby. Especially not Mr. Truman.

Besides, he sort of liked having this secret. It was better than trains.

He watched the wet day, half expecting to catch a brief glimpse of a villain skulking across the estate, obscured by rain and mist.

After Mysterious Caller's number had rung maybe a hundred times without being answered, Fric returned to the phone and terminated the call.

He had work to do. Preparations to make.

A bad thing was coming. Fric intended to be ready to meet it, greet it, defeat it.

CHAPTER 19

Under a black umbrella, Ethan Truman walked the grassy avenue of graves, his shoes squishing in the saturated turf.

Giant drooping cedars mourned with the weeping day, and birds, like spirits risen, stirred in the cloistered branches when he passed near enough to worry them.

As far as he could see, he alone walked in these mortal fields. Respect for the loved and lost was usually paid on sunny days, with remembrances as bright as the weather. No one would choose to visit a cemetery in a storm.

No one but a cop whose mainspring of curiosity had been wound tight, who had been born with a compulsive need to know the truth. A clockwork mechanism in his heart and soul, designed by fate and granted as a birthright, compelled him to follow wherever suspicion and logic might lead.

In this case, suspicion, logic, and dread.

Intuition wove in him the strange conviction that he would prove to be not the first visitor of the day and that in this bastion of the dead, he would discover something disturbing, though he had no idea what it might be.

Headstones of time-eaten granite, mausoleums crusted with lichen and stained by settled smog, memorial columns and obelisks tilted by ground subsidence: None of that traditional architecture identified this as a cemetery. The marker at each of these graves—a bronze plaque on a pale granite plinth—had been set flush with the grass. From a distance the burial ground appeared to be an ordinary park.

Radiant and unique in life, Hannah was here remembered with the same drab bronze that memorialized the thousands of others who slept eternal in these fields.

Ethan visited her grave six or seven times a year, including once at Christmas. And always on their anniversary.

He didn't know why he came that often. Hannah didn't lie here, only her bones. She lived in his heart, always with him.

Sometimes he thought he traveled to this place less to remember her—for she was not in the least forgotten—than to gaze at the empty plot beside her, at the blank granite tablet on which a cast-bronze plaque with his name would one day be fixed.

At thirty-seven, he was too young a man to welcome death, and life continued to hold the greater promise for him. Nevertheless, five years after losing Hannah, Ethan still felt that something of himself had died, as well.

Through twelve years of marriage, they delayed having children. They had been so young. No need to hurry.

No one expected a vibrant, beautiful, thirty-two-year-old woman to be diagnosed with a virulent cancer, to be dead four months later. When it took her, the malignancy also claimed the children they might have brought into the world, and the grandchildren thereafter.

In a sense, Ethan *had* died with her: the Ethan who would have been a loving father to the children blessed with her grace, the Ethan who would have known the joy of her company for decades yet to come, who would have known the peace and the purpose of growing old at her side.

Perhaps he would have been surprised to find her grave torn open, empty.

What he found instead of grave robbery, though unexpected, did not surprise him.

At the base of her bronze plaque lay two dozen fresh long-stemmed roses. The florist had wrapped them in a cone of stiff cellophane that partly protected the blooms from the pelting rain.

These were hybrid tea roses, a golden-red variety named Broadway. Of all the roses that Hannah loved and grew, Broadway had been her favorite.

Ethan turned slowly in a full circle, studying the cemetery. No figure moved anywhere on those gently sloped green acres.

He peered with special suspicion at every cedar,

every oak. As best he could tell, those trunks didn't shelter a lurking observer.

No traffic moved on the narrow winding road that served the cemetery. Ethan's Expedition—white as winter, glimmering like ice—was the only vehicle parked along the lane.

Beyond the boundaries of the cemetery, urban vistas loomed in veils of rain and fog, less like a real city than like a metropolis in a dream. No rumble of traffic, no bleat of horn penetrated from its maze of streets, as though all its citizens had long ago gone horizontal in these silent grassy acres surrounding Ethan.

He looked down at the bouquet once more. In addition to bright color, the Broadway rose offers a fine fragrance. It flourishes in any sun-drenched garden and is more resistant to mildew than are many other varieties.

Two dozen roses found on a grave would not be admitted as evidence in a court of law. Yet Ethan regarded these colorful blooms as proof enough of a strange courtship of the dead, by the dead.

CHAPTER 20

Eating a mamoul, washing it down with coffee from a thermos, Hazard Yancy sat in an unmarked sedan directly in front of Rolf Reynerd's apartment house in West Hollywood.

The early winter twilight would not descend for another thirty minutes, but under the pall of the storm, the city had an hour ago settled into a prolonged dusk. Activated by photoelectric sensors, streetlamps glowed, painting a steely sheen on the needles of rain that stitched the gauzy gray sky ever closer to the earth.

Although it might appear that Hazard lingered over cookies on the city's time, he was considering his approach to Reynerd.

After lunch with Ethan, he had returned to his desk in Homicide. In a couple hours, on the Internet and off, working both the keyboard and the phone, he had learned more than a little about his subject.

Rolf Reynerd was an actor who only intermittently made a living at his craft. Between occasional multi-episode supporting roles as a bad boy on one cheesy soap opera or another, he endured long periods of unemployment.

In an episode of *The X-Files,* he'd played a federal agent driven psychotic by an alien brain leech. In an episode of *Law & Order,* he had been a psychotic personal trainer who killed himself and his wife near the end of the first act. In a TV commercial for a deodorant, he had been cast as a psychotic guard in a Soviet gulag; the spot had never gone national, and he'd made only a little money from it.

An actor unlucky enough to be typecast usually didn't fall into that career trap until he'd experienced great success in a memorable role. Thereafter, the public had difficulty accepting him as any character type other than the one that had made him famous.

In Reynerd's case, however, he seemed to have been typecast even in failure. This suggested to Hazard that certain qualities of the man's personality and demeanor allowed him to portray only mentally unbalanced characters, that he played screw-loose well because several of his own screws had stripped threads.

Despite an unreliable flow of income, Rolf Reynerd lived in a spacious apartment in a handsome building, in a good neighborhood. He dressed well, frequented the hottest nightclubs with young actresses who had a taste for Dom Perignon, and drove a new Jaguar.

According to former friends of Reynerd's widowed mother, Mina, she doted on her son, believed that one day he would be a star, and subsidized him with a fat monthly check.

They were her *former* friends because Mina Reynerd had died four months ago. She'd first been shot in the foot, then beaten to death with a marble lamp encrusted with ornate ormolu mountings.

Her killer remained unknown. Detectives had turned up no leads in her case.

Not surprisingly, the sole heir to her estate had been her only child, poor typecast Rolf.

The actor had a dead-solid perfect alibi for the evening of his mother's murder.

This didn't either surprise Hazard or convince him of Reynerd's innocence. Sole heirs usually had airtight alibis.

According to the medical examiner, Mina had been bludgeoned to death between 9:00 and 11:00 P.M. She'd been struck with such brutal force that patterns of the bronze ormolu had been deeply imprinted on her flesh, even crushed into the bone of her forehead.

Rolf had been partying with his current girlfriend and four other couples from seven o'clock that evening until two o'clock in the morning. They had been a flashy, noisy, memorable group at the two trendy nightclubs between which they had divided their time.

Anyway, even though Mina's murder remained unsolved, and even if Rolf's alibi had been only that he'd stayed home alone, playing with himself,

Hazard would have had no excuse to give the man a once-over. The case belonged to another detective.

By happy chance, one of Reynerd's party pals that night—Jerry Nemo—was known to Hazard from another case, which opened a door.

Two months ago, a drug dealer named Carter Cook had been shot in the head. Apparently the murder had been incidental to robbery; Cook had been loaded with merchandise and cash.

Reynerd's buddy, Jerry Nemo, had placed a call to Cook's cell phone an hour before the murder. Nemo was a customer, a cokehead. He set up a meet with Cook to score some blow.

Nemo was no longer under suspicion. No one in Los Angeles or anywhere on Planet Earth was still under suspicion. The Cook murder qualified as classic shitcan, a case unlikely ever to be solved.

Nevertheless, by pretending that Nemo remained a suspect, Hazard had an excuse to approach Reynerd and scope him out for Ethan.

He didn't need an excuse for the purpose of satisfying Reynerd. Using just badge and bluster, Hazard could spin a hundred stories convincing enough to persuade the party boy to open the door and answer questions.

Should Reynerd directly or indirectly disclose his obsession with Channing Manheim, however, or in the unlikely event that Reynerd revealed an intent to harm the movie star, Hazard would have to refer the situation outside the Homicide Division for investigation. Then he would need a credible intradepartmental explanation as to why he had been interviewing Reynerd in the first place, when information regarding Manheim had fallen into his lap.

By pretending that Reynerd's snow-blowing buddy, Nemo, remained a suspect in the Carter Cook murder, Hazard could cover his ass.

After licking powdered sugar and mamoul crumbs from his fingers, he got out of the car.

He didn't bother with an umbrella. Considering that he presented nearly two linebackers' worth of surface area to the rain, he would have needed a bumbershoot the size of a beach umbrella to shelter himself completely.

Approaching the apartment house, he proceeded briskly but did not run through the downpour. The building didn't set far back from the street.

Besides, Hazard seldom accommodated himself to the world, for the world usually moved out of his way. He hardly noticed the rain.

Inside, he ignored the elevator and climbed the stairs.

He'd once been shot at in an elevator. He'd ridden up to the sixth floor, the doors had slid aside, and the perp had been waiting.

Targeted in an elevator, you don't have much room to dodge: As a place in which to be shot at, only a telephone booth and a parked car offered worse circumstances.

Hazard had been shot at while sitting in a parked

car, but never while standing in a telephone booth. He expected that it was only a matter of time.

Waiting outside the elevator, the shooter had been packing a 9-mm pistol. And he'd been pants-wetting nervous.

If the freak had been either calm or armed with a shotgun, the outcome for Hazard would have been much bleaker than what happened.

The first round had slammed into the cabin ceiling. The second blew a hole in the back wall. The third winged the stranger who had shared the elevator with Hazard.

As it turned out, the stranger, an IRS agent, was the intended target. Hazard had just been in the wrong place at an inconvenient time, marked for death only because he was a witness.

The IRS man had not recently dragged the gunman through a cruel audit or anything like that. He'd been jumping the shooter's wife.

Instead of returning fire, Hazard had gone in under the pistol. He wrenched it away from the assailant, drove him across the hallway, hammered him into the wall, and compacted his testicles with a knee. Not accidentally, he broke the guy's arm.

Later, for a few months during the divorce proceedings, he dated the shooter's wife. She wasn't a bad woman. She'd just gotten mixed up with bad men.

Now, Hazard climbed to the second floor of the apartment house, not entirely comfortable with the confining nature of the stairwell.

At Apartment 2B, he rang the bell without hesitation.

When Rolf Reynerd opened the door, he proved to be a perfect match for Ethan's description, down to the methamphetamine shine in his cold blue eyes and to the tiny flecks of foamy spittle in the corners of his mouth, which suggested that he was so routinely amped that he might, in a moment of toxic psychosis, spin wildly around his apartment under the misapprehension that he was Spiderman squirting silky filaments from his wrists.

Hazard flashed his ID, spread a garden-growing load of crap about Jerry Nemo being a suspect in the death of Carter Cook, and got into the apartment so fast that rain still dripped from his earlobes.

A product of weight training and protein powders, Reynerd looked as if he would have to eat a dozen raw eggs every morning merely to sustain the muscle mass in his right triceps.

Of the two of them, Hazard Yancy was the bigger and no doubt the smarter, but he cautioned himself to remain wary, alert.

Reynerd closed the apartment door and escorted Hazard into the living room, expressing a sincere desire to cooperate, as well as a sincere conviction that his good friend Jerry Nemo was incapable of harming a fly.

Regardless of how fly-loving Nemo might or might not be, Reynerd troweled on the sincerity as thickly as he might have done had he been wearing a purple-dinosaur costume, teaching little life lessons to preschoolers on an early-morning TV program.

If his acting had been this dreadful when he'd appeared on those soap operas, the writers must have been frantic to script Reynerd into a deadly car accident or a lightning-quick terminal brain tumor. The audience might have preferred a bloody end for him, by shotgun in an elevator.

Furniture, carpet, blinds, photographs of birds: Everything in the apartment was black-and-white. On the TV, in an old black-and-white movie, Clark Gable and Claudette Colbert showed Reynerd how it ought to be done.

In black slacks and a black-and-white sport shirt, the sincere friend of Jerry Nemo had coordinated his wardrobe with the decor.

At the suggestion of his host, Hazard settled in an armchair. He perched on the edge, the better to get up fast.

Reynerd plucked the remote control off the coffee table, pausing Gable in midspeech and Colbert in reaction. He sat on the sofa.

The only color in the room was provided by Reynerd's blue eyes and by the bright designs that enlivened the two bags of potato chips that flanked him on the sofa.

The bag to his left offered Hawaiian-style chips. The bag to his right held a sour-cream-and-chive variety. Mr. Gourmet.

Hazard had not forgotten Ethan's enigmatic but intense warning about snack-food containers.

Both bags were open, standing upright, plump

enough to be full. Hazard detected the faint oily aroma of the chips.

If the bags contained handguns as well as chips, Hazard wasn't able to smell the weapons. He couldn't see them, either, because the bags, made of foil, were not transparent.

Reynerd sat with his hands palms-down on his thighs, licking his lips, as though he might reach for a salty treat at any moment.

With a nod to indicate the frozen image on the TV, the actor said, "That's the perfect medium for me. I was born too late. I should have lived back then."

"When's that?" Hazard asked, for he knew that suspects often revealed the most when they seemed to be rambling.

"The 1930s and '40s. When all films were black-and-white. I'd have been a star in those days."

"Is that right?"

"I'm too strong a personality for color films. I explode off the screen. I overwhelm the medium, the audience."

"I can see where that would be a problem."

"In the color era, the most successful stars have all been flat personalities, shallow. They're an inch wide, half an inch deep."

"And why is that?"

"The color, the depth of field made possible by modern cameras, surround-sound technology— all that stuff makes flat personalities bigger than life, provides them with a powerful illusion of substance and complexity."

"You, on the other hand—"

"I, on the other hand, am wide and deep and so *alive* to begin with that the further enhancement of modern film technology puts me over the top, makes a caricature of me."

"That must be frustrating," Hazard commiserated.

"You can't imagine. In black-and-white film, I would fill the screen without overwhelming the audience. Where are the Bogarts and Bacalls of our age, the Tracys and Hepburns, the Cary Grants and the Gary Coopers and the John Waynes?"

"We don't have them," Hazard acknowledged.

"They couldn't succeed today," Reynerd assured him. "They would be too powerful for modern film, too deep, entirely too glamorous. What did you think of *Moonshaker*?"

Hazard frowned. "Of what?"

"*Moonshaker*. Channing Manheim's latest hit. Two hundred million dollars at the box office."

Perhaps Reynerd was so obsessed with Manheim that sooner or later in *any* conversation, he would bring the subject around to the star.

Wary nonetheless, Hazard said, "I don't go to the movies."

"Everybody goes."

"Not really. Fewer than thirty million tickets have to be sold to generate two hundred million bucks. Maybe just ten percent of the country."

"All right, but other people see it on TV, on DVD."

"Maybe another thirty million. Pick any particular

movie—at least eighty percent of the country never sees it. They have lives to live."

Reynerd seemed to boggle at the notion that movies were not the hub of the world. Although he didn't reach for a gun in either of the chip-bag holsters, his displeasure with this turn in the conversation was evident.

Hazard got back in the actor's good graces by saying, "Now, in the black-and-white era you're talking about, half the country went to the movies once a week. Stars were *stars* in those days. Everybody knew Clark Gable's movies, Jimmy Stewart's."

"Exactly," Reynerd agreed. "Manheim would have faded away in the black-and-white era. He would have been too thin for the medium, too flat. He'd be forgotten now. Worse than forgotten—he'd be *unknown*."

The doorbell rang.

Sounding puzzled and mildly annoyed, Reynerd said, "I'm not expecting anyone."

"Me neither," Hazard said dryly.

Reynerd glanced at the windows, where the sodden gray twilight slowly expired beyond the glass.

He shifted his attention to the television. Gable and Colbert remained frozen in flirtatious argument.

At last Reynerd rose from the sofa, but then hesitated, looking down at the bags of potato chips.

Watching this peculiar performance, Hazard wondered if the actor was approaching that amped-out condition in which a meth freak can slide precipitously from a peak of hyperacute awareness down into a haze of disorientation, into crushing exhaustion.

When the bell rang again, Reynerd finally crossed the living room. "These geeks are always coming around selling Jesus," he said irritably, wearily, and opened the door.

From the armchair, Hazard couldn't see who fired the shots. The hard *boom, boom, boom* of three rapid reports, however, told him that the killer was packing a high-caliber piece, maybe a .357, or bigger.

Unless Seventh Day Adventists had adopted hard-sell techniques, Reynerd had been mistaken about the purpose of the caller.

Hazard came up from the armchair on the second *boom*, reached for his holstered pistol on the third.

As mortal now as even Gable and Bogart had proved to be, Reynerd jolted backward, went down, casting a Technicolor splatter across the black-and-white apartment in which he had been so wide, so deep, so *alive*.

Moving toward the actor, Hazard heard running footsteps in the public hall.

Reynerd had taken three rounds point-blank in his broad chest, including one that must have punched significant scraps of his heart muscle through an exit wound in his back. He'd been mortuary material even as he fell.

The death-blinded blue of the actor's shock-widened eyes seemed less cold than they had been in life. He looked as if he needed some Jesus now.

Hazard stepped over the body, out of the apartment. He saw the shooter reach the end of the hallway. The guy leaped down the stairs two at a time. Hazard went after him.

CHAPTER 21

Above the city, as the retreating day shed its grizzled beard in wet ravelings of mist and drab drizzles, the hard face of night had not quite yet appeared.

On a west-side street of art galleries, of high-end
shops, of restaurants in which elitist attitude was
served more efficiently than the food, Ethan
tucked the Expedition tight up against a red curb,
two wheels in a flooded gutter, confident that the
parking patrol issued tickets far less enthusiastically in foul weather than in fair.

The businesses in this neighborhood, seeking a
sophisticated and exclusive clientele, stood behind shop fronts without flash, relying on subdued
signage. Mere money shouts; wealth whispers.

The retail shops were not yet closed, and most
restaurants were an hour away from opening their
doors. Early lamplight gilded the dripping leaves of
curbside trees and transformed the wet sidewalk
into a path paved with pirates' treasure.

Without umbrella, Ethan moved in the shelter of

shop awnings, all of which were tan or forest-green, silver or black, except for that in front of Forever Roses, which was a deep coral-pink.

The florist's shop might as aptly have been named Only Roses, for beyond the glass doors of the coolers that lined the big front room, no flowers other than roses could be seen, along with supplies of cut ferns and other greenery that were used to soften bright bouquets and arrangements.

Because of Hannah's gardening interests, now even five years after she had been laid to rest under mounded roses, Ethan could identify many of the varieties in the coolers.

Here was a rose so dark red that it almost appeared to be black, with petals that looked like velvet, earning its name: Black Magic.

And here, the John F. Kennedy rose: white petals so thick and glossy that they resembled sculpted wax.

The Charlotte Armstrong: large, fragrant, deep pink blooms. The Jardins de Bagatelle, the Rio Samba, the Paul McCartney rose, the Auguste Renoir, the Barbara Bush, the Voodoo, and the Bride's Dream.

Behind the customer counter stood an exceptional rose who looked as Hannah might have looked had she lived to be sixty. Thick salt-and-pepper hair cut short and shaggy. Large dark eyes brimming with life and delight. Time had not faded this woman's beauty, but had enriched it with a patina of experience.

Reading the name tag on the clerk's blouse,

Ethan said, "Rowena, most of what I see in these coolers are hybrid tea varieties. Do you also like climbing roses?"

"Oh, yes, all kinds of roses," Rowena said, her voice musical and warm. "But we seldom use climbing roses. Varieties with longer stems work better in arrangements."

He introduced himself and, as was his habit in such situations, explained that he'd once been a homicide detective but recently had gone to work as an assistant to a high-profile celebrity.

Los Angeles and environs were acrawl with poseurs and frauds who claimed association with the rich and famous. Yet even those who had been made cynical by this city of deception neverthe-less believed what Ethan told them, or pretended that they did.

Hannah had said that people trusted him easily because combined in him were the quiet steely strength of Dirty Harry Callahan and the earnest in-nocence of Huck Finn. *That,* he had replied, was a movie he *never* wanted to see.

Rowena, whether responding to the Harry-Huck of him or to other qualities, seemed to accept Ethan for who and what he claimed to be.

"If I guess your favorite variety of climbing rose," he said, "will you answer a few questions about a customer you served earlier this afternoon?"

"Is this police or celebrity business?"

"Both."

"Oh, delicious. I love running a rose shop, but

194

DEAN KOONTZ

there's more fragrance than excitement in it. Make your guess."

Because in Rowena he saw Hannah as she might have been at sixty, he spoke the name of the climbing rose that his lost wife had loved best: "Saint Joseph's Coat."

Rowena seemed genuinely surprised and pleased. "That's exactly right! You put Sherlock to shame."

"Now your half of the bargain," Ethan said, leaning with both arms on the counter. "This afternoon a man came in here and bought a bouquet of Broadway roses."

The dazzling golden-red blooms on Hannah's grave had been wrapped in a cone of stiff cellophane. Instead of Scotch tape or staples, a series of six peel-and-press stickers had been applied to seal cellophane to cellophane and thus ensure that the cone kept its shape. Each fancy foil sticker bore the name and address of Forever Roses.

"We had just two dozen," Rowena said, "and he took them all."

"You remember him then?"

"Oh, yes. He was . . . quite memorable."

"Would you describe him for me?"

"Tall, athletic but a bit on the thin side, wearing an exquisite gray suit."

Duncan Whistler owned uncounted fine suits, all custom-tailored at great cost.

"He was a handsome man," Rowena continued, "but terribly pale, as though he hadn't seen the sun in months."

Comatose for twelve weeks, Dunny had developed a hospital pallor subsequently seasoned by at least an hour of morgue time.

"He had the most magnetic gray eyes," Rowena said, "with flecks of green. Beautiful."

She had given a perfect description of Dunny's eyes.

"He said that he wanted the roses for a special woman."

At her funeral, Dunny had seen the Broadway roses.

Rowena smiled. "He said an old friend would be around before long, asking what kind of roses he'd bought. I gather you're in competition for the same girl."

Neither the winter day outside nor the cool air here in the flower shop was responsible for the chill that might have rattled Ethan's teeth if he hadn't clenched them.

He suddenly realized that Rowena's smile had a curious tilt, as though tempered by uncertainty or uneasiness.

When she recognized how deeply her revelation troubled him, her tentative smile faltered, vanished.

"He was a strange man," she said.

"Did he say anything else?"

Rowena broke eye contact and looked toward the windows at the front of the shop, as though expecting to see someone familiar—and unwelcome—at the door.

Ethan gave her an opportunity to consider her

words, and at last she spoke: "He said you think he's dead."

Images swelled to the foreground of memory: the empty gurney and the tangled shroud in the hospital morgue; the elusive phantom in the steam-blurred bathroom mirror; the lizard on the driveway, struggling to ascend in spite of its broken back, confronted by a cruel degree of incline and by sluicing water as cold and insistent as the flow of time. . . .

"He said you think he's dead," Rowena repeated, shifting her gaze from the shop door to Ethan once more. "And he said I should tell you that you're right."

CHAPTER 22

Hazard in the hallway, Hazard on the stairs, acutely aware of what an easy target a big man made in a narrow space, threw himself nonetheless into the hot pursuit. When you took the job, you knew it wasn't part of the deal that you could pick and choose the places where you would put your life on the line.

Besides, like most cops, he operated on the superstitious conviction that the greatest risk came with hesitation, came in the moment when nerve was briefly lost. Survival depended on boldness seasoned with just enough fear to discourage outright recklessness.

Or so it was easy to believe until a bit of boldness got you killed.

In the movies, cops were always yelling "Halt! Police!" when they knew that the dirtbags running away from them weren't going to obey, but also when a shout would reveal their presence before absolutely necessary and even before every bad guy on the game board realized that badges were in play.

Hazard Yancy, who had recently escaped being shot at while in an armchair, didn't bellow either a command or a threat at the gunman who had killed Rolf Reynerd. He just plunged down the stairs after the guy.

By the time Hazard reached the midfloor landing, the shooter had thundered to the bottom of the lower flight, losing his balance as he flew off the last step into the public foyer. He slipped on the Mexican-tile floor, windmilled his arms, but avoided a fall.

Running, the perp never looked back, suggesting that he was oblivious of being pursued.

As he gave chase, Hazard was in the guy's head. Expecting Reynerd to be home alone, the rent-a-killer gink comes in to do a quick pop, he drops the sucker with a heart-buster, manages to avoid getting lit up in the process, breaks hard for the street, and now he's already thinking about smoking some good bo with some long-legged fresh who's waiting for him in his crib.

The shooter hit the front door, and at the same moment, Hazard landed in the foyer, but the shooter was making too much noise to hear doom closing from behind, and Hazard didn't slip as his quarry had done, so he was gaining.

When Hazard reached the door, the shooter was already out in the night, down the exterior steps, maybe thinking about spending some of his hit money on fancy chrome laces for the wheels on his bucket, some on 24-carat flash to drape his lady.

Not much wind, cold rain, Hazard on the steps, shooter on the walk: The gap between them closed as inevitably as that between a speeding truck and a brick wall.

Then the car horn blared. One long bleat, two short.

A signal. Prearranged.

In the street, not at the curb, stood a dark Mercedes-Benz, headlights on, engine running, exhaust pluming from the tailpipe. The front passenger door stood open to welcome the shooter. This was a getaway bucket with style, maybe a G-ride, a gangster ride, stolen out of a driveway in Beverly Hills, and behind the wheel sat the shooter's ace kool, his backup homey, ready to shave the tires bald in a pedal-jammed escape.

The one long bleat followed by two short must have signaled the rabbit that he had a wolf on his ass, because he made a sudden break to the left, off the sidewalk. He torqued himself around so hard that he should have stumbled, should have fallen, but didn't, and instead brought up the piece with which he'd popped Reynerd.

Having lost the advantage of surprise, Hazard finally shouted "Police! Drop it!" just like in the movies, but of course the shooter had already earned life without possibility of parole, maybe even the death penalty, by chilling Reynerd, and he had nothing to lose. He would be no more likely to drop his weapon than he would be likely to drop his pants and bend over.

The piece looked big, not a trey-eight or a .357, but a four-five. Loaded with wicked ammo, a four-five would reliably bust bone and tenderize meat for the undertaker, but it required stability and calculation to compensate for the kick.

In a bad stance, from panic rather than poise, the perp squeezed off a shot. His pull was actually more jerk than squeeze, and the round went so wild that Hazard stood at less risk of being drilled by this bullet than of being pulverized by an asteroid.

The instant he saw the muzzle spit fire into the rain and heard the slug shatter a window in the apartment house behind him, however, Hazard was only partly driven by training, partly by duty, and mostly by blood. The shooter wouldn't be sloppy twice. All the sensitivity instruction, all the earnest lectures in social policy and political consequences, all the police-commission directives to meet violence with patience, understanding, and measured response were impediments to survival when, in the quick, you had to kill or be killed.

The sound of bullet-battered glass was still ringing through the rain when Hazard got a two-hand grip on his gun, assumed the stance, and answered fire with fire. He placed two rounds with little concern for the stern judgment of the *Los Angeles Times* in matters of police deportment, but with every concern for the safety of Mother Yancy's favorite baby boy.

The first shot took the killer down, and the second rapped him hammer-hard even as his knees were still buckling.

Reflexively, the perp fired the .45 not at Hazard, but into the grass in front of his own feet. The recoil broke his weakened grip, and the gun flew from his hand.

He met the ground with one knee, in the briefest genuflection, then with two knees, then with his face.

Hazard kicked the dropped .45 away from the killer, into shrubs and shadows, and he ran toward the street, toward the Mercedes.

The driver gunned the engine an instant before he let up on the brakes. Shrieking tires spun off clouds of vaporized rain, and smoke that stank of burnt rubber.

Maybe Hazard was at risk of being shot by the driver, who could get a line on him through the open front passenger's door, but that was a risk worth taking. An ace-kool wheelman specialized in flight, not fight, and although the guy would be packing heat for use in a cornered-rat situation, he wouldn't likely draw down on anyone when he had an open street, gas in the tank, and ignition.

Splashing along the puddled pavement, Hazard reached his sedan. Before he could get around that parked vehicle, into the street, the spinning tires of the getaway car bit blacktop and bolted forward with a bark. Momentum slammed shut the passenger's door.

He hadn't gotten a look at the driver.

The figure behind the wheel had been little more than a shadow. Hunched, distorted, somehow . . . *wrong.*

To Hazard's surprise, the ragged fingernails of superstition scratched at the inner hollows of his bones, where usually it lay buried, quiet, forgotten. But he didn't know what had stirred his fear or why a sense of the uncanny suddenly possessed him.

As the Mercedes roared away, Hazard didn't squeeze off a few shots at it, as a movie cop would have done. This was a peaceful residential neighborhood in which people watching reruns of *Seinfeld* and other people cleaning vegetables for dinner had every right not to expect to be shot dead over their TV remotes and their cutting boards by the stray rounds of a reckless detective.

He ran after the car, however, because he couldn't get a clear take on the license number. Exhaust vapors, street spray, falling rain, and the gloom of day's end conspired to shroud the rear plate.

He persisted, anyway, glad that he regularly used a treadmill. Although the Mercedes soon pulled away from him, a couple streetlamps and a clearing crosswind revealed the plate number in pieces.

Most likely the car had been stolen. The driver would dump it. Nevertheless, having the number was better than not having it.

Giving up the chase, Hazard headed back to the front lawn at the apartment house. He hoped that he'd shot the shooter dead instead of merely wounding him.

Minutes from now, an Officer Involved Shooting team would be on the scene. Depending on the personal philosophies of team members, they would either vigorously build a defense of Hazard's actions and strive to exonerate him without any genuine search for the truth, which was fine by him, or they would seek the tiniest of meaningless inconsistencies and screw him to a cross of bogus evidence, haul him into the court of public opinion, and encourage the media to build a fire at his feet and give him the Saint Joan treatment.

The third possibility was that the OIS team might arrive without preconceptions, might examine the facts analytically, and might come to a dispassionate conclusion based on logic and reason, which would be jake with Hazard because he'd done nothing wrong.

Of course, he'd never heard of such a thing actually occurring, and he considered it far less likely than being eyewitness to eight flying reindeer and an elf-piloted sleigh three nights hence.

If the shooter was alive, he might assert that Hazard had killed Reynerd and then tried to frame him for it. Or that he'd been in the neighborhood, collecting donations to Toys for Tots, when he'd been caught in a cross fire, giving the *real* shooter a chance to escape.

Whatever he claimed, cop haters and aggressively brainless citizens would believe him.

More important, the shooter would find an attorney to file suit against the city, eager to feed at the public trough. A settlement would be reached, regardless of the merits of the case, and Hazard would probably be sacrificed as part of the package. Politicians were no more protective of good law-enforcement officers than they were of the young interns whom they regularly abused and sometimes killed.

The shooter posed far less of a problem dead than alive.

Hazard could have *moseyed* back to the scene, giving the perp a chance to bleed out another critical pint, but he ran.

The killer lay where he'd fallen, face planted in the wet grass. A snail had ascended the back of his neck.

People were at windows, looking down, expressions blank, like dead sentinels at the gates of Hell. Hazard expected to see Reynerd at one of the panes, black-and-white, too glamorous for his time.

He turned the shooter faceup. Somebody's son, somebody's homey, in his early twenties, with a shaved head, wearing a tiny coke spoon for an earring.

Hazard was glad to see the mouth stretched in a death rictus and the eyes full of eternity, but at the same time he was sickened by the sense of relief that flooded through him.

Standing in the storm, swallowing a hard-to-repress sludge of half-digested mamoul that burned in his throat, he used his cell phone to call the division and report the situation.

After making the call, he could have gone inside

to watch from the foyer, but he waited in the downpour.

City lights reflected in every storm-glazed surface, yet when night swallowed twilight, darkness swelled in threatening coils, like a well-fed snake.

The rat-feet tap of palm-pelting rain suggested that legions of tree rodents scurried through the masses of arching fronds overhead.

Hazard saw two snails on the dead man's face. He wanted to flick them off, but he hesitated to do so.

Some onlookers at the windows would suspect him of tampering with evidence. Their sinister assumptions might charm the OIS team.

That scratching in his bones again. That sense of *wrongness.*

One dead upstairs, one dead here, sirens in the distance.

What the hell is going on? What the hell?

CHAPTER 23

Rowena, mistress of the roses, recalled Dunny Whistler's words again, but obviously more for her consideration than for Ethan's: "He said you think he's dead, and that you're right."

A rattle of hinges, a faint jingle of shop bells turned Ethan toward the front door. No one had entered.

The vagrant wind, having wandered out of the storm for a while, had here returned, blustering at the entrance to Forever Roses, trembling the door.

Behind the counter, the woman wondered, "What on earth could he mean by such a bizarre statement?"

"Did you ask him?"

"He said it after he paid for the roses, on his way out of the shop. I didn't have a chance to ask. Is it a joke between the two of you?"

"Did he smile when he said it?"

Rowena considered, shook her head. "No."

From the corner of his eye, Ethan glimpsed a figure that had silently appeared. Turning toward it, breath caught in his throat, he discovered that he had been tricked by his own reflection in the glass door of a cooler.

In pails of water, on tiered racks, the chilled roses bloomed so gloriously that you could easily forget they were in fact already dead, and in a few days would be wilted, spotted brown, and rotting.

These coolers, where Death concealed himself in petals bright, reminded Ethan of morgue drawers, in which the deceased lay much as they had looked in life, and in whom Death dwelt but did not yet manifest himself in all the gaudy details of corruption.

Although Rowena was personable and lovely, although this realm of roses ought to have been pleasant, Ethan grew anxious to leave. "Did my . . . my friend have any other message for me?"

"No. That was all of it, I think."

"Thank you, Rowena. You've been helpful."

"Have I really?" she asked, looking at him strangely, perhaps as puzzled by this odd encounter as by her conversation with Dunny Whistler.

"Yes," he assured her. "Yes, you have."

Wind rattled the door again as Ethan put his hand upon the knob, and behind him Rowena said, "One more thing."

When he turned to her, although they were now almost forty feet apart, he saw that his questioning had left her more pensive than she had been when he'd first approached her.

"As your friend was leaving," she said, "he stopped in the open doorway, on the threshold there, and said to me, 'God bless you and your roses.' "

Perhaps this had been a peculiar thing for a man like Dunny to have said, but nothing in those six words seemed to explain why the memory of them clouded Rowena's face with uneasiness.

She said, "Just as he finished speaking, the lights pulsed and dimmed, went off—but then came on again. I didn't think anything about it at the time, not with the storm, but now it somehow seems . . . significant. I don't know why."

Years of experience with interrogations told Ethan that Rowena had not finished, and that his patient silence would draw her out more surely and more quickly than anything he could say.

"When the lights dimmed and went off, your friend laughed. Just a little laugh, not long, not loud. He glanced at the ceiling as the lights flick-ered, and he laughed, and then he left."

Ethan waited.

Rowena appeared to be surprised that she had said this much about such a small moment, but then she added, "There was something terrible about that laugh."

The beautiful dead roses behind walls of glass.

A beast of wind snuffling at the door.

Rain gnashing at the windows.

Ethan said, "Terrible?"

"I don't have the words to explain it. No humor in that laugh, but some terrible . . . quality."

Self-conscious, she brushed at the spotless

countertop with one hand, as if she saw dust, debris, a stain.

Clearly, she had said all that she wished to say, or could.

"God bless you and your roses," Ethan told her, as though he were countering a curse.

He didn't know what he would have done had the lights flickered, but they burned steadily.

Rowena smiled uncertainly.

Turning to the door again, Ethan encountered his reflection and closed his eyes, perhaps to guard against the sight of an impossible phantom figure sharing the glass with him. He opened the door, then opened his eyes.

In a growl of wind and a jingle of overhead bells, he stepped out of the shop into the cold teeth of the December night, and drew the door shut behind him.

He waited in the entry alcove, between the display windows, as a young couple in raincoats and hoods passed on the sidewalk, led by a golden retriever on a leash.

Relishing the rain and wind, the soaked retriever pranced on webbed paws, snout lifted to savor mysterious scents upon the chilly air. Before it fully passed, it looked up, and its eyes were as wise as they were liquid and dark.

The dog halted, pricked its floppy ears as much as they would prick, and cocked its head as though not entirely sure what kind of man stood here in the shelter of the coral-pink awning, between the roses and the rain. The tail wagged, but only twice, and tentatively.

Stopped by their canine companion, the young couple said, "Good evening," and Ethan replied, and the woman spoke to the dog, "Tink, let's go."

Tink hesitated, searching Ethan's eyes, and only moved on when the woman repeated the command.

Because the couple and the dog were headed in the direction of his SUV, Ethan waited briefly, to avoid following on their heels.

The leaves of the curbside trees were still gilded by lamplight, and from their pointed tips flowed drips and drizzles as glimmerous as molten gold.

In the street, the traffic appeared to be lighter than it should have been at this hour, moving faster than the weather warranted.

Awning by awning, Ethan approached the Expedition, fishing keys from his jacket pocket.

Ahead, Tink twice slowed to an amble, looked back at Ethan, but didn't stop.

The ozone-scented cascades of rain couldn't rinse away the yeasty aroma of freshly baked bread, which issued from one of the glittery restaurants preparing to open their doors for dinner.

At the end of the block, the dog halted once more, turning its head to stare.

Though her voice was muffled by distance, screened by the sizzle of rain and the swish of passing traffic, the woman could be heard saying, "Tink, let's go." She repeated the command twice before the dog began to move again, picking up the slack in its leash.

The trio disappeared around the corner.

Arriving at the red zone near the end of the block, where he had parked illegally, Ethan hesitated under the last awning. He monitored the approaching traffic until he saw a long gap between vehicles.

He stepped into the rain and crossed the sidewalk. He jumped over the dirty racing current in the gutter.

Behind his SUV, he thumbed the lock-release button on his key fob. The Expedition chirruped at him.

Having waited until there was no passing traffic to splash him, he rounded the back of the vehicle while a chance remained that he could avoid an immediate need for a dry cleaner.

Approaching the driver's door, he realized that he had not taken a close look at the SUV itself from the shelter of the final awning, and suddenly he was convinced that *this* time, when he got behind the wheel, he would discover Dunny Whistler, dead or alive, waiting for him in the passenger's seat.

The real threat lay elsewhere.

Entering from the cross street at too high a speed, a Chrysler PT Cruiser fishtailed in the intersection. The driver tried to resist the slide instead of steering into it, the wheels locked, and the Cruiser spun out.

In the spin, the left front bumper rapped Ethan

hard. Clipped, flipped, he slammed into the Expedition, shattering the side window with his face.

He wasn't aware of ricocheting off the SUV, collapsing to the pavement, but then he was down on the wet blacktop, tumbling, with the smell of exhaust fumes, with the taste of blood.

He heard brakes shriek, but not the Cruiser. Air brakes. Loud and shrill.

Something loomed, huge, a truck, loomed and immediately *arrived,* tremendous weight on his legs, hideous pressure, bones snapping like dry sticks.

CHAPTER 24

Bunked three-high along the walls, like travelers in a railroad sleeping car, the corpses lay in open berths, the journey from death to grave having been delayed by this unscheduled stop.

After switching on the light, Corky Laputa quietly closed the door behind him.

"Good evening, ladies and gentlemen," he said to the assembled cadavers.

In any circumstances, he could reliably amuse himself.

"The next station on this line is Hell, with cozy beds of nails, hot and cold running cockroaches, and a free continental breakfast of molten sulfur."

To his left were eight bodies and one empty berth. Seven bodies and two empty berths to his right. Five bodies and one empty berth at the end of the room. Twenty cadavers, with accommodations available to serve four more.

These dreamless sleepers lay not on mattresses but on stainless-steel pans. The bunks were actually open racks designed to facilitate air circulation.

This refrigerated chamber provided a dry environment no colder than five—and no higher than eight—degrees above freezing. Corky's exhalations issued from his nostrils in twin ribbons of pale vapor.

A sophisticated ventilation system continuously drew air out of the room through exhausts near the floor. Fresh air pumped in through wall vents just below the ceiling.

Although the smell wasn't conducive to a romantic candlelight dinner, it wasn't instantly repulsive, either. You could half deceive yourself that this odor was not significantly different in character from the stale-sweat, foot-fungus, shower-mold bouquet common to many high-school locker rooms.

None of the resident dead was bagged. The low temperature and the strictly controlled humidity slowed decomposition almost to a halt, but the inevitable process *did* continue at a much reduced rate. A vinyl bag would trap the slowly released gases, becoming a heat-filled balloon and defeating the purpose of the refrigeration.

Instead of vinyl cocoons, loose white cotton shrouds draped the reclining dead. Except for the chill and the smell, they might have been the pampered guests at an exclusive health spa, taking a group nap in a sauna.

In life, few if any of them had ever been pampered. If one had seen the inside of a health spa, he had surely at once been ejected by security guards and warned never to trespass again.

These were life's losers. They had died alone and unknown.

Those who perished at the hand of another were required by law to undergo autopsy. So were those who died by accident, by apparent suicide, from an illness not confidently diagnosed, and from causes that were not apparent and that were, therefore, suspicious.

In any big city, especially in one as dysfunctional as current-day Los Angeles, bodies often arrived at the morgue faster than the medical examiner's overworked staff could deal with them. Priority was given to victims of violence, to possible victims of medical malpractice, and to those among the deceased who had families waiting to receive their remains for burial.

Vagrants without families, often without identification, whose bodies had been discovered in alleyways, in parks, under bridges, who might have succumbed from drug overdoses or from exposure to the elements, or from simple liver failure, were parked here for a few days, for a week, maybe even longer, until the medical examiner's staff had time to conduct at least cursory postmortems.

In death, as in life, these castaways were served last.

A telephone hung on the wall to the right of the door, as though considerately provided to enable the deceased to order pizza.

Most lines permitted only in-facility communication, functioning as intercom links. The last of six lines allowed outgoing calls.

Corky keyed in Roman Castevet's cell-phone number.

Roman, a pathologist on the medical examiner's staff, had just come on duty for the evening shift. He was probably in an autopsy room elsewhere in the building, preparing to cut.

More than a year ago, they had met at an anarchists' mixer at the university where Corky taught. The catered food had been second-rate, the drinks slightly watered down, and the flower arrangements less than inspired, but the company had been engaging.

On the third ring, Roman answered, and after Corky identified himself, he said, "Guess where I am?"

"You've crawled up your own ass and can't get out," Roman said.

He had an unconventional sense of humor.

"It's a good thing this isn't a pay phone," Corky said. "I don't have any change, and none of the cheap stiffs here will lend me a quarter."

"Then it must be a faculty function. Nobody's more miserly than a bunch of anticapitalist academics wallowing in the high life with fat checks from the taxpayers."

"Some might see a wide vein of meanness in your humor," Corky said with a severe note that wasn't characteristic of him.

"They wouldn't be mistaken. Cruelty is my creed, remember?"

Roman was a Satanist. Hail the Prince of Darkness, that kind of stuff. Not all anarchists were also Satanists, but many Satanists were also anarchists.

Corky knew one Buddhist who was an anarchist—a conflicted young woman. Otherwise, in his experience, the vast majority of anarchists were atheists.

In his considered opinion, pure anarchists didn't believe in the supernatural, neither in the powers of Darkness nor in the powers of Light. They put all their faith in the power of destruction and in the new and better order that might arise from ruin.

"Considering your backlog of work," said Corky, "it seems to me academics aren't the only ones who don't always earn their fat checks from the taxpayers. What do you guys do here on the evening shift—just play poker, swap ghost stories?"

Roman must have been only half listening. He didn't pick up on the word *here.* "Banter isn't your strong suit. Get to the point. What do you want? You always want something."

"And I always pay well for it, don't I?"

"The ability to pay cash in full is the virtue I admire most."

"I see you people have solved the rat problem."

"What rat problem?"

Two years ago, the media had given extensive grisly coverage to the fact that sanitary and pest-control conditions in this very room and elsewhere in this facility had been deplorable.

"The place must be rat-proof now. I'm looking around," Corky said, "and I don't see any lowbrow cousins of Mickey Mouse noshing on anyone's nose."

The silence of shocked disbelief greeted this statement. When Roman Castevet could speak, he said, "You can't be where I think you are."

"I'm exactly where you think I am."

The smug self-satisfaction and sarcasm in Roman's voice abruptly vaporized into a whisper fierce with self-concern. "What're you doing to me, coming here? You're not authorized. You don't belong anywhere in the morgue, and especially not in *there*."

"I have credentials."

"The hell you do."

"I could leave here and come to you. Are you in one of the autopsy rooms or still at your desk?"

Roman's whisper grew softer but even more intense: "Are you nuts? Are you trying to get me fired?"

"I just want to place an order," Corky said.

Recently Roman had supplied him with a jar containing tissue preservative and ten foreskins harvested from cadavers destined for cremation.

Corky had given the jar to Rolf Reynerd with instructions. In spite of his congenital stupidity, Reynerd had managed to pack the container in a black gift box and send it to Channing Manheim.

"I need another ten," Corky said.

"You don't come *here* to talk about it. You *never* come here, you moron. You call me at home."

"I thought this would be a hoot, give you a laugh."

Shakily, Roman said, "Dear Jesus."

"You're a Satanist," Corky reminded him.

"Idiot."

"Listen, Roman, where exactly are you? How do I get to you from here? We need to do some business."

"Stay right where you are."

"I don't know. I'm getting a little claustrophobic. This place is beginning to spook me."

"Stay right where you are! I'll be there in two minutes."

"I just heard something weird. I think one of these corpses might be alive."

"None of them is alive."

"I'm sure this one guy, over toward the corner, just said something."

"Then he said you're an idiot."

"Maybe you've got a live one in here by mistake. I'm really starting to get creeped out."

"Two minutes," Roman insisted. "You wait right where you are. Don't come blundering out of there, drawing attention to yourself, or I'll harvest *your* foreskin."

Roman terminated the call.

In the vault of the unknown and penniless dead, Corky hung up the phone.

Surveying his shrouded audience, he said, "With

all humility, I could teach Channing Manheim a thing or two about acting."

He expected and needed no applause. A perfect performance was its own reward.

CHAPTER 25

Snow fell on the city of angels.

Unprecedented, the shepherd wind drove white flocks out of the dark meadows above the world, gently harried them between ficus trees and palms, along avenues that had never known a snowy Christmas.

Dazzled, Ethan gazed up into the fleecy night.

Abed in his room, he realized that the roof must have been lifted off the house by a prying wind. Snowdrifts would bury the furniture, ruin the carpet.

Soon he would have to rise, go along the hall to his parents' room. Dad would know what to do about the missing roof.

First, however, Ethan wanted to enjoy this spectacle: Above him, the snowfall hung an infinite crystal chandelier, its beautiful swags of cut beads and beveled pendants in perpetual glittering movement.

His eyelashes were frosted.

Flakes delivered cold kisses to his face, melted on his cheeks.

When his vision fully focused, he discovered that in truth the December night was full of raindrops, to which his troubled eyes had imparted crystalline structures and mysterious hieroglyphic forms.

Once soft, his bed had been spellcast into black-top.

He felt no discomfort, except that his feather pillow pressed like hard pavement against the back of his head.

The rain on his face fell as cold as snow, imparting an equal chill to his upturned left hand.

His right hand lay exposed, as well, but with it he could not feel the cold or the tap-and-trickle of the rain.

He couldn't feel his legs, either. Couldn't move them. Could not move anything other than his head and left hand.

If his roofless room filled with rain, and if he were unable to move, he might drown.

In the pool of dreamy speculation on which Ethan had been drifting, sudden terror darted sharklike through the depths beneath him, rising.

He closed his eyes to avoid seeing a bigger and more terrible truth than that the snowflakes were actually raindrops.

Voices approached. Dad and Mom must be coming to put the roof back where it belonged, to fluff his stone pillow into comfortable plumpness once more, and to set all wrongness right.

He surrendered himself to their loving care, and

like a feather, he drifted down into darkness, toward the Land of Nod, not the Nod to which Cain had fled after killing Abel, but the Nod to which dreaming children journeyed to find adventure and from which they woke safely in the golden dawn.

Still descending through the darkness north of Nod, he heard the words "spinal injury."

Opening his eyes a minute or ten minutes later, he discovered the night aswarm with pulsing-revolving red and yellow lights, and blue, as if he were in an open-air discotheque, and he knew that he would never dance again, or walk.

To the tuneless broken songs of police-radio crackle, flanked by paramedics, Ethan glided through the rain on a gurney toward an ambulance.

On the white van, in red letters trimmed in gold, under the bold word AMBULANCE, glowed the smaller words OUR LADY OF ANGELS HOSPITAL.

Maybe they would give him a bed in Dunny's old room.

That prospect filled him with a choking dread.

He closed his eyes for what seemed a blink, heard men warning one another "careful" and "easy, easy," and when he looked again, he had blinked himself into the ambulance.

He became aware that a needle already pierced his right arm, served by an IV tube and a dangling bag of plasma.

For the first time, he heard his breathing—full of wheeze and rush and rattle—whereupon he knew that more than his legs had been crushed. He suspected that one or both of his lungs struggled against the confinement of a partially collapsed rib cage.

He wished for pain. Anything but this terrible lack of feeling.

The paramedic at Ethan's side spoke urgently to his teammate, who stood in the rain, beyond the open doors: "We're gonna need speed."

"I'll burn asphalt," the rain-lashed medic promised, and he slammed shut the doors.

Along both side walls, near the ceiling, taut garlands of red tinsel sparkled. At the ends and in the middle of each garland, small silver bells, three per set, dangled brightly. Christmas decorations.

The bells in each group were strung concentrically on the same string. The top bell, also the largest, overhung the middle bell, which overhung the third—which was also the smallest—in the set.

When the door slammed, the tiny bells on each string jiggled against one another, producing a silvery ringing as faint as fairy music.

The paramedic fitted Ethan with an oxygen mask.

As cool as autumn, as sweet as springtime, a rich blend of air soothed his hot throat, but his wheezing did not in the least abate.

Having climbed behind the steering wheel in the front of the ambulance, the driver slammed his door, again causing the red tinsel to shimmer and the bells to ring.

"Bells," Ethan said, but the oxygen mask muffled the word.

In the process of fitting the binaurals of a stethoscope to his ears, the paramedic paused. "What
did you say?"

The sight of the stethoscope inspired in Ethan
the realization that he could hear his heartbeat,
and that what he heard was ragged, uneven,
alarming.

Listening, he knew that he was hearing not just
his heart, but also the knock-hoofed canter of
Death's horse approaching.

"Bells," he repeated, as throughout his mind the
doors to a thousand fears flew open.

The ambulance began to move, and as it rolled,
the siren found its shrill voice.

Ethan couldn't hear the bells above the banshee
wail, but he could see the nearest three trembling
on their string. Trembling.

He raised his left hand toward the dangling cluster but couldn't reach that far. His hand grasped at
empty air.

This terrible intensity of fear brought with it a
clouding confusion, and perhaps he was utterly
delirious; nevertheless, the bells seemed to be
more than mere decorations, seemed mystical in
their shiny smoothness, in their glimmering curves,
the embodiment of hope, and he desperately
needed to hold them.

Apparently the paramedic understood the urgency
of Ethan's need to have the bells, if not the reason for
it. He plucked a small pair of scissors from a kit, and
swaying with the movement of the vehicle, he clipped

the knot that secured the nearest cluster to the garland of tinsel.

Given the string of bells, Ethan clutched them in his left hand with a grip both tender and ferocious.

He was exhausted, but he dared not close his eyes again, for he feared that when he opened them, darkness would remain and never go away, that he would henceforth see nothing of this world.

The paramedic picked up the stethoscope once more. He inserted the binaural tips in his ears.

With the fingers of his left hand, Ethan counted the bells on the string, from tiniest to largest, to tiniest again.

He realized that he held these ornaments as he'd held a rosary in the hushed hospital room during the last few nights of Hannah's life: with equal measures of despair and hope, with an unexpected awe that sustained the heart and with a stoicism that armored it. His hope had been unrealized, his stoicism essential, when he had found it necessary to survive her loss.

Between thumb and forefinger, he had tried to pinch mercy from the rosary beads. Now he smoothed the curvatures of bell, bell, and bell, seeking mercy less than understanding, seeking a revelation deaf to the ear but resonant in the heart.

Although Ethan did not close his eyes and bring the darkness down, seeping shadows encroached from the periphery of vision, like ink spreading through the fibers of a blotter.

Apparently the stethoscope captured rhythms that alarmed the paramedic. He loomed close, but his voice came from a distance, and though his face was a mask of calm professionalism, he spoke with an urgency that revealed the depth of his concern for his patient. "Ethan, don't leave us here. Hang tight. Hold on, damn it."

Cinched by a knot of darkness, Ethan's vision narrowed as the cords pulled tighter, tighter.

He detected the astringent scent of rubbing alcohol. A coolness below the crook of his left arm preceded the sting of a needle.

Within him, the knocking hooves of one-horse Death gave way to the thunder of an apocalyptic herd in chaotic gallop.

The ambulance still rocketed toward Our Lady of Angels, but the driver gave the siren a rest, evidently trusting to the swiveling beacons on the roof.

In the absence of the banshee shriek, Ethan thought he heard bells again.

These were not the worry-bead bells that in his hand he smoothed and smoothed, nor were they the strings of ornamental bells suspended from the red sparkling tinsel. These chimes arose at some distance, calling him with a silvery insistence.

His vision irised to a dim spot of light, and then the mortal knot drew tighter still, blinding him completely. Accepting the inevitability of death and endless darkness, at last he closed his eyelids.

He opened the door, then opened his eyes.

In a growl of wind and a jingle of overhead bells,

he stepped out of Forever Roses into the cold teeth of the December night, and drew the door shut behind him.

In shock to find himself alive, in disbelief that he stood on legs unbroken, he waited in the entry alcove, between the display windows, as a young couple in raincoats and hoods strolled by on the sidewalk, led by a golden retriever on a leash.

The dog looked up at Ethan, its eyes as wise as they were liquid and dark.

"Good evening," the couple said.

Unable to speak, Ethan nodded.

"Tink, let's go," the woman urged, and then repeated the command when the dog hesitated.

The soaked retriever pranced away, snout lifted to savor the chilly air, followed by its companions.

Ethan turned to peer at the florist who still stood behind the counter, past the glass coffins full of roses.

Rowena had been staring after him. Now she quickly looked down as though attending to a task.

On legs as shaky as his reason, Ethan retraced the route that he had taken to this place, under the sheltering awnings of shops and restaurants, toward the Expedition in the red zone.

Ahead, Tink twice glanced back, but didn't stop.

Passing a restaurant bejeweled with candlelight and sparkling tableware, breathing in the yeasty fragrance of freshly baked bread, Ethan thought, *The staff of life.*

At the end of the block, the dog looked back

once more. Then the trio disappeared around the corner.

In the street, the traffic was lighter than usual at this hour, moving faster than the weather warranted.

Arriving at the red zone near the end of the block, Ethan stood under the last awning—and thought that he might stand there, well and safely back from the street, until dawn reclaimed the city from the night.

A long gap appeared in the approaching traffic.

With his trembling right hand, he fished his keys from a jacket pocket and thumbed the lock-release button on the fob. The Expedition chirruped at him, but he didn't approach it.

Turning his attention toward the intersection, Ethan saw the headlights of the PT Cruiser as the vehicle approached at far too high a speed on the cross street.

The Cruiser fishtailed in the intersection, and its wheels locked. In the spinout, the car rotated past the parked Expedition, mere inches from a collision.

Had Ethan stood there, he would have been battered between the vehicles, like a pinball between warring flippers.

Here came the crushing truck, the shrill blast of air brakes.

With a sharp stuttering bark of tires against wet blacktop, the Cruiser spun into the far lanes where it belonged.

Parting the rain where the Cruiser had just

whipped through it, the truck shook and shuddered to a stop.

When the driver of the Cruiser regained control, he raced away, at a lower but still reckless speed.

The agitated trucker blew his horn. Then he continued on the route that he'd been following before the near miss, toward whatever destination unhindered fate had planned for him.

In the wake of the truck, the gap in traffic had closed.

The signal light changed at the intersection. In two directions, traffic came to a halt, but in two others, it began to move again.

Drenching the night: the delicious aroma of baking bread.

Golden lamplight spending doubloons upon the pavement.

The rush and rustle of the rain.

Perhaps the signal light changed twice again or even three times before Ethan became aware of an aching in his left hand. The cramping pain had begun to spread into the muscles of his forearm.

Tangled through the fiercely clenched fingers of his fist was the string of three small silvery bells clipped from the ambulance tinsel and given to him by a compassionate paramedic.

CHAPTER 26

As if they were the degenerate elite of ancient Rome, reclining in midbacchanal, their togas scandalously disarranged, the nameless dead revealed here a smooth and creamy shoulder, here the pale curve of a breast, here a blue-veined thigh, here a hand with the fingers curled in a subtle obscene gesture, here a delicate foot and slender ankle, and here half a profile in which one open eye stared with milky lust.

The least-superstitious witness to this grotesque display might be inclined to suspect that in the absence of a living observer, these unidentified vagrants and teenage runaways would visit bunk to bunk. In the most lonely hours after midnight, might not the restless dead pair up in a cold and hideous parody of passion?

If Corky Laputa had believed in a moral code or even if he had believed that good taste required certain universal rules of social conduct, he might have passed his two-minute wait by rearranging these carelessly draped shrouds, insisting upon modesty even among the deceased.

Instead, he enjoyed the scene because in this chamber was the ultimate fruit of anarchy. Besides, with considerable excitement, he anticipated the arrival of the usually unflappable Roman Castevet, who would be fully flapped on this occasion.

Almost two minutes to the tick, the lever-action door handle clicked, creaked, and eased down. The door cracked open, but only an inch.

As though he expected to discover that Corky awaited him with a camera crew and a pack of muckraking reporters, Roman peered through the gap, his one revealed eye as wide as that of a startled owl.

"Come in, come, come," Corky encouraged. "You're among friends here, even though it *is* your intention eventually to dissect some of them."

Opening the door only wide enough to accommodate his thin frame, Roman slipped into the cadaver vault, pausing to peer back worriedly at the hallway before closing himself in with Corky and the twenty naughty members of the toga party.

"What the hell are you wearing?" asked the nervous pathologist.

Corky turned in place, flaring the skirt of his yellow slicker. "Fashionable rain gear. Do you like the hat?"

"How did you slip by security in that ludicrous outfit? How did you slip by security at all?"

"No slipping necessary. I presented my credentials."

"What credentials? You teach empty-calorie modern fiction to a bunch of self-important sluts and brain-dead, snot-nosed wonderboys."

Like many in the sciences, Roman Castevet held a dim view of the liberal-arts departments in contemporary universities and of those students who sought, first, truth through literature and, second, a delayed entry into the job market.

Taking no offense, in fact approving of Roman's nasty antisocial vitriol, Corky explained: "The pleasant fellows at your security desk think I'm a visiting pathologist from Indianapolis, here to discuss with you certain deeply puzzling entomological details related to the victims of a serial killer operating throughout the Midwest."

"Huh? Why would they think that?"

"I have a source for excellent forged documents."

Roman boggled. *"You?"*

"Frequently, it's advisable for me to carry first-rate false identification."

"Are you delusional or merely stupid?"

"As I've explained previously, I'm not just an effete professor who gets a thrill from hanging out with anarchists."

"Yeah, right," Roman said scornfully.

"I promote anarchy at every opportunity in my daily life, often at the risk of arrest and imprisonment."

"You're a regular Che Guevara."

"Many of my operations are as clever and shocking as they are unconventional. You didn't think I wanted those ten foreskins just for some sick personal use, did you?"

"Yeah, that's exactly what I thought. When we met at that boring university mixer, you seemed like the grand pooh-bah of the demented, a moral and mental mutant of classic proportions."

"Coming from a Satanist," Corky said with a smile, "that could be taken as a compliment."

"It's not meant as one," Roman replied impatiently, angrily.

At his best, groomed and togged and breath-freshened for serious socializing, Castevet was an unattractive man. Anger made him uglier than usual.

Slat-thin, all bony hips and elbows and sharp shoulders, with an Adam's apple more prominent than his nose and with a nose sharper than any Corky had ever seen on another member of the human species, with gaunt cheeks and with a fleshless chin that resembled the knob of a femur, Roman appeared to have a serious eating disorder.

Every time that he met Castevet's bird-keen, reptile-intense eyes, however, and whenever he caught the pathologist, for no apparent reason, sensuously licking his lips, which were the only ripe feature of that scarecrow face and form, Corky suspected that a fearsome erotic need spun the wheels of the man's metabolism almost fast enough to cause smoke to issue from various orifices. Had there been a betting pool regarding the average number of calories that Roman burned up every day in obsessive self-abuse alone, Corky would have wagered heavily on at least three thousand—and he would no doubt have ensured a comfortable retirement with his winnings.

"Well, whatever you think of me," Corky said, "nevertheless, I would like to place an order for another ten foreskins."

"Hey, get it through your head—I'm not doing business with you anymore. You're reckless, coming here like this."

Partly as a profitable sideline, but also partly from a sense of religious duty and as an expression of his abiding faith in the King of Hell, Roman Castevet provided—only from cadavers—selected body parts, internal organs, blood, malignant tumors, occasionally even entire brains to other Satanists. His customers, other than Corky, had both a theological and a practical interest in arcane rituals designed to petition His Satanic Majesty for special favors or to summon actual demons out of the fiery pit. Frequently, after all, the most essential ingredients in a black-magic formula could not be purchased at the nearest Wal-Mart.

"You're overreacting," Corky said.

"I'm *not* overreacting. You're imprudent, you're foolhardy."

"*Foolhardy?*" Corky smiled, nearly laughed. "All of a sudden you seem awfully prissy for a man who believes plunder, torture, rape, and murder will be rewarded in the afterlife."

"Lower your voice," Roman demanded in a fierce whisper, though Corky had continued to speak in a pleasant conversational tone. "If somebody finds you here with me, it could mean my job."

"Not at all. I'm a visiting pathologist from Indianapolis, and we're discussing your current manpower shortage and this deplorable backlog of unidentified cadavers."

"You'll ruin me," Roman moaned.

"All I've come here to do," Corky lied, "is to order ten more foreskins. I don't expect you to collect them while I wait. I just placed the order in person because I thought it would give you a chuckle."

Although Roman Castevet appeared too emaciated, too juiceless to produce tears, his feverish black eyes grew watery with frustration.

"Anyway," Corky continued, "there's a bigger threat to your job than being caught here with me—if someone discovers you people have mistakenly penned up a living man in this place with all these dead bodies."

"Are you wired on something?"

"I already told you on the phone, a few minutes ago. One of these unfortunate souls is still alive."

"What kind of mind game is this?" Roman demanded.

"It's not a game. It's true. I heard him murmuring *'Help me, help me,'* so soft, barely loud enough to hear."

"Heard who?"

"I tracked him down, peeled the shroud back from his face. He's paralyzed. Facial muscles distorted by a stroke."

Hunching closer, bristling like the collection of dry sticks in a bindle of kindling, Roman *insisted* on eye-to-eye conversation, as if he believed the fierceness of his gaze would convey the message that his words had failed to deliver.

Corky blithely continued: "The poor guy was probably comatose when they brought him in here, then he regained consciousness. But he's awfully weak."

A crack of uncertainty breached Roman Castevet's armor of disbelief. He broke eye contact and swept the bunks with his gaze. "Who?"

"Over there," Corky said brightly, indicating the back of the vault, where the light from the overhead fixture barely reached, leaving the recumbent dead shrouded in gloom as well as in white cotton cloth. "Seems to me I'm saving *all* your jobs by alerting you to this, so you ought to fill my order for free, out of gratitude."

Moving toward the back of the vault, Roman said, "Which one?"

Stepping close behind the pathologist, Corky replied, "On the left, the second from the bottom."

As Roman bent to peel the shroud off the face of the corpse, Corky raised his right arm, revealing the hand that until now had been concealed in the sleeve of his yellow slicker, and the ice pick in the hand. With judicious aim, great force, and utter

confidence, he drove the weapon into the pathologist's back.

Placed with precision, an ice pick can penetrate
atriums and ventricles, causing such a convulsive
shock in cardiac muscle that the heart stops in an
instant and forever.

With a rustle of clothes and a quiet knockety-
knock of folding limbs, Roman Castevet collapsed
without a cry to the floor.

Corky didn't need to check for a pulse. The gaping mouth, from which no breath escaped, and the
eyes, as fixed as the glass orbs in a fine work of
taxidermy, confirmed the perfection of his aim.

Preparation paid off. At home, using this same
ice pick, Corky had practiced on a CPR dummy
that he had stolen from the university medical
school.

If he'd needed to stab twice, three, four times, or
if Roman's heart had continued to pump for even a
short while, the assault could have proved messy.
For that reason, he'd worn the stainproof slicker.

In the unlikely event that one of the vault's properly chilled treasures sprung an unfortunate leak,
the tile floor featured a large drain. Near the door, a
collapsible vinyl hose on a reel was attached to a
wall spigot.

Corky knew about this janitorial equipment from
the articles that he had read two years ago, when
the rat scandal had made the front page. Happily,
he didn't need the hose.

He lifted Roman into one of the empty bunks

along the back wall of the vault, where the shadows served his scheme.

From a deep inner pocket of his slicker, he withdrew the sheet that earlier he'd purchased in a department store at the mall. He draped the sheet over Roman, being careful to cover him entirely, for he needed to conceal both the identity of the corpse and the fact that, unlike the others here, it was fully clothed.

Because death had been instantaneous and the wound had been minute, no blood seeped forth to stain the sheet and thus call attention to the freshness of this carcass.

In a day or two, or three, Roman would most likely be found by a morgue employee taking inventory or withdrawing a cadaver for an overdue autopsy. Another front-page story for the medical examiner.

Corky regretted having to kill a man like Roman Castevet. As a good Satanist and a committed anarchist, the pathologist had served well in the campaign to destabilize the social order and hasten its collapse.

Soon, however, ghastly events at Channing Manheim's estate would make big headlines worldwide. Authorities would commit extraordinary resources to discover the identity of the man who'd sent the taunting gifts in the black boxes.

Logic would send them to private mortuaries and public morgues, in search of the source of the ten foreskins. If Roman had come under suspicion during that investigation, he would have tried to save his own hide by fingering Corky.

Anarchists labored under no obligation of loyalty to one another, which was as it should be among champions of disorder.

Indeed, Corky had other loose ends to tie up before the yuletide celebrations could begin.

Considering that his hands were sheathed in latex gloves, which had been hidden from his victim in the roomy sleeves of his slicker, he could have left the ice pick in the vault without worrying that he might provide police with incriminating fingerprints. Instead, he returned it to its sheath and then to a pocket not only because it might serve him well again, but also because it now had sentimental value.

Leaving the morgue, he said a friendly good-bye to the night security men. They had a thankless job, protecting the dead from the living. He even paused long enough to share with them an obscene joke about an attorney and a chicken.

He had no fear that eventually they would be able to provide the police with a useful description of his face. In his droopy hat and tentlike slicker, he was an eccentric and amusing figure about whom no one would remember more than his costume.

Later, in a fireplace at home, while he enjoyed a brandy, he would burn all the ID that had established him as a pathologist from Indianapolis. He possessed numerous additional sets of documentation for other identities if and when he needed them.

Now he returned to the night, the rain.

And so the time had come to deal with Rolf Reynerd, who by his actions had shown himself to be every bit as unfit for life as he had proved to be unfit for soap-opera stardom.

CHAPTER 27

If Aelfric Manheim's Monday-evening dinner had been reported upon in *Daily Variety*, the colorful trade paper of the film industry, the headline might have been FRIC CLICKS WITH CHICK.

On the grill, the plump breast had been basted with olive oil and sprinkled with sea salt, pepper, and a delicious mixture of exotic herbs known around Palazzo Rospo as the McBee McSecret. In addition to the chicken, he had been served pasta, not with tomato sauce, but with butter, basil, pine nuts, and Parmesan cheese.

Mr. Hachette, the Cordon Bleu–trained chef who was a direct descendent of Jack the Ripper, didn't work Sundays and Mondays, so that he might stalk and slash innocent women, toss rabid cats into baby carriages, and indulge in whatever other personal interests currently appealed to him.

Mr. Baptiste, the happy cook, was off Mondays and Tuesdays; therefore, on Mondays the kitchen was, in show-biz lingo, dark. Mrs. McBee had prepared these delicacies herself.

By the softly pulsing light of electric fixtures tricked up to look like antique oil lamps, Fric ate in the wine cellar, alone at the refectory table for eight in the cozy tasting room, which was separated from the temperature-controlled portion of the cellar by a glass wall. Beyond the glass, in aisles of shelves, were fourteen thousand bottles of what his father sometimes identified as "Cabernet Sauvignon, Merlot, Pinot Noir, claret, port, Burgundy—and the blood of critics, which is a bitter vintage."

Ha, ha, ha.

When Ghost Dad was home, they usually ate in the dining room, unless the dinner guests—the old man's buddies, business associates, or various personal advisers from his spiritual counselor to his clairvoyance instructor—felt uncomfortable having a ten-year-old kid listening to their gossip and rolling his eyes at their trash talk.

In Ghost Dad's absence, which was most of the time, Fric could choose to have dinner not just in his private rooms, where he usually ate, but virtually anywhere on the estate.

In good weather, he might dine outdoors by the swimming pool, grateful that in his father's absence no hopelessly dense, tiresomely giggly, embarrassingly half-naked starlets were there to pester him with questions about his favorite subject in school, his favorite food, his favorite color, his favorite world-famous movie star.

They were always trying to cadge some Ritalin or antidepressants from Fric. They refused to believe that his only prescription was for asthma medication.

If not by the pool, he might dine dangerously with fine china and antique silverware at a table in the rose garden, keeping his inhaler ready on a dessert plate in the event that a breeze stirred up enough pollen to trigger an asthma attack.

Sometimes he ate from a lap tray while ensconced in one of the sixty comfortable armchairs in the screening room, which had recently been remodeled using the ornate Art Deco–style Pantages Theater, in Los Angeles, as inspiration.

The screening-room equipment could handle film, all formats of videotape, DVDs, and broadcast-television signals, projecting them onto a screen larger than many in the average suburban multiplex.

To watch videos and DVDs, Fric didn't need the assistance of a projectionist. Sitting in the center seat in the center row, adjacent to the control console, he could run his own show.

Sometimes, when he knew that no cleaning had been scheduled in the theater, when he was certain that no one would come looking for him, he locked the door to ensure privacy, and he loaded the DVD player with one of his father's movies.

Being *seen* watching a Ghost Dad movie was unthinkable.

Not that they sucked. Some of them sucked, of course, because no star rang the big bell every time. But some were all right. Some were cool. A few were even amazing.

If anyone were to *see* him watching his father's movies under these circumstances, however, he would be the National Academy of Nerds' choice for Greatest Nerd of the Decade. Maybe of the century. The Pathetic Losers Club would vote him a free lifetime membership.

Mr. Hachette, the psychopathic chef related to the Frankenstein family, would mock him with sneers and by drawing sly comparisons between Fric's sticklike physique and his father's maximum buffness.

Anyway, in the only occupied seat of sixty, with the ornate Art Deco ceiling soaring thirty-four feet overhead, Fric sometimes sat in the dark and ran Ghost Dad's movies on the huge screen. Drenched in Dolby surround sound.

He watched certain films for the stories, though he'd seen them many times. He watched others for blow-out-the-walls special effects.

And always in his father's performances, Fric looked for the qualities, the charms, the expressions, and the bits of business that made millions of people all over the world love Channing Manheim.

In the better films, such moments abounded. Even in the suckiest of the sucky, however, there were scenes in which you couldn't help but like the guy, admire him, want so much to hang out with him.

When citing the brightest moments in his finest films, critics had said that Fric's father was magical. "Magical" sounded stupid, like gooey girl gush, embarrassing, but it was the right word.

Sometimes you watched him on the big screen, and he seemed more colorful, more *real* than anyone you'd ever known. Or ever would know.

This super-real quality couldn't be explained by the giant size of his projected image or by the visual genius of the cameraman. Nor by the brilliance of the director—most being no more brilliant than a boiled potato—nor by the layered details achieved through digital technology. Most actors, including stars, didn't have the Manheim magic even when they worked with the best directors and technicians.

You watched him up there, and he seemed to have been everywhere, to have seen everything, to know all that could be known. He seemed to be wiser, more caring, funnier, and braver than anyone, anywhere, ever—as though he lived in six dimensions while everyone else had to live in only three.

Fric had studied certain scenes over and over again, scores of times, maybe a hundred times in some cases, until they seemed as real to him as any moments he had actually spent with his father.

Once in a while, when he went to bed drag-ass tired, but was able to settle only on the twilight edge of sleep, or when he woke incompletely in the middle of the night yet continued to skate upon the surface of a temporarily frozen dream, those special movie scenes with his father *did* seem real to Fric. They played in memory not as though he'd viewed them from a theater seat, but as though they were true-life experiences that he and his father had shared.

These dreamy spells of half-sleep were some of the happiest moments of Fric's life.

Of course, if he ever *told* anyone that those were some of the happiest moments of his life, the Pathetic Losers Club would erect a thirty-foot statue of him, emphasizing his uncombable hair and his skinny neck, and they would spotlight it on the same hill that held the HOLLYWOOD sign.

So on this Monday evening, though Fric might have preferred to eat in the theater while watching his father beat the crap out of bad guys and save an entire orphanage full of waifs, he dined in the wine cellar because in the pre-Christmas bustle, little privacy could be found elsewhere in Palazzo Rospo.

Ms. Sanchez and Ms. Norbert, the maids who lived on the estate, had been away on an early Christmas leave for the past ten days. They would not return until Thursday morning, December 24.

Mrs. McBee and Mr. McBee would be gone Tuesday and Wednesday, to have an early Christmas with their son and his family in Santa Barbara. They, too, would return to Palazzo Rospo on December 24, to ensure that the biggest movie star in the world was met with the proper pomp when he arrived from Florida later that afternoon.

Consequently, here on Monday evening, the other four maids and the porters were working late, under the firm direction of the busy McBees, alongside a few outsourced services that included a six-man floor-cleaning crew specializing in the care of marble and limestone, an eight-person holiday-decorating team, and an emergency feng-shui facilitator who would make certain that various Christmas trees and other seasonal displays were arranged and festooned in such a way as not to interfere with the proper energy flow of the great house.

Madness.

Far from the hum of floor-polishing machines and the jolly laughter of the Christmas-besotted decorating team, Fric took refuge deep underground in the wine cellar. Within these brick walls, under this low, vaulted brick ceiling, the only sounds were those he made swallowing and the clink of his fork against his plate.

And then: *Ooodelee-ooodelee-oo.*

Muffled but audible, the phone rang inside a keg.

Because the temperature in the tasting room was too high for wine storage, the barrels and bottles in this chamber, on the warmer side of the glass wall, were strictly decorative.

Ooodelee-ooodelee-oo.

Stacked floor to ceiling along one brick wall, several of the enormous barrels featured hinged bottoms that could be swung open, doorlike. Some barrels had shelves inside, on which were stored wineglasses, linen napkins, corkscrews, other items. Four contained televisions, allowing a wine connoisseur to view multiple channels simultaneously.

Ooodelee-ooodelee-oo.

Fric opened the phone keg and answered his private line in the usual Frician style, determined not to sound intimidated. "Pete's Pest Control and School of Home Canning. We'll rid your house of rats and teach you how to preserve them for future holiday feasts."

"Hello, Aelfric."

"Do you have a name yet?" Fric asked.

"Lost."

"Is that a first name or last name?"

"Both. Are you enjoying your dinner?"

"I'm not eating dinner."

"What did I tell you about lying, Aelfric?"

"That it won't get me anything but misery."

"Do you eat in the wine cellar often?"

"I'm in the attic."

"Don't seek misery, boy. Enough of it will find you without your help."

"In the movie business," Fric said, "people lie twenty-four hours a day, and all it gets them is rich."

"Sometimes the misery follows swiftly," Mysterious Caller assured him. "More often it takes a lifetime to arrive, and then at the end, there's a great roaring *sea* of it."

Fric was silent.

The stranger matched his silence.

At last Fric drew a deep breath and said, "I've got to admit, you're a spooky son of a bitch."

"That's progress, Aelfric. A little truth."

"I found a place where I can hide and never be found."

"Do you mean the secret room behind your closet?"

Fric had never imagined that any creepy creatures lived in the hollows of his bones, but now he seemed to feel them crawling through his marrow.

Mysterious Caller said, "The place with steel walls and all the hooks in the ceiling—is that where you think you can hide?"

CHAPTER 28

With murder on his mind but not on his conscience, Corky Laputa, fresh from the vault of the nameless dead, crossed the city in the night rain.

As he drove, he thought about his father, perhaps because Henry James Laputa had squandered his life as surely as the vagrants and teenage runaways bunking at the morgue had squandered theirs.

Corky's mother, the economist, had believed in the righteousness of envy, in the power of hatred. Her life had been consumed by both, and she had worn bitterness as though it were a crown.

His father believed in the *necessity* of envy as a motivator. His perpetual envy led inevitably to chronic hatred whether he believed in the power of hatred or not.

Henry James Laputa had been a professor of American literature. He had also been a novelist with dreams of worthy fame.

He chose the most acclaimed writers of his time to envy. With fierce diligence, he begrudged them every good review, every word of praise, every honor and award. He seethed at news of their successes.

Thus motivated, he produced novels in a white-hot passion, works meant to make the fiction of his contemporaries appear shallow and pallid and puerile by comparison. He wanted to humble other writers, humiliate them by example, inspire in them an envy greater than any he'd directed against them, for only then could he let go of his own envy and at last enjoy his accomplishments.

He believed that one day these literati would be so jealous of him that they'd be unable to take any pleasure in their own careers. When they coveted his literary reputation with such intensity that they were *avaricious* for it, when they burned with shame that their greatest efforts were fading embers compared to the bonfire of his talent, then Henry Laputa would be happy, fulfilled.

Year after year, however, his novels had received only lukewarm praise, and much of this had flowed from the pens of critics who were not of the highest tier. The expected award nominations never came. The deserved honors were not conferred. His genius went unrecognized.

Indeed, he detected that many of his literary contemporaries patronized him, which led him to recognize, at long last, that they were all members of a club from which he'd been blackballed. They *did* recognize the superiority of his talent, but they conspired to deny him the laurels that he had earned, for they were intent on keeping the pieces of the pie that they had cut for themselves.

Pie. Henry realized that even in the literary community, the god of gods was money. Their dirty little secret. They handed awards back and forth, blathering about art, but were interested only in using these honors to pump their careers and get rich.

This insight into the conspiratorial greed of the literati was fertilizer, water, and sunshine to the garden of Henry's hatred. The black flowers of antipathy flourished as never before.

Frustrated by their refusal to accord him the acclaim that he desired, Henry set out to earn their envy by writing a novel that would be an enormous commercial success. He believed that he knew all the tricks of plotting and the many uses of treacly sentimentality by which such hacks as Dickens manipulated the unwashed masses. He would write an irresistible tale, make millions, and let the phony literati be consumed by jealousy.

This commercial epic found a publisher but not an audience. The royalties were meager. Instead of showering him with money, the god of mammon left him standing in a manure storm, which was exactly what one major critic called his novel.

As more years passed, Henry's hatred thickened into a malignity of pure, persistent, and singularly venomous quality. He cherished this malignity, and in time it soured and festered into rancor as virulent and implacable as pancreatic cancer.

At the age of fifty-three, while delivering a caustic

speech full of fire and outrage to an indifferent crowd of academics at the Modern Language Association's annual convention, Henry James Laputa suffered a massive heart attack. He fell instantly dead with such authority that some audience members thought he'd daringly punctuated a point with a pratfall, and they applauded briefly before realizing that here was death indeed, not shtick.

Corky had learned so much from his parents. He had learned that envy alone does not constitute a philosophy. He'd learned that a fun lifestyle and cheerful optimism cannot exist in the face of all-consuming, all-embracing hatred without surcease.

He'd also learned not to trust in laws, idealism, or art.

His mother had trusted in the laws of economics, in the ideals of Marxism. She ended as a bitter old woman, without hope or purpose, who seemed almost relieved when her own son had beaten her to death with a fireplace poker.

Corky's father had believed that he could use art like a hammer to beat the world into submission. The world still turned, but Dad had gone to ashes, scattered in the sea, dispersed, as if he'd never existed.

Chaos.

Chaos was the only dependable force in the universe, and Corky served it with the confidence that it would, in turn, always serve him.

Across the glistening city, through the night and

unrelenting rain, he drove to West Hollywood, where the undependable Rolf Reynerd needed to die.

Both ends of the block where Reynerd lived were closed off by police barricades. Officers in black rain slickers with fluorescent yellow stripes used chemical-light torches to redirect traffic.

In the basic colors of emergency, bright skeins of rain raveled through the pulsing ambulance beacons and knitted urgent patterns on the puddled pavement.

Corky drove past the barricade. Within two blocks, he found a parking place.

Perhaps the official bustle on Rolf Reynerd's street had no connection with the actor, but Corky's intuition insisted otherwise.

He wasn't worried. Whatever mess Rolf Reynerd had gotten himself into, Corky would find a way to use the situation to further his own agenda. Tumble and tumult were his friends, and he was confident that in the church of chaos, he was a favored child.

CHAPTER 29

Fric felt that by some magical influence of the brick floor under his feet and the brick walls around him and the low brick vaults overhead, he had been transformed into brick himself as he listened to the soft voice of this stranger.

"The secret room concealed behind your closet isn't as secret as you think, Aelfric. You won't be safe there when Robin Goodfellow pays a visit."

"Who?"

"Previously I called him the Beast in Yellow. He styles himself Robin Goodfellow, but he's darker than that. In truth, he's Moloch, with the splintered bones of babies stuck between his teeth."

"That'll take some heavy-duty dental floss," said Fric, though a tremor in his voice belied the flippancy of his words. He hurried on, hoping that Mysterious Caller had failed to detect his fear. "Robin Goodfellow, Moloch, baby bones—you aren't making any sense."

"You have a great library in your house, don't you, Aelfric?"

"Yeah."

"And you must have a good dictionary in that library."

"We have a whole shelf of dictionaries," said Fric, "just to prove how scholarly we are."

"Then look it all up. Know your enemy, prepare yourself for what is coming, Aelfric."

"Why don't you *tell* me what's coming? I mean just plain, simple, easy to understand."

"That's not within my power. I'm not licensed to take any direct action."

"So you aren't James Bond."

"I'm authorized to work only by indirection. Encourage, inspire, terrify, cajole, advise. I influence events by every means that is sly, slippery, and seductive."

"What're you—an attorney or something?"

"You're an interesting young man, Aelfric. I'll genuinely be sorry if you're disemboweled and nailed to the front door of Palazzo Rospo."

Fric almost hung up.

Wrapped around the handset of the phone, his palm became greasy with perspiration.

He would not have been surprised if the man on the far end of the line had smelled this sweat and had commented on the salty scent.

Returning to the subject of a deep and special secret place, Fric mustered a steady voice. "We have a panic room in the house," he said, referring to a hidden high-security haven armored to keep out even the most determined kidnappers or terrorists.

"Because the house is so large, you actually have two panic rooms," Mysterious Caller said, which was true. "Both are known, and neither will keep you safe on the night."

"And when is the night?"

Enigmatically, the man said, "It's a fur vault, you know."

"A what?"

"Long ago, your nice suite of rooms was occupied by the original owner's mother."

"How do you know which rooms are mine?"

"She had a collection of expensive fur coats. Several minks, sable, white fox, black fox, chinchilla."

"Did you know her?"

"That steel-lined room was meant to keep the fur coats safe from burglars, moths, and rodents."

"Have you been in our house?"

"The fur vault is a bad place to have an asthma attack—"

Stunned, Fric said, "How could you know about that?"

"—but it'll be an even worse place to be trapped by Moloch when he comes. Time is running out, Aelfric."

The line went dead, and Fric stood alone in the wine room, surely alone, but feeling watched.

CHAPTER 30

If the sky opened to disgorge a deluge of fanged and poisonous toads, if the wind blew hard enough to flay the skin to bloody ruin and to blind the unprotected eye, even such cataclysmic weather would fail to dissuade ghouls and gossips from gathering at the scenes of spectacular accidents and shocking crimes. By comparison, a steady drizzle on a cool December night was picnic weather to this crowd that followed misery as others might follow baseball.

On the front lawn of an apartment house, cater-corner across the intersection from the police barricade, twenty to thirty neighborhood residents gathered to share misinformation and gory details. The majority were adults, but half a dozen energized children capered among them.

Most of these sociable vultures were outfitted in rain gear or carried umbrellas. Two bare-chested and barefoot young men, however, wore only blue jeans and appeared to be so steeped in a marinade of illegal substances that the night could not chill them, as though they were being cooked flamelessly like fish fillets in lime juice.

An air of carnival had settled upon this gathering, expectations of fireworks and freaks.

In all his glistening yellowness, Corky Laputa moved among the onlookers, like a buzzless bumblebee patiently gathering a morsel of nectar here, a morsel there. From time to time, to blend better with the swarm and to win friends, he offered a taste of ersatz honey, inventing florid details of the vicious crime that he claimed to have heard from cops manning the second barricade at the farther end of the block.

He quickly learned that Rolf Reynerd had been killed.

The gossips and the ghouls weren't sure if the victim's first name was Ralph or Rafe, Dolph or Randolph. Or Bob.

They were pretty sure that the luckless fellow's last name was either Reinhardt or Kleinhard, or Reiner like the film director, or maybe Spielberg like another famous director, or Nerdoff, or possibly Nordoff.

One of the bare-chested young men insisted that everyone had confused the victim's first name, surname, and nickname. According to this wizard of deductive reasoning, the dead man's true identity was Ray "the Nerd" Rolf.

All agreed that the murdered man had been an actor whose career had recently rocketed toward stardom. He had just completed a film in which he played Tom Cruise's best buddy or younger brother. Paramount or DreamWorks had hired him to costar with Reese Witherspoon. Warner Brothers offered him the title role in a new series of Batman movies, Miramax wanted him to play a transvestite sheriff in a sensitive drama about anti-gay bigotry in Texas circa 1890, and Universal hoped he would sign a ten-million-dollar deal for two films that he would also write and direct.

Evidently, in this new millennium and in the popular imagination of those who dwelt on the glamorous west side of L.A., no failure ever died young, and Death came early only to the famous, the rich, the adored. Call it the Princess Di Principle.

Whether the man who had killed Ray "the Nerd" Rolf had also been an actor on the brink of superstardom, no one knew for certain. The murderer's name remained unknown, unmangled.

Indisputably, the killer himself had been gunned down. His body lay on the lawn in front of Rolf's apartment house.

Two pairs of binoculars circulated among the onlookers. Corky borrowed one pair to study Rolf's apparent executioner.

In the darkness and the rain, even with magnification, he was unable to discern any identifying details of the corpse sprawled on the grass.

Crime-scene investigators, busy with scientific instruments and cameras, crouched alongside the cadaver. In black raincoats draped like folded wings, they had the posture and the intensity of crows pecking at carrion.

In every version of the story viewed with credibility among the gossips, the killer himself had been killed by a police officer. The cop had been passing by in the street at the right moment, by sheer happenstance, or he had lived in Rolf's building, or he'd come there to visit his girlfriend or his mother.

Whatever had occurred here this evening, Corky was reasonably confident that it would not compromise his plans or cause the police to turn a gimlet eye on him. He had kept his association with Reynerd secret from everyone he knew.

He believed that Reynerd had been likewise discreet. They had committed crimes together and had conspired to commit others. Neither of them had anything to gain—and much to lose—by revealing their relationship to anyone.

Stupid in uncounted ways, Rolf had not been entirely reckless. To impress a woman or his witless friends, he might wish to reveal that he'd had his mother killed by proxy or that he was partner to a murderous conspiracy involving the biggest movie star in the world, but he would never go that far. He would just invent a colorful lie.

Although Ethan Truman, incognito, had visited earlier this very day, the possibility that Reynerd's death was connected in any way to Channing Manheim and the six gifts in black boxes remained unlikely.

Being an apostle of anarchy, Corky understood that chaos ruled the world and that in the rough and disorderly jumble-tumble of daily events, meaningless coincidences like this frequently occurred. Such apparent synchronisms encouraged lesser men than he to see patterns, design, and meaning in life.

He had wagered his future and, in fact, his existence, on the belief that life was meaningless. He owned a lot of stock in chaos, and at this late date, he wasn't going to second-guess his investment by selling chaos short.

Reynerd had fancied himself not only a potential movie star of historic proportions, but also something of a bad boy, and bad boys made enemies. For one thing, more in search of thrills than profits, he had dealt drugs to a refined list of entertainment-industry clients, mostly cocaine and meth and Ecstasy.

More likely than not, tougher men than pretty-boy Reynerd had decided that he was poaching in their fields. With a bullet in the head, he'd been discouraged from further competition.

Corky had needed Reynerd dead.

Chaos had obliged.

No more, no less.

Time to move on.

Time, in fact, for dinner. Aside from a candy bar in the car and a double latte at the mall, he had eaten nothing since breakfast.

On good days filled with worthwhile endeavors, his work provided nourishment enough, and he often skipped lunch. Now, after busy hours of useful enterprise, he was famished.

Nevertheless, he tarried long enough to serve chaos. The six children were a temptation that he could not resist.

All were six to eight years old. Some were better dressed for the rain and the cold than others were, but all remained unflaggingly exuberant, dancing-playing-chasing in the nasty night, as though they were storm petrels born to wet wind and turbulent skies.

Focused on the hubbub of cops and ambulances, the adults stood oblivious of their offspring. The kids were wise enough to understand that as long as they played on the lawn behind their elders and kept their chatter below a certain volume, they could prolong their night adventure indefinitely.

In this paranoid age, a stranger dared not offer candy to any child. Even the most gullible among them would shriek for the cops at the offer of a lollipop.

Corky had no lollipops, but he traveled with a bag of luscious, chewy caramels.

He waited until the kids' attention turned elsewhere, whereupon he extracted the bag from a deep inner pocket of his slicker. He dropped it on the grass where the children were sure to find it when their games brought them in this direction again.

He hadn't laced the candy with poison, but only with a potent hallucinogenic. Terror and disorder could be spread through society by means more subtle than extreme violence.

The amount of drug infused in each sweet morsel was small enough that even a child who greedily stuffed his face with six or eight of them would not risk toxic overdose. By the third piece, the waking nightmares would begin.

Corky mingled a while longer with the adults, surreptitiously observing the children, until two girls found the bag. Being girls, they at once generously shared the contents with the four boys.

This particular drug, unless taken in concert with a mellowing antidepressant like Prozac, was known to cause hallucinations so horrific that they tested the user's sanity. Soon, the kids would believe that mouths, bristling with sharp teeth and serpent tongues, had opened in the earth to swallow them, that alien parasites were bursting from their chests, and that everyone they knew and loved now intended to rend them limb from limb. Even after they recovered, flashbacks would trouble them for months, possibly for years.

Having sown these seeds of chaos, he returned to his car through the refreshingly cool night and cleansing rain.

If he had been born in an earlier century, Corky Laputa would have followed the original trail of Johnny Appleseed, killing one by one all the trees that the fabled orchardist had planted on this continent.

CHAPTER 31

If Fric had suspected that the wine cellar was haunted or that something less than human prowled its channels and chambers, he would have eaten dinner in his bedroom.

He proceeded without caution.

Likening the separation noise of the rubber seal to the sucking sound made by popping the lid off a vacuum-packed can of peanuts, Fric opened the thick glass door in the insulated-glass wall.

He stepped out of the wine-tasting room into the wine cellar proper. Here the temperature was maintained at a constant fifty-five degrees.

Fourteen thousand bottles required a lot of racks—a *maze* of racks. These weren't simply arranged like aisles in a supermarket. Instead, they lined a cozy brick labyrinth of vaulted passageways that intersected at circular grottoes ringed by more racks.

Four times each year, every bottle in the collection was gently rotated a quarter turn—ninety degrees—in its niche. This ensured that no edge of any cork would dry out and that the sediment would settle properly to the bottom of each punt.

The two porters, Mr. Worthy and Mr. Phan, were able to attend to the turning of the wine bottles for only four hours a day due to the tediousness of the work, the measured care that it required, and the havoc that it caused with neck and shoulder muscles. Each man could properly rotate between twelve hundred and thirteen hundred bottles per four-hour session.

Through a flow of cool dry air that pumped ceaselessly from ceiling vents, Fric followed a narrow dome-vaulted passageway of Pinot Noir to a wider groin-vaulted corridor of Cabernet, circled a curiously coved grotto of Lafitte Rothschild stocked with various vintages, continued through a tunnel of Merlot, in search of a place where he would be able to hide without fear of discovery.

Arriving in an elongated-oval gallery stocked with French Burgundy, he thought he heard footsteps other than his own, elsewhere in the maze. He froze, listened.

Nothing. Just the whispery voice of the perpetual wine-cooling draft lazily entering the gallery by one passageway, leaving by a second.

The fluttering false flames of the fake gas lamps, which were wall-mounted in some places but also hung from grotto ceilings where height allowed, caused shimmers of light to chase twists of shadow along the racks and brickwork. This meaningless but spooky movement teased the mind into hearing footsteps that probably weren't there.

Probably.

Proceeding less boldly than before, occasionally glancing over his shoulder, he moved on with the gentle draft.

Other wine cellars might be musty dens in which time shed skin after skin of dust, leaving a record of its unending progress. In fact a dusty film on the bottles was often considered good ambience.

Fric's father had an almost obsessive aversion to dust, however, and none could be found in this place. Taking special care not to disturb the bottles, the staff vacuumed the racks once a month, as well as the ceiling, walls, and floor.

Here and there in the corners of the passageways and more often in the shadowed curves of the masonry ceiling vaults were delicate spider webs. Some were simple, others elaborate.

No eight-legged architects could be glimpsed at home in these constructions. Spiders were not tolerated.

When at work, the housekeepers kept the vacuum cleaner away from these gossamer architectures, which had been made not by spiders but by a specialist in set decoration from Ghost Dad's favorite film studio. Nevertheless, the webs deteriorated. Twice a year, Mr. Knute, the set decorator, swabbed them off the bricks and then rebuilt them as good as new.

The wine itself was real.

Turn by turn through the labyrinth, Fric calculated how long his father could stay blind drunk on wine before exhausting the contents of this cellar.

Certain assumptions had to be made, the first being that Ghost Dad would sleep eight hours a night. Perpetually soused, he might sleep longer; however, in the interest of keeping these calculations simple, an arbitrary number must be selected. Eight.

Also assume that a grown man could stay seriously drunk by consuming one bottle of wine every three hours. To establish a state of inebriation, the first bottle might have to be slugged down in an hour or two, but after that, one every three hours.

This was actually not an assumption but hard knowledge. Fric had on numerous occasions been in a position to observe actors, writers, rock stars, directors, and other famous drunks with a taste for fine wine, and while some could pour it down faster than one bottle every three hours, those aggressive drinkers always passed out.

Okay. Five bottles spread over each sixteen-hour day. Divide fourteen thousand by five. Twenty-eight hundred.

The contents of this cellar ought to keep Ghost Dad shitfaced for twenty-eight hundred days. So then divide 2,800 by 365 . . .

Over seven and a half years. The old man could stay blind drunk until Fric had graduated from high school and had run away to join the United States Marine Corps.

Of course, the biggest movie star in the world never drank more than one glass of wine with dinner. He didn't use drugs at all—not even pot, which everyone else in Hollywood seemed to think was just a health food. "I'm far from perfect," he'd once told a reporter for *Premiere* magazine, "but all my faults and failures and foibles tend to be spiritual in nature."

Fric had no idea what *that* meant, even though he'd spent more than a little time trying to figure it out.

Maybe Ming du Lac, his father's full-time spiritual adviser, could have explained the quote. Fric never dared to ask him for a translation because he found Ming nearly as scary as Mr. Hachette, the extraterrestrial predator disguised as their household chef.

Arriving in the last grotto, the point farthest from the wine-cellar entrance, he heard footsteps again. As before, when he cocked his head and listened intently, he detected nothing suspicious.

Sometimes his imagination went into overdrive.

Three years ago, when he'd been seven, he'd been convinced that something strange and green and scaly crawled out of the toilet bowl in his bathroom every night and waited to devour him if ever he went for a postmidnight pee. For months, when Fric woke in the middle of the night with a bloated bladder, he left his suite and used safe bathrooms elsewhere in the house.

In his own monster-occupied bath, he'd left a cookie on a plate. Night after night, the cookie remained untouched. Eventually he had substituted a chunk of cheese for the cookie, and then a package of lunch meat in place of the cheese. A monster might have no interest in cookies, might even turn its nose up at cheese, but surely no carnivorous beast could resist pimento-loaf bologna.

When the bologna went unmolested for a week, Fric used his own bathroom again. Nothing ate him.

Now nothing followed him into the final grotto. Nothing but the cool draft and the flicker of light and shadow from fake gas lamps.

The entrance and exit passages more or less divided the grotto in half. To Fric's right were yet more racks of wine bottles. To his left, stacked floor to ceiling along the wall, were sealed wooden cases of wine.

According to the stenciled names, the cases contained a fine French Bordeaux. In fact they were filled with cheap vino that only gutter-living bums would drink, and the contents had no doubt turned to vinegar decades before Fric had been born.

The wooden cases had been stacked here partly for decoration and partly to conceal the entrance to the port-wine closet.

Fric pressed a hidden latch-release button. One stack of wooden cases swung inward.

Beyond lay a room the size of a walk-in closet. At the back was a rack of port wines fifty, sixty, and seventy years old.

Ports were dessert wines. Fric preferred chocolate cake.

He assumed that even in the late 1930s, when this house had been built, the nation had not been plagued by gangs of port-wine thieves. The closet had most likely been concealed just for the fun of it.

This secret chamber, smaller than the fur vault, might make an adequate hiding place—depending on how long he would need to remain hidden. The space would be comfortable enough for a few hours.

If he had to stay in here for two or three days, however, he would start to feel that he'd been buried alive. He'd collapse into a screaming fit of claustrophobia and eventually, descending into madness, he would probably eat himself alive, beginning with his toes and working upward.

Unnerved by the direction their second conversation had taken, he'd forgotten to ask Mysterious Caller how long he could expect to be under siege.

He retreated from the port closet and pulled shut the clever wine-case door.

Turning, Fric saw movement in the passageway by which he had entered this last grotto. Not just the throb of fake gas flames.

A large, strange, spiral silhouette wheeled across the racks and vaulted brick ceiling, layering itself over the familiar flicker of small pennants of light and small flags of shadow. It was approaching the grotto.

Quite unlike his father in a big-screen pinch, Fric seized up with fear and could neither attack nor flee.

Eerily shapeless, shifting, gently tumbling, the shadow billowed closer, closer, and then the fear-

some source appeared at the mouth of the passageway: a spirit, a ghost, an apparition, ragged
and milky, semitransparent and vaguely luminous,
drifting slowly toward him by supernatural loco-
motion.

Fric frantically stepped backward, stumbled, fell
hard enough to remind himself that his butt was as
scrawny as his biceps.

Out of the passageway and into the grotto came
the apparition, gliding like a stingray in ocean
depths. Lambent light and pulsing shadow played
upon the phantom form, lending it a greater mystery, an aura of veiled or bearded evil.

Fric raised his hands protectively before his face
and peered up between his spread fingers as the
spirit arrived above him. For a moment, weightless
and slowly revolving, the apparition reminded him
of the Milky Way galaxy, with its gossamer spiral
arms—and then he recognized it for what it was.

Lazily drifting on the cool draft, a fake web, fabri-
cated by Mr. Knute, had come unanchored. Floating with all the ghostly grace of a jellyfish, it followed the air currents across the grotto toward the
next passageway.

Mortified, Fric scrambled to his feet.

Passing out of the grotto, the airborne web
snared on one of the wall-mounted lamps, tangled
upon itself, and hung there, flimsy and aflutter, like
something from Tinkerbell's lingerie drawer.

Angry with himself, Fric fled the wine cellar.

He was in the tasting room, closing the heavy
glass door behind himself, before he realized that

the spider web could not have come loose all by it-self. A draft alone would not have spun it free, up, and away.

Someone would have had to brush against it, at the least, and Fric didn't believe that he himself had done so.

He suspected that someone close behind him in the wine maze had patiently worked the web loose from its corner, careful not to shred or wad it, and had set it afloat upon the draft, to taunt him.

On the other hand, he remembered too well the toilet-spawned, scaly, green monster that had not even been real enough to nibble on a slice of bologna.

He stood for a moment, frowning at the refectory table. While he had been wandering the wine cel-lar, his dinner dishes had been taken away.

One of the maids might have cleaned up after him. Or Mrs. McBee, though as busy as she was this evening, she would probably send the mister.

Why any of them would have followed him into the wine cellar without calling out to him, why they would have set the Knute-spun cobweb afloat, he couldn't begin to understand.

Fric felt that he was at the center of a web not manufactured by Mr. Knute, an invisible web of conspiracy.

CHAPTER 32

Upon receiving the call, Dunny Whistler at once responds to it, driving directly to Beverly Hills.

He doesn't need the car anymore. Nevertheless, he enjoys being behind the wheel of a well-engineered automobile, and even the simple pleasure of driving has a new poignancy in light of recent events.

En route, traffic lights turn green just when needed, gaps in traffic repeatedly open for him, and he makes such speed that dark wings of water plume from his tires most of the way. He should feel exhilarated, but many concerns weigh on his mind.

At the hotel, where the arriving and departing vehicles seem to be those makes that retail for six figures, he leaves his car with valet parking. He tips the attendant twenty bucks, going in, because he's not likely to be around long enough to spend all his cash on pleasures for himself.

The sumptuous luxury of the lobby embraces him with such warmth of color, texture, and form that Dunny could easily forget that the night outside is cold and rainy.

Richly paneled, expensively appointed, lighted for romance, a textbook on glamorous decor, the hotel bar is huge, but crowded in spite of its size.

Every woman in sight, regardless of age, is beautiful, by either the grace of God or the knife of a good surgeon. Half the men are as handsome as movie stars, and the other half *think* they are.

Most of these people work in the entertainment industry. No actors, but agents and studio executives, publicists and producers.

In another hotel, elsewhere in the city, you might hear several foreign tongues, but in this place only English is spoken, and only that narrow but colorful version of English known as the dialect of the deal. Connections are being secured here; money is being made; sexual excesses are being plotted.

These people are energetic, optimistic, flirtatious, loud, and convinced of their immortality.

In the manner that Cary Grant once navigated crowded parties in the movies, as though skating while everyone around him walked with leg weights, Dunny glides past the bar, among the crowded tables, directly to a prized corner table for four where only one man sits.

This man's name is Typhon, or so he would have you believe. He pronounces it *tie-fon,* and tells you on first meeting that he bears the name of a monster from Greek mythology, a beast that traveled in storms and spread terror wherever the rain took it.

Then he laughs, perhaps in recognition that his name is dramatically at odds with his appearance, his genteel business style, and his polished manners.

Nothing about Typhon appears the least monstrous or stormy. He is plump, white-haired, with a sweet androgynous face that would serve well in a movie as either that of a beatific nun or that of a saintly friar. His smile comes easily and often, and seems sincere. Soft-spoken, a good listener, irresistibly likable, the man can make a friend in a minute.

He is impeccably dressed in a dark blue suit, white silk shirt, blue-and-red club tie, and red display handkerchief. His thick white hair has been cut by a stylist to stars and royalty. Unblemished skin smoothed by expensive emollients, bleached teeth, and manicured nails suggest that he takes pride in his appearance.

Typhon sits facing the room, pleasantly regal in demeanor, as might be a kindly monarch holding court. Although he must be known to this crowd, no one bothers him, as though it is understood that he prefers to see and be seen rather than to talk with anyone.

Of the four chairs at the table, two face the room. Dunny takes the second.

Typhon is eating oysters and drinking a superb Pinot Grigio. He says, "Dine with me, please, dear boy. Have anything you wish."

As if conjured by a sorcerer, a waiter instantly appears. Dunny orders double oysters and a bottle of

"All right. You're more than fair. And I'm grateful to have another chance."

"Ah, now, there's no need for gratitude, Dunny." Typhon smiles broadly, his merriment regained. "If you succeed, then *I* succeed. Your interests are my own."

To reassure his benefactor that they are in full understanding of each other, Dunny says, "I'll do everything I possibly can for Ethan Truman—always keeping a low profile, of course. But I won't make any move against Corky Laputa."

"What an appalling piece of work *he* is." Typhon clucks his tongue, but his eyes twinkle. "The world desperately needs God's mercy as long as there are men like Corky in it."

"Amen."

"You know that Corky would most likely have killed Reynerd anyway if you hadn't interfered."

"I know," Dunny says.

"Then why show up with Hector X?"

"Laputa wouldn't have killed him with witnesses, certainly not with Hazard Yancy present. When Reynerd died in front of Yancy, then Yancy was *involved,* and more deeply than he'd have been otherwise. For Ethan's sake, I want him involved."

"Your friend *does* need all the help he can get," Typhon acknowledges.

For a minute or two, they enjoy the oysters and the fine wine in a mutual, comfortable silence.

Then Dunny says, "The incident with the PT Cruiser came as a surprise."

Raising his eyebrows, Typhon says, "You don't think our people were involved with that, do you?"

"No," Dunny says. "I understand how these things work. It came as a surprise, that's all. But I was able to use it to my advantage."

"Leaving him with the three little bells was a clever move," Typhon agrees. "Though you've driven him to drink."

Smiling, nodding, Dunny agrees: "I probably have."

"No 'probably' about it," says Typhon. Pointing, he adds: "Poor Ethan is at the bar right now."

Although Dunny's chair faces most of the room, about a third of the long bar is to his back. He turns to look where Typhon points.

Past intervening tables where breachers of contracts socialize like friends, Ethan Truman sits on a stool at the bar, in profile to Dunny, staring into a glass that might contain high-quality Scotch.

"He'll see me," Dunny worries.

"Most likely not. He's too distracted. In a sense, he doesn't see anyone right now. He might as well be here alone."

"But if he does—"

"If he does," Typhon says reassuringly, "then you'll manage the situation one way or another. I'm here for guidance if you need it."

Dunny stares at Ethan for a moment, then turns his back to him. "You chose this place knowing he was here?"

The only response from Typhon is a winning smile with a sly twist, which seems to say that he knows he's been naughty but simply couldn't resist.

"You chose this place *because* he was here."

Typhon says, "Did you know that Saint Duncan, for whom you were named, is the patron saint of guardians and protectors of many kinds, and that he will help you be steadfast and resourceful in your work if you petition him?"

Smiling thinly, Dunny says, "Is that so? Ironic, huh?"

Patting Dunny on the arm, Typhon reassures him: "From everything I've seen, you're an amazingly resourceful man to begin with."

Dunny communes with the Pinot Grigio for a while, but then says, "Do you think he's going to come through this alive?"

After finishing his last oyster, Typhon says, "Ethan? To some extent, that's up to you."

"But only to some extent."

"Well, you know how these things work, Dunny. More likely than not, he'll be dead before Christmas. But his situation isn't entirely hopeless. No one's ever is."

"And the people at Palazzo Rospo?"

With his white hair, plump features, and sparkling blue eyes, Typhon is but a beard away from being Santa Claus. His sweet face isn't made for grim expressions. He appears disconcertingly merry when he says, "I don't think any experienced oddsmaker would give them much of a chance, do you? Not against the likes of Mr. Laputa. He has the violent temperament and the reckless determination to get what he wants."

"Even the boy?"

"Especially the boy," says Typhon. "Especially him."

CHAPTER 33

Fed, frightened, and frustrated, Fric went directly from the wine cellar to the library, proceeding by an indirect route least likely to result in an encounter with a member of the house staff.

Like a spirit, like a phantom, like a boy wearing a cloak of invisibility, he passed room to hall to stair to room, and no one in the great house registered his passage, in part because he carried a rare gene for catlike stealth, but in part because no one, with the possible exception of Mrs. McBee, cared where the hell he was or ever wondered what the hell he was up to.

Being small, thin, and ignored was not always a curse. When the forces of evil were rising up against you in vast dark battalions, having a low profile improved your chances of avoiding evisceration, decapitation, induction into the soulless legions of the living dead, or whatever other hideous fate they might have planned for you.

The last time that Nominal Mom had visited, which wasn't quite as far back in the mists of time as mastodons and sabertooths, she had told Fric that he was a mouse: "A sweet little mouse that no one ever realizes is there because he's so quiet, so quick, so quick and so gray, as quick as the gray shadow of a darting bird. You're a little mouse, Aelfric, an almost invisible perfect little mouse."

Freddie Nielander said a lot of stupid things.

Fric didn't hold any of them against her.

She'd been so beautiful for so long that nobody really listened to her. They were overwhelmed by the visuals.

When no one ever listened to you, really listened, you could begin to lose the ability to tell whether or not you were making sense when you talked.

Fric understood this danger because no one really listened to him, either. In his case, they weren't overwhelmed by the visuals. They were underwhelmed.

Without exception, people loved Freddie Nielander on sight, and they wanted her to love them in return. Even if they *had* listened to her, therefore, they wouldn't have disagreed with her, and even when she made no sense whatsoever, people praised her wit.

Poor Freddie didn't get any truthful feedback from anything but a mirror. No explanation short of a miracle explained why she hadn't gone as crazy as a nuclear-waste-dump rat a long time ago.

Arriving in the library, Fric discovered that the furniture in the reading area nearest the entrance had been slightly rearranged to accommodate a twelve-foot Christmas tree. The fresh forestal smell of evergreens was so strong that he expected to see squirrels sitting in the armchairs and busily storing acorns in the antique Chinese vases.

This was one of nine massive spruces erected this very evening in key rooms throughout the mansion. Flawlessly shaped, perfectly symmetrical, greener-than-green clone trees.

Each of the nine evergreens would be decorated with a different theme. Here the subject was angels.

Every ornament on the tree was an angel or featured an angel in its design. Baby angels, child angels, adult angels, blond angels with blue eyes, African-American angels, Asian angels, noble-looking American Indian angels with feathered headdresses as well as halos. Angels smiling, angels laughing, angels using their halos as Hula-Hoops, angels flying, dancing, caroling, praying, and skipping rope. Cute dogs with angel wings. Angel cats, angel toads, an angel pig.

Fric resisted the urge to puke.

Leaving all the angels to glitter and glimmer and dangle and grin, he went into the book stacks, directly to the shelf that held the dictionaries. He sat on the floor with the biggest volume—*The Random House Dictionary of the English Language*—and paged to ROBIN GOODFELLOW, because Mysterious Caller had said that the man from whom Fric would soon need to hide "styles himself as Robin Goodfellow."

The definition was a single word: *Puck*.

To Fric, this appeared to be an obscenity, although he didn't know what it meant.

Dictionaries were full of obscenities. This didn't bother Fric. He assumed that the people who compiled dictionaries weren't just a bunch of foul-mouthed gutter scum, that they had scholarly reasons for including trash talk.

When they started providing one-word obscene definitions that made no sense, however, maybe the time had come for the publisher to start smelling their coffee to see if it was loaded with booze.

Many of his father's associates used so many obscenities per sentence that they probably owned dictionaries that contained nothing but foul language. Yet *Puck* was so obscure none of them had ever spoken it in Fric's presence.

Fric paged forward through the volume, pretty sure he would discover that *Puck* meant "Screw you, we're tired of defining words, make up your own meaning."

Instead, he learned that Puck was a "mischievous sprite" in English folklore and a character in Shakespeare's *A Midsummer Night's Dream.*

Most words had more than one meaning, and that was true of *Puck*. The second definition proved to be less cheerful-sounding than the first: "a malicious or mischievous demon or spirit; a goblin."

Mysterious Caller had said that the guy Fric needed to worry about had a darker side than

Robin Goodfellow, alias Puck. A darker side than a malicious demon or goblin.

Ugly clouds were gathering over Friclandia.

Fric paged farther forward in the dictionary, looking for a guy named M-o-e L-o-c-k. Instead, after some searching, he found MOLOCH. He read the definition twice.

Not good.

Moloch had been a deity, mentioned in two books of the Bible, whose worshipers were required to sacrifice children. Obviously, he had not been a Bible-approved deity.

The last four words of the definition particularly disturbed Fric: ". . . the sacrifice of children *by their own parents.*"

This seemed to be carrying child sacrifice one step too far.

He didn't for a moment believe that Ghost Dad and Nominal Mom would strap him down on an altar and chop him to pieces for Moloch.

For one thing, with their superstar schedules, they'd probably never again be together in the same place at the same time.

Besides, while they might not be the kind of parents who tucked you in bed at night and taught you how to throw a baseball, they were not monsters, either. They were just people. Confused. Trying to do the best they knew how.

Fric had no doubt they cared about him. They had to care. They'd made him.

They just didn't express their feelings well. Images, not words, were your average supermodel's strength. Naturally, the biggest movie star in the world, being an actor, was better with words than Freddie was, but only when someone wrote them for him.

For a while, just to have something to do that didn't require thinking about being brutally murdered, Fric looked up obscene words in the dictionary. It was an amazingly dirty book.

Eventually he began to feel ashamed of himself for reading all these filthy definitions in the same room with a tree full of angels.

After returning the dictionary to its shelf, he went to the nearest telephone. Because the library was a humongous space, three phones were distributed among its armchair-furnished reading areas.

On those rare occasions when Ghost Dad invited a magazine journalist to interview him at home rather than on a set or some other neutral ground, he usually noted that the library contained more than twice as many books as there were bottles of wine in the wine cellar. Then he said, "When I'm a has-been, at least I'll be a pleasantly wasted, well-educated has-been."

Ha, ha, ha.

Fric sat on the edge of a chair, picked up the phone beside it, pressed the access button for his private line, and keyed in *69. He had forgotten to do this in the wine-tasting room, after Mysterious Caller had hung up on him.

Previously, when he'd tried this trick, the call-back number had rung and rung, and no one had ever answered it.

This time, someone answered. Someone picked up on the fourth ring, but didn't say anything.

"It's me," said Fric.

Though he didn't receive a reply, Fric knew he wasn't listening to a dead line. He could sense a presence at the other end.

"Are you surprised?" Fric asked.

He could hear breathing.

"I used star sixty-nine."

The breathing grew strange, a little ragged, as though the idea of being tracked down with *69 excited the guy.

"I'm calling you from the crapper in my father's bathroom," he lied, and waited to see if his weird phone buddy would warn him about the misery with which lying was rewarded.

Instead, he just got breathed at some more.

The guy was obviously trying to spook him. Fric refused to give the pervert the satisfaction of knowing that he had succeeded.

"What I forgot to ask you is how long I'll need to hide from this Puck when he shows up."

The longer he listened to the breathing, the more Fric realized that this had peculiar and disturbing qualities far different from the standard pervert-on-the-phone panting that he'd heard in movies.

"I looked up Moloch, too."

This name seemed to excite the freak. The breathing grew rougher and more urgent.

Abruptly Fric became convinced that the heavy breather was not a man, but an animal. Like a bear, maybe, but worse than a bear. Like a bull, but nothing as ordinary as a bull.

Up the coiled cord, into the handset, into the ear piece, into Fric's right ear, the breathing squirmed, a serpent of sound, seeking to coil inside his skull and set its fangs into his brain.

This didn't seem at all like Mysterious Caller. He hung up.

Instantly, his line rang: *Ooodelee-ooodelee-oo.*

He didn't answer it.

Ooodelee-ooodelee-oo.

Fric got up from the armchair. He walked away.

He passed quickly along aisles of bookshelves to the front of the library.

His personal call tone continued to mock him. He paused to stare at the phone in this main reading area, watching as the signal light burned bright with each ring.

Like all the members of the household and the staff who enjoyed dedicated phone lines, Fric had voice mail. If he didn't pick up by the fifth ring, the call would be recorded for him.

Although his voice mail was currently activated, the phone had rung fourteen times, maybe more.

He circled the Christmas tree, opened one of the two tall doors, and stepped out of the library, into the hall.

At last the phone stopped taunting him.

Fric glanced to his left, then to his right. He stood alone in the hall, yet the feeling of being watched had once more settled over him.

In the library, among the hundreds of tiny white

sion on his face at once made them choke on their unvoiced reprimands.

By the time Ethan stepped out of the bar, Dunny had vanished.

Hurrying into the adjacent lobby, Ethan saw guests standing at the registration desk, others at the concierge desk, people walking toward the elevator alcove. Dunny wasn't among them.

To Ethan's left, the marble-clad lobby opened to an enormous drawing room furnished with sofas and armchairs. There, guests could attend high tea every afternoon; and at this later hour, drinks were being served to those who preferred an atmosphere gentler than that in the bar.

At a glance, Dunny Whistler couldn't be seen among the crowd in the drawing room.

Nearer, to Ethan's right, the revolving door at the hotel's main entrance was slowly turning to a stop, as though someone had recently gone in or out, but its quadrants were deserted now.

He pushed through the door, into the night chill under the roof of the porte-cochere.

Sheltering their charges with umbrellas, the doorman and a busy squad of parking valets escorted visitors to and from arriving and departing vehicles. Cars, SUVs, and limousines jostled for position in the crowded hotel-service lanes.

Dunny wasn't standing with those who were waiting for their cars. Nor did he appear to be hurrying through the downpour in the company of any of the escorts.

Several Mercedes in various dark colors idled

among the other vehicles, but Ethan was pretty sure none of them was Dunny's wheels.

The ring of his cell phone might not have been audible above the chatter of the people under the porte-cochere, the car engines, and the hiss and sizzle of the drizzling night. Set for a silent signal, however, it vibrated in a jacket pocket.

Still surveying the night for Dunny, he answered the phone.

Hazard Yancy said, "I've got to see you right now, man, and it's got to be somewhere the elite don't meet."

CHAPTER 35

Dunny takes the hotel elevator up to the fourth floor in the company of an elderly couple. They hold hands as though they are young lovers.

Overhearing the word "anniversary," Dunny asks how long they have been married.

"Fifty years," the husband says, aglow with pride that his bride has chosen to spend most of her life with him.

They are from Scranton, Pennsylvania, here in Los Angeles to celebrate their anniversary with their daughter and her family. The daughter has paid for the hotel honeymoon suite, which is, according to the wife, "so fancy we're afraid to sit on the furniture."

From L.A., they'll fly to Hawaii, just the two of them, for a romantic week-long idyll in the sun.

They are unaffected, sweet, clearly in love. They have built a life of the kind that Dunny for so long disdained, even mocked.

In recent years, he's come to want their brand of happiness more than anything else. Their devotion and commitment to each other, the family they have built, the life of mutual striving, the memories of shared challenges and hard-won triumphs: Here is what matters, in the end, not the things that he has pursued with single-minded strategy and brutal tactics. Not power, not money, not thrills, not control.

He has tried to change, but he's gone too far along a solitary road to be able to turn back and find the companionship for which he yearns. Hannah is five years gone. Only when she had been on her deathbed had he realized that she'd been the best chance he'd ever had of finding his way from the wrong road to the right one. As a young hothead, he had rejected her counsel, had believed that power and money were more important to him than she was. The shock of her early death forced him to face the hard truth that he'd been wrong.

Only on this strange, rainy day has he come to understand that she was also his *last* chance.

For a man who once believed that the world was clay from which he could make what he wished, Dunny has arrived at a difficult place. He has lost all power, for nothing he does now can change his life.

Of the money he withdrew from the wall safe in his study, he still has twenty thousand dollars. He could give ten of it to this elderly couple from Scranton, tell them to stay a full month in blue Hawaii, to dine well and drink well, with his blessings.

Or he could stop the elevator and kill them.

Neither act would change his future in any meaningful way.

He bitterly envies their happiness. There would
be a certain savage satisfaction in robbing them of
their remaining years.

Whatever else may be wrong with him—the list
of his faults and corruptions is long—he can't kill
solely out of envy. Pride alone prevents him, more
than mercy.

On the fourth floor, their accommodations are at
the opposite end of the hotel from his. He wishes
them well and watches them walk away, hand-in-
hand.

Dunny is using the presidential suite. This grand
space has been booked on a twelve-month basis
by Typhon, who will not be needing it for the next
few days, as business will take him elsewhere.

Presidential implies an understated democratic
grandeur. These large rooms are so rich and so
sensual, however, that they are less suitable for a
steward of democracy than for royalty or
demigods.

Inlaid marble floors, Oushak rugs in tones of gold
and red and apricot and indigo, bubinga paneling
soaring sixteen feet to coffered ceilings . . .

Dunny wanders room to room, moved by humanity's desire to make beautiful its habitat and
thereby bravely to deny that the roughness of the
world must be endured. Every palace and every
work of art is only dust as yet unrealized, and time
is the patient wind that will wither it away. Nevertheless, men and women have given great

thought, effort, and care to making these rooms appealing, because they hope, against all evidence, that their lives have meaning and that in their talents lies a purpose larger than themselves.

Until two years ago, Dunny never knew this hope. Three years of anguish over her loss, ironically, made him *want* to believe in God.

Gradually, during the years following her funeral, an unexpected hope grew in him, desperate and fragile but enduring. Yet he remains too much the old Dunny, mired in old habits of thought and action.

Hope is a cloudy radiance. He has not learned how to distill it into something pure, clear, more powerful.

And now he never will.

In the master bedroom, he stands at a rain-washed window, gazing northwest. Beyond the storm-blurred city lights, beyond the lushly landscaped and mansioned slopes of Beverly Hills, lies Bel Air and Palazzo Rospo, that foolish yet nonetheless brave monument to hope. All who ever owned it have died—or will.

He turns from the window and stares at the bed. The maid has removed the spread, turned down the sheets, and left a tiny gold box on one of the pillows.

The box holds four bonbons. Elegantly formed and decorated, they appear to be delicious, but he doesn't sample them.

He could call any of several beautiful women to share the bed with him. Some would expect money; others would not. Among them are women for whom sex is an act of love and grace, but also women who revel in their own debasement. The choice is his, any tenderness or any thrill that he desires.

He cannot recall the taste of the oysters or the bouquet of the Pinot Grigio. The memory has no savor, offers less stimulation to his senses than might a photograph of oysters and wine.

None of the women he could call would leave a greater impression than the food and drink that, still settling in him, seems to be a meal imagined. The silken texture of their skin, the smell of their hair would not linger with him past the moment when, in leaving, they closed the door behind them.

He is like a man living through the night before doomsday, with full knowledge that the sun will go nova in the morning, yet unable to enjoy the precious pleasures of this world because all his energy is devoted to wishing desperately that the foreseen end will not, after all, come to pass.

CHAPTER 36

Ethan and Hazard met in a church, for at this hour on a Monday night, the pews were empty, and no chance whatsoever existed that they would be seen here together by politicians, by members of the Officer Involved Shooting team, or by other authorities.

In the otherwise deserted nave, they sat side by side in a pew, near a side aisle where neither the overhead nor the footpath lights were aglow, veiled in shadows. The stale but pleasant spice of long-extinguished incense perfumed air as still as that in a sealed jar.

They spoke less in conspiratorial whispers than in the hushed voices of men humbled by awesome experience.

"So I told the OIS team I went to see Reynerd to ask about his friend Jerry Nemo, who happens to be a suspect in the murder of this coke peddler name of Carter Cook."

"They believe you?" Ethan asked.

"They seem like they want to. But suppose tomorrow I get a lab report that superglues Blonde in the Pond to that city councilman I told you about."

"That girl dumped in the sewage plant."

"Yeah. So the bastard councilman will start looking for a way to get at me. If any guys on the OIS team can be bought or blackmailed, they'll turn that homey hit man with the coke-spoon earring into a crippled choirboy who got shot in the back, and my mug will be on the front pages under the nine-letter headline."

Ethan knew what the nine-letter headline would be—KILLER COP—because they had talked about the power of anti-cop prejudice over the years. When a dirty politician and the sensation-hungry press discovered a shared agenda in any case, truth was stretched tighter than the skin of any Hollywood dowager with four face-lifts, and the blindfold over Lady Justice's eyes was ripped away and shoved into her mouth to shut her up.

Hazard hunched forward, forearms on his thighs, hands clasped almost as if in prayer, staring at the altar. "The media love this councilman. His rep is he's a reformer, got all the right sympathies and positions on the issues. They ought to love me, too, 'cause I'm so lovable, but that crowd would rather cut off their lips than kiss a cop. If they see a chance to save him by crucifying me, every hardware store in the city will be sold out of nails."

"I'm sorry I got you into this."

"You couldn't know some fool would whack Reynerd." Hazard turned his gaze from the altar, and his eyes met Ethan's as though searching for the Judas taint: "Could you?"

"Some ways this looks bad for me."

"Some ways," Hazard agreed. "But even you aren't dumb enough to work for some movie-star asshole who settles business like he's a rap-music mogul."

"Manheim doesn't know about Reynerd or the black boxes. And if he did know, he'd figure all Reynerd needed to improve his psychology was a little aromatherapy."

"But there *is* something you're not telling me," Hazard pressed.

Ethan shook his head, but not in denial. "Oh, man, this has been one long day in a monkey barrel."

"For one thing, Reynerd was sitting on his sofa between two bags of potato chips. Turns out he kept a loaded piece in each bag."

"Yet when the shooter rang the bell, Reynerd answered the door unarmed."

"Maybe 'cause he figured I was the true threat, and already through the door. My point is you were right about the potato chips."

"Like I told you, a neighbor said he was paranoid, kept a pistol close to him, stashed it in odd places like that."

"The talky neighbor—that's bullshit," Hazard said. "There was no talky neighbor. You knew some other way."

They were at a crossroads of trust and suspicion. Unless Ethan spilled more than he had revealed thus far, Hazard wasn't going to follow him one step farther. Their friendship would not be finished, but without greater disclosure, it would never be the same.

"You're gonna think I'm mental," Ethan said.

"Already do."

Ethan inhaled more incense, exhaled inhibition, and told Hazard about being shot in the gut by Reynerd, opening his eyes to discover he wasn't shot after all, and in the absence of a wound, nevertheless finding blood under his fingernails.

Throughout all this, Hazard's eyes neither swam out of focus nor shifted toward some far point of the church, as they would have done if he'd decided that Ethan was either jiving or psychotic. Only when Ethan finished did Hazard look down at his folded hands again.

Eventually the big man said, "Well, for sure I'm not sitting here beside a ghost."

"When you choose an institution for me," Ethan said, "I'd prefer one with a good arts-and-crafts program."

"Other than having your blood tested for drugs, you cooked up any theories about this?"

"You mean, besides I'm in the Twilight Zone? Or I really did die from that gut shot, and this is Hell?"

Hazard took the point. "Aren't a whole lot of theories come to mind, are there?"

"Not the kind you can explore with what the suits at the police academy call 'conventional investigative techniques.'"

"You don't seem nuts to me," Hazard said.

"I don't seem nuts to me, either. But then the nut is always the last to know."

"Besides, you were right about the pistol in the potato chips. So it was at least like . . . a psychic experience."

"Clairvoyance, yeah. Except that doesn't explain the blood under my nails."

Hazard had absorbed this bizarre revelation with quiet trust and remarkable equanimity.

Nevertheless, Ethan had no intention of telling him about being run down by the PT Cruiser and the truck. Or about dying in the ambulance.

If you reported having seen a ghost, you were a regular guy who'd had an uncanny experience. If you reported seeing *another* ghost at another place and time, you were at best an eccentric whose every statement would thereafter be taken with enough salt to crust the rims of a million margarita glasses.

"The shooter who killed Reynerd," Hazard said, "was a gangbanger called himself Hector X. Real name was Calvin Roosevelt. He's a high cuzz in the Crips, so you figure his accomplice must've been driving a set of wheels they boosted right before the hit."

"Standard," Ethan agreed.

"But there's no stolen-car report on the Benz they used. I got the number on the tags, and you won't believe who it belongs to."

Hazard looked up from his folded hands. He met Ethan's eyes.

Although Ethan didn't know what was coming, he knew it couldn't be good. "Who?"

"Your boyhood pal. The notorious Dunny Whistler."

Ethan didn't look away. He didn't dare. "You know what happened to him a few months ago."

"Some guys drowned him in a toilet, but he didn't quite die."

"Few days after that, his lawyer contacted me, told me Dunny's will named me executor, and his *living* will gives me the right to make medical decisions for him."

"You never mentioned this."

"Didn't see any reason. You know what he was. You understand why I didn't want him in my life. But I accepted the situation out of . . . I don't know . . . because of what he meant to me when we were kids."

Hazard nodded. He withdrew a roll of hard caramels from a coat pocket, peeled back the wrapping, and offered to share.

Ethan shook his head. "Dunny died this morning at Our Lady of Angels."

Hazard pried a caramel from the roll, popped it in his mouth.

"They can't find his body," Ethan said, for suddenly he sensed that Hazard already knew all this.

Carefully folding the loose end of the wrapper over the exposed candy, Hazard said nothing.

"They swear he was dead," Ethan continued, "but considering how things work at the hospital morgue, he couldn't have gotten out of there any way but on his own two feet."

Hazard returned the roll to his coat pocket. He sucked on the caramel, moving it around his mouth.

"I'm sure he's alive," Ethan said.

Finally Hazard looked at him again. "All this happened before we had lunch."

"Yeah. Listen, man, I didn't mention it because I didn't see how Dunny could be connected to Reynerd. I *still* don't see how. Do you?"

"You were one self-possessed dude at lunch, considering all this was churning through your head."

"I thought I was going crazy, but I didn't see how you'd be more likely to help me if I virtually *told* you I was losing my mind."

"So what happened *after* lunch?"

Ethan recounted his visit to Dunny's apartment, leaving nothing out except the strange elusive shape in the steam-clouded mirror.

"Why'd he keep a photo of Hannah on his desk?" Hazard asked.

"He'd never gotten over her. Still hasn't. I guess that's why he ripped it out of the frame today and took it with him."

"So he drives out of the garage in his Mercedes—"

"I assumed it was him. I couldn't get a look at the driver."

"And then what?"

"I had to think about it. Then I visited Hannah's grave."

"Why?"

"Gut feeling. Thought I might find something there."

"And what did you find?"

"Roses." He told Hazard about the two dozen Broadways and his subsequent visit to Forever Roses. "The florist described Dunny as good as I could've. That's when I was sure he was alive."

"What'd he mean when he told her that you thought he was dead—and you were right?"

"I don't know."

Hazard crunched the half-finished caramel.

"You can break a tooth that way," Ethan warned.

"Like that's my biggest problem."

"Just friendly advice."

"Whistler wakes up in a morgue, realizes he's been mistaken for dead, so then he puts his clothes on, goes home without saying boo to anyone, takes a shower. That make sense to you?"

"No. But I thought he might be brain-damaged."

"He drives to a florist, buys some roses, visits a grave, hires a hit man. . . . For a guy who comes out of a coma with brain damage, he seems to get around pretty well."

"I've given up the brain-damage theory."

"Good for you. So what happened after you left the florist?"

Operating on the two-ghost theory of credibility, Ethan didn't tell him about the PT Cruiser, but said, "I went to a bar."

"You're not a guy who looks for answers in a glass of gin."

"This was Scotch. Didn't find any answers there either. Might try vodka next."

"So that's everything? You've come clean with me now?"

With all the conviction that he could muster, Ethan said, "What—this whole mess isn't *X-Files* enough already? You want there should be some aliens in it, vampires, werewolves?"

"What're you—dodging the question?"

"I'm not dodging anything," Ethan said, regretting that he was going to be forced to lie boldly rather than by indirection. "Yeah, that was everything, through the flower shop. I was drinking Scotch when I got your call."

"Truth?"

"Yeah. I was drinking Scotch, I got your call."

"Remember, you're in a church here."

"The whole world's a church if you're a believer."

"Are you a believer?"

"I used to be."

"Not since Hannah died, huh?"

Ethan shrugged. "Maybe I am, maybe I'm not. It's a day-to-day thing."

After giving him a look that could have peeled an onion layer by layer to the pearl at the core, Hazard said, "Okay. I believe you."

Feeling low enough to slide under a snake, Ethan said, "Thanks."

Hazard turned in the pew to survey the nave, to be sure that a lost soul had not entered in need of a God fix. "You've come clean, so I'll tell you something, but you've got to forget you heard it."

"Already I don't even remember being here."

"Not much of interest in Reynerd's apartment. Spare furnishings, everything black-and-white."

"He seemed to live like a monk, but a monk with style."

"And drugs. He had a big stash of coke packaged for resale and a notebook of names and numbers that's probably a customer list."

"Famous names?"

"Not really. Some actors. Nobody big. The thing you need to know about is the screenplay he was writing."

"In this town," Ethan said, "guys writing screenplays outnumber those cheating on their wives."

"He had twenty-six pages in a pile beside his computer."

"That's not even enough for a first act."

"You know about screenplays, huh? You writing one?"

"No. I've still got some self-respect."

Hazard said, "Reynerd was writing about this young actor goes to a special acting class, makes what he calls 'a deep intellectual connection' with his professor. They both hate this character named Cameron Mansfield, who happens to be the biggest movie star in the world, so they decide to kill him."

Under a weight of weariness, Ethan had slouched in the corner of the pew. Now he sat up straight. "What's their motivation?"

"That's not clear. Reynerd has lots of handwritten notes in the margin, trying to figure that out. Anyway, sort of to prove to each other that they've got the guts to do this, each agrees to give the other guy the name of someone to kill *before* they do the movie star together. The actor wants the professor to kill his mother."

"Why's this sound so Hitchcock?" Ethan wondered.

"It's sort of like his old film, *Strangers on a Train*. The idea is by swapping killings, each guy can have a perfect alibi for the murder he might otherwise be convicted of."

"Let me guess. Reynerd's mother was actually murdered."

"Four months ago," Hazard confirmed. "On a night when her son had an alibi more airtight than a space-shuttle window."

The church seemed to turn at a lazy six or eight revolutions per minute, as if the Scotch might be having a delayed effect on Ethan, but he knew this vertigo was caused less by the Scotch than by these latest weird revelations. "What kind of idiot does these things, then writes them up in a screenplay?"

"An arrogant idiot actor. Don't tell me you think he's unique."

"And who did the professor want Reynerd to kill?"

"A colleague at the university. But Reynerd hadn't written that part yet. He'd just completed the scene featuring the murder of his mother. In real life, her name was Mina, and she was shot once in the right foot and then beaten to death with a marble-and-bronze lamp. In the script, her name's Rena, and she's stabbed repeatedly, beheaded, dismembered, and incinerated in a furnace."

Ethan winced. "Sounds like his mom's days were numbered whether or not Reynerd ever met the professor."

They were silent. The well-insulated church roof lay so far overhead that the storm's voice was barely audible, less like the drumming of rain than like the whispery wings of some hovering flock.

"So," Hazard eventually said, "even with Reynerd dead, maybe Chan the Man had better be looking over his shoulder. The professor—or whatever he might be in real life—is still out there somewhere."

"Who's working Mina Reynerd's murder?" Ethan wondered. "Anyone I know?"

"Sam Kesselman."

Sam had been a detective with Robbery/Homicide when Ethan still carried a badge.

"What's he make of the screenplay?"

Hazard shrugged. "He hasn't heard about it yet. They probably won't drop a Xerox on him till tomorrow."

"He's a good man. He'll be all over it."

"Maybe not fast enough for you," Hazard predicted.

At the front of the church, teased by a draft, votive-candle flames squirmed in ruby glasses. Chameleons of light and shadow wriggled across a sanctuary wall.

"What're you going to do?" Hazard asked.

"Reynerd's shooting will be in the morning newspaper. They're sure to mention his mother's murder. That'll give me an excuse to go to Kesselman, fill him in on those packages Reynerd has been sending to Manheim. He'll have read the partial screenplay—"

"About which you don't know jack," Hazard reminded him.

"—and he'll realize there's an ongoing threat to Manheim until the professor is identified. That'll accelerate the investigation, and I might even get police protection for my boss in the meantime."

"In a perfect world," Hazard said sourly.

"Sometimes the system works."

"Only when you don't expect it to."

"Yeah. But I don't have the resources to investigate Reynerd's friends and associates fast enough to matter, and I don't have the authority to dig through his personal records and effects. I've got to rely on the system whether I want to or not."

"What about our lunch today?" Hazard asked.

"It never happened."

"Someone might've seen us. And there's a credit-card trail."

"Okay, we had lunch. But I never mentioned Reynerd to you."

"Who's going to believe that?"

Ethan couldn't think of anyone sufficiently gullible.

"You and I have lunch," Hazard said, "I cook up a reason to visit Reynerd the same day, and it just so happens he gets killed while I'm there. *Then* it just so happens the shooter's getaway car belongs to Dunny Whistler, your old buddy."

"My head hurts," Ethan said.

"And I haven't even kicked it yet. Man, they'll expect us to know what's going on here, and when we claim we don't—"

"Which we don't."

"—they're going to be sure we're lying. I was them, *I'd* think we were lying."

"Me too," Ethan admitted.

"So they'll dream up a screwy scenario that sorta-kinda explains things, and we'll wind up accused of offing Reynerd's mother, wasting Reynerd, pinning it on Hector X, then popping him, too. Before it's over, the bastard D.A. will be trying to pin us for the disappearance of the dinosaurs."

The church didn't seem like a sanctuary anymore. Ethan wished he were in another bar, where he might have a chance of finding solace, but not a bar that Dunny, dead or alive, would be likely to visit.

"I can't go to Kesselman," he decided.

Hazard would never sigh with relief and concede the intensity of his concern. A mirror held under his nostrils might have revealed a sudden bloom of condensation, but otherwise his relaxation of tension was marked by only a slight settling of his mountainous shoulders.

Ethan said, "I'm going to have to take extra measures to protect Manheim, and just hope Kesselman finds Mina's killer quickly."

"If the preliminary OIS opinion doesn't move me off the Reynerd case," Hazard said, "I'll turn this city inside out to find Dunny Whistler. I've got to believe he's the key to all this."

"I think Dunny will find me first."

"What do you mean?"

"I don't know." Ethan hesitated, sighed. "Dunny was there."

Hazard frowned. "There where?"

"At the hotel bar. I only noticed him when he left. I went after him, lost him in the crowd outside."

"What was he doing there?"

"Drinking. Maybe watching me. Maybe he followed me there, intended to approach me, then decided against it. I don't know."

"Why didn't you tell me first thing?"

"I don't know. It seemed . . . like one ghost too many."

"You think it all gets too rich, I won't believe it? Have some faith, man. We go back, don't we? We been shot at together."

They chose to leave the church separately.

Hazard got up first and moved away. From the farther end of the pew, in the center aisle, he said, "Like old times, huh?"

Ethan knew what he meant. "Covering each other's ass again."

For such a big man, Hazard made little noise as he walked from the nave to the narthex, and out of the church.

Having a reliable friend to watch your back is a comfort, but the consolation and support provided by even the best of friends is no match for what a loving wife can be to a husband, or a loving husband to a wife. In the architecture of the heart, the rooms of friendship are deeply placed and strongly built, but the warmest and most secure retreat in Ethan's heart was the one that he had shared with Hannah, where these days she lived only as a precious ghost, a sweet haunting memory.

He could have told her everything—about the phantom in the mirror, about his second death outside Forever Roses—and she would have believed him. Together they'd have sought some understanding.

During the five years that she'd been gone, he had never missed her more than he missed her at this moment. Sitting alone in a silent church, keenly aware of the soft beating of the rain on the roof, of the lingering fragrance of incense, of the ruby light of the votive candles, but unable to detect the faintest whisper, whiff, or glimmer of God, Ethan longed not for evidence of his Maker, but for Hannah, for the music of her voice and the beautiful geometry of her smile.

He felt homeless, without hearth or anchor. His apartment in the Manheim house awaited his return, offering many comforts, but it was merely a residence, not a place endeared to him. He had felt the tug of home only once in this long strange day: when he'd stood at Hannah's grave, where she lay beside an empty plot to which he held the deed.

CHAPTER 37

From alternating bronze-ball and bronze-flame finials, from cast panels of arabesques, from darts and twists and frets and scallops and leaves, from griffins and heraldic emblems, black and silver rain dripped and drizzled off the Manheim gate.

Ethan braked to a stop beside the security post: a five-foot-high, square, limestone-clad column in which were embedded a closed-circuit video camera, an intercom speaker, and a keypad. He put down his window and keyed in his six-digit personal code.

Slowly, with the Expedition's headlight beams rippling across its ornate surfaces, the massive gate began to roll aside.

Each employee of the estate had a different code. The security staff maintained computerized records of every entrance.

Remote-control units such as typical garage-door openers or coded transponders, assigned to each vehicle, would have been more convenient than a key-entry system, especially in foul

weather; however, such devices would have been
accessible to garage mechanics, valet-parking attendants, and anyone else in temporary custody of
a vehicle. One dishonest person among them
might easily compromise the security of the estate.

If Ethan had been a visitor lacking a personal
gate-entry code, he would have pushed the intercom button on the post and would have announced himself to the guard in the security office
at the back of the property. If the visitor was expected or was a family friend on the permanent-
access list, the guard would open the gate from
his command board.

As he waited for the massive bronze barrier to
roll out of the way, Ethan was under surveillance
by the camera on the security post. Entering the
property, he would be scrutinized through a series
of tree-mounted cameras angled in such a manner
as to reveal anyone who might be lying on the floor
of the SUV to avoid detection.

All videocams included night-vision technology
that transformed the faintest moonlight into a revealing glow. A sophisticated bit of software filtered out most of the veiling and the distortion effects produced by falling rain, ensuring a clear
real-time image on the security-office screens.

Had he been a repairman or deliveryman arriving
in an enclosed van or truck, Ethan would have
been asked to wait outside the gate until a security
guard arrived. The guard would then look inside

the vehicle to ensure that the driver was not, under duress, bringing any bad guys with him.

Palazzo Rospo was not a fortress either by modern definition or by the moat-and-drawbridge standards of medieval times. Neither was the estate a cupcake served on a plate to be easily plucked by any hungry thief.

Explosives could bring down the gate. The property wall could be scaled. But the grounds couldn't easily be entered by stealth. Intruders would be identified and tracked almost at once by cameras, motion detectors, heat sensors, and other devices.

The thirty-foot-wide bronze gate, more solid than open, weighed over eight thousand pounds. The motor that operated the chain drive was powerful, however, and the barrier rolled aside with apparent ease and with more speed than one might expect.

A five-acre plot qualified as a large piece of land in most residential communities. In *this* neighborhood, where an acre could bring upwards of ten million dollars, a five-acre property was the equivalent of an English country estate of baronial scale.

The long driveway looped around a reflection pond in front of the great house, which was not Baroque, like the bronze gate, but a limestone-clad, three-story Palladian structure with simple classic ornamentation, huge yet elegant in its proportions.

Just before reaching the pond, the driveway split, and Ethan took the branch that led around to the side of the house. When it split again, one artery led to the groundskeeper's building and the security office, while the other led down a ramp to the underground garage.

The garage had two levels. In the upper, the Face stored thirty-two vehicles in his personal collection, ranging from a new Porsche to a series of Rolls-Royces from the 1930s, to a 1936 Mercedes-Benz 500K, to a 1931 Duesenberg Model J, to a 1933 Cadillac Sixteen.

The lower garage housed the fleet of workaday vehicles owned by the estate and provided parking for cars belonging to employees.

Like the upper garage, the lower featured a beige matte-finish ceramic-tile floor and walls of glossy tile in a matching color. Supporting columns were decorated with free-flowing mosaics in various shades of yellow.

Few high-end automobile sales facilities, catering to the very wealthy, were as beautifully appointed as this lower garage.

The pegboard for car keys hung on the wall outside the elevator, and Fric sat on the floor under the board, holding the same paperback fantasy novel that he'd been reading in the library this morning. He got to his feet as Ethan approached.

To a degree that surprised Ethan, the sight of the boy gladdened him. Nothing else had done so in this long, gray, dismal day.

He wasn't entirely sure why the kid lifted his spirits. Maybe because you expected the son of the Face, raised in such wealth and with such indifference, to be spoiled rotten or to be dysfunctionally neurotic, or both; and because instead Fric was basically decent and shy, tried to cover his shyness with a seen-it-all air, but could not conceal a fundamental modesty as rare in his glamorous world as pity was rare among the scaly denizens of a crocodile swamp.

Indicating the paperback, Ethan said, "Has the evil wizard found the tongue of an honest man for his potion?"

"No luck yet. But he just sent his brutal assistant, Cragmore, to visit a lying politician and harvest his testicles."

Ethan winced. "He *is* an evil wizard."

"Well, it's just a politician. Some of them come around here now and then, you know. After they leave, Mrs. McBee does an inventory of the valuable items in the rooms they visited."

"So . . . what're you doing down here? Planning to go for a drive?"

Fric shook his head. "There's no point making a break for it until I'm sixteen. First I've got to get my driver's license, have enough time to put together a stash of cash big enough to start over with, research the perfect small town to hide in, and design a series of really cool impenetrable disguises."

Ethan smiled. "That's the plan, huh?"

Failing to match Ethan's smile, with bone-dry seriousness, Fric said, "That's the plan."

The boy pressed the button to call the elevator. The machinery hummed into motion, the noise only partly muffled by the shaft walls.

"I've been hiding out from the decorating crew," Fric revealed. "They're still putting up trees and stuff all over the house. This is your first Christmas here, so you don't know, but they all wear these stupid Santa hats, and every time they see you, they shout, 'Merry Christmas,' grinning like lunatics, and they want to give you these sucky little candy canes. They don't just decorate, they like make a performance out of it, which I guess most people want, otherwise they wouldn't have a business, but it's enough to turn you into an atheist."

"Sounds like a memorable holiday tradition."

"It's better than the paid carolers on Christmas Eve. They dress like characters out of Dickens, and between songs they talk to you about Queen Victoria and Mr. Scrooge and whether you're going to have goose and suet pudding for Christmas dinner, and they call you 'm'lord' and 'young master,' and you've got to be there because Ghost . . . because my father thinks it's all so cool. After about half an hour, you're sure you're either going to shit or go blind, and there's *another* half-hour to get through. But then it's okay, because after the carolers is the magician who does this act with dwarfs dressed up like Santa's elves, and he's radically hilarious."

Aelfric seemed to be concealing a nervous and urgent concern that he unintentionally expressed in a flood of words set loose with a quality akin to babble. He wasn't a tight-lipped boy by nature, but neither was he a nonstop talker.

The elevator arrived and the doors opened.

Ethan followed the boy into the wood-paneled cab.

After pushing the button for the ground floor, Fric said, "In your experience, are phone perverts really dangerous or are they just all talk?"

"Phone perverts?"

To this point, the boy had made eye contact. Now he watched the light on the floor-indicator board and didn't even glance at Ethan. "Guys that call up and breathe at you. Do they mainly get their kicks from just that, or do they sometimes actually come around and want to grope you and stuff?"

"Has someone called you, Fric?"

"Yeah. This freak." The boy made heavy, ragged panting sounds, as if Ethan might be able to identify the pervert from the unique signature of his breathing patterns.

"When did this start?"

"Just today. First when I was in the train room. Then he called again when I was in the wine cellar, eating dinner."

"He called on your private line?"

"Yeah."

On the board, the indicator light blinked from the lower garage to the higher garage. The elevator moved slowly upward.

"What did this guy say to you?"

Fric hesitated, shuffling his feet slightly on the inlaid-marble floor. Then: "He just breathed. And made some . . . some almost like animal sounds."

"That's all?"

"Yeah. Animal sounds, but I don't know what

they were supposed to be, 'cause he wasn't like *talented* at it or anything."

"You're sure he didn't say something to you? Didn't even use your name?"

Remaining focused on the indicator board, Fric said, "Just that stupid breathing. I star sixty-nined him, figuring maybe the pervert still lives with his mother, see, and she'd answer, and I could tell her what her precious sicko son was up to, but then I just got him breathing at me."

They arrived at the ground floor. The doors opened.

Ethan stepped into the hall, but Fric remained in the elevator.

Blocking the doors with one arm, Ethan said, "Calling him back—that wasn't a good idea, Fric. When someone's trying to harass you, what gives them a kick is knowing they got under your skin. The best thing to do is hang up as soon as you realize who it is, and if the phone rings again right away, don't answer it."

Looking at his wristwatch, adjusting the time with the stem, busying himself, Fric said, "I thought you'd have a way to find out who he is."

"I'll give it a try. And Fric?"

The boy continued to fiddle with the watch. "Yeah?"

"It's important that you tell me everything about this."

"Sure."

"You *are* telling me everything, aren't you?"

Holding the watch to one ear, as if listening for ticking, Fric said, "Sure. It was this breather."

The boy was withholding information, but putting pressure on him at this time would only ensure that he would guard his secret all the more fiercely.

Recalling how he himself had responded to Hazard's interrogation in the church, Ethan relented. "If it's all right with you, when your line rings tonight or anytime tomorrow while I'm here, I'd like to answer it myself."

"Okay."

"Your line doesn't ring in my apartment, but I'll just go into the house computer and change that."

"When?"

"Right now. I'll pick it up on the first few rings, but if a call comes in tomorrow when I'm not here, then just let it go to your voice mail."

The boy made eye contact at last. "Okay. You know what my ring sounds like?"

Ethan smiled. "I'll recognize it."

With a look of consternation, Fric said, "Yeah, it's dorky."

"And you think the first nine notes of 'Dragnet' makes me feel like I'm getting an important call?"

Fric smiled.

"If you need to call me anytime, day or night," Ethan said, "on one of my house lines or my cell phone, don't hesitate, Fric. I don't sleep all that much anyway. You understand?"

The boy nodded. "Thanks, Mr. Truman."

Ethan stepped backward into the hallway once more.

Self-conscious, Fric chewed solemnly on his lower lip as he pushed a control-panel button, probably for the third floor where he had his rooms.

Because of the boy's diminutive stature, the elevator, as big as any in a high-rise building, seemed to be even larger than usual.

Although short and slender for his age, Fric possessed a quiet determination and a courage, apparent in his posture and in his daily attitude, that were surprising for his years and bigger than his small body. The boy's strange and lonely childhood had already begun to steel him for adversity.

In spite of his wealth and wit and growing wisdom, adversity would come to him sooner or later. He was a human being, after all, and therefore heir to his share of misery and misfortune.

The elevator doors slid shut.

As Fric disappeared from view and as machinery purred, Ethan looked at the indicator board above the door. He watched until he saw the light change from the ground floor to the second, listened as the lift mechanism continued to grind.

In his mind's eye, Ethan saw the elevator doors open on the third floor, revealing an empty cab, Fric having vanished forever between floors.

Such peculiar dark imaginings were not common to him. On any day but this one, he would have wondered where such a disturbing twist of thought had come from, and he would have at once smoothed it out of his mind as easily as pressing a wrinkle from a shirt.

This was the day it was, however, so utterly unlike any other that Ethan felt inclined to take seriously even the most unlikely presentiments and possibilities.

The back staircase wrapped the elevator shaft. He was tempted to race up four flights. The elevator rose so slowly that he might beat it to the third floor.

When the doors slid open, revealing Fric unharmed, the boy would be startled to be greeted with such alarm. Breathing hard from his frantic ascent, Ethan wouldn't be able to conceal his concern from Fric—nor would he be able to explain it.

The moment passed.

His clenched throat relaxed. He swallowed, breathed.

The indicator light blinked from the second to the third floor. The elevator motor fell silent.

Surely Fric had arrived safely at the top of the house. He had not been consumed and digested by demonically possessed machinery.

As best he could, Ethan smoothed that bizarre idea from his mind as he went to his apartment in the west wing.

CHAPTER 38

Hurrying the length of the long north hall, Fric more than once looked worriedly over his shoulder, for he had always half believed that ghosts lurked in the lonelier corners of the great house. On *this* night, he was all but certain of their presence.

As he passed a gilded mirror set above an old-as-dirt console, he thought he glimpsed *two* figures in the age-discolored glass: he himself, but also someone taller, darker, hurrying just behind him.

In a tapestry that probably dated from before the last ice age, threatening-looking horsemen on dark steeds seemed to turn their heads to watch him pass. Peripherally, he thought he saw the horses—eyes wild, nostrils flared—begin to gallop through that fabric field and forest, as if intent on bolting out of their woven world and into the third-floor hallway.

Considering his current state of mind, Fric was not suited for work in a graveyard, a mortuary, a morgue, or in a cryogenics facility where gaggles of dead people were frozen in expectation that one day they could be thawed and returned to life.

In a movie, Ghost Dad had played Sherlock Holmes, who had turned out to be the first man ever to have his body scientifically frozen upon death. Holmes was revived in the year 2225, where a utopian society needed his help to solve the first murder in a hundred years.

Deleting either the evil robots or the evil aliens, or the evil mummies, would have made it a better movie. Sometimes a film could be *too* imaginative.

At this moment, however, Fric had no difficulty believing that Palazzo Rospo might be seething with ghosts, robots, aliens, mummies, and some unnameable thing worse than all the others, especially here on the third floor, where he was alone. Not *safely* alone, perhaps, but alone in the sense that he was the only living human presence.

His father's bedroom and the suite of rooms related to it were on this level, in the west wing and along part of the north corridor. With Ghost Dad in residence, Fric had company in this high retreat, but most nights he dwelt alone here on the third floor.

Like now.

At the junction of the north and the east hallways, he stood as still as a corpsicle in a cryogenic vat, listening to the house.

Fric more imagined than heard the patter of rain. The roof was slate, well insulated, and far above even this high hallway.

The faint and inconstant sough of winter wind

was but a memory from another time, for this was largely a windless night.

In addition to Fric's suite, along the east hall were other chambers. Seldom-used guest bedrooms. A walk-in linen closet. An electric-utilities room crammed with equipment mysterious to Fric but reminiscent of Frankenstein's laboratory. There was a small sitting room, richly furnished and well maintained, in which no one ever sat.

At the end of the hall lay the door to a set of back stairs that went down five stories, all the way to the lower garage. Another set of stairs, at the end of the west hall, also descended to the bottom of Palazzo Rospo. Neither was as wide or as grand, of course, as the main staircase, which featured a crystal chandelier at each landing.

The actress Cassandra Limone—born name, Sandy Leaky—who had lived with Fric's father for five months, staying in the house even when he was absent, had churned up and down every stair-case fifteen times a day, as part of her workout regimen. A well-equipped gym on the second floor offered a StairMaster among numerous machines, but Cassandra said the "authentic" stairs were less boring than the make-believe stairs and had a more natural effect on leg and butt muscles.

Slathered in sweat, grunting, squinting, grimac-ing, cursing like the possessed girl in *The Exorcist,* screeching at Fric if he happened onto the stairs when she was using them, climbing Cassandra would not have been recognizable to the editors at

People magazine. They had twice selected her as one of the most beautiful people in the world.

Apparently, however, all the effort had been worthwhile. Ghost Dad had more than once told Cassandra that she was a deadly weapon because her calf muscles could crack a man's skull, her thigh muscles could break any heart, and her butt could drive a man crazy.

Ha, ha, ha. Instead of testing your sense of humor, some jokes tested your gag reflex.

One day near the end of her stay, Cassandra had fallen down the back west stairs and broken an ankle.

Genuinely funny.

Now Fric followed the east hall not to his suite, but to the last room on the right before the stairs.

This inelegant space, measuring about twelve feet by fourteen, had a sturdy plank floor and bare white walls. Empty at the moment, it served as a staging point for the transferral of goods in and out of the attic.

A spacious dumbwaiter, driven by an electric motor, could carry up to four hundred pounds, allowing for the storage of heavy boxes and large objects in the vastness above. A door opened to a spiral staircase that also led to the attic.

Fric used the stairs. He climbed carefully, with one hand always on the railing, concerned that his amusement regarding Cassandra's broken ankle would jinx him with a shattered leg of his own.

The attic extended the entire length and breadth of the mansion. The space was finished, not rough: plaster walls, solid plank floor covered with linoleum for easy cleaning.

Colonnades of massive vertical beams supported an elaborate trusswork of rafters that held up the roof. No partitions had been constructed between these beams, so the attic remained one great open room.

In practice, you could not see easily from one end of the high chamber to another, for suspended by wires from the rafters were hundreds of enormous, framed movie posters. Every one of them bore the name and giant image of Channing Manheim.

Fric's father had made just twenty-two films, but he collected career-related items in every language. His movies were big box office worldwide, and any one project produced dozens of posters.

The hanging posters formed walls of a kind, and aisles, as did hundreds of stacked boxes packed full of Channing Manheim memorabilia that included T-shirts bearing his likeness and/or catchphrases from his films, wristwatches on which time ticked across his famous face, coffee mugs bearing *his* mug, hats, caps, jackets, drinking glasses, action figures, dolls, hundreds of different toys, lingerie, lockets, lunchboxes, and more merchandise than Fric could remember or imagine.

At every turn were life-size and larger-than-life, freestanding cardboard figures of Ghost Dad. Here he was a roughneck cowboy, there the captain of a spaceship, here a naval officer, there a jet pilot, a jungle explorer, a nineteenth-century cavalry officer, a doctor, a boxer, a policeman, a fire-fighter. . . .

More elaborate cardboard dioramas featured the biggest star in the world in whole sets from his movies. These had been displayed in theater lobbies, and many of them, if supplied with batteries, would prove to have moving parts and flashing lights.

Cool props from his films lay on open metal shelves or leaned against the walls. Futuristic weapons, firemen's helmets, soldiers' helmets, a suit of armor, a robot spider the size of an armchair . . .

Larger props, like the time machine from *Future Imperfect,* were stored at a warehouse in Santa Monica. That facility and this attic featured museum-quality heating and humidifying systems to ensure the least possible deterioration of the items in the collection.

Ghost Dad had recently bought the estate next door to Palazzo Rospo. He intended to tear down the existing house on that adjacent property, connect the two parcels of land, and build a museum in the architectural style of Palazzo Rospo, to display his memorabilia.

Although his father had never said as much, Fric suspected that the intention was for the estate to be opened to the public one day, in the manner of Graceland, and that Fric himself would be expected to manage this operation.

If that day ever came, he would, of course, have to blow his brains out or throw himself off a tall building, or both, if he had not already successfully started a new, secret life under an assumed identity in Goose Crotch, Montana, or in some other town so remote and simple that the locals still referred to movies as "magic-lantern shows."

Once in a while when he climbed into the attic to wander the Manheim maze, Fric was enchanted. Sometimes he was even thrilled to be a part of this almost-legendary, nearly magical enterprise.

At other times, he felt at most an inch tall and shrinking, an insignificant bug of a boy, in danger of being stepped on, smashed flat, and forgotten.

This evening, he felt neither inspired nor discouraged by the collection, for he toured it solely in search of a hiding place. In this labyrinth, surely he would discover a pocket of sanctuary among the memorabilia, where he could conceal himself and be protected by his father's omnipresent face and name, which might ward off evil in much the way that garlic and a crucifix discouraged vampires.

He came to a seven-foot-high mirror in a frame of carved and hand-painted snakes writhing in jewel-colored tangles. In *Black Snow,* Fric's father had seen glimpses of his future in this mirror.

Fric saw Fric, and Fric alone, squinting at his reflection as he sometimes did, trying to blur his image into someone taller and tougher than who he really was. As usual, he failed to fool himself into feeling heroic, but he was glad that the mirror didn't reveal scenes from *his* future, confirming what a hopeless geek he would still be at thirty, forty, fifty.

As Fric stepped back from the mirror and began to turn away, the glass appeared to ripple, and a man came *through* it, a big man, looking plenty tough without having to squint. The grinning brute reached for Fric, and Fric ran for his life.

CHAPTER 39

Troubled as never before by the darkness beyond the windows, Ethan went through his apartment, closing the drapes and shutting out the rainy night as if, in fact, it had a thousand eyes.

In his study, at his desk, he switched on the computer and engaged the house-control program. On the screen, icons appeared for the heating-cooling controls, the pool and spa heaters, the landscape watering and lighting, the interior lighting, the interlinked audio-video equipment, the electronic security apparatus, the telephones, and other systems.

Using his mouse, he clicked the telephone icon. A request for his password appeared, and he entered it.

Among everyone on the household staff, only Ethan could access *and* reprogram the security and the telephone systems.

The screen changed, offering him a new set of options.

The phones in his apartment featured all twenty-four lines, but only two were accessible to him. He could not eavesdrop on anyone's calls, and they were likewise unable to overhear his.

Furthermore, when calls came through to other lines in the house, Ethan heard no ringing in his rooms. The indicator light above the number of each line did, however, flutter when a call was coming in, and it burned steadily when a conversation was being conducted.

Having entered the telephone program, Ethan edited the controls to make Line 23, Fric's line, henceforth accessible to his apartment phones. It would also ring here using Fric's personal tone.

With this task completed, he perused the day's phone log.

Every incoming call to Palazzo Rospo and all outgoing calls as well were automatically logged— although not voice recorded. Note was made of the time that each connection had been effected and of the duration of each conversation.

For every outgoing call, the phone number was also preserved on the computer log. Incoming caller numbers were noted as well, except in those instances when they had Caller ID blocking to protect their privacy.

He entered his name and saw that he had received only one call while he'd been out of the house. The calls he'd made and received on his cell phone were not included in these records.

He snatched up the phone to check his voice mail. The call had been from the hospital, informing him of Dunny's death.

When Ethan cleared his name and typed Ael-fric's, the computer reported that the boy had received no calls at any time on this date, Monday, December 21.

According to Fric, the breather had phoned twice. And at least once, the boy had tracked him back with *69. All three occurrences should have been noted.

Ethan jumped from Fric's file to the master log, which listed all phone-line activity since the previous midnight in the order that the calls had been placed and received. The list was long because the staff had been busy making Christmas preparations.

Carefully scrolling through the log, Ethan found no calls to or from Fric's line.

Unless the record-keeping system had erred, which it had never done before in Ethan's experience, the inescapable conclusion had to be that Fric lied about receiving obscene calls.

His respect for the boy motivated Ethan to scroll through the phone log again, bottom to top this time. The result was the same.

As difficult as it might be to believe that the system had failed to note the calls that Fric reported, Ethan found it almost equally hard to accept that the kid had concocted the story of the heavy breather. Fric was not a self-dramatizer and certainly not an attention-seeker.

Besides, he had seemed genuinely disturbed when he'd recounted those calls. *He just breathed. And made some . . . some almost like animal sounds.*

Aware of a winking brightness at the periphery of his vision, Ethan turned from the computer and saw the indicator light fluttering on Line 24. As he watched, the call was answered, a connection made, and the light burned steadily.

Line 24, the last line on the board, was set aside to receive phone calls from the dead.

CHAPTER 40

When a fierce-looking guy comes out of a mirror as though it's a doorway, and when he grabs for you and snags your shirt with his fingertips, you could be excused for wetting your pants or for losing total control of your sphincter, so Fric was amazed that he didn't instantly void from every orifice, that he reacted quickly enough to slip free of the snagging fingers, and that he raced away into the memorabilia maze in a totally dry and stink-free condition.

He turned left, right, right, left, vaulted over a low stack of boxes from one aisle into another, knocking between two huge posters as he went, raced past a life-size Ghost-Dad-as-1930s-detective, pushed between more posters, dodged around a realistic-looking Styrofoam unicorn from the one film in the Manheim credit list that no one dared talk about in his father's presence, turned left, left, right, and halted when he realized that he had lost track of where he'd come from and that he might be returning in a circle to the serpent-embraced mirror.

In his wake, across a significant portion of the wide attic, the framed posters swung like giant pendulums. He had stirred some of them during his flight, but the wind of those dozen fanned others into gentler motion, perpetrating a wider disturbance.

Among all this movement, the approach of the mirror man was more difficult to discern than it would have been in an attic steeped in stillness. Fric couldn't catch a glimpse of him.

Unless you were a skulking fiend with a sympathy for shadows, the lighting here was troublesome. Wall lamps ringed the perimeter of the attic, while others were mounted to some of the columns that supported the trusswork, though the number and brightness of them left much to be desired. The hanging palisades of posters, arrayed like flags from the many nations of Manheim, thwarted the even flow of light from aisle to aisle.

Crouched warily in gloom, Fric drew a deep breath, held it, listened.

At first he could hear nothing but the *didop-da-bidda-boom* of his skipping-drumming heart, but near the useful end of that banked breath, he began to hear, as well, the dash of rain on slate.

Aware that by his every noise he would locate himself for the stalking predator, Fric *eased* out the dead breath, coaxed in a live one, held it.

Higher in the house, he was also higher in the

storm. Here the lonely sighing of the rain swelled into the whispers of a multitude exchanging sinister secrets in the sea of night that now submerged Palazzo Rospo.

Yet in the same way that he had focused himself to hear the rain above the drumbeat of his heart, he tuned in to the footsteps of the mirror man. The attic architecture, the pendulum motion of the giant posters, and the whiffle of the rain served to distort the sound, to make it seem that the intruder was going away from Fric, then coming closer, then going, when in fact he most likely made steady progress toward his quarry.

Fric had heeded Mysterious Caller's advice to find a deep and secret hiding place. He had believed that he would need a refuge soon, but he hadn't realized that he would need it *this* soon.

Learning to breathe and listen at the same time, he took to heart his dotty mother's insistence that he was "an almost invisible perfect little mouse." He crept with quiet quickness past the red-and-gold cardboard spires of a futuristic city over which his father—in cardboard—towered with a fearsome laser rifle at the ready.

At an intersection of aisles, Fric looked both ways, turned left. He scurried onward, analyzing the sound of the heavy footsteps as he went, calculating what route might best put distance between him and the man from the mirror.

The intruder made no effort at stealth. He

seemed to *want* Fric to hear him, as though confident that the boy couldn't evade capture.

Moloch. This must be Moloch. Looking for a child to take as a sacrifice, a child to kill, perhaps to eat.

He's Moloch, with the splintered bones of babies stuck between his teeth. . . .

Fric refrained from screaming for help, certain that he would not be heard by anyone other than the man-god-beast-thing who stalked him. The walls of the house were thick, the floors thicker than the walls, and no one was nearer than the second floor down in the middle of the mansion.

He might have sought a window and risked a ledge or a three-story drop. The attic had no windows.

A fake stone sarcophagus stood on end, decorated with carved hieroglyphics and the image of a dead pharaoh, no longer inhabited by the evil mummy that had once done battle with the biggest movie star in the world.

A steamer trunk, in which a ruthless and clever murderer (played by Richard Gere) had once crammed the corpse of a gorgeous blonde (actually the live body of the aforementioned Cassandra Limone), now stood empty.

Fric wasn't tempted to hide in those containers, nor in the black-lacquered coffin, nor in the trick box in which a magician's assistant could be made to disappear with the help of angled mirrors. Even the ones that weren't coffins *seemed* like coffins, and he was sure that crawling into any of them would mean certain death.

The wise thing to do would be to keep moving, mouse-quick and mouse-quiet, staying low, staying loose, always several twists and turns ahead of the mirror man. Eventually he could circle back to the spiral staircase, descend from the attic, and flee to lower floors where help could be found.

Suddenly he realized that he could no longer hear the footsteps of his pursuer.

No cardboard Ghost Dad stood more still, no mummy under Egyptian sands rested any more breathless with its shriveled lungs, than Fric as he began to suspect that this new silence was a bad development.

A shadow floated overhead, treading air as though it were water.

Fric gasped, looked up.

The roof-supporting trusses rested atop the attic columns, five feet above his head. From one truss line to another, above the movie posters, a figure flew across the aisle, wingless but more graceful than a bird, leaping with the slow and weightless form exhibited by any astronaut in space, contemptuous of gravity.

This was no caped phantom, but a man in a suit, the one who had stepped out of the mirror, executing an impossible aerial ballet. He landed on a horizontal beam, pivoted toward Fric, and swooped down from his high perch, not like a plummeting stone, but like a feather, grinning exactly as Fric had imagined that evil Moloch, hungry for a child, would grin.

Fric turned and ran.

Although Moloch's descent had been feather-slow, suddenly he was *here*. He seized Fric from behind, one arm around his chest, one hand over his face.

Fric tried desperately to wrench loose but was lifted off his feet as a mouse might be snatched off the ground by the talons of a hunting hawk.

For an instant, he thought that Moloch would fly up into the rafters with him, there to rip at him with fierce appetite.

They remained on the floor, but Moloch was already moving. He strode along as if certain of where each turning of the maze would take him.

Fric struggled, kicked, kicked, but seemed to be fighting nothing more substantial than water, caught in the dreamy currents of a nightmare.

The hand on his face pressed up from beneath his chin, a clamp that jammed teeth to teeth, forcing him to swallow his scream, and pinching shut his nose.

He was overcome by the panic familiar from his worst asthma attacks, the terror of suffocation. He couldn't open his mouth to bite, couldn't land a kick that mattered. Couldn't *breathe*.

And yet a worse fear gripped him, clawed him, tore at his mind as they passed the mummy's sarcophagus, passed a cardboard cop with Ghost Dad's face: the horrifying thought that Moloch would carry him through the mirror and into a world of perpetual night where children were fattened like cattle for the pleasure of cannibal gods, where you wouldn't find even the paid kindness of Mrs. McBee, where there was no hope at all, not even the hope of growing up.

CHAPTER 41

Ethan glanced at his wristwatch, then at the indicator light on Line 24, timing the telephone call.

He didn't believe a dead person had dialed up Palazzo Rospo, dropping metaphysical coins into a pay phone on the Other Side. Dependably, this would be either a wrong number or a solicitation from a salesman with such a high-pressure approach that he would rattle out his spiel even to the answering machine that recorded these messages.

When Ming du Lac, spiritual adviser to the Face, had explained Line 24, Ethan had been perceptive enough to realize that Ming would be impatient with even so much as a raised eyebrow, and hostile to any expression of disbelief. He had managed to keep a straight face and a solemn voice.

Only Mrs. McBee on the household staff and only Ming du Lac among Manheim's other associates had the influence to get the great man to fire Ethan. He knew exactly with whom he must tread softly.

normal researchers were what motivated Channing Manheim to maintain Line 24 strictly for the
convenience of the chatty dead.

Every day, wherever they were in the world, Manheim and Ming du Lac used part of their meditation
periods to broadcast mentally the area code plus
the seven-digit number for Line 24, casting this
baited hook into the sea of immortality with the
hope that it would catch a spirit.

Thus far, over a period of three years, they had
recorded only wrong numbers, sales pitches, and
a series of calls from a hoaxer who, before Ethan's
arrival, had proved to be a security guard on the
estate. He had been let go with generous severance pay and, according to Mrs. McBee, with a
lecture from Ming du Lac to the effect that he
would be wise to put his spiritual house in order.

The signal light winked off. This call had lasted
one minute and twelve seconds.

Sometimes Ethan wondered how the Channing
Manheim who managed an acting career so brilliantly and who had proved himself an investment
wizard could be the same man who employed
Ming du Lac and also a feng-shui adviser, a clairvoyance instructor, and a past-life researcher who
spent forty hours a week tracking the actor's rein-
carnations backward through the centuries.

On the other hand, the singular events of this day
left him less certain of his usual skepticism.

He turned his attention to the computer screen
once more, to the telephone log. He frowned,

wondering why Fric would have invented the heavy breather.

If someone had in fact made obscene calls to the boy, chances were good that this related to the implied threats against Manheim that had come in those black boxes. Otherwise, there were two sources of threats that had arisen simultaneously. Ethan didn't believe in coincidences.

The heavy breather might be the real-life inspiration for the "professor" mentioned in Reynerd's partial screenplay, the man who had conspired to send the black gift boxes and to kill Manheim. If so, he had somehow acquired at least one of the house's unlisted numbers: a disturbing development.

Yet the phone log had never failed to record any call in the past. And though they might err, machines didn't lie.

The recent incoming call to Line 24 was now the last item on the day's log. As it should be.

Ethan had timed the call at one minute twelve seconds. The monitoring software registered one minute fourteen seconds. He had no doubt that the two-second error was his.

According to the log, Caller ID blocking prevented notation of the point-of-origin number. That was peculiar if the call had been from a phone-sales agent, a breed now forbidden by law to block their ID, not peculiar at all if it had been a wrong number.

Neither was it unusual for a wrong number to have tied up the line for a minute or longer. The outgoing greeting on the special answering machine that serviced Line 24 was not an elaborate hello to those in the spirit world, but a simple "Please leave a message." Some callers, failing to realize that they hadn't reached the desired number, complied with that invitation.

Anyway, whoever called Line 24 wasn't the issue. The question was if the ever-dependable machine had erred or lied in failing to record the calls that the boy claimed to have received.

Logically, Ethan could only conclude that the machine couldn't be faulted. In the morning, he would have a talk with Fric.

On the desk beside the computer were the three silvery bells from the ambulance. He stared at them for a long time.

Beside the bells was a nine-by-twelve manila envelope that had been left here for him by Mrs. McBee. She had printed his name in matchless calligraphy.

As with all things McBee, her graceful penmanship made Ethan smile. She knew the best and most elegant way that every task ought to be performed, and she held herself to her own high standards.

He opened the envelope and confirmed a truth that he already knew: Freddie Nielander, Fric's mother, was a braying jackass.

CHAPTER 42

Fantastically yellow from head to foot, Corky Laputa accepted the shocking-pink plastic bag from Mr. Chung.

He was aware that he evoked smiles from other customers, and he supposed that in his yellow-and-pink flamboyance, he must be the most cheerful-looking anarchist in the world.

The bag bulged with containers of Chinese food, and Mr. Chung overflowed with good will. He effusively thanked Corky for his continuing patronage and wished him all the best that fortune had to offer.

After a typically busy day in the pursuit of social collapse, Corky seldom found himself in the mood to make dinner. He got takeout from Mr. Chung as often as three or four times a week.

In a better world, instead of resorting repeatedly to Chinese takeout, he would have preferred to dine frequently in upscale restaurants. If an establishment offered fine cuisine and excellent service, however, there were invariably enough customers to ruin the experience.

With but few exceptions, human beings were tedious, self-deluded bores. He could tolerate them individually or in classroom situations where he set the rules, but in crowds they were not conducive to the enjoyment of a good meal or to proper digestion.

He drove home through the rain with his pink bag, and he left it unopened on the kitchen table. Mouthwatering aromas flooded the room.

After changing into a comfortable Glen-plaid cashmere robe suitable to a drizzly December evening, Corky mixed a martini. Only a trace of vermouth, two olives.

In the sublime afterglow of a day well spent, he often liked to walk his spacious home and admire the richness of its Victorian architecture and ornamentation.

His parents, both from well-to-do families, had purchased the property shortly after their marriage. Had they not been the people they were, the beautiful house would have been alive with wonderful family memories and with a sense of tradition.

Consequently, his only fine family memory, the one that warmed him most, was associated with the living room, especially with the area around the fireplace, where he had separated his mother from his inheritance by the application of an iron poker.

He stood there for only a minute or two, basking in the fire, before going upstairs again. This time, martini in hand, he went to the back guest bedroom, to check on Stinky Cheese Man.

He didn't even bother to lock the door these days. Old Stinky wasn't going anywhere under his own power ever again.

The room would have been dark in daylight, for the two windows were boarded over. The wall switch by the door controlled the lamp on the nightstand.

The tinted bulb and the apricot silk shade provided an appealing glow. Even in this flattering light, Stinky appeared paler than pale, so gray that he seemed to be petrifying into stone.

His head, shoulders, and arms were exposed, but the rest of him remained covered by a sheet and blanket. Later, Corky would enjoy the entire show.

Stinky had once been a trim 200 pounds, in excellent condition. If he could have gotten on a scale now, he probably would have weighed less than 110.

All bone, skin, hair, and pressure sores, he was barely strong enough to lift his head an inch off his pillow, too weak by far to get out of bed and onto a scale, and the depth of his despair had weeks ago broken his will to resist.

Stinky was no longer semi-sedated. His sunken eyes met Corky's, darkly shining with a desperate petition.

On the IV tree, the dangling twelve-hour bag of glucose and saline solution had drained completely. The slow drip of glucose, vitamins, and minerals that kept Stinky alive also infused a drug

that ensured mental vagueness and reliable do-
cility.

Corky put down his martini, and from a small refrigerator well stocked with full infusion bags, he
plucked a replacement for the empty container.
With practiced hands, he removed the collapsed
bag and installed the plump one.

The current drip included no drug. Corky wanted
his withered guest to have a clear head later.

After picking up his martini and taking a sip, he
said, "I'll rejoin you after dinner," and he left the
bedroom.

In the living room once more, Corky stopped by
the fireplace to finish his drink and to remember
Mama.

Unfortunately, the historic poker was not here to
be polished, hefted, and admired. Years ago, on
the night of the event, police had taken it away
with many other items, intent on collecting evidence, and had never brought it back.

Corky had been too wise to request its return,
leery that the police might suspect that it had sentimental value to him. All the fireplace tools had
been purchased new following his mother's death.

Reluctantly, he had replaced the carpet as well. If
the homicide detectives had for any reason returned in the months following the murder, upon
seeing the bloodstained carpet still in place, they
might have at least raised an eyebrow.

In the kitchen, he heated the Chinese food in the
microwave. Moo goo gai pan. Mu shu pork. Beef

and red pepper. Rice, of course, and pickled cabbage.

He could not eat all this food himself. Ever since he'd begun methodically to starve Stinky Cheese Man in the guest room, however, Corky had been buying too much takeout.

Evidently, the spectacle of Stinky's ghastly decline was not merely entertaining but subconsciously disturbing. It raised in Corky a deep-seated fear of being underfed.

In the interest of good mental health, therefore, he continued to purchase too much takeout and enjoyed the therapeutic pleasure of feeding the excess to the garbage disposal.

This evening, as had been the case more often than not in recent months, Corky ate at the dining-room table, on which were stacked the complete blueprints of Palazzo Rospo. These prints had been produced from a set of diskettes developed by the architectural firm that had overseen the six-million-dollar renovation of the mansion soon after Manheim had purchased the estate.

In addition to receiving new electrical, plumbing, heating, air-conditioning, and audio-video systems, the enormous house had been computerized and fitted with a state-of-the-art security package designed for continual, easy upgrading. According to one source on whom Corky was relying, that package had indeed been upgraded at least once in the past two years.

As if the night were a living thing, and moody, it rose out of its sodden lethargy and worked up a peevish wind, hissing at the windows, clawing at the house walls with prosthetic hands that it fashioned from tree limbs, and by the shaking of its great black coat, rattled barrages of rain against the glass.

In his warm dining room, wrapped in Glen-plaid cashmere, with a Chinese feast before him, with worthwhile and exciting work to occupy his mind, Corky Laputa had seldom felt so cozy or more glad to be alive.

CHAPTER 43

The McBee report was detailed and businesslike, as usual, yet also friendly, presented in calligraphy that made it a minor work of art and lent to it the aura of a historical document. Sitting at the desk in his study, Ethan could hear in his mind the musical lilt and the faint Scottish brogue of the house-keeper's voice.

After an initial greeting to the effect that she hoped Ethan had enjoyed a productive day and that the Christmas spirit buoyed him as much as it did her, Mrs. McBee reminded him that she and Mr. McBee would be off to Santa Barbara early in the morning. They were spending two days with their son and his family, and were scheduled to return at 9:00 A.M. on the twenty-fourth.

She further reminded him that Santa Barbara lay but an hour to the north and that she remained on call in the event that her counsel was needed. She supplied her cell-phone number, which Ethan already knew, and her son's phone number. In addition, she provided her son's street address and the information that less than three blocks from his house was a large, lovely park.

The park features many stately old California live oaks and other trees of size, she wrote, *but within its boundaries are also at least two generous meadows, either of which will accommodate a helicopter in the event there should arise a household emergency of such dire proportions that I must be ferried home in the style of a battlefield surgeon.*

Ethan would not have believed that anyone could make him laugh out loud at the end of this distressing day. With her dry sense of humor, Mrs. McBee had done so.

She reminded him that in her and Mr. McBee's absence, Ethan would serve *in loco parentis,* with full responsibility for and authority over Fric.

During the day, if Ethan needed to be away from the estate, Mr. Hachette, the chef, would be next in the succession of command. The porters and maids could attend to the boy as needed.

After five o'clock, the day maids and the porters would be gone. Following dinner, Mr. Hachette would depart, as well.

Because the other live-in staff members were off on an advance Christmas holiday, Mrs. McBee advised Ethan that he must be certain to return before Mr. Hachette went home for the day. Otherwise Fric would be alone in the house, with no adults nearer than the two guards in the security office at the back of the estate.

Next, in her memo, the housekeeper addressed the issue central to Christmas morning. Early this day, after speaking with the boy in the library, before driving to West Hollywood to investigate Rolf Reynerd, Ethan had raised with Mrs. McBee the matter of Fric's Christmas gifts.

Any kid would have thrilled to the idea that he could submit a list of wanted items as extensive as he wished and that he would receive on Christmas morning everything he requested, precisely those items, nothing less, but nothing more. Yet it seemed to Ethan that this robbed Christmas morning of its delicious suspense and even of some of its magic. As this would be his first Christmas at Palazzo Rospo, he had approached Mrs. McBee in her office off the kitchen to inquire as to the protocol of leaving an unexpected gift under the tree, for Fric.

"God bless you, Mr. Truman," she had said, "but it's a bad idea. Not quite as bad as shooting yourself in the foot to observe the effect of the bullet, but nearly so."

"Why?" he had wondered.

"Every member of the staff receives a generous Christmas bonus, plus a small item from Neiman Marcus or Cartier, of a more personal nature—"

"Yes, I read that in your *Standards and Practices*," Ethan had said.

"And staff members are thoughtfully forbidden to exchange gifts among themselves because there are so many of us that shopping would take too much time and would impose a financial burden—"

"That's in *Standards and Practices* as well."

In fact, their entire telephone relationship was so secret that even Fric didn't know about it.

Freddie described Fric as "an exuberant, self-assured boy, very athletic like his father, wonderful with horses, a superb rider."

Horses?

Ethan would have bet a year's pay that if Fric ever had dealings with horses, they had been the kind that never left droppings and ran always to calliope music.

By manufacturing this false Fric, Freddie seemed to suggest that the real qualities of her son either did not impress her or possibly even embarrassed her.

Fric was smart enough and sensitive enough to draw that very conclusion.

The thought of the boy reading this hurtful drivel moved Ethan not to toss the magazine in the trash basket beside his desk, but to throw it angrily toward the fireplace, with the intention of burning it later.

Freddie would probably argue that in an interview with *Vanity Fair,* she needed to calculate each statement to enhance her image. How super could a supermodel be, if from her loins had sprung any but a supernaturally super son?

Burning those pages of the magazine that featured photographs of Freddie would be *especially* satisfying. Make-believe voodoo.

Line 24 was still engaged.

He looked at the computer, where the telephone log continued to be displayed. This call, too, appeared to be from a number screened by Caller ID blocking.

Because the connection had not been broken, the time continued to change in the column headed LENGTH OF CALL. Already it was over four minutes.

That was a long message to leave on an answering machine if the caller was either a salesman or someone who'd unknowingly reached a wrong number. Curious.

The indicator light blinked off.

CHAPTER 44

Fric woke to the sight of a multitude of fathers on all sides of him, a guardian army in which every soldier had the same famous face.

He lay flat on his back, and not in bed. Although he remained cautiously still, pressing with something akin to desperation against the hard smooth surface under him, his mind turned lazily, lazily, in a whirlpool of confusion.

Huge they were, these fathers, sometimes full towering figures and sometimes only disembodied heads, but giant heads, like balloons in the Macy's Thanksgiving parade.

Fric had the impression that he'd passed out for lack of air, which meant a terrible asthma attack. When he tried to breathe, however, he experienced no difficulty.

Often these enormous father faces wore noble expressions, expressions of fearless determination, of squint-eyed ferocity, but some smiled. One winked. One laughed soundlessly. A few gazed fondly or dreamily not at Fric but at famous women with equally huge heads.

As his mind turned at a steadily slower speed, toward stability, Fric abruptly remembered the man who had come out of the mirror. He sat straight up on the attic floor.

For a moment, his slowly spinning mind spun faster.

The urge to puke overcame him. He successfully resisted it and felt semiheroic.

Fric dared to tip his head back to scan the rafters for the wingless phantom. He expected a glimpse or more of a gray wool suit in flight, black wing-tip shoes skating across the air with an ice-dancer's grace.

He spied no flying freak, but saw everywhere the guardian fathers in full color, in duochromatic schemes, in black-and-white. They advanced, they receded, they encircled, they loomed.

Paper fathers, all of them.

A daredevil of modest ambition, he got to his feet and stood for a moment as if he were balancing on a high wire.

He listened and heard only the rain. The incessant, besieging, all-dissolving rain.

Too quick for caution, too slow for courage, Fric found his way through the memorabilia maze, seeking the attic stairs. Perhaps inevitably, he came to the serpent-framed mirror.

He intended to give it a wide berth. Yet the silvered glass exerted a dark and powerful attraction.

voodoo dofunny, a black-magic jiggumbob, a satanic polywhatsit, or any of the weird and grisly
items you might have expected to receive from
something that lived inside mirrors would have
been less surprising and less mystifying than this
creased photograph. He couldn't imagine who this
woman was, what her picture was meant to sig-
nify, how he could proceed to identify her, or what
he might have to gain or lose by learning her
name.

His fright had been diluted by the calming effect
of the woman's face in the photograph, but when
he lifted his gaze from the picture to the evergreen,
fear concentrated in him again. Something moved
in the tree.

Not branch to branch, not lurking in the green
shadows of the boughs: Instead, this movement
manifested in the ornaments. Each silver ball, silver trumpet, silver pendant was a three-
dimensional mirror. A formless shadowy reflection
flowed across those curved and shiny surfaces,
back and forth, up the tree, and down.

Only something flying around the rotunda, repeatedly approaching and retreating from the glittering tree, could possibly have cast such a reflection. No great bird, no bat with wings the size of
flags, no Christmas angel, no Moloch plied this air,
however, and so it seemed that the swooping
darkness flowed *within* the ornaments, rippling up
one flank of the tree, cascading down another.

Less bright, murkier than the silver decorations,
the red were mirrors, too. The same pulsing

shadow traveled through those candy-apple curves and ruby planes, inevitably suggesting the spurt and flow of blood.

Fric sensed that what stalked him now—if in fact anything did—was what had stalked him in the wine cellar earlier in the evening.

The skin tightened on his scalp, puckered on the back of his neck.

In one of the fantasy novels he loved, Fric had read that ghosts could appear by an act of their own will, but could not long sustain material form if you failed to focus on them, that your wonder and your fear empowered and sustained them.

He'd read that vampires could not enter your home unless someone inside invited them to cross the threshold.

He'd read that an evil entity can escape the chains of Hell and enter a person in this world through the trivet of a Ouija board, not if you simply ask questions of the dead, but only if you're careless enough to say something like "come join us" or "come be with us."

He'd read a shitload of stupid things, in fact, and most of them were probably just made up by stupid novelists trying to make a buck while they peddled their stupid screenplays to stupid producers.

Nevertheless, Fric convinced himself that if he didn't look away from the Christmas tree, the apparition in the blown glass would move faster, faster, growing in power by the second until, like bandoliers of grenades, every ornament would at once explode, piercing him with ten thousand splinters, whereupon every jagged shard would carry into his flesh a fragment of this pulsing darkness, which would flourish in his blood and soon become his master.

He ran past the tree, out of the rotunda.

He pressed a light switch in the north hall, and squeaked his rubber-soled sneakers along an avenue of newly polished limestone floor. Past drawing room, tea room, intimate dining room, grand dining room, breakfast room, butler's pantry, kitchen, to the end of the north wing he raced, and did not look back this time, or left, or right.

In addition to the dayroom in which the household staff took breaks and ate their lunch, and also the professionally equipped laundry, the ground-floor west wing housed the rooms and apartments of the live-in staff members.

The maids, Ms. Sanchez and Ms. Norbert, were away until the morning of the twenty-fourth. He wouldn't have gone to them, anyway. They were nice enough, but one had a giggle problem and the other was full of tales of her native North Dakota, which to Fric seemed even less interesting than the island nation of Tuvalu with its thrilling coconut-export industry.

Mrs. McBee and Mr. McBee had put in an especially long hard day. By now they might be asleep, and Fric was reluctant to disturb them.

Arriving at the door of the apartment assigned to Mr. Truman, who had so recently invited him to call for help at any hour of the day or night, and to whom he had intended to go from the moment that he'd fled the attic, Fric abruptly lost his nerve. A man stepping out of a mirror; the same man flying among the attic rafters; some spirit that lived in, watched from, and might explode out of the ornaments on a Christmas tree: Fric could not imagine that such a fantastic and incoherent story would be believed by anyone, especially not by an ex-cop who'd probably grown cynical after listening to a million crazy tales from uncounted lying sleazeballs and deluded fruitcakes.

Fric worried a little about being put in a booby hatch. No one had ever before suggested that he belonged in one. But at least one booby hatch was a part of his family history. Someone would remember a certain experience of Nominal Mom's, and maybe they would look at Fric and think, *Here's a booby in need of a hatch.*

Worse, he had earlier lied to Mr. Truman, and now he would have to admit to that lie.

He had not reported his weird conversations with Mysterious Caller because even *that* stuff had seemed too wickedly strange to be believed. He had hoped that if he just talked about a heavy-breathing pervert, Mr. Truman would track back the calls, find the scumbag—assuming that Mysterious Caller *was* a scumbag—and get to the bottom of this bizarreness.

Mr. Truman had asked if Fric was telling him everything, and Fric had said, "Sure. It was this breather," which is where the lie had been told.

Now Fric would have to admit that he'd not been what cops called "entirely forthcoming," and cops on TV weren't happy with dirtbags who withheld information. From then on, Mr. Truman would be rightly suspicious of him, wondering if the son of the biggest movie star in the world was actually just another sleazeball in the making.

Yet he had to tell Mr. Truman about Mysterious Caller in order to tell him about the Robin Goodfellow who was actually Moloch, and he had to tell him about Moloch in order to prepare him for the story of the totally insane events that had happened in the attic.

This seemed like way too much crazy stuff to explain to anyone in one big load, let alone to a cynical ex-cop who had seen it all twice too often and who hated unforthcoming slopbuckets. By not telling Mr. Truman the full truth earlier in the evening, Fric had dug a hole for himself, just like stupid people in stupid cop shows were always digging holes for themselves, innocent and guilty alike.

Lying won't get you anything but misery.

Yeah, yeah, yeah.

The sole proof of his tale was the crumpled photograph of the pretty lady with the gentle smile, which had been thrust into his hands by the man in the mirror.

He stared at the door to Mr. Truman's apartment.

He looked at the photograph.

The photograph didn't prove anything. He could have gotten it from anyone, from anywhere.

If the man in the mirror had given him a magic ring that allowed him to turn into a cat, or had given him a two-headed toad that spoke English out of one head and French out of the other, and sang Britney Spears tunes out of its butt, *that* would have been proof.

The photo amounted to nothing. Just a crumpled picture. Nothing more than a portrait of a pretty lady with a great smile, a stranger.

If Fric reported what had happened in the attic, Mr. Truman would think that he'd been smoking weed. He would lose whatever credibility he currently had.

Without knocking, he turned away from the door.

In this battle, he stood alone. Standing alone was nothing new, but it sure was getting tiresome.

rattle: a voice like wind-driven sand scouring across ancient stone, like the brittle whispery click of scuttling scarabs. The sound of his voice scared Stinky these days, and speaking had become painful; evening by evening he said less.

In the early days, to prevent him from crying out loud enough to make the neighbors curious, his mouth had been taped shut. Tape was no longer necessary, for he could not project a worrisome volume of sound.

Initially, although maintained in a state of semi-paralysis with drugs, Stinky had been chained to the bed. With the severe withering of his body, with the total collapse of his physical strength, the chains had become superfluous.

In Corky's absence, the captive's glucose drip always included drugs to keep him docile, as insurance against an unlikely escape.

Evenings, he was allowed a clear mind. For their sessions.

Now his fright-stricken eyes alternately avoided Corky and were drawn to him by magnetic dread. He lay in terror of what was to come.

Corky had never struck this man, had never employed physical torture. He never would.

With words and words alone he had broken his captive's heart, had shattered his hope, had crushed his sense of self-worth. With words he would break his mind, as well, if in fact Stinky was not already insane.

Stinky's real name was Maxwell Dalton. He had

been a professor of English at the same university where Corky still enjoyed tenure.

Corky taught literature from a deconstructionist perspective, instilling in students the belief that language can never describe reality because words only refer to other words, not to anything real. He taught them that whether a piece of writing is a novel or a law, each person is the sole arbiter of what that writing says and what it means, that all truth is relative, that all moral principles are fraudulent interpretations of religious and philosophical texts that actually have no meaning other than what each person *wants* them to mean. These were deliciously destructive ideas, and Corky took great pride in his work as a teacher.

Professor Maxwell Dalton was a traditionalist. He believed in language, meaning, purpose, and principle.

For decades, Corky's like-minded colleagues had controlled the English Department. In the past few years, Dalton had attempted to mount a revolt against meaninglessness.

He was a nuisance, a pest, a threat to the triumph of chaos. He admired the work of Charles Dickens and T. S. Eliot and Mark Twain. He was an unspeakably vile man.

Thanks to Rolf Reynerd, Dalton had been imprisoned in this bedroom for more than twelve weeks.

When Corky and Reynerd had sworn that together they would make a statement to the world by making a well-planned assault on Channing Manheim's tightly guarded estate, they had also agreed that to prove the seriousness of their pledge, each would first commit a capital crime on behalf of the other. Corky would murder Reynerd's mother; in return, the actor would kidnap Dalton and deliver him to Corky.

Keeping in mind how his intention to smother his own mother with a minimum of mess had so easily degenerated into a frenzied clubbing with a fire-place poker, Corky had obtained an untraceable handgun with which to despatch Mina Reynerd quickly, professionally, with a shot through the heart to ensure that there would be little blood.

Unfortunately, at that time, he'd not been expert in the use of firearms. His first shot hit her not in the heart, but in the foot.

Mrs. Reynerd had begun to scream in pain. For reasons that Corky still didn't fully understand, instead of proceeding with the gun, he eventually discovered himself flailing away furiously with an antique marble-and-bronze lamp, which he severely damaged.

Later, he had apologized to Rolf for diminishing the value of this lovely heirloom.

True to his word, the actor had subsequently kidnapped Maxwell Dalton. He delivered the professor, unconscious, to this bedroom, where Corky had been waiting with a stock of refrigerated infusion bags and a supply of drugs required to keep his captive docile during the early weeks when Dalton still possessed the physical potential for resistance.

Since then, he had methodically starved his colleague, providing him with only sufficient nutrients, by intravenous drip, to keep him alive. Evening after evening, sometimes in the morning, he subjected Dalton to extreme psychological torment.

The good professor believed that his wife, Rachel, and his ten-year-old daughter, Emily, had been kidnapped as well. He thought that they were being kept in other rooms of this house.

Daily, Corky regaled Dalton with accounts of the indignities, abuses, and torments to which he had most recently subjected lovely Rachel and tender Emily. His reports were graphic, exquisitely crude, gloriously obscene.

His talent for pornographic invention surprised and delighted Corky, but he was more surprised that Dalton so readily accepted his stories as truth, withering with grief and despair when he listened to them. Had he been tending to *three* captives in addition to the demands of daily life, had he committed a fraction of the atrocities on Rachel and Emily that he claimed to have enjoyed, he would have been nearly as thin and weak as the starving man in the bed.

Corky's mother, the economist and vicious academic infighter, would have been astonished to know that her son had proved to be a greater terror to at least one colleague than she had ever dreamed of being to one of hers. She would not have been capable of devising and executing such a complex and clever scheme as the one with which he had brought down Maxwell Dalton.

Mother had been motivated by envy, hatred.

cluded a sofa. Fric was about to stretch out on this makeshift bed when the silence gave way to a cheerful child-pleasing sound suitable for the nursery or the bedrooms of younger children.

Ooodelee-ooodelee-oo.

The telephone stood on a piece of furniture that Mrs. McBee referred to as an "escritoire," but which was still a writing desk to Fric. He stood beside it, watching the signal light flutter at his private line each time that the phone rang.

Ooodelee-ooodelee-oo.

He expected Mr. Truman to answer the call by the third ring.

Ooodelee-ooodelee-oo.

Mr. Truman didn't respond.

The phone rang a fourth time. A fifth.

The voice-mail system didn't take the call, either. Six rings. Seven.

Fric refused to pick up the handset.

Ooodelee-ooodelee-oo.

In his apartment, Ethan had retrieved the six black-box items from a cabinet and had arranged them on his desk in the order that they had been received.

He had switched off the computer.

The phone was near at hand, where he could intercept calls to Fric should that line in fact ring, and where he would notice the indicator light on Line 24 if it signaled additional incoming calls. Traffic on this messages-from-the-dead line seemed to be increasing, which disturbed him for reasons he could not articulate, and he wanted to keep an eye on the situation.

Sitting in his desk chair with a can of Coke, he considered the elements of the riddle.

The small jar containing twenty-two dead lady-bugs. *Hippodamia convergens,* of the family Coc-cinellidae.

Another, larger jar into which he had transferred the ten dead snails. An uglier sight by the day.

A pickle-relish jar holding nine foreskins in formaldehyde. The tenth had been destroyed by the lab in the process of analysis.

The closed drapes muffled the snap of rain on glass, the threat of wind enraged.

Beetles, snails, foreskins . . .

For some reason, Ethan's attention drifted to the phone, though it hadn't rung. No indicator light burned on Line 24 or on any of the first twenty-three.

He tipped the Coke can, took a swallow.

Beetles, snails, foreskins . . .

Ooodelee-ooodelee-oo.

Maybe Mr. Truman had slipped and fallen and hit his head, and maybe he lay unconscious, oblivious of the ringing. Or maybe he had been carried off into a land beyond a mirror. Or maybe he had just forgotten to modify the system to receive Fric's private calls.

The caller would not give up. After twenty-one

repetitions of the stupid child-pleasing tones, Fric decided that if he didn't pick up the phone, he would have to listen to it ringing all night.

The slight tremor in his voice dismayed him, but he persevered: "Vinnie's Soda Parlor and Vomitorium, home of the nine-pound ice-cream sundae, where you splurge and then purge."

"Hello, Aelfric," said Mysterious Caller.

"I can't make up my mind whether you're a pervert or a friend like you say. I'm leaning toward pervert."

"You're leaning wrong. Look around you for the truth, Aelfric."

"Look around me at what?"

"At what's there with you in the library."

"I'm in the kitchen."

"By now you ought to realize that you can't lie to me."

"My deep and secret hiding place is going to be one of the bigger ovens. I'll crawl inside and pull the door shut behind me."

"You better baste yourself in butter, because Moloch will just turn on the gas."

"Moloch has already been here," Fric said.

"That wasn't Moloch. That was me."

Receiving this revelation, Fric almost slammed down the phone.

Mysterious Caller said, "I paid you a visit because I wanted you to understand, Aelfric, that you really *are* at risk, and that time really *is* running out. If I'd been Moloch, you'd be toast."

"You came out of a mirror," said Fric, his curiosity

and sense of wonder for the moment outweighing his fear.

"And I went back into one."

"How can you come out of a mirror?"

"For the answer, look around you, son."

Fric surveyed the library.

"What do you see?" asked Mysterious Caller.

"Books."

"Oh? You have a lot of books there in the kitchen?"

"I'm in the library."

"Ah, truth. There's hope that you'll avoid at least some misery, after all. What else do you see besides books?"

"A writing desk. Chairs. A sofa."

"Keep looking."

"A Christmas tree."

"There you go."

"There I go where?" asked Fric.

"What dingles and what dangles?"

"Huh?"

"And is spelled almost like *angles*."

"Angels," Fric said, surveying the radiant white flock that gathered with trumpets and harps upon the tree.

"I travel by mirrors, by mist, by smoke, by doorways in water, by stairways made of shadows, on roads of moonlight, by wish and hope and simple expectation. I've given up my car."

Amazed, Fric clenched the phone so hard that his hand ached, as if he might squeeze a few more revealing words from the mirror man.

"You've a good memory. I know what's coming, but I may influence events only by means that are sly—"

"—slippery, and seductive," Fric finished.

"I may not interfere directly with Moloch's pursuit of his own damnation. Just as I may not interfere with any heroic policeman who is about to sacrifice his life to save another, and therefore raise himself forever high."

"I guess I understand that. You're like a director who doesn't get final cut of the film."

"I'm not even a director. Think of me as just another studio executive who gives notes for suggested revisions of the script."

"The kind of notes that always make screenwriters so pissy and turn them into drunks. They'll bore your butt off talking about that, like a ten-year-old kid could care, like *anyone* could care."

"The difference," said the maybe-angel, "is that my notes are always well intended—and based on a vision of the future that may be too true."

Fric thought about all this for a moment as he pulled the chair out from the kneehole of the desk. Sitting down, he said, "Wow. Being a guardian angel must be frustrating."

"You can't begin to know. *You* control the final cut of your life, Aelfric. It's called free will. You've got it. Everyone here has it. And in the end, I can't act for you. That's what you're here to do . . . to make choices, right or wrong, to be wise or not, to be courageous or not."

"I guess I can try."

"I guess you better. What've you done with the photo I gave you?"

"The pretty lady with the nice smile? She's folded in my back pocket."

"It won't be any good to you there."

"What do you expect me to do with it?"

"Think. Use your brain, Aelfric. Even in your family, that's possible. Think. Be wise."

"I'm too drag-ass tired to think right now. Who is she—the lady in the picture?"

"Why don't you play detective? Make inquiries."

"I did make an inquiry. Who is she?"

"Ask around. That's not a question for me to answer."

"Why isn't it?"

"Because I have to abide by the sly-slippery-seductive rule, which sometimes makes any guardian angel a pain in the ass."

"Okay. Forget it. Am I safe tonight? Can I wait till morning to find that deep and special secret place to hide?"

"First thing in the morning will be all right," the guardian said. "But don't waste any more time. Prepare, Aelfric. Prepare."

"Okay. And, hey, I'm sorry for what I called you."

"You mean earlier—an attorney?"

"Yeah."

"I've been called worse."

"Really?"

"Much worse."

"And I'm sorry for trying to track you back."

"What do you mean?"

"It seems like a sneaky thing to do to an angel. I'm sorry for star sixty-nining you."

Mysterious Caller fell silent.

An indefinable quality of the silence made it different from any hush that Fric had ever heard.

This was a *perfect* silence, for one thing, and it sucked away not only all the noise on the open line but also every whisper of sound in the library, until he seemed to have gone deafer than deaf.

The silence felt deep, too, as though the guardian were calling from the bottom of an oceanic trench. Deep and so *cold.*

Fric shuddered. He could not hear his teeth chatter or his body quake. He could not hear his exhalation, either, although he felt the breath rush from him, hot enough to dry his teeth.

Perfect, deep, cold silence, yes, but more and stranger than simply perfect, deep, and cold.

Fric imagined that such a silence might be cast like a spell by *any* angel with supernatural powers, but that it might be a trick most characteristic of the Angel of Death.

The Mysterious Caller drew a breath, inhaling the very silence and letting sound into the world once more, beginning with his voice, which resonated with an ominous note of concern: "When did you use star sixty-nine, Aelfric?"

"Well, after you called me in the train room."

"And also after I called you in the wine cellar?"

"Yeah. Don't you know all this . . . being who you are?"

"Angels don't know everything, Aelfric. Now and then, some things are . . . slipped by us."

"The first time, your phone just rang and rang—"

"That's because I used the telephone in my old apartment, where I lived before I died. I didn't enter your number, just thought of you, but I *did* pick up the phone. I was still learning . . . learning what I can do now. I'm getting smoother at this by the hour."

Fric wondered if he was more tired even than he realized. The conversation wasn't always making sense. "Your old apartment?"

"I'm a relatively new angel, son. Died this morning. I'm using the body I used to live in, though it's . . . more flexible now, with my new powers. What happened the second time you used star sixty-nine?"

"You really don't know?"

"I'm afraid I might. But tell me."

"I got this pervert."

"What did it say to you?"

"Didn't say anything. He just breathed heavy . . . and then made these like animal sounds."

The Mysterious Caller was quiet, but this proved to be a far different silence from the death-deep stillness of a moment ago. This hush had in it a host of half-heard twitches, the moth-wing vibration of fluttering nerves, the so-soft tensing of muscles.

"At first, I thought he was you," Fric explained. "So I told him I'd looked up Moloch in the dictionary. The name excited him."

"Don't ever use star sixty-nine after I call, Aelfric. Not ever, ever again."

"Why?"

With hard insistence, revealing a degree of alarm that seemed to be too mortal in character for an immortal guardian angel, the caller said, "Not *ever* again. Do you understand?"

"Yes."

"Do you promise me you'll never again try to call me back with star sixty-nine?"

"All right. But why?"

"When I called you in the wine cellar, I didn't use a phone, the way I did the first time. I don't require a phone to ring you up any more than I need a car to travel. I need only the *idea* of a phone."

"The idea of a phone? How's that work?"

"My current position comes with certain supernatural abilities."

"Being a guardian angel, you mean."

"But when I use only the idea of a phone, star sixty-nine might connect you with a place you must not go."

"What place?"

The guardian hesitated. Then he said, "The dark eternity."

"Doesn't sound good," Fric agreed, and uneasily surveyed the library.

In the labyrinth of shelves, monsters both human and not abided between the covers of so many books. Perhaps one beast prowled not in those paper worlds but in this one, breathing not ink fumes but air, waiting for a small boy to find it along one turning or another of those quiet aisles.

"The dark eternity. The bottomless abyss, the darkness visible, and all that dwells there," the guardian elaborated. "You were lucky, son. It didn't talk to you."

"It?"

"What you called 'the pervert.' If they talk to you, they can wheedle, persuade, charm, sometimes even command."

Fric glanced at the tree again. The angels seemed to be watching him, every one.

"When you press star sixty-nine," the guardian said, "you open a door to them."

"Who?"

"Do we need to speak their sulfurous name? We both know who I mean, do we not?"

Being a boy with a taste for fantasy in his reading, with a home theater in which he could watch everything from kid flicks to R-rated monster fests, with an imagination stropped sharp by solitude, Fric was pretty sure he knew who was meant.

The caller said, "You open a door to them, and then, with one wrong word, you might unintentionally . . . invite them in."

"In here, to Palazzo Rospo?"

"You might invite one of them into *you,* Aelfric. When invited, they can travel by the telephone connection, by that fragile link of spirit to spirit, much the way that I can travel through one mirror to another."

"No lie?"

aware of anyone but themselves, anyway, and the other half were intently focused on the handful of directors, agents, and studio honchos who could make them either filthy rich or filthier rich than they already were.

During one of these spells of invisibility, Fric had heard it said of the third—or possibly the fourth—biggest movie star in the world that "the stupid prick will kill himself with women, the way he's going." Fric had no slightest idea how one could kill oneself with women, or why a suicidal person would not just buy a pistol.

That intriguing statement had remained with him, however, and he intended to be careful. These days, when he met new women, he studied them surreptitiously for indications that they were the potentially dangerous type.

Until this weird night, he had likewise never imagined that death could be rung up just by pressing *69.

Maybe what came through the phone would not kill him. Maybe it would imprison his soul and take control of his body and make him so miserable that he would *wish* he were dead.

Or perhaps it would take control of him and run him headfirst into a brick wall, into an open cesspool (assuming an open cesspool could be found in Bel Air), off the roof of Palazzo Rospo, or into the arms of a deadly blonde (with which Bel Air apparently was infested).

His quandary was that he didn't know whether to believe anything that Mysterious Caller had said.

On the one hand, the entire rap about being a guardian angel, about moving by mirrors and moonlight—it might all be a shitload of nonsense. A bigger pile even than Ghost Dad's unicorn movie.

On the other hand—and there was always another hand—Mysterious Caller *had* walked out of a mirror. He *had* flown through the rafters. His performance in the attic—and later in the shiny surfaces of the Christmas-tree ornaments—had been so incredible that it had earned him some credibility.

Yet what kind of guardian angel wore a suit and tie straight out of a big-bucks Rodeo Drive shop, had skin as pale as fish flesh, looked a lot less holy than scary, and had gray eyes as cold as ashes in ice?

Possibly Mysterious Caller, for reasons unknown, had been lying, leading Fric toward wrong conclusions, setting him up.

He'd once overheard his father say that virtually everyone in this town was setting someone up for a fall, that if they weren't doing it for money, then they were doing it for sport.

Mysterious Caller said Fric must not use *69 because it would connect him with the dark eternity. Maybe the *truth* was that the guy just didn't want Fric to try tracking him.

Still belly-down on the sofa, leaning out toward the phone, Fric picked up the handset. He pressed the button for his private line.

He listened to the dial tone.

The angels on the tree *looked* like angels. You could trust an angel with a harp, with a trumpet, wearing white, sporting wings.

He pressed * and 6 and 9.

The phone was picked up not on the fourth ring, as it had been previously, but on the first. No one said hello. As before, only silence greeted him.

Then, after a few seconds, he heard breathing.

Fric intended to outwait the breather, make the pervert speak first. After twenty or thirty seconds, however, he grew so nervous that he said, "It's me again."

His concession didn't bring a response.

Trying to strike a light and somewhat jokey tone, but largely failing, Fric asked, "How're things in the dark eternity?"

The breathing grew rougher, heavier.

"You know—the dark eternity?" Fric asked tauntingly but also with a faint tremor that he could not control and that put the lie to his pose of bold self-assurance. "Also known on some maps as the bottomless abyss. Or the darkness visible."

The freak continued to breathe at him.

"You don't sound so good. You have a bad sinus thing going on there," said Fric.

With his head hanging over the edge of the sofa, he began to feel a little dizzy.

"I'll give you my doctor's name. He'll write a prescription. You'll be able to breathe better. You'll thank me."

A croaking-grinding voice, issuing from a throat clogged with razor blades, drier than the ashes of ashes twice burnt, arising from a terrible depth, through crevices in the broken stones of strange ruins, said just one word: *"Boy."*

In Fric's ear, the word crawled as if it were an insect, maybe one of those earwigs that legend said could find its way into your brain and lay eggs in there, transforming you into a walking hive filled with squirming legions.

Remembering all those posters of his father looking noble and brave and full of steely resolve, Fric held fast to the phone. He summoned an iron weight of determination to press the wrinkles of fear from his voice, and he said, "You don't scare me."

"Boy," the other repeated, *"boy,"* and additional voices arose on the phone, initially just four or five, at a lower volume than the first, male and female, punctuating their gabble with *"boy . . . boy."* Their voices were urgent, eager. Desperate. Voices whispery and smooth, voices rough. ". . . who's there?" ". . . the way, he's the way . . ." ". . . sweet flesh . . ." ". . . stupid little piglet, easy for the taking . . ." ". . . ask me in . . ." ". . . ask *me* . . ." ". . . no, ask *me* . . ." In seconds their numbers swelled to a dozen, a score, a crowd. Maybe because they were all talking at once, their speech sounded as though it descended into bestial mutterings and snarls, and what words remained were as often as not obscenities strung together in incoherent sequences. Chilling cries of fear, pain, frustration, and raw anger sewed these rags of raucous noise into a tapestry of *need.*

Fric's strong heart rapped hard against his ribs, pulsed in his throat, throbbed in his temples. He had claimed not to be scared, but he was scared, all right, too scared to come up with a single smart-ass remark or to speak at all.

Yet the churning voices intrigued him, compelled his attention. The hunger in them, the intense yearning, the pitiful desperation, the melancholy longing wove a poignant song that strummed the cords of his abiding loneliness, that *spoke* to him and assured him that he need not suffer solitude, that companionship was his for the asking, that purpose and meaning and family were all his if only he would open his heart to them.

Even when wordless, when bursting with ripe obscenities that ought to have repelled Fric, the guttural chorus, full of growl and hiss, steadily soothed his terror. His heart continued to pound, but moment by moment, the power driving its frenzied hammering was less fear than excitement. Everything could change. Utterly. Completely. Now and forever. Change in an instant. He could have a new life and a better one simply for the asking, a life from which all loneliness would be banished, all uncertainty, all confusion and self-doubt and weakness. . . .

Fric opened his mouth to issue what all but certainly would have been an invitation similar to those that users of a Ouija board were well advised to avoid. Before he could speak, he was distracted by movement at the periphery of his vision.

When he turned to look at what had drawn his

attention, Fric saw that the stretchy, coiled cord between the handset and the telephone, once a clean white length of vinyl-coated wires, now appeared to be organic, pink and slick, like that rope of tissue that tied a mother to a newborn baby. A pulse throbbed through the cord, slow and thick, but strong, moving from the phone box on the floor to the handset that he held, toward his ear, as if in anticipation of the invitation that trembled on his tongue.

Sitting at the desk in his study, eating a ham sandwich, trying to puzzle meaning from Reynerd's six taunting gifts, Ethan found his thoughts drifting repeatedly to Duncan Whistler.

In the garden room at Our Lady of Angels, when he had initially learned that Dunny's body had gone missing, he had known intuitively that the uncanny events at Reynerd's apartment and Dunny's dead-man-walking stunt were related. Later, Dunny's apparent involvement in the murder of Reynerd, though unexpected, had been no surprise.

What *did* surprise Ethan, the more he thought about it, was the close encounter with Dunny in the hotel bar.

More than coincidence must be involved. Dunny had been in the bar because Ethan was in the bar. He had been *meant* to see Dunny.

If he'd been meant to see Dunny, then he'd been meant to follow him. Perhaps he had also been meant to catch up with Dunny.

could not be sure, but he sensed a presence on the line.

During the years that he had carried a badge, he'd conducted enough stakeouts to learn patience. He listened to the listener, trading silence for silence.

Time passed. Ham waited. Still hungry, Ethan also grew thirsty for a beer.

Eventually, he heard a cry, repeated three times. The voice was faint neither because it whispered nor because it was feeble but because it arose from a great distance, so fragile that it might have been merely a mirage of sound.

More silence, more time, and then the voice rose again, no less frail than before, so ephemeral that Ethan could not confidently say whether it was the voice of a man or a woman. Indeed, it might have been the mournful cry of a bird or an animal, repeated three times again, with a damped quality similar to that provided by a filter of fog.

He had ceased to expect heavy breathing.

Although no louder than before, the quiet hiss of static had acquired a menacing quality, as though each soft tick represented the impact of a radioactive particle on his eardrum.

When the voice came a third time, it didn't resort to the short cry that it had previously repeated. Ethan detected patterns of sound surely meant to convey meaning. Words. Not quite comprehensible.

As though broadcast from a distant radio station into an ether troubled by storms, these words were distorted by fading, by drift, by scratchy atmospherics. A voice out of time might sound like this, or one sent by spacefarers from the night side of Saturn.

He didn't remember leaning far forward in his chair. Neither did he recall when his arms had slid off the arms of the chair nor when he had propped his elbows on his knees. Yet here he sat in this compacted posture, both hands to his head, one holding the phone, like a man humbled by remorse or bent by despair upon the receipt of terrible news.

Although Ethan strained to capture the content of the faraway speaker's conversation, it continuously sifted through him without sticking, as elusive as cloud shadows projected by moonlight upon a rolling seascape.

Indeed, when he struggled the hardest to find meaning in these might-be words, they receded farther behind a screen of static and distortion. He suspected that if he relaxed, the flow of speech might clarify, the voice grow stronger, but he could not relax. Although he pressed the handset to his head with such force that his ear ached, he was unable to relent, as if a brief moment of less-intense focus would prove to be the very instant when the words would come clearly, but only to he who faithfully attended them.

The voice possessed a plaintive quality. Although unable to grasp the words and deduce their meaning, Ethan detected an urgent and beseeching tone, and perhaps a yearning sadness.

When he assumed that he had spent five minutes striving without success to net those words from the sea of static and silence, Ethan glanced at his wristwatch. 12:26. He had been riveted to the phone for nearly half an hour.

Having been crushed so long against the ear-piece, his ear burned and throbbed. His neck felt stiff, his shoulders ached.

Surprised and somewhat disoriented, he sat up straight in his chair. He had never been hypno-tized; but he imagined that this must be how it would feel to shake off the lingering effects of a trance.

Reluctantly, he put down the phone.

The suggestion of a voice in the void might have been that and nothing more, merely a suggestion, an audial illusion. Yet he had pursued it with the single-minded sweaty expectation of a submarine sonar operator listening for the *ping* of an ap-proaching battleship as it off-loaded depth charges.

He didn't quite understand what he'd done. Or why.

Although the room was not excessively warm, he blotted his brow with his shirt sleeve.

He expected the phone to ring again. Perhaps he would be wise not to answer it.

That thought disturbed him because he didn't understand it. Why not answer a ringing phone?

His gaze traveled across the six items from Reynerd, but his attention settled longest on the three small bells from the ambulance in which he'd never ridden.

When the phone had not rung after two or three minutes, he switched on the computer and again accessed the telephone log. The most recent entry was the call that he had placed to the hotel to inquire about Dunny Whistler.

Subsequently, the call that he'd received, which had lasted nearly half an hour, had not registered in the log.

Impossible.

He stared at the screen, thinking about Fric's calls from the heavy breather. He'd been too quick to dismiss the boy's story.

When Ethan glanced at the phone, he discovered the indicator light aglow at Line 24.

Sales call. Wrong number. And yet . . .

Had it been easy to satisfy his curiosity, he would have gone up to the third floor where the answering machine serving Line 24 was isolated in a special chamber behind a locked blue door. By the very act of entering that room, however, he would be surrendering his job.

To Ming du Lac and Channing Manheim, the room behind the blue door was a sacred place. Entry by anyone but them had been forbidden.

In the event of an emergency, Ethan was authorized to use his master key anywhere in the house. The only door that it didn't open was the blue one.

A flock of angels, the pleasant smell of spruce, and the comfort of the huge armchair could not lull Fric into sleep.

wasn't set afire. His wonderful new mother poured him another glass of lemonade to cool him off, and they continued to talk about favorite books as he ate a fat slice of the homemade chocolate cake that she had baked for him.

In a tumultuous darkness filled first with gunfire and the roar of approaching engines, then with a voice crying out of a void, Ethan turned and turned, tumbling across wet blacktop, until he turned one last time into a quiet darkness of damp tangled sheets.

Sitting up in bed, he said, "Hannah," for in sleep, where all his psychological defenses were removed, he had recognized her voice as the one that he had heard on the telephone.

Initially, she had repeated the same cry three times, and then three times again. In sleep, he had recognized the word, his name: *"Ethan . . . Ethan . . . Ethan."*

What else she had said to him, the urgent message that she had struggled to convey across the gulf between them, continued to elude him. Even in sleep, that room next door to death, he had not been close enough to Hannah to hear more than his name.

As the shrouds of sleep slipped off him, Ethan was overcome by a conviction that he was being watched.

Every child knows well the feeling of waking from a dream to the perception that the bedroom darkness grants cover to vicious fiends of innumerable descriptions and appetites. The presence of demons seemed so real that many a small hand had hesitated on a lamp switch, for fear that seeing would be even worse than the images that the fevered imagination provided; yet always the terrors evaporated in the light.

Ethan wasn't sure that light would banish unreason this time. He sensed that what watched him were owls and crack-beaked crows, ravens and fierce-eyed hawks, that they perched not on his furniture but in somber black-and-white photographs on the walls, pictures that hadn't hung there when he'd gone to sleep. Although hours ago the night had melted into the predawn blackness of a new day, he had no reason to suppose that Tuesday would be less stained by irrationality than Monday had been.

He didn't reach for the lamp switch. He reclined once more, head upon his pillows, resigned to the presence of whatever the darkness might conceal.

He doubted that he would be able to doze off again. Sooner than later, however, his eyes grew heavy.

On the rim of sleep's whirlpool, as Ethan drifted lazily around, around, he heard from time to time a *tick-tick-tick* that might have been the talons of sentinel crows as they shifted position on an iron fence. Or perhaps it was only claws of cold rain scratching at the windows.

As he began to revolve more rapidly around the relentless pull of black-hole gravity that was sleep, Ethan's eyes fluttered one last time, and he noticed a small light in the lampblack gloom. The phone. Without investigation, he couldn't with certainty identify the number of the indicator light, but he knew instinctively that it must be Line 24.

He slid off the rim of the whirlpool, into the vortex, down into whatever dreams might come.

CHAPTER 48

Free of envy, free of hatred, buoyant in the service of chaos, Corky Laputa began his day with a cinnamon-pecan roll, four cups of black coffee, and a pair of caffeine tablets.

Anyone who would bring the social order to ruin must embrace anything that gives him an additional edge, even at the risk of destroying his stomach lining and instigating chronic intestinal inflammation. Fortunately for Corky, periodically consuming massive quantities of caffeine seemed to increase the bitter potency of his bile without causing acid indigestion or other regrettable symptoms.

Washing down caffeine with caffeine, he stood at his kitchen window, smiling at the low somber sky and at the trailing beard of night fog that had not entirely been shorn away by the blunt gray dawn. Bad weather was again his co-conspirator.

The current pause in the rain would be brief. Rushing in fast on the heels of the departing tempest, a new and reportedly stronger storm would wash the city and justify the wearing of rain gear, regardless of how elaborate it might be.

Corky had already reloaded the weatherproof interior pockets of his yellow vinyl slicker, which hung now from a hook in the garage.

He carried his last cup of coffee upstairs to the guest room, where he finished it while informing Stinky Cheese Man that his beloved daughter, Emily, was dead.

The previous night he'd reported the final torture and savage murder of Rachel, Stinky's wife, who was still alive, of course, and not in Corky's custody. The invented details were so imaginative and vivid that Stinky had been reduced to uncontrollable tears, to sobs that sounded weirdly inhuman—and quite disgusting—coming from his withered voice box.

Although crushed by despair, Stinky had not suffered the heart attack for which Corky had been hoping.

Rather than coddle the man with a sedative, Corky had introduced a powerful hallucinogenic through a port in the IV line. His hope was that Stinky would be unable to sleep and would pass the darkest hours between midnight and dawn in a hell of drug-induced visions featuring his brutalized wife.

Now, regaling his guest with an even more outrageous tale of the many crude violations and cruel acts of violence visited upon young Emily, Corky grew weary of the tears and anguish that were replayed here yet again. Under the circumstances, a massive cardiac infarction didn't seem too much to ask, but Stinky would not cooperate.

For a man who supposedly loved his wife and daughter more than life itself, Stinky's determination to survive was unseemly now that he'd been told that his family was nothing more than rotting meat. Like most traditionalists, with all their loudly expressed belief in language and meaning and purpose and principle, Stinky was probably a fraud.

Now and then, Corky glimpsed rage underlying Stinky's grief. Into the man's eyes came hatred hot enough to sear with a look, but then at once vanished under pools of tears.

Perhaps Stinky clung to life only for the hope of revenge. The guy was delusional.

Besides, hatred only destroys the hater. By the example of her wasted life, Corky's mother had proved the truth of that contention.

With facility and efficiency, Corky changed infusion bags after doctoring the new one with a drug that would induce a semiparalytic state. Stinky had so little muscle tissue left that an artificially induced paralysis seemed unnecessary, but Corky was loath to let anything to chance.

Ironically, to serve chaos well, he needed to be well organized. He required a strategy for victory and the carefully planned tactics necessary to fulfill that strategy.

Without strategy and tactics, you weren't a true agent of chaos. You were just Jeffrey Dahmer or some crazy lady who kept a hundred cats and fire that might soon be breathed out in dazzling, jagged plumes.

A tentative drizzle fell, but cataracts were sure to follow, vertical rivers, torrents, Niagaras, a deluge.

CHAPTER 49

Protected by the tree of angels and by the photo of the unknown pretty lady, Fric woke unharmed, with his body and soul intact.

Over the center of the library, the elaborate stained-glass dome brightened with the dawn, but the colors were muted because the early light fell weak and gray.

After studying the photograph of his dream mother for a moment, Fric folded it and returned it to a back pocket of his jeans.

He got up from the armchair. He yawned and stretched. He took a moment to be amazed that he was alive.

At the back of the library, he removed the bracing chair from under the knob of the powder-room door. He did not, however, enter that mirrored space to use the facilities.

Following a quick look around to be certain that he remained unobserved, he peed on the potted palm that he had begun to kill the previous evening. The experience was satisfying for him, but surely not for the tree.

He could think of no water closet in the mansion that could be reached without going through a bathroom with mirrors.

This unconventional toileting would be all right for a while, but only as long as he could stand up to do what needed to be done. The moment sitting was required, he would be in trouble.

If the rain ended at last—or if it didn't—he might venture outside to the grouping of deodar cedars beyond the rose garden. There he could do what bears did in the woods, by which he didn't mean hibernate or guzzle honey from bee hives.

Security guards would see him going to and from the cedars. Fortunately, no cameras were positioned inside that little grove.

If anyone asked why he'd gone out in the rain to the woods, he would say without hesitation that he'd been bird watching. He must remember to take with him a pair of binoculars for cover.

No one would doubt his story. People *expected* a geeky-looking kid like him to be a bird watcher, a math whiz, a builder of plastic model-kit monsters, a secret reader of body-building magazines, and a collector of his own boogers, among other things.

With his toilet strategy now devised, he plugged in the library phone, which he had unplugged the previous night. He expected his line to ring at once, but it didn't.

He dragged the armchair away from the Christmas tree and returned it to its proper position. After turning out the lights, he left the library.

As he closed the door, some of the dangling angels glimmered softly in the gloom, barely touched by storm light filtering through the stained-glass dome.

Moloch was coming.

Preparations must be made.

He went down the main stairs, across the rotunda, and along the hall to the kitchen. En route, he switched off the lights that he had left on during the night.

The post-dawn stillness in the great house was deeper even than the silence that, during the long night, had made it seem like such a perfect haunt for ghosts of all intentions.

In the kitchen, passing a window, he noticed a lull in the rain, and he glimpsed the grove of cedars in the distance. At the moment, however, he felt no urge to engage in any bird watching.

Usually Fric avoided the kitchen on days when Mr. Hachette, the diabolical chef, was on the job. Here be the lair of the beast, where the many ovens could not help but bring to mind Hansel and Gretel and their close call, where you were reminded that a rolling pin was also a wicked bludgeon, where you expected to discover that the knives and the cleavers and the meat forks were engraved with the words PROPERTY OF THE BATES MOTEL.

This morning, the territory was safe because Mr. Hachette—late of the Cordon Bleu school of culi-

442 DEAN KOONTZ

types than you would find in a bakery, three widely separated cooking areas with a total of twenty high-intensity gas burners, a planning station, a baking station, a clean-up station with four sinks and four dishwashers, three islands, prep tables, and a shitload of restaurant-quality equipment.

A Beverly Hills caterer and forty of his employees could work here with Mr. Hachette and the household staff, with little sense of being crowded. At a party, they prepared, plated, and served three hundred sit-down dinners, on a timely basis, from this space. Fric had seen it happen many times, and it never failed to dazzle him.

If two or even three ordinary people had set out to search the kitchen for him, Fric's chances of eluding them would have been good. Mrs. McBee was in no way ordinary.

Holding his breath, he thought that he could hear her sniffing the air. *Fee-fie-fo-fum*.

He was glad that he had not turned on the kitchen lights, though she was certain to smell the fresh water that remained in the central sink.

Footsteps.

Fric almost bolted to his feet, almost announced his presence, which seemed a wiser course of action than waiting here to be found lurking like a sleazeball criminal, stripped to the waist and clearly up to no good.

Then he realized the footsteps were moving away from him.

He heard the butler's-pantry door swing shut.

The footsteps faded into silence.

Stunned and strangely dismayed to discover that Mrs. McBee was fallible, Fric breathed again.

After a while, he crept to the hall door, which he cracked open. He stood listening.

When he heard the distant hum of the service elevator, he knew that Mrs. McBee and Mr. McBee were descending to the lower garage. Soon they would be off to Santa Barbara.

He waited a few minutes before he ventured from the kitchen to the laundry room in the nearby west wing, which also contained the McBees' apartment.

Whereas the kitchen was gigantic, the laundry was only huge.

He liked the smell of this place. Detergent, bleach, starch, the lingering scent of hot cotton under a steam iron . . .

Fric would happily have worn the same jeans and shirt a second day. But he worried that Mr. Truman might notice, and inquire.

Mrs. McBee would have noticed in an instant. She would have insisted on knowing the reason for this slovenliness.

Mr. Truman couldn't help but be slower on the uptake than Mrs. McBee. Still, he *was* an ex-cop, so he wouldn't long overlook day-old, dirty, rumpled clothes.

The possibility might be slim that something evil and supremely slimy was waiting for Fric in his suite, but he didn't intend to find out anytime soon. He would not return there to change clothes.

Monday had been a scheduled wash day. Mrs.

Carstairs, one of the day maids and in fact the laundress, processed laundry one day and returned it promptly to family members and to staff the following morning.

Fric found his pressed blue jeans, pants, and shirts hanging from a cart similar to those with which hotel bellmen move suit bags and luggage. His folded underwear and socks were arranged under the hanging items, on the bed of the cart.

Red-faced, feeling like a pervert for sure, he stripped naked right there in the laundry. He changed into fresh underwear, jeans, and a blue-and-green checkered flannel shirt with a straight-cut tail that allowed it to be worn out, Hawaiian style.

He transferred his wallet and the folded photograph from his old jeans before dropping the soiled garments into the collection basket under the laundry chute that served the second and third floors.

Emboldened by having successfully toileted, bathed, and changed clothes under these desperate wartime conditions, Fric returned to the kitchen.

He entered cautiously, expecting to find Mrs. McBee waiting for him: *Ah, laddie, did ya truly think I was such a fool as to be that easily deceived?*

She had not returned.

From the appliance pantry, he fetched a small stainless-steel cart with two shelves. He traveled the kitchen, loading the cart with items that he would need in his deep and special secret place.

He considered including a six-pack of Coke among his provisions, but warm cola didn't taste good. Instead, he selected a four-pack of Stewart's Diet Orange 'N Cream soda, which was fabulous even at room temperature, and six twelve-ounce bottles of water.

After he put a few apples and a bag of pretzels on the cart, he realized his mistake. When hiding from a demented psycho killer who had the sharply honed senses of a stalking panther, eating noisy food was no wiser than singing Christmas songs to pass the time.

Fric replaced the apples and pretzels with bananas, a box of chocolate-covered doughnuts, and several chewy granola bars.

He added a quart-size Hefty OneZip plastic bag in which to store the peels after he ate the fruit. Left in the open air, peels would give off an intense banana scent as they darkened. According to the movies, every serial killer had a sense of smell keener than that of a wolf. Banana peels might be the death of Fric if he didn't stow them in an airtight container.

A roll of paper towels. Several foil-wrapped moist towelettes. Even in hiding, he would want to be neat.

From a cupboard filled with Rubbermaid containers, he chose a pair of one-quart, soft-plastic jars with screw-on lids. They would serve in place of the library palm tree.

Shoveling manure over the seed of truth that he'd spoken, hoping to grow a half-convincing lie from it, Fric said, "Well, you know, my dad keeps a special phone for messages from ghosts. I just meant like maybe one of them called the wrong line."

Mr. Truman stared at him as though trying to decide whether he could be as stupid as he was pretending to be.

Not as great an actor as his father, Fric knew he couldn't long stand up to interrogation by an ex-cop. He was so nervous that in a minute he'd need to take a leak in one of the Rubbermaid jars.

"Ummm, well, gotta go, things to do, things up in my room, you know," he muttered, once more sounding like a cousin from the feeble-minded branch of the Hobbit clan.

He swung the cart around Mr. Truman and pushed it east along the main hall. He didn't look back.

CHAPTER 50

The dome light atop Our Lady of Angels Hospital was a golden beacon. High above the dome, at the top of the radio mast, the red aircraft-warning lamp winked in the gray mist, as if the storm were a living beast and this were its malevolent Cyclopean eye.

In the elevator, on the way from the garage to the fifth floor, Ethan listened to a lushly orchestrated version of a classic Elvis Costello number tricked up with violins and fulsome French horns. This cable-hung cubicle, ascending and descending twenty-four hours a day, was a little outpost of Hell in perpetual motion.

The physicians' lounge on the fifth floor, to which he'd been given directions by phone, was nothing more than a dreary windowless vending-machine room with a pair of Formica-topped tables in the center. The orange plastic items that surrounded the tables qualified as chairs no more than the room deserved the grand name on its door.

Having arrived five minutes early, Ethan fed coins

to one of the machines and selected black coffee. When he sipped the stuff, he knew what death must taste like, but he drank it anyway because he'd slept only four or five hours and needed the kick.

Dr. Kevin O'Brien arrived precisely on time. About forty-five, handsome, he had the vaguely haunted look and the well-suppressed but still-apparent nervous edge of one who had spent two-thirds of his life in arduous scholarship, only to find that the hammers wielded by HMOs, government bureaucracy, and greedy trial attorneys were daily degrading his profession and destroying the medical system to which he'd dedicated his life. His eyes were pinched at the corners. He frequently licked his lips. Stress lent a gray tint to his pallor. Unfortunately for his peace of mind, he seemed to be a bright man who would not much longer be able to delude himself into believing that the quicksand under his feet was actually solid ground.

Although he was not Duncan Whistler's personal internist, Dr. O'Brien had been the physician on duty when Dunny had gone flatline. He had overseen resuscitation procedures and had made the final call to cease heroic efforts. The death certificate carried his signature.

Dr. O'Brien brought with him the complete patient file in three thickly packed folders. During their discussion, he gradually spread the entire contents across one of the tables.

They sat side by side in the orange pseudochairs, the better to review the documents together.

Dunny's coma resulted from cerebral hypoxia, a lack of adequate oxygen to the brain for an extended period of time. Results revealed on EEG scrolls and by brain-imaging tests—angiography, CT scanning, MRI—led inescapably to the conclusion that if he had ever regained consciousness, he would have been profoundly handicapped.

"Even among patients in the deepest comas," O'Brien explained, "where there's little or no apparent activity in the cerebrum, there is usually enough function in the brain stem to allow them to exhibit some automatic responses. They continue to breathe unaided. Once in a while they might cough, blink their eyes, even yawn."

Throughout most of his hospitalization, Dunny had breathed on his own. Three days ago, his declining automatic responses required that he be connected to a ventilator. He'd no longer been able to breathe without mechanical assistance.

In his early weeks at the hospital, although deeply comatose, he had at times coughed, sneezed, yawned, blinked. Occasionally he had even exhibited roving eye movements.

Gradually, those automatic responses declined in frequency until they ceased to be observed at all. This suggested a steady loss of function in the lower brain stem.

The previous morning, Dunny's heart had stopped. Defibrillation and injections of epinephrine restarted the heart, but only briefly.

CHAPTER 51

Corky parked on the wrong street and walked two blocks through the cold rain to the home of the three-eyed freak.

Windier than Monday's storm, this one snapped weak fronds off queen palms, tumbled an empty plastic trash can down the center of the street, tore a window awning and loudly flapped the loose length of forest-green canvas.

Melaleucas lashed their willowy branches as though trying to whip themselves to pieces. Stone pines were stripped of dead brown needles that bristled through the churning air and gave it the power to prick, to blind.

As Corky walked, a dead rat bobbed past him on the racing water in the gutter. The lolling head rolled toward him, revealing one dark empty socket and one milky eye.

The grand and lovely spectacle made him wish that he had time to join in the celebration of disorder, to spread some prankish chaos of his own. He longed to poison a few trees, stuff mailboxes with hate literature, spread nails under the tires of parked cars, set a house afire. . . .

This was a busy day of a different kind, however, and he had numerous scheduled tasks to which he must attend. Monday he had been a devilish rascal, an amusing imp of nihilism, but this day he must be a serious soldier of anarchy.

The neighborhood was an eclectic mix of two-story Craftsman houses with raised front porches and classic single-story California bungalows that borrowed from many styles of architecture. They were maintained with evident pride, enhanced with brick walkways, picket fences, beds of flowers.

By contrast, the bungalow of the three-eyed freak sat behind a half-dead front lawn, skirted by masses of unkempt shrubbery, at the end of a cracked and hoved concrete walkway. Under the Mexican-tile roof, the filthy tangles of long-empty birds' nests dripped from the eaves, and the stucco walls were cracked, chipped, in need of paint.

The structure looked like the residence of a troll who had grown weary of living under bridges, without amenities, but who had neither the knowledge nor the industry, nor the sense of pride, needed to maintain a house.

Corky rang the doorbell, which produced not sweet chimes but the sputtering racket of a broken, corroded mechanism.

He loved this place.

Because Corky had called ahead and promised

money, the three-eyed freak was waiting by the door. He answered the tubercular cough of the bell even before the sound finished grating on Corky's ear.

Yanking the door open, looming, one great grizzled grimace with a pendulous gut and size-thirteen bare feet, wearing gray sweat pants and a Megadeth concert T-shirt, Ned Hokenberry said, "You look like a damn mustard pot."

"It's raining," Corky observed.

"You look like a pimple on Godzilla's ass."

"If you're worried about getting the carpet wet—"

"Hell, scuzzy as this carpet is, a bunch of pukin'-drunk hobos with bad bladders couldn't do it any harm."

Hokenberry turned away, lumbering into the living room. Corky stepped inside and closed the door behind himself.

The carpet looked as if previously it had been wall-to-wall in a barn.

Should the day arrive when mahogany-finish Formica furniture with green-and-blue-striped polyester upholstery became prized by collectors and museums, Hokenberry would be a wealthy man. The two best items in the living room were a recliner littered with crushed corn chips and a big-screen TV.

The small windows were half covered by drapes. No lamps were aglow; only the TV screen cast light.

Corky was comfortable with the gloom. In spite

of his affinity for chaos, he hoped never to see the interior of this house in bright light.

"The last batch of information you gave me checks out, as far as I'm able to check it," Corky said, "and it's really been helpful."

"Told you I know the estate better than that candy-ass actor knows his own dick."

Until he'd been dismissed, with generous severance pay, for leaving prank messages on the answering machine that his employer had dedicated to phone calls from the dead, Ned Hokenberry had been a security guard at Palazzo Rospo.

"You say they got a new security chief. I can't guarantee he didn't change some procedures."

"I understand."

"You have my twenty thousand?"

"I have it right here." Corky withdrew his right arm from the voluminous sleeve of the slicker, and reached to an interior pocket for the packet of cash, his second payment to Hokenberry.

Even framed by the snugly buttoned yellow collar of his slicker and the drooping yellow brim of his rain hat, Corky's face must have revealed more of his contempt than he intended.

Hokenberry's bloodshot eyes blurred with self-pity, and his doughy face kneaded itself into more and deeper folds as he said, "I wasn't always a sorry damn wreck, you know. Didn't used to have this gut. Shaved every day, cleaned up real nice. Front lawn used to be green. Bein' fired by that son of a bitch is what ruined me."

archic survivalist with deep ties to an aggressive
group of anti-veal activists who manufactured the
suppressors both for their own use and as a fund-
raising activity. Each of the shots made a quiet
sound like someone pronouncing the word *supper*
with a lisp.

This was the weapon with which he had shot
Rolf Reynerd's mother in the foot.

Considering Hokenberry's intimidating size,
Corky hadn't trusted the ice pick to do the job.

He moved closer to the beef and shot him three
more times, just to be certain no punch remained
in Rocky and Bullwinkle.

CHAPTER 52

Two windows presented a solvent sky and a city dissolving in drips, drizzles, and vapors.

Most of the large records room at Our Lady of Angels was divided into aisles by tall banks of filing cabinets. Near the windows lay a more open area with four work stations, and people were busy at two.

Dr. O'Brien settled at one of the unused stations and switched on the computer. Ethan pulled up a chair beside him.

Inserting a DVD into the computer, the physician said, "Mr. Whistler began to experience difficulty breathing three days ago. He needed to be put on a ventilator, and he was moved into the intensive care unit."

When the DVD was accessed, WHISTLER, DUNCAN EUGENE appeared on the screen with Dunny's patient number and other vital information that had been collected by the admissions office.

"While he was in the ICU," O'Brien continued, "his respiration, heartbeat, and brain function were continuously monitored and sent by telemetry to the unit nurses' station. That's always been standard procedure." He used the mouse to click on a series of icons and numbered choices. "The rest is relatively new. The system digitally records data collected by the electronic monitoring devices during the patient's entire stay in the ICU. For later review."

Ethan figured they kept a digital record as evidence to defend against frivolous lawsuits.

"Here's Whistler's EEG when first admitted to the ICU at four-twenty P.M. last Friday."

An unseen stylus drew a continuous line left to right across an endlessly scrolling graph.

"These are the brain's electrical impulses as measured in microvolts," O'Brien continued.

A monotonous series of peaks and valleys depicted Dunny's brain activity. The peaks were low and wide; the valleys were comparatively steep and narrow.

"Delta waves are the typical pattern of normal sleep," O'Brien explained. "These are delta waves but not those associated with an ordinary night's rest. These peaks are broader and much lower than common delta waves, with a smoother oscillation into and out of the troughs. The electrical impulses are few in number, attenuated, weak. This is Whistler in a deep coma. Okay. Now let's fast-forward to the evening of the day before his death."

"Sunday night."

"Yes."

On the screen, as hours of monitoring flew past in a minute, the uncommon delta waves blurred and jumped slightly, but only slightly because the variation from wave to wave was minuscule. An hour of compressed data, viewed in seconds, closely resembled any minute of the same data studied in real time.

Indeed, the sameness of the patterns was so remarkable that Ethan would not have realized how many hours—days—of data were streaming by if there hadn't been a time display on the screen.

"The event occurred at one minute before midnight, Sunday," O'Brien said.

He clicked back to real-time display, and the fast-forwarding stopped at 11:23:22, Sunday night. He speeded the data again in two quick spurts, until he reached 11:58:09.

"Less than a minute now."

Ethan found himself leaning forward in his chair.

Shatters of rain clattered against the windowpanes, as though the wind, in wounded anger, had spat out broken teeth.

One of the people at the other work stations had left the room.

The remaining woman murmured into her phone. Her voice was soft, singsong, slightly spooky, as might be the voices that left messages on the answering machine that served Line 24.

"Here," said Dr. O'Brien.

At 11:59, the lazy, variant delta waves began to spike violently into something different: sharp, irregular peaks and valleys.

"These are beta waves, quite extreme beta waves. The low, very fast oscillation indicates that the patient is concentrating on an external stimulus."

"What stimulus?" Ethan asked.

"Something he sees, hears, feels."

"External? What can he see, hear, or feel in a coma?"

"This isn't the wave pattern of a man in a coma. This is a fully conscious, alert, and disturbed individual."

"And it's a machine malfunction?"

"A couple people here think it has to be machine error. But . . ."

"You disagree."

O'Brien hesitated, staring at the screen. "Well, I shouldn't get ahead of the story. First . . . when the ICU nurse saw this coming in by telemetry, she went directly to the patient, thinking he'd come out of his coma. But he remained slack, unresponsive."

"Could he have been dreaming?" Ethan asked.

O'Brien shook his head emphatically. "The wave patterns of dreamers are distinctive and easily recognizable. Researchers have identified four stages of sleep, and a different signature wave for each stage. None of them is like this."

The beta waves began to spike higher and lower than before. The peaks and valleys were mere needle points instead of the former rugged plateaus, with precipitous slopes between them.

"The nurse summoned a doctor," O'Brien said.

"That doctor called in another. No one observed any physical evidence that Whistler had ascended by any degree from deep coma. The ventilator still handled respiration. Heart was slow, slightly irregular. Yet according to the EEG, his brain produced the beta waves of a conscious, alert person."

"And you said 'disturbed.' "

The beta tracery on the screen jittered wildly up and down, valleys growing narrower, the distance between the apex and nadir of each pattern increasing radically, until it was reminiscent of the patterns produced on a seismograph during a major earthquake.

"At some points you might accurately say he appears 'disturbed,' at others 'excited,' and in this passage you're watching now, I'd say without any concern about being melodramatic, that these are the brain waves of a terrified individual."

"Terrified?"

"Thoroughly."

"Nightmare?" Ethan suggested.

"A nightmare is just a dream of a darker variety. It can produce radical wave patterns, but they're nevertheless recognizable as those of a dream. Nothing like this."

O'Brien speeded the flow of data again, forwarding through eight minutes' worth in a few seconds.

When the screen returned to real-time display, Ethan said, "This looks the same . . . yet different."

"These are still the beta waves of a conscious person, and I would say this guy is still frightened, although the terror may have declined here to high anxiety."

The serpent-voiced wind, singing in a language of hiss-shriek-moan, and the claw-tap of rain on window glass seemed to be the perfect music to accompany the jagged images on the screen.

"Although the overall pattern remains one of conscious anxiety," Dr. O'Brien continued, "within it are these irregular subsets of higher spikes, each followed by a subset of lower spikes."

He pointed at the screen, calling examples to Ethan's attention.

"I see them," Ethan said. "What do they mean?"

"They're indicative of conversation."

"Conversation? He's talking to himself?"

"First of all, he isn't talking *aloud* to anyone, not even to himself, so we shouldn't be seeing these patterns."

"I understand. I think."

"But what these represent is not arguable. During the subsets of higher spikes, the subject should be speaking. During the subsets of lower spikes, he should be listening. A subject having a bit of *mental* give-and-take with himself, even when he's awake, produces no such subsets. After all, for one thing, when you're talking to yourself, conducting a little interior debate—"

"Technically, you're always talking," Ethan said. "You're both sides of the debate. You're never really listening."

"Exactly. These subsets are indicative of *con-*

scious conversation between this individual and another person."

"What other person?"

"I don't know."

"He's in a coma."

"Yes."

Frowning, Ethan said, "Then how is he talking to anyone? By telepathy?"

"Do we believe in telepathy?" O'Brien asked.

"I don't."

"Neither do I."

"Then why couldn't this be a malfunctioning machine?" Ethan wondered.

O'Brien accelerated the data flow until the brain-wave patterns disappeared from the screen, replaced by the words DATA INTERRUPT.

"They took Whistler off the EEG, the one they thought must be malfunctioning," the doctor said. "They connected him to a different machine. The switchover took six minutes."

He fast-forwarded through the gap, until the patterns appeared once more.

"They look the same on the new machine," Ethan said.

"Yeah, they are. Beta waves representing consciousness, lots of anxiety, and with subsets suggesting vigorous conversation."

"A second malfunctioning machine?"

"There's one holdout who still thinks so. Not me. These wave patterns ran nineteen minutes on the first EEG, apparently for six minutes between hookups, and then thirty-one minutes on the second machine. Fifty-six minutes total before they abruptly stopped."

"How do you explain it?" Ethan asked.

Instead of answering him, O'Brien worked the keyboard, calling up a second display of data, which appeared above the first: another moving white line on the blue background, spiking from left to right. In this case, all the spikes were above the base line, none below.

"This is Whistler's respiration synchronized with the brain-wave data," O'Brien said. "Each spike is an inhalation. Exhalation takes place between spikes."

"Very regular."

"Very. Because the ventilator is breathing for him."

The physician tapped the keys again, and a third display shared the screen with the first two.

"This is heart function. Standard three-phase action. Diastole, atrial systole, ventricular systole. Slow but not too slow. Weak but not too weak. Slight irregularities, but nothing dangerous. Now look here at the brain waves."

The beta waves were doing the earthquake jitterbug once more.

Ethan said, "He's terrified again."

"In my opinion, yes. Yet there's no change in heart function. It's the same slow, somewhat weak beat with tolerable irregularities, exactly his deep-coma pattern ever since he was first admitted to the hospital almost three months ago. He's in a state of terror . . . yet his heart is calm."

"The heart's calm because he's comatose. Right?"

"Wrong. Even in a profound coma, Mr. Truman, there isn't this complete disconnect between the mind and body. When you're having a nightmare, the terror is imagined, not real, but heart function is affected just the same. The heart races during a nightmare."

For a moment, Ethan studied the violently jumping beta waves and compared them to the slow, steady heartbeat. "After fifty-six minutes of this, his brain activity returned to the long, slow delta waves?"

"That's right. Until he died the next morning."

"So if it's not two machines malfunctioning, how do you explain all of this, Doctor?"

"I don't. I can't. You asked me if there was anything unusual in the patient's file. Specifically, something . . . *uncanny*."

"Yes, but—"

"I don't have a dictionary handy, but I believe *uncanny* means something not normal, something extraordinary, something that can't be explained. I can only tell you what happened, Mr. Truman, not a damn thing about *why*."

Tongues of rain licked the windows.

With snuffle, growl, and keening petition, the wolfish wind begged entry.

Across the fabled city rolled a low protracted rumble.

Ethan and O'Brien looked toward the windows, and Ethan supposed that the physician, too, had envisioned a terrorist attack somewhere, women and babies murdered by the fascistic Islamic radicals who fed on wickedness and crawled the modern world with demon determination.

They listened to the sound slowly fade, and finally Dr. O'Brien said with relief, "Thunder."

"Thunder," Ethan agreed.

Thunder and lightning were not common to storms in southern California. This peal, in place of bomb blast, suggested a turbulent day ahead.

Beta waves, as jagged as lightning, struck repeatedly across the computer screen.

Comatose, Dunny had experienced a terrifying encounter that had occurred neither in this world nor in the land of dreams, but in some realm mysterious. He had engaged in a conversation without spoken words, as if he'd breathed in a ghost that had traveled to his lungs and thence into his arteries, by blood from heart to brain, there to haunt him in the shadowy rooms of his mind for fifty-six minutes.

CHAPTER 53

Like an Arab sheik in yellow kaffiyeh and yellow cloak, brought here by the rubbing of a lamp and the magic of a genie, Corky Laputa was a bright whirl in the otherwise dismal house of the three-eyed freak.

Singing "Reunited" and then "Shake Your Groove Thing," both Peaches and Herb hits, he searched these cluttered chambers, rating them on a crud scale—cruddy, cruddier, cruddiest—as he sought what might remain of the first twenty thousand dollars that he had given Hokenberry a few weeks ago.

The beefy one might have written Corky's name in an address book, on an index card—even on a wall, considering how much these shabby walls resembled those of the grungiest public restroom. Corky didn't care about that. He hadn't given Hokenberry his real name, anyway.

Surely, with a memory about as reliable as that of a chuck steak, Hokenberry had scribbled Corky's phone number on a piece of paper somewhere in the bungalow. Corky wasn't worried about that, ei-

or meaning. He believed only in the power of chaos.

Nonetheless, he chose to believe that the thunder should be taken as an omen, signifying that his trip this coming evening to Palazzo Rospo would unfold as planned and that he would return to his home with the sedated boy.

The universe might be a dumb machine, clattering nowhere but moving fast, with no purpose other than its own eventual cataclysmic destruction. Yet even so, it might from time to time cast off a bolt or a broken gear from which a thoughtful person could foretell its next turn of direction. The thunder was such a broken gear, and based upon the timbre and duration of it, Corky confidently predicted the success of his scheme.

If the biggest movie star in the world, living behind fortified walls and an electronic moat, with full-time security and bodyguards, could not keep his family safe, if the only son of the Face could be plucked from his Bel Air estate and spirited away, even though the actor had been explicitly warned by the delivery of six packages wrapped in black, then no family was safe *anywhere*. Neither the poor nor the rich. Neither the unknown nor the famous. Neither the godless nor the God-fearing.

That message would penetrate the public hour by hour, day by grueling day, as Channing Manheim's long and excruciating ordeal unfolded.

Corky intended first to destroy the captive boy emotionally, then mentally, and last of all physically. He would videotape this process, which he expected to take weeks. He would edit the tape, make copies on equipment that he had acquired for this project, and periodically pepper selected publications and television-news operations with evidence of Aelfric's brutalization.

Certain media would be loath to show any of the video or even still frames from it, but others would recognize the competitive advantage of acting without conscience or taste, and with noble words would justify a plunge into the grossly sensational. Thereafter, some of the squeamish would do likewise.

The boy's terror-stricken face would haunt the nation, and yet another blow in a long series would be struck at the foundations of America's order and stability. Millions of citizens would be robbed of their already shaky sense of security.

Two streets from Hokenberry's bungalow, as Corky approached his BMW, a lance of lightning pierced the clouds, thunder cracked, and a boil in the heavens burst. Rain that had drizzled suddenly fell by the ton, weight enough to press half the huff out of the wind.

If thunder alone had been an omen of his triumph, more thunder preceded by lightning was confirmation that he'd properly interpreted that first rolling peal.

The sky blazed again, and growled. Fat leaf-snapping droplets of cold rain roared through the trees and pounded, *pounded* the pavement.

For a sweet half-minute, Corky capered like

Gene Kelly, singing "Shake Your Groove Thing," not caring who might see him.

Then he got in the car and drove away from there, for he had much work to do on this most important day of his life to date.

CHAPTER 54

As Ethan waited for music that would wither the soul and for the hospital elevator that would bring it, his cell phone rang.

"Where are you?" Hazard Yancy asked.

"Our Lady of Angels. About to leave."

"You in the garage?"

"On my way down now."

"Upper or lower level?"

"Upper."

"What're you driving?"

"A white Expedition, like yesterday."

"Wait there. We have to talk." Hazard hung up.

Ethan rode the elevator alone and without music. Apparently the sound system was malfunctioning. Nothing but hiss-pop-crackle came from the ceiling speaker.

He had descended one floor when he thought that he detected a faint voice behind the static. Quickly it became less faint, though still too weak to convey meaning.

By the time he traveled three floors, he convinced himself that this was the eerie voice to which he had listened for half an hour on the phone the previous night. He had been so intent on understanding what it was saying that he'd fallen into something like a trance.

Drifting down from the ceiling speaker, in a fall of static as soft as snow, came his name. He heard it as if from a great distance but distinctly.

"Ethan . . . Ethan . . ."

On a foggy winter day at the beach or harbor, sea gulls in flight, high in muffling mist, sometimes called to one another with two-syllable cries that seemed part alarm and part searching signal issued in mournful hope of a reply, the most forlorn sound in the world. This call of *"Ethan, Ethan,"* as though echoing down to a ravine from a lofty peak, had that same quality of melancholy and urgency.

Listening to gulls, however, he had never imagined that he heard his name in their desolate voices. Nor had he ever thought that their plaints in the fog sounded like Hannah, as the far voice behind the speaker static sounded like her now.

She no longer called his name, but she cried out something not quite decipherable. Her tone was the same that you might use to shout a warning at a man standing on a sidewalk in complete ignorance of a terrible weight of broken cornice falling toward him from atop the building at his back.

Between the lobby and the upper level of the garage, half a floor from his destination, Ethan pressed STOP on the control panel. The cab braked, sagging slightly and rebounding on its cables.

Even if this was indeed a voice speaking to him—and to him alone—through the overhead speaker, rather than proof of mental imbalance, he couldn't allow himself to be hypnotized by it as he had been on the phone.

He thought of fogbound nights and the unwary sailors who heard the singing of the Lorelei. They turned their ships toward her voice, seeking to understand the alluring promise of her words, steered onto her rock, wrecked their vessels, and drowned.

This voice was more likely to be that of the Lorelei than that of his lost Hannah. To desire what is forever beyond reach, to seek it in disregard of reason, is the fateful rock in an endless fog.

Anyway, he hadn't brought the elevator to a halt in order to puzzle out the words of the might-be warning. Heart knocking, he pressed STOP because he'd suddenly been overcome with the conviction that when the doors slid open, the garage would not lie beyond them.

Crazily, he expected thick fog and black water. Or a precipice and a yawning abyss. The voice would be out there, beyond the water, beyond the chasm, and he would have nowhere to go but toward it.

In another elevator, Monday afternoon, ascending toward Dunny's apartment, he had been stricken by claustrophobia.

Here again, the four walls crowded closer than

old girl that's all over the news, no time for anything else."

"Man, the world gets sicker by the week."

"By the hour. Otherwise, we'd be unemployed. They call Mina Reynerd's case Vamp and the Lamp 'cause in pictures of her when she was younger, she looked like one of those vamps in the old movies, like Theda Bara or Jean Harlow. The file is strictly on Kesselman's desk, along with other active cases."

"So even after Christmas, he might not get to it first thing."

Hazard stared at the concrete wall beyond the windshield, as if stocking a menagerie of his own. Maybe he saw gazelles and kangaroos. More likely, he could not avoid seeing battered children, strangled women, the bodies of men torn by gunfire.

Memories of innocent victims. His ghost family. Always with him. They were as real to him as the badge he carried, more real than the pension that he might never live to collect.

"After Christmas isn't soon enough," Hazard said. "I had this dream."

Ethan looked at him, waited. Then: "What dream?"

Rolling his Paul Bunyan shoulders, shifting on the seat to gain legroom, looking as uncomfortable as Babe the Blue Ox in a canary cage, Hazard stared at the concrete wall while he said matter-of-factly, "You were with me in Reynerd's apartment. He shot you in the gut. Next, we're in an ambulance. You're not gonna make it. They have these Christmas decorations in the ambulance. Tinsel, little bells. You ask me for a set of the bells. I take one set down, try to give them to you, but you're gone, you're dead."

Ethan turned his attention to the parking-garage wall once more. Among the decomposing corpses that his imagination identified in the stains and subtleties of texture, he expected to see his own face.

"I wake up," Hazard continued, still focused on the mottled concrete, "there's someone in the room with me. Standing over the bed. A darker shape in the dark. Some guy. I'm up, I'm at him, but he's not there. Now he's across the room. I go after him. He moves. He's quick. He doesn't walk, he like *glides*. My piece is in my holster, hanging on a chair. I get it. He keeps moving, quick, too quick, gliding, like he's playing with me. We circle the room. I get to a light switch, click on a lamp. He's at my closet doors, his back to me. Mirrored closet doors. He walks into the mirror. Disappears into the mirror."

"This is still the dream," Ethan suggested.

"I told you, *I wake up,* there's someone in the room with me," Hazard reminded him. "I didn't get a good look at him, his back to me, just a glimpse in the mirror, but I think it was Dunny Whistler. I open the closet door. He's not in there. Where is he—in the damn *mirror*?"

"Sometimes in a dream," Ethan said, "you wake

up, but the waking up is just part of the nightmare, and you're really still dreaming."

"I search the apartment. Don't find anybody. Back in the bedroom what I *do* find are these."

Ethan heard the sweet silvery ringing of small bells.

He looked away from the concrete wall.

Hazard held up an array of three concentrically strung bells like those that had hung in the ambulance.

Their eyes met.

Ethan knew that Hazard had instantly read not the nature of his secrets but certainly the fact that he *had* secrets.

The astonishing things that had happened to Ethan in less than thirty hours, and now also to Hazard, plus the inexplicable case of dead Dunny walking and possibly orchestrating the murder of Reynerd: All this had to be connected somehow to the contents of the six black boxes and the threat against Manheim.

"What aren't you telling me," Hazard demanded.

After a long pause, Ethan said, "I have a set of bells, too."

"You get yours in a dream like I did?"

"I got mine just before I died in an ambulance late yesterday afternoon."

CHAPTER 55

Free of both insipid music and voices from Beyond, four flights of stairs led down to the lowest of the three subterranean levels of the hospital.

Ethan and Hazard followed the familiar, brightly lighted white corridor past the garden room to a set of double doors. Beyond lay the ambulance garage.

Among other vehicles belonging to the hospital, four van-type ambulances stood side by side. Empty parking stalls suggested that additional units in the fleet were at work in the rainy day.

Ethan went to the nearest ambulance. He hesitated, then opened the rear door.

Inside, red tinsel was strung at the ceiling along both the left and right sides of the compartment. Six clusters of tiny bells hung here, as well, one set at the beginning, another at the middle, and a third at the end of each garland of tinsel.

At the second ambulance, Hazard said, "Here."

Ethan joined him at the open back door.

Two lengths of red tinsel. Only five sets of bells. The missing set, in the middle of the right-hand gar-

"We're wondering what happened to them."

Puzzlement worked Sheen's face into a squint. "You are? Those little bells? Don't recall anything happening to them during my watch. Maybe one of the guys on another shift could help you."

At a glance from Hazard, Ethan shrugged. Hazard slammed shut the ambulance door.

Sheen's puzzlement resolved into amazement. "You don't mean they send two detectives 'cause maybe someone stole a two-dollar Christmas ornament?"

Neither Ethan nor Hazard had an answer for that.

Sheen should have let it go then, but like a lot of people these days, his ignorance of the true nature of a cop's work allowed him to feel smugly superior to anyone with a badge. "What's it take to get a kitten out of a tree—a SWAT team?"

Hazard said, "The missing ornament isn't simply a matter of two dollars, is it, Detective Truman?"

"No," Ethan agreed, falling into their old rhythm, "it's the principle of the thing. And it's a hate crime."

"Definitely a felony hate crime under the California Criminal Code," Hazard deadpanned.

"For the duration of the season," Ethan said, "we're assigned to the Ornament and Manger Scene Defacement Response Team."

"That's a division," Hazard added, "of the Christmas Spirit Task Force established pursuant to the Anti-Hate Act of 2001."

A tentative smile crept across Sheen's face as he

cocked his head first at Ethan, then at Hazard. "You're goofing me, right, doing *Dragnet*."

Employing the intense and disapproving stare with which he could wither everything from hard-case thugs to flower arrangements, Hazard said, "Are you a Christian hater, Mr. Sheen?"

Sheen's creeping smile froze before it fully formed. "What?"

"Do you," Ethan asked, "believe in freedom of religion or are you one of those who think the United States Constitution guarantees you freedom *from* religion?"

Blinking the smile out of his eyes, licking it off his lips, the paramedic said, "Sure, of course, freedom of religion, who doesn't believe in it?"

"If we were to obtain a warrant to search your residence right now," Hazard said, "would we find a collection of anti-Christian hate literature, Mr. Sheen?"

"What? Me? I don't hate anybody. I'm a get-along guy. What're you talking about?"

"Would we find bomb-making materials?" Ethan asked.

As Sheen's smirk had frozen and cracked apart under Hazard's cold stare, so now the color drained from his face, leaving him as gray as the unpainted concrete walls of the ambulance garage.

Backing away from Hazard and Ethan, raising his hands as if to call a time-out, Sheen said, "What is this? Are you serious? This is crazy. What—there's a two-dollar Christmas ornament missing, so I should get a lawyer?"

"If you have one," Hazard said solemnly, "maybe you'd be smart to give him a call."

Still not sure what to believe, Sheen backed away another step, two, then pivoted from them and hurried toward the dayroom in which ambulance crews waited to be dispatched.

"SWAT team, my ass," Hazard grumbled.

Ethan smiled. "You da man."

"*You* da man."

Ethan had forgotten how much easier life could be with backup, especially backup with a sense of humor.

"You should rejoin the force," Hazard said as they crossed the garage toward the doors to the garden-room corridor. "We could save the world, have some fun."

On the stairs to the upper level of the public garage, Ethan said, "Supposing all this craziness stops sooner or later—being gut shot but not, the bells, the voice on the phone, a guy walking into your closet mirror. You think it's possible just to go back to the usual cop stuff like nothing strange ever happened?"

"What am I supposed to do—become a monk?"

"Seems like this ought to . . . change things."

"I'm happy who I am," Hazard said. "I'm already as cool as cool gets. Don't you think I'm cool to the chromosomes?"

"You're walking ice."

"Not to say I don't have heat."

"Not to say," Ethan agreed.

"I've got plenty of heat."

"You're so cool, you're hot."

"Exactly. So there's no reason for me to change unless maybe I meet Jesus, and He slaps me upside the head."

They weren't in a graveyard, weren't whistling, but the tenor of their words, echoing off the crypt-cold walls of the stairwell, brought to Ethan's mind old movie images of boys masking their fear with bravado as they journeyed through a cemetery at high mid night.

CHAPTER 56

On a grindstone of self-denial, with the diligence of a true obsessive, Brittina Dowd had sharpened herself into a long thin blade. When she walked, her clothes seemed certain to be cut to shreds by the scissoring movement of her body.

Her hips had been honed until they were almost as fragile as bird bones. Her legs resembled those of a flamingo. Her arms had no more substance than wings stripped of their feathers. Brittina seemed to be determined to whittle herself until a brisk breeze could carry her aloft, high into the realm of wren and sparrow.

She was not a single blade, in fact, but an entire Swiss Army knife with all its cutting edges and pointed tools deployed.

Corky Laputa might have loved her if she had not also been ugly.

Although he didn't love Brittina, he made love to her. The disorder into which she had shaped her skeletal body thrilled him. This was like making love to Death.

Only twenty-six, she had assiduously prepared herself for early-onset osteoporosis, as though she yearned to be shattered in a fall, reduced to fragments as completely as a crystal vase knocked off a shelf onto a stone floor.

In their passion, Corky always expected to be punctured by one of her knees or elbows, or to hear Brittina crack apart beneath him.

"Do me," she said, "do me," and managed to make it sound less like an invitation to sex than like a request for assisted suicide.

Her bed was narrow, suitable only for a sleeper who did not toss and turn, who lay as unmoving as the average occupant of a casket, by far too narrow for the wild rutting of which they both were capable.

She had furnished the room with a single bed because she'd never had a lover and had expected to remain a virgin. Corky had romanced her as easily as he could have crushed a hummingbird in his fist.

The narrow bed stood in a room on the top floor of a narrow two-story Victorian house. The lot was deep but too narrow to qualify as a residential building site under current city codes.

Almost sixty years ago, just after the war, an eccentric dog fancier had designed and built the curious place. He lived in it with two greyhounds and two whippets.

Eventually he'd been paralyzed by a stroke. After several days passed during which their master had not fed them, the starving dogs ate him.

That had been forty years ago. The subsequent history of this residence at times had been as colorful and on occasion nearly as grisly as the life and ghastly death of its first owner.

The vibe of the house caught Brittina's attention just like the high-frequency shriek of a dog whistle might have pricked the ears of a whippet. She'd purchased it with a portion of an inheritance that she received from her paternal grandmother.

Brittina was a graduate student at the same university that had provided multigeneration employment for the Laputa family. In another eighteen months, she would earn a doctorate in American literature, which she largely despised.

Although she had not blown her entire inheritance on the house, she needed to supplement her investment income with other revenue. She had served as a graduate assistant to keep herself in chocolate-flavored Slim-Fast and ipecac.

Then, six months ago, Channing Manheim's personal assistant had approached the chairperson of the university's English department to explain that a new tutor would be required for the famous actor's son. Only academicians of the highest caliber need apply.

The chairperson consulted Corky, who was vice-chairperson of the department, and Corky recommended Ms. Dowd.

He'd known that she would be hired because, first of all, the idiot movie star would be impressed by her dramatic appearance. Cadaverous paleness, a gaunt face, and the body of an anorexic nun would be seen as proof that Brittina cared little for the pleasures of the flesh, that she enjoyed largely a life of the mind, that she was therefore a genuine intellectual.

In the entertainment business, only image mattered. Manheim would believe, therefore, that appearance equaled reality in other professions, as well.

Furthermore, Brittina Dowd was an intellectual snob who peppered her speech with academic jargon more impenetrable than the lab-speak of microbiologists. If the young woman's emaciation didn't convince the movie star of her intellectual credentials, her big words would.

The evening before Brittina went to her job interview, Corky poured on charm as thick as clotted cream, and she at once proved to be famished not only for food but also for flattery. She allowed herself to indulge her appetite for adoration, and Corky bedded her then for the first time.

Ultimately, she became Aelfric Manheim's tutor in English and literature, making regularly scheduled visits to Palazzo Rospo.

Prior to this, Rolf Reynerd and Corky had discussed, in general terms, the blow that might be struck in the name of social disorder by proving that even a celebrity of worldwide renown was vulnerable to the agents of chaos. They had not been able to settle on an ideal target until Corky's lover was hired by Channing Manheim.

From Brittina, in bed and out, Corky had learned much about the Manheim estate. Indeed, she dis-

CHAPTER 57

During the years they'd been official partners, Ethan and Hazard had gone by the book as much as it is ever possible to go by a book that is written largely by people who have never done the job.

On this December day, however, unofficially partners once more, they were bad boys. Being bad boys made Ethan uneasy, but it gave him the comforting feeling that at least they were taking control of the situation.

A notice on Rolf Reynerd's door warned that Apartment 2B was the site of an ongoing police investigation. The premises remained off-limits to all but authorized personnel of the police department and the district attorney's office.

They ignored the warning.

The deadbolt lock on Rolf Reynerd's apartment door was covered with a police seal. Ethan cracked it, peeled it.

Hazard had with him a Lockaid lock-release gun, an item sold exclusively to law-enforcement agencies. In ordinary circumstances, he would have

requisitioned this device with the proper paperwork, specifying the exact intended use, virtually
always with reference to an existing search warrant.

These were not ordinary circumstances.

Hazard had gotten his hands on one of the department's Lockaids by unconventional means. He
would be walking a razor's edge between righteousness and ruin until he returned the device to
the equipment locker where it belonged.

"When you're up against some mojo man who
fades into mirrors," he said, "your ass is hanging
over a cliff anyway."

Hazard slid the thin pick of the Lockaid into the
key channel of the deadbolt, under the pin tum-
blers. He squeezed the trigger four times before
the steel spring in the gun managed to lodge all
the pins at the shear line and thereby fully disen-
gage the lock.

Ethan followed Hazard into the apartment, closing the door behind them. He tried to step around
and over the stains—Reynerd's blood—that
marred the white carpet just inside the threshold.

He had spilled rivers of his own blood on this
carpet. Died on it. The experience rose in memory,
too vivid to have been a dream.

The black-and-white furnishings, art, and decorations proved to be as he remembered them.

On the walls, a flock of pigeons was frozen in
midwhirl. Like white chalk checks on gray slate,
geese flew across a somber sky, and a parliament

of owls perched on a barn roof, deliberating over the fate of mice.

Hazard had been present the previous night during the first search of the apartment. He knew what had been collected as possible evidence and what had been left behind.

He went directly to that corner of the living room in which stood a black-lacquered desk with faux-ivory drawer pulls. "What we need is probably here," he said, and searched the drawers from top to bottom.

Crows on an iron fence, an eagle on a rock, a fierce-eyed heron as prehistoric as a pterodactyl: All peered into this living room from other times, other places.

Paranoid and unashamed of it, Ethan sensed that when he looked away from the large photographs, the birds therein turned their heads to watch him, all aware that he ought to be dead and that the man who had collected their images should be alive to admire them.

"Here," Hazard said, withdrawing a shoebox from one of the desk drawers. "Bank statements, canceled checks."

They sat at the stainless-steel and black-Formica dinette table to review Reynerd's financial records.

Beside the table: a window. Beyond the window: the tumultuous day, entirely in shades of gray, wind-whipped, awash, now without the thunder and lightning, yet still foreboding, dark and dire.

The light proved too dim to facilitate their work.

Hazard got up and switched on the small black-and-white ceramic chandelier over the table.

Eleven bundles of checks had been bound with rubber bands, one for each month of the current year from January through November. The canceled checks from the current month would not be forwarded by the bank until mid-January.

When they finished, they would have to return everything to the shoebox and replace the box in the desk drawer exactly as Hazard found it. Sam Kesselman, the detective assigned to Mina Reynerd's murder, would no doubt review these same checks when he recovered from the flu, returned to work after Christmas, and read the dead actor's partial screenplay.

If they waited for Kesselman, however, Channing Manheim might by then be dead. And Ethan, too.

They needed to look through only those checks written in the first eight months of the year, prior to Mina Reynerd's murder.

Hazard took four months' worth of checks. He pushed four packets across the table to Ethan.

In the screenplay, an out-of-work and underappreciated actor had taken an acting class at a university, where he'd met a professor with whom he had devised a scheme to kill the biggest movie star in the world. If the fictional academic had been inspired by a murderous professor in real life, a tuition check might suggest an institution of higher learning at which the search should begin.

Soon they discovered that Rolf Reynerd had been a fiend for continuing education. His entries hind evidence that would convict him of murder. Semen, hair, fingerprints—all must be eliminated.

From the day that he'd begun visiting this pinched place, months previously, he had gone without the latex gloves that he customarily wore at the scenes of capital crimes. Even though Brittina Dowd was nothing if not an eccentric, she would surely have grown suspicious of a lover who at all times wore surgical gloves.

Steeper and narrower stairs than any others in the house led down from the kitchen to a garage in which three of the four walls were underground. Gloom gathered here as luxuriously as ever it had coiled in any catacomb or dungeon.

Corky could almost hear a multitude of spiders plucking their silken harp strings.

Four small windows in the garage door would have admitted some sun on a classic California day. Now the gray storm gloom could not penetrate the dusty glass.

He switched on a bare bulb overhead, providing hardly enough light by which to drain the god of Zoroastrianism.

The god of Zoroastrianism is Ahura Mazda. Brittina's car was a Mazda, without the Ahura, but Corky enjoyed his little joke anyway.

From the trunk, he removed four hairspray-size aerosol cans with any one of which a stranded motorist could inflate a flat tire and at the same time seal the puncture in it. He set these aside and then took from the trunk a pair of empty two-gallon gasoline cans.

He had purchased these items for Brittina, in addition to road flares and a yellow pennant emblazoned with EMERGENCY in bold black letters, and had insisted that she keep them in the trunk of her Zoroastrian god at all times.

She had been touched by his concern and had said that diamonds would not have proved his love as surely as did these humble gifts. They were, in fact, part of his preparations to dispose of her body when the day arrived to kill her.

Corky would never deny that he could be brilliantly romantic when required, but greater than his flair for romance was his talent for meticulous preparation. Whether he was roasting a Thanksgiving turkey or murdering an inconvenient lover, or scheming to kidnap the son of the biggest movie star in the world, he approached the task with considerable thought and patience, taking all the time necessary to develop a flawless strategy as well as tactics certain to ensure success.

She had never asked why *two* fuel cans, when one would have been all that she could easily carry. He had *known* that she would not ask or even wonder, for she had been a woman of images and memes and utopian dreams, not one with an interest in math or logic.

He set the empty two-gallon cans on the floor. He fed a shorter end of rubber tubing into the fuel port of the car. A suck on the longer end was required to prime the siphon.

Much practice at this sort of thing ensured that Corky drew as little fumes into his lungs as possible and that none of Shell Oil's finest got in his mouth. The flow came quickly as he tucked the longer end into the first can.

When four gallons had been drawn and both cans filled, Corky carried the containers up to the ground floor. He left the trailing end of the siphon to spill a stream of gasoline on the garage floor.

He returned for the four aerosol cans. In the kitchen, he placed two of these on the lowest rack of the bottom oven. He left the other two on the lowest rack of the top oven.

On his way upstairs with one of the two-gallon cans, he switched off the thermostat on the main floor, and then the thermostat on the upper floor. This would prevent the electric starter from striking a spark in the natural-gas furnace and possibly triggering an explosion of accumulated gasoline fumes before Corky had left the house.

Leaving the cap on the can, pouring from the spout, he liberally splashed the pale naked body of Brittina Dowd. Her long hair offered tinder, but she didn't have much fat to feed the fire.

After pouring no more than a quart of fuel in the bathroom, he distributed perhaps half a gallon over the rumpled bedclothes. He didn't prime the two other small upstairs rooms because he'd never been in them and because he didn't need to saturate every corner to achieve the effect he wanted.

From the bedroom he drizzled an uninterrupted gasoline trail into the narrow upstairs hallway and down the stairs to the ground floor. At the bottom of the steps, he cast aside the empty can and picked up the full one.

He continued in a looping fashion through the living room and the dining room, to the kitchen doorway. There he set the can on the threshold. He unscrewed the cap and tossed it aside.

From a jacket pocket, he retrieved the black-and-red object that was about the size of a single-serving yogurt container: a chemical-action detonator.

The casing of the detonator was somewhat pliable. He shaped it into the hole that had been covered by the screw-on cap, plugging the two-gallon can in which approximately half a gallon of gasoline remained.

He popped a ring tab off the red cap. This initiated a chemical process that would rapidly generate heat and, in four minutes, an explosion fiery enough to ignite the remaining contents of the two-gallon can and the trail of fuel leading away from it to the bedroom on the second floor, to the corpse.

This would be a bad time for the doorbell to ring.

No chimes sounded, of course, because in addition to his fine strategy, solid tactics, and meticulous preparation, he could count on Laputa luck. His guardian angel was chaos, and he was always at the safe calm eye of its world-destroying force.

He returned to the ovens and latched both doors as required to initiate the self-cleaning cycle. On each he pressed a button marked CLEAN.

Heat would rapidly expand the pressurized contents

CHAPTER 59

From the more remote rooms in Palazzo Rospo, Fric gathered earthquake lights in a picnic hamper.

The mansion and the outlying buildings had been re-engineered for seismic security and retro-fitted with structural reinforcements that were supposed to ensure little or no damage even from a two-minute shaker peaking at 8.0 on the Richter scale.

Generally, 8.0 was considered to be the kiss-your-ass-good-bye number. Earthquakes that big struck only in movies.

If a humongous killer quake knocked out the city's power supply, Palazzo Rospo would be able to rely on gasoline-fueled generators in a subterranean vault that had two-foot-thick, poured-in-place, steel-reinforced walls and ceiling. Following a regional catastrophe, the mansion should remain fully lighted, the computers should continue to run, the elevators should still be operating, the refrigerators should remain cold.

In the rose garden, the carved-granite fountain of

urinating cherubs should continue to sprinkle eternally.

This backup would be less useful if heretofore unknown volcanoes erupted under Los Angeles and disgorged rivers of molten lava that turned hundreds of square miles into a smoldering wasteland or if an asteroid smashed into Bel Air. But even a star as famous and rich as Ghost Dad could not protect himself from cataclysm on a planetary scale.

If the Swiss-made generators in the bunker were disabled, then Frankenstein-castle banks of twenty-year batteries, each as big as a casket standing on end, instantly came into service. These supported limited emergency lighting, all computers, the security system, and other essential equipment for as long as ninety-six hours.

Should the city's electric power fail, should the generators be wrecked, should the giant twenty-year batteries prove useless, there were many earthquake lights distributed throughout the house. Personally, Fric figured such a series of failures was likely only in the event of an invasion of extraterrestrials with magnetic-pulse weapons.

Anyway, according to Mrs. McBee, there were 214 quake lights, which meant you could safely bet your life that there were not 213 or 215.

These small but potentially bright, battery-powered flashlights were at all times plugged into electrical outlets in the baseboard, continuously charging. If the power failed, the quake lights at once switched on, providing enough pathway illumination to allow everyone to exit safely from the mansion in the darkest hours of the deepest night. Furthermore, they could be unplugged and carried as though they were ordinary flashlights.

Like the cover plate on the electrical outlet in which it was seated, the plastic casing of each flashlight matched the color of the baseboard on which it rested: beige against limestone base-board, dark brown against mahogany, black against black marble. . . . During ordinary times, they were meant to be inconspicuous. When you lived with them day after day, you soon ceased to notice them.

No one but Mrs. McBee would be likely to realize that a dozen of those 214 were missing. Mrs. McBee wouldn't return from Santa Barbara until Thursday morning.

Nevertheless, Fric filched quake lights only from remote and little-used rooms where their disap-pearance was less likely to cause inquiry. He needed them for his deep and special secret hid-ing place.

He stowed the lights in the picnic hamper be-cause it had a hinged lid. As long as he kept the lid closed, the contents could not be seen if he unex-pectedly encountered a member of the staff.

If anyone asked what was in the hamper, he would lie and say "Sandwiches." He would tell them that he was going to camp out under a blan-ket tent in the billiards room, where he would pre-tend that he was a Blackfoot Indian living back in maybe 1880.

The whole concept of playing Blackfoot in the billiards room was monumentally stupid, of course. But most grownups believed that geeky ten-year-old boys did stupid, geeky things like that, so he would be believed, and probably pitied.

Having people pity you was better than having them think that you were as crazy as Barbra Streisand's two-headed cat.

That was one of Ghost Dad's expressions. When he thought someone didn't have both oars in the water, he said, "The guy's as crazy as Barbra Streisand's two-headed cat."

Years ago, Ghost Dad had signed a deal to make a movie directed by Barbra Streisand. Something had gone terribly wrong. Eventually, he backed out of the project.

He had never said a negative word about Ms. Streisand. But that didn't mean they were as friendly and as eager for mutual adventures as all the little animals in *The Wind in the Willows.*

In the entertainment business, everyone pretended to be friends even if maybe they hated each other's guts. They were kissy-faced, gushy-lovey, always hugging and backslapping, praising one another so convincingly that Sherlock Holmes couldn't have figured out which of them really wanted to kill which others.

According to Ghost Dad, no one in the business dared tell the truth about anyone else in the business because each of them knew that any of the others was capable of conducting a bloody vendetta of such viciousness that it would have scared the shit out of the meanest Mafioso.

Barbra Streisand didn't actually have a two-headed cat. This was just a "metaphor," as Fric's father called it, for some story element or character that she had wanted to add to her movie after Ghost Dad signed up based on a script *without* the two-headed cat.

He thought the two-headed cat was a totally crazy idea, and Ms. Streisand thought that it would win the picture a shitload of Oscars. So they agreed to disagree, kissed, hugged, swapped praise, and backed away from each other unbloodied.

This morning, in the hallway outside the kitchen, when Fric had almost told Mr. Truman about the mirror man and Moloch and all of it, he had come perilously close to being considered as crazy as Barbra Streisand's two-headed cat. He wouldn't make that mistake again.

His mother had once been committed to a booby hatch.

They would think, *Like mother, like son.*

His mother had been released after ten days.

If Fric started talking about mirror men, they would *never* let him out. Not in ten days, not in ten years.

Worse, if he were in the booby hatch, Moloch would know *exactly* where to find him. There was no place to hide in a padded cell.

Carrying the picnic hamper as if he were on an Easter-egg hunt, stealthily collecting quake lights in a back staircase, in a back hall, in the tea room, in the meditation room, Fric kept reminding himself, "Sandwiches, sandwiches," because he worried that when he finally encountered a maid or porter, he would become tongue-tied and forget what lie he had meant to tell.

By nature, he was not a good liar. In a time and place where you needed to lie merely to pass for normal, in a place and time when *he* needed to lie to survive, being a lousy liar could get him killed.

"Sandwiches, sandwiches."

He was a moronically bad liar.

And he was alone. Even with some kind of half-assed guardian angel, he was really *alone.*

Every time he passed a window, he was reminded also that the stormy day was melting away rapidly and that Moloch would most likely come in the night.

Short for his age, thin for his age, a bad liar, alone, *tick-tick-tick:* He had nothing going for him.

"Pandwiches," he muttered to himself. "Just some jellybutter-and-seanut pandwiches."

He was doomed.

"Didn't check. If I've got the true goods on my city councilman, it'll just make me squirmy, having to leave him walking around full of himself, the way he is, like he's the Lord by election, which is even more infuriating when you think how many ballot boxes his thugs stuffed for him. I'll call the lab tomorrow, the day after, whenever it is we settle the situation we're in."

"Sorry about this," Ethan said.

"If you're sorry for that nose of yours, get it fixed. Anything else you're sorry for, you shouldn't be."

"Lunch and a few mamouls didn't pay you for this much trouble."

"It wasn't *you* turned my world upside down. Some guy gives me a set of dream bells out of a nightmare, then disappears into a mirror, I tend to get shook up without your help."

Hazard reached under his jacket with both hands, tugging on his cotton sweater, and Ethan said, "You bulked up since yesterday?"

"Yeah. Had me a breakfast of Kevlar."

"Never knew you to wear protection."

"I've been thinking maybe I've dodged more bullets than any man has a right to. Doesn't mean I'm not still fearless."

"Didn't say you weren't."

"I'm scared shitless, but I'm still fearless."

"That's the right psychology."

"Survivor's psychology," Hazard said.

"Anyway, what's wrong with my nose?"

"What isn't?"

The hard rain abruptly began to fall harder, and Ethan cranked the windshield-wiper speed to the highest setting.

Hazard said, "Feels like the end of the world."

CHAPTER 61

After receiving a frantic telephone call from Captain Queeg von Hindenburg, Corky Laputa had to undertake an unexpected journey to the farther reaches of Malibu.

The man in Malibu currently called himself Jack Trotter. Trotter owned property, carried a valid driver's license, and paid as few taxes as possible under the name Felix Greene. Greene, alias Trotter, had once used the names Lewis Motherwell, Jason Barnes, Bobby Domino, and others.

When Jack-Felix-Lewis-Jason-Bobby had been born forty-four years ago, his proud parents had named him Norbert James Creezel. They had no doubt loved him and, being simple Iowa farm folk, could never have imagined that Norbert would grow up to be a wigged-out piece of work like Captain Queeg von Hindenburg.

Corky called him Captain Queeg because the guy exhibited the paranoia and megalomania to be found in the character of the same name in Herman Wouk's *The Caine Mutiny*. Von Hindenburg suited him in part because—like the German zep-pelin that had taken thirty-six to their deaths in Lakehurst, New Jersey, in 1937—he was a gasbag and, if left to his own devices, he would one day crash and burn spectacularly.

On his way to Malibu, Corky stopped at a garage that he rented in Santa Monica. This was one of forty double-stall units accessed by an alleyway in an industrial area.

He held the lease on the garage under the name Moriarity and paid the monthly bill in cash.

A black Land Rover occupied the first stall. Corky owned this vehicle under the name Kurtz Ivory International, a nonexistent but well-docu-mented corporation.

He parked the BMW beside the Land Rover, got out, put down the garage door, and switched on the lights.

Redolent of the crisp limy scent of cold concrete, the sweet-and-sour fragrance of old motor-oil stains, and the faint but still lingering astringency of insecticide from a termite fumigation that had been conducted a month ago, this drab space was, to Corky, the essence of magic and adventure. Here, like troubled Bruce Wayne in the Batcave, Corky became a dark knight, though with an agenda that might appeal more to the Joker than to Bruce in cape and tights.

In the war between Heaven and Earth, armies of rain marched across the corrugated-steel roof, raising such a battle roar that he could not have clearly heard himself singing if he'd chosen to break into "Shake Your Groove Thing."

After switching on an electric space heater, he took off his rain hat and yellow slicker. He hung them on a wall peg.

On the left side of the garage, toward the back, four tall metal lockers were bolted to the wall. Corky opened the first of these.

Two zippered vinyl wardrobe bags hung from a rod. On a shelf above the bags, a large Tupperware container held socks, neckties, a few items of men's inexpensive jewelry, a wristwatch, and other personal effects of a false identity. On the floor was a selection of shoes.

After pulling off his rain boots and a double layer of socks, after stripping to his underwear, Corky dressed in gray cords, a black turtleneck, black socks, and black Rockports.

The elaborate combination workbench and tool-storage cabinet at the back of the double garage featured a spacious secret drawer that Corky himself had designed. This drawer contained a selection of handguns and packets of false identification in six names.

Over the turtleneck, he strapped on a shoulder holster. He stuffed the holster with a 9-mm Glock.

He swapped his wallet for one that was filled with everything that he needed to hit the road as a different man: driver's license, social-security card, a couple of credit cards in his new name, and photographs of a wife and family that were entirely invented. The wallet was even preloaded with five hundred dollars in cash.

The packet also included a birth certificate, a passport, and a leather ID fold containing fake FBI credentials. For the task at hand, he required none of those items.

He did, however, take with him a second slim leather fold that contained fake but convincing credentials identifying him as an operative of the National Security Agency. This was who Queeg von Hindenburg believed him to be.

The NSA identification would reduce the average civilian to a swoon of cooperation, but wouldn't withstand determined verification by any authority. Corky would never dare flash it at a cop.

Because it was real, the driver's license in this false name could endure close scrutiny by any police officer who might stop Corky. In addition, it credited him with a spotless driving record.

Years ago, the state of California had lost control of many of its bureaucracies, including the Department of Motor Vehicles. Certain corrupted DMV employees sold tens of thousands of valid driver's licenses every year to men like Mick Sachatone, the multimillionaire anarchist who also regularly supplied Corky with disposable cell phones in fake account names.

Mick—and other middlemen like him—made substantial money by obtaining driver's licenses for illegal immigrants, for convicted felons who had served their time and who earnestly hoped to begin fresh criminal lives uninhibited by their arrest records, for chaos activists like Corky, and for many others.

Sufficiently IDed, with the Glock in a holster under his left arm, Corky shrugged into a stylish black leather coat tailored to conceal the bulge of the weapon. He tucked two spare magazines of ammunition into the coat pockets.

He closed the locker, closed and locked the secret drawer in the workbench, and switched off the space heater.

Behind the wheel of the Land Rover, he clicked the remote to roll up the garage door. He backed into the rain-swept alley.

He had arrived in Santa Monica as Corky Laputa. He was leaving as Robin Goodfellow, agent of the NSA.

After waiting to be sure that the garage door went all the way down, he pressed a second button on the remote, engaging an electric lock that doubly secured the premises.

The CD player in the Land Rover was loaded with the symphonies and operas of Richard Wagner, which was his preferred music when he was being Robin Goodfellow. He fired up *Götterdämmerung* and set out through the storm for Malibu, to have a serious face-to-face talk with the man who this evening would get him onto the Manheim estate undetected.

Corky loved his life.

CHAPTER 62

"Sandwiches," said Fric.

Stupid, stupid, stupid.

After conveying the dozen quake lights to his deep and special secret place, Fric had decided to return the empty picnic hamper to the lawn-and-patio-storage room, where he had originally gotten it. He had undertaken this task for some reason that had seemed logical at the time, though he could not now recall what it had been.

Mr. Devonshire, one of the porters—the one with the English accent, the bushy eyebrows, and the weak left eye that tended to drift toward his temple—had encountered Fric in the ground-floor west hall, at the end of which lay the lawn-and-patio-storage room. By way of friendly small talk, Mr. Devonshire had said, "What've you got there, Fric?"

Sandwiches, Fric had said. Now he said again, "Sandwiches."

This was a stupid, stupid, stupid thing to say, let alone to repeat, because when Mr. Devonshire had first seen him, Fric had been swinging the hamper as he walked along the hall, swinging it in such a way that its light weight—and therefore its emptiness—must have been instantly apparent.

"What kind of sandwiches?" Mr. Devonshire asked.

"Ham," said Fric, for this was a simple response that he could not screw up in the nine thousand ways that he could probably mangle the words *peanut butter and jelly.*

"So you're having a picnic, are you?" Mr. Devonshire asked, his left eye slowly drifting out of alignment as though he expected to be able to look behind himself while simultaneously studying Fric.

When the porter had first come to work at Palazzo Rospo, Fric had thought that he possessed an evil eye and could cast curses with a glance. Mrs. McBee had corrected this childish misapprehension and had suggested that he do some research.

Fric now knew that Mr. Devonshire suffered from amblyopia. This was a little-known word. Fric liked knowing things that most people didn't.

Long ago Fric had learned to look at Mr. Devonshire's good eye when talking to him. Right now, however, he wasn't able to meet the porter's good eye because he felt so guilty for lying; consequently, he found himself gazing stupidly at the amblyopic eye.

To avoid embarrassing Mr. Devonshire and himself, he stared instead at the floor and said, "Yes, a picnic, just me, something different to do, you know, ummm, not the old routine."

"Where will you have your picnic?" Mr. Devonshire asked.

"The rose garden."

Sounding surprised, Mr. Devonshire said, "In this rain?"

Stupid, stupid, stupid.

Fric had forgotten the rain. He said, "Ummm, I mean the rose *room.*"

The rose room, as members of the staff continued to refer to it, was a small ground-floor reception parlor. Its windows presented a view of the former site of the rose garden.

A few years ago, at the urging of their feng-shui consultant, the rose garden had been moved farther from the house. Where the old rose garden had been, grass grew, and from the grass soared a massive piece of contemporary sculpture that Nominal Mom had given to Ghost Dad on the ninth anniversary of their wedding, at which time they had been divorced for eight years.

Nominal Mom described the sculpture as "futuristic organic Zen" in style. To Fric it looked like a giant heap of road apples produced by a herd of Clydesdales.

"The rose room seems like an odd place for a picnic," said Mr. Devonshire, no doubt thinking about the Zen turd pile beyond the windows.

"Ummm, well, I feel close to my mom there," Fric said, which was so lame that it was almost clever.

Mr. Devonshire was silent for a moment, and then he said, "Are you all right, Fric?"

"Ummm, sure, I'm swell, just a little, you know, bummed out by all the rain."

After another but thankfully shorter silence, the porter said, "Well, enjoy your ham sandwiches."

"Thank you, sir. I will. I made them myself. From scratch." He was the world's worst liar. "With ham."

Mr. Devonshire walked toward the north hall, and Fric just stood there, stupidly holding the hamper as if it were *heavy*.

After the porter disappeared at the intersection of the west and north halls, Fric continued to stare after him. He was convinced that Mr. Devonshire was hiding just out of sight and that the man's eerie left eye would turn so far to one side that it would be hanging out of his head when he peeked around the corner.

The lawn-and-patio-storage room, to which Fric had been headed, was not set aside for the storage of lawns and patios. Rather, the cushions for the hundred or more outdoor chairs and sun lounges—and sometimes the furniture as well—were moved there in anticipation of bad weather. The big room also held lawn umbrellas, croquet sets, outdoor games, and such associated paraphernalia as picnic hampers.

Following his conversation with the porter, Fric could no longer simply return the hamper to the storage room. If Mr. Devonshire saw him without it anytime soon, he would be exposed as a devious liar who was actually up to some kind of no good.

Suspicious, the staff might surreptitiously watch him, even as shorthanded as they were at the moment. Without realizing it, he might reveal his deep and special secret place to a keen observer.

Now that he had committed himself to the picnic story, he must follow through. He would have to lug the hamper to the rose room and sit by the windows, gazing out at the rose garden that wasn't there anymore, pretending to eat ham sandwiches that didn't exist.

Mysterious Caller had warned him about lying.

If he wasn't ready to handle nice Mr. Devonshire, Fric wondered how he could expect to deceive and hide out from Moloch.

Finally he decided that the porter and his lazy eye were not lurking just around the corner, after all.

Certain that he appeared too grim for a picnicker, but unable to force a smile, he carried the damn hamper all the way from the southwest corner of the house to the northeast corner, to the rose room.

visit had he not believed that Corky, as Robin Goodfellow, knew the location of every one of his bolt-holes and would descend on him in his hide-away with a company of cutthroat mailmen who would show no mercy.

Toward the east end of the property, away from the house, stood an ancient unpainted barn and a prefab steel building of more recent construction. Corky knew only some of what Trotter was up to in those structures, but he pretended to have full knowledge.

In the fierce heat of summer, the real threat to Trotter would be fire, not a wicked government cabal. The steep slopes behind his property, as well as half the narrow valley both up-canyon and down-canyon, bristled with wild brush that, by late August, would be as ready for burning as Brittina Dowd's house had proved to be with the application of a little gasoline.

Now, of course, the steep slopes were so super-saturated with rain that the risk was a mud slide. In this terrain, a canyon wall could descend in a tidal wave of muck with such suddenness that even a wild-eyed paranoid with every nerve fully cocked might not be able to outrun it. If he broke into a sprint at first rumble, Trotter could still wind up buried alive, but alive only briefly, sharing his grave with an ark's worth of crushed and smothered wildlife.

Corky loved southern California.

Not yet crushed and smothered, Trotter waited

for his visitor on the veranda. If at all possible, he hoped to keep Corky out of the house.

On one of his previous visits, deeply into his role as a rogue government agent who used the United States Constitution as toilet paper, Corky had misbehaved. He had shown no respect for Trotter's property rights. He had been a brute.

On this twenty-second day of December, Corky didn't find himself to be mellowed out by holiday good will. He was a punk-mean elf.

Although he parked ten steps from the veranda, he didn't hurry through the downpour because Robin Goodfellow, too cool for jackboots but wearing them in spirit, was not a man who noticed the weather when he was in a foul mood.

He climbed the three steps to the veranda, drew the Glock from his shoulder holster, and pressed the muzzle to Trotter's forehead.

"Repeat what you told me on the phone."

"Damn," Trotter said nervously. "You know it's true."

"It's bullshit," Corky said.

Trotter's hair was as orange as that of the Cheshire Cat who had toyed with Alice in Wonderland. He had the pinned-wide, protuberant eyes of the Mad Hatter. His nose twitched nervously, reminiscent of the White Rabbit. His bloated face and his huge mustache recalled the famous Walrus, and he was in general as brillig, slithy, and mimsy as numerous of Lewis Carroll's characters rolled into one.

"For God's sake, Goodfellow," Trotter all but blubbered, "the storm, the *storm*! We can't do the job in this. It's impossible in weather like this."

Still pressing the Glock to Trotter's forehead, Corky said, "The storm will break by six o'clock. The wind will die completely. We'll have ideal conditions."

"Yeah, they're saying it might break, but what do they know? Do any of their predictions ever turn out right?"

"I'm not relying on the TV weathermen, you cretin. I'm relying on supersecret Defense Department satellites that not only study the planet's weather patterns but *control* them with microwave energy pulses. We will *make* the storm end when we need it to end."

This crackpot assertion played well with the paranoid Trotter, whose pinned-wide eyes stretched even wider. "Weather control," he whispered shakily. "Hurricanes, tornadoes, blizzards, droughts—an untraceable weapon as terrible as nuclear bombs."

In reality, Corky was counting on nothing more than chaos to be his ally, to bring the storm to an end when he needed calm skies.

Chaos never failed him.

"Rain or no rain, wind or no wind," he told Trotter, "you will be in Bel Air, at the rendezvous point, at seven o'clock sharp, as originally planned."

"Weather control," Trotter muttered darkly.

"Don't even think about not coming. Do you know how many eyes are on us right now—up in those hills, out in those fields?"

"Lots of eyes," Trotter guessed.

"My people are everywhere in this canyon, ready to keep you honest or blow your brains out, whichever you want."

In fact, the only eyes on them were those of the crows, hawks, sparrows, and other members of the feathered community gathered in the ancient California live oaks that sheltered the house.

Jack Trotter had fallen for these lies not because of the phony NSA credentials, not because of Corky's bravura performance as Agent Robin Goodfellow, but because Corky had known so much about Trotter's many aliases and at least a few things about his thus far successful career as a bank robber and a distributor of Ecstasy. He believed that Corky had learned about him by means of the ruling cabal's all but omniscient intelligence-gathering apparatus.

What Corky had learned about Trotter, however, he had heard from Mick Sachatone, the hacker and multimillionaire anarchist who traded in forged documents, untraceable cell phones, and other illegal paperwork, objects, substances, and information. Mick had provided Trotter with the identities that subsequently he revealed to Corky.

Ordinarily, Mick would never disclose to one client the affairs of another. Considering the kind of people he did business with, such a lack of discretion would result, if he were lucky, in his death or, if he were unlucky, in the excision of his eyes, the extraction of his tongue, the severing of his thumbs, and castration with pliers.

Because Mick had reason to hate Trotter with an intensity nearly homicidal, he had risked sharing information with Corky. Jealous rage of operatic proportions had caused him to violate his usual standards of client confidentiality.

For his part, Trotter had earned Mick's enmity, though he seemed unaware of it. He had stolen Mick's girlfriend.

Mick's girlfriend had been a porn-movie star renowned in certain jerky circles for the inhuman flexibility of her body.

Perhaps Trotter didn't think that anyone could become profoundly emotionally attached, on evenings and weekends, to a woman who did two, six, and even ten men at a time in front of a camera, during her regular business hours.

Since the age of thirteen, however, Mick's most cherished dream had been to have a porn star for a girlfriend. He felt that Trotter had robbed him of his heart's one true desire and had thwarted his destiny.

After four months with Trotter, the woman had disappeared. Mick was of the opinion that, having tired of her, Trotter had killed her either because she had learned too much about his illegal activities or merely for sport, and had buried her deep in the canyon.

Now she was of no use to anyone, and this pointless waste of her exceptional flexibility further infuriated Mick.

Lowering the Glock from Trotter's forehead, Corky said, "Let's go inside."

"Please, let's not," Trotter pleaded.

"Need I remind you," Corky said, lying with delightful panache, "that your cooperation with me could earn you erasure from all public records, from all tax records, making you the freest man who ever lived, a man *utterly unknown to the government*?"

"I'll be there tonight. Seven o'clock sharp. Wind or no wind. I swear I will."

"I still want to go inside," Corky said. "I still feel the need to make my point with you."

A sadness came into Trotter's Mad Hatter eyes. His walruslike face drooped.

Resigned, he led Corky into the house.

The bullet holes in the walls, from the previous occasion when Corky had needed to teach Trotter a lesson, had not been repaired; however, the living-room display shelves had been filled with a new collection of Lladro porcelains—statuettes of ballerinas, princesses dancing with princes, children capering with a dog, a lovely farm maiden feeding a flock of geese gathered at her feet. . . .

That a paranoid, conspiracy-drunk, bank-robbing, drug-peddling survivalist with bolt-holes leading from here to the Canadian border should have a weak spot for fragile porcelains didn't surprise Corky. Regardless of how rough we may appear on the exterior, each of us has a human heart.

Corky himself had a weakness for old Shirley Temple movies, in which he indulged once or twice a year. Without embarrassment.

As Trotter watched, Corky emptied the 9-mm

ed with apples and fed to unsuspecting Bowery bums on Thanksgiving.

Eventually, everyone had left him alone.

He still didn't know whether it had been a hospital, sanitarium, or booby hatch.

His mother had been to Palazzo Rospo only once since then, but she hadn't mentioned the incident. That was the visit in which she told Fric that he was an almost perfect invisible little mouse.

Then they had gone riding on a pair of great black stallions, and Fric had been exuberant, self-assured, athletic like his father, and a superb rider.

Ha, ha, ha.

Sitting here in the rose room, gazing through the windows, he had gotten so lost in the past that he hadn't noticed when Mr. Yorn, the groundskeeper, had entered the picture. Wearing green rain togs and black wading boots, Mr. Yorn must have been checking the lawn drains or investigating a clogged downspout. Now he stared through the rose-room windows at Fric, from a distance of six feet, looking puzzled, perhaps worried.

Maybe Mr. Yorn had waved and Fric, lost in the past, had not waved back, and so Mr. Yorn had waved again, and still Fric had not waved back; and now maybe Mr. Yorn thought Fric was in a trance.

To prove that he was neither a rude little snot nor hypnotized, Fric waved, which seemed to be the right thing to do, whether Mr. Yorn had been standing there unacknowledged for ten seconds or five minutes.

Fric waved a little too vigorously, which might have been what caused the groundskeeper to step closer to the windows and say, "Are you all right, Fric?"

"Yes, sir. I'm fine. I'm just having some ham sandwiches."

Apparently the leaded glass panes and the roar of the rain filtered some of the sense out of Fric's voice, for Mr. Yorn edged closer still and spoke again: "What did you say?"

"Ham sandwiches!" Fric explained, raising his voice almost to a shout.

For a moment Mr. Yorn continued to peer in at him, as though studying a curious bug trapped in a specimen jar. Then he shook his head, causing the brim of his rain hat to flap comically, and he turned away.

Fric watched the groundskeeper walk past the bronze bowel movement. Mr. Yorn receded into the storm, dwindling across the immense lawn until he appeared to be no bigger than a garden gnome, until he was finally gone like a ghost.

Fric figured he knew exactly what Mr. Yorn was thinking: *Like mother, like son.*

Rising from the chair, stretching, shaking stiffness out of his legs, Fric accidentally kicked the picnic hamper, knocking it over.

The lid fell open, revealing something inside: a whiteness.

The hamper had been empty. No quake lights, no ham sandwiches, no anything.

Fric scoped the parlor. He saw no place in which

an unsuspected companion might be hiding. The door to the hall remained closed, as he had left it.

Hesitantly, he stooped. Cautiously, he reached into the hamper.

He withdrew a folded newspaper and shakily opened it. The *Los Angeles Times*.

The headline was too bold, too black, too incredible to miss: FBI ENTERS MANHEIM KIDNAPPING.

A chill shuttled and wove in Fric.

A sudden brine moistened his palms, as if he had dipped his hands into a supernatural sea, and his fingers stuck to the paper.

He checked the date of the issue. December 24. The day after tomorrow.

On the front page, under the frightening headline, were two photographs: a publicity shot of Ghost Dad, and the front gate of the estate.

Reluctant to read the report for fear that reading it would make it come true, Fric glanced at the bottom of the column and saw that the story continued on page 8. He turned to page 8 in search of the picture most important to him.

And there he was.

Under his photo were these words: *Aelfric Manheim, 10, missing since Tuesday night.*

As he stared in shock at the photo, his black-and-white image morphed into that of the mirror man, Mysterious Caller, his guardian angel: the cold face, the pale gray eyes.

Fric tried to throw the *Times* down, but was unable to let go of it, not because his hands were moist with fear but because the newspaper seemed to have acquired a static charge, and clung to him.

In the picture, Mysterious Caller became animated, as if this were not a newspaper photo but a miniature TV screen, and he spoke warningly from the *Los Angeles Times: "Moloch is coming."*

Then with no recollection of having taken a step, Fric found that he had crossed the rose room to the door.

He gasped for breath, though not because of his asthma. His heart boomed louder than the thunder that earlier had knocked through the sky.

The *Times* lay on the floor by the overturned hamper.

As Fric watched, the newspaper exploded off the Persian carpet as if caught in a wild wind, although not so much as a faint draft could be felt. The several sections of the *Times* unfolded, blossomed; in seconds, they rumpled and swirled and noisily assembled themselves into a tall human figure, as if an invisible man had been standing there all the time and as if the blown newsprint had adhered to his heretofore unseen form.

This did not have the aura of a guardian angel, though surely it was. This felt . . . *menacing.*

The paper man turned from Fric and flung himself at the bay windows. When the crackling newsprint hit the glass, it ceased to be paper anymore, became a shadow, a flowing darkness, that swarmed through the beveled panes in the very way that it had pulsed through the ornaments on the Christmas tree the previous night.

The phantom faded, vanished, as though it had traveled by glass into the rain, and then had ridden on the rain to some place far away and unthinkable.

Fric was alone once more. Or seemed to be.

CHAPTER 65

Dr. Jonathan Spetz-Mogg lived in a pricey West-wood neighborhood, in a fine Nantucket-style house with cedar-shingle siding so silvered by time that not even the rain could darken it, which suggested that the silvering might be an applied patina.

Spetz-Mogg's British accent was eccentric enough to be captivating, inconsistent enough to have been acquired during a long visit to those shores rather than by birth and upbringing.

The professor welcomed Ethan and Hazard into his home, but less graciously than obsequiously. He answered their questions not in a spirit of thoughtful cooperation, but in a nervous, wordy gush.

He wore a roomy FUBU shirt and baggy low-rider pants with snap pockets on the legs, looking as ridiculous as any white man trying to dress like a homey from the hood, twice as ridiculous be-cause he was forty-eight. Every time he crossed his legs, which he did frequently, the baggy pants rustled loudly enough to interrupt conversation.

Perhaps he affected sunglasses indoors more often than not. He wore them on this occasion.

Spetz-Mogg removed the shades and put them on again nearly as often as he recrossed his legs, though these two nervous tells were not synchronized. He seemed unable to decide whether he had a better chance of surviving interrogation by presenting an open and guileless image or by hiding behind tinted lenses.

Although the professor clearly believed that every cop was a brutal fascist, he'd never be one to climb a barricade to shout the accusation. He wasn't incensed that two agents of the repressive police state were in his home; he was simply, quietly terrified.

In answer to every question, he vomited up a mess of information with the hope that garrulous responses would wash Ethan and Hazard out of his door before they produced brass knuckles and truncheons.

This was not the professor for whom they were searching. Spetz-Mogg might encourage others to commit crimes in the name of one ideal or another, but he was too gutless to do so himself.

Besides, he didn't have time for crime. He had written ten works of nonfiction and eight novels. In addition to teaching his classes, he organized conferences, workshops, and seminars. He wrote plays.

In Ethan's experience, industrious people, regardless of the quality of what their labor produced, rarely committed violent crimes. Only in movies did successful businessmen routinely indulge in murder and mayhem in addition to corporate responsibilities.

Criminals were likely to be failures in the workplace or just lazy. Or their material possessions had come through inheritance or by other easy means. Idleness gave them time to scheme.

Dr. Spetz-Mogg had no memory of Rolf Reynerd. On average, three hundred struggling actors attended one of his weekend conferences. Not many of them left a lasting impression.

When Ethan and Hazard rose to leave without suggesting that they torture the professor with electric wires to his genitals, Spetz-Mogg accompanied them to the door with visible relief. When he closed the door behind them, he no doubt bolted for the bathroom, his pretense of British equanimity belied by shuddering bowels.

In the Expedition, Hazard said, "I should have punched the son of a bitch on general principles."

"You're getting cranky in midcareer," Ethan said.

"What was that accent?"

"Adam Sandler playing James Bond."

"Yeah. With a twist of Schwarzenegger."

From Spetz-Mogg's house in Westwood, they wasted far too much time tracking down Dr. Gerald Fitzmartin, who had organized the screenwriting conference attended by Reynerd.

According to the university at which he taught, Fitzmartin was home for the holidays, not traveling. When Hazard called, all he got was an answering machine.

Fitzmartin lived in Pacific Palisades. They traveled surface streets, which seemed less well suited for SUVs than for gondolas.

No one answered the bell at the Fitzmartin place. Maybe he was Christmas shopping. Maybe he was too busy to come to the door because he was wrapping a hate gift in a black box for Channing Manheim.

The neighbor told a different story: Fitzmartin had been rushed to Cedars-Sinai Medical Center on Monday morning. He wasn't sure why.

When Hazard called Cedars-Sinai, he found that patient privacy was more important to the hospital than were police relations.

Under a sky as bruised as the battered body of a boxer, Ethan drove back toward the city. The wind fought with trees, and sometimes trees lost, dropping branches into the streets, hampering traffic.

The traffic matched the turbulence of the heavens. At one intersection, car had punched car, and both had gone down for the count. Five blocks farther, a truck had broadsided a paneled van.

He drove with caution that grew into an inhibiting wariness. He couldn't help thinking that if he had been run down and killed in traffic once, he might die again on another street. This time, maybe he would not get up again from death.

En route, Hazard worked the phone, tracking down the name of the professor, at yet another institution, who had organized the one-day seminar on publicity and self-promotion.

Taking neither hand off the wheel, Ethan glanced at his watch. The day was draining away faster than rain into storm culverts.

He had to be back at Palazzo Rospo before 5:00. Fric could not be left alone in the great house, especially not on this strange day.

Cedars-Sinai Medical Center was on Beverly Boulevard in a part of Los Angeles that wanted to be Beverly Hills. They arrived at 2:18.

They located Dr. Gerald Fitzmartin in the ICU, but they weren't permitted to see him. In the waiting room, the professor's son was pleased to have a distraction, though he couldn't imagine why police officers would want to talk to his father.

Professor Fitzmartin was sixty-eight years old. After a life of honest living, older men rarely turned to crime in their retirement. It interfered with gardening and with passing kidney stones.

Besides, just this morning, Fitzmartin had undergone quadruple heart-bypass surgery. If he *was* Rolf Reynerd's conspirator, he would not be killing movie stars in the immediate future.

Ethan checked his watch. 2:34. *Tick, tick, tick.*

CHAPTER 66

Mick Sachatone, the anarchist multimillionaire, didn't live in a glitzy neighborhood of multimillionaires because he never wanted to have to explain the origins of his wealth to the tax authorities. When you make it in cash, you live without flash.

He laundered enough income to justify a spacious four-bedroom, two-story house of no architectural distinction in a clean and pleasant upper-middle-class neighborhood in Sherman Oaks.

Only a handful of Mick's most trusted customers of long standing knew his address. Mostly he transacted business on public beaches and in public parks, coffee shops, and churches.

Without stopping at the garage in Santa Monica to change from his Robin Goodfellow costume into his regular-guy clothes and yellow slicker, Corky went directly from Jack Trotter's funky digs in Malibu to Sherman Oaks. Thanks to Queeg von Hindenburg, collector of broken porcelains, Corky's schedule was screwed up. He had much yet to do on this most important but fast-vanishing day of his life.

He parked in the driveway and ran a few quick steps through the rain to the cover of the front porch.

Mick's voice came from an intercom speaker beside the bell push, "Be right there," and Mick Sachatone himself came to the door with unusual alacrity. Sometimes, you had to wait here on the porch two or three minutes, or longer, between when Mick spoke to you via the intercom and when he greeted you in person, so routinely preoccupied was he with work or with other interests.

As usual when at home, Mick was barefoot and dressed in pajamas. Today the jammies were red, decorated with images of the cartoon character Bart Simpson. Mick bought some peejays off the rack but had others custom tailored.

Even before Mick had achieved puberty, he had been enchanted by the story of Hugh Hefner, founder of *Playboy*. Hef had discovered a way to grow up, be a success, and yet remain a big child, indulging any whim or desire to whatever degree he wished, making of his life one long party, living more days than not in pajamas.

Mick, who worked mostly at home, owned more than 150 pairs of peejays. He slept in the nude but sported pajamas during the day.

He considered himself an acolyte of Hef. A mini-Hef. Mick was forty-two going on thirteen.

"Hey, Cork, super-hip threads," Mick declared

CHAPTER 67

The professor who had organized the one-day seminar on publicity and self-promotion was Dr. Robert Vebbler. He preferred to be called Dr. Bob, as he was known on the motivational-speaking circuit, where he promised to turn ordinary, self-doubting men and women into doubt-free dynamos of self-interest and superhuman achievement.

Ethan and Hazard found the professor on the mostly deserted campus, in his office, preparing for a January speaking tour. The walls of the two-room space were papered with portrait posters of Dr. Bob in a size popularized by Joseph Stalin and Mao Tse-tung.

He had a shaved head, a handlebar mustache, a red-bronze tan that established his contempt for melanoma, and laser-whitened teeth brighter than irradiated piano keys. With the exception of his red snakeskin boots, everything he wore—as in the posters—was white, including his watch, which had a white band and a plain white face without any numbers or checks to indicate the hours.

Dr. Bob managed so successfully to turn the answer to every question into a mini-lecture on self-esteem and positive thinking that Ethan wanted Hazard to arrest him on charges of felony cliche and practicing philosophy without an idea.

He was just as quacky as Donald Duck, but he was no more a murderer than was that excitable mallard. He hungered to be famous, not infamous. Donald *had* on occasion attempted to kill Chip and Dale, that pair of pesky chipmunks, but Dr. Bob would instead motivate them to give up their rodent ways and become successful entrepreneurs.

He signed for Ethan and Hazard two paperback copies of his latest collection of motivational speeches and declared that he would be the first ever to pyramid a series of self-help books into a Nobel prize for literature.

By the time they escaped Dr. Bob's office, located a trash can in which to ditch the paperbacks, and returned to the Expedition, the instrument-panel clock and Ethan's watch showed a synchronized 3:41.

At five o'clock, the last of the household staff would leave for the day. Fric would be alone in Palazzo Rospo.

Ethan considered calling the guards in the security office at the back of the estate. One of them could go to the house and stay with the boy.

That would leave one man to monitor cameras and other detection systems, with no one to conduct the scheduled foot patrols. Ethan was reluctant to spread his resources thin in the current circumstances.

He continued to believe that Reynerd's unknown partner, if still determined to act, would not do so until Thursday afternoon at the earliest, when the Face returned from the location shoot in Florida. Manheim's whereabouts were public knowledge and much written about. Anyone sufficiently obsessed with the star to want to kill him would most likely know when he was expected to return to Bel Air.

Most likely . . . but not absolutely.

The element of doubt, and Hazard's intuitive sense that they didn't have until Thursday, troubled Ethan. He worried that someone would discover a way to penetrate the estate's defenses, regardless of how tightly the grounds were sealed, and lie in wait undetected until Manheim's return.

Even the most drum-tight security plan was a human enterprise, after all, and every human enterprise, due to the nature of the beast, was imperfect. A clever enough lunatic, driven by obsession and by a vicious homicidal impulse, could find a crack even in the wall of protection around a President of the United States.

From what Ethan knew of Reynerd, the man hadn't been clever, but the person who had inspired the character of the professor in the screenplay might be a higher-caliber crackpot.

"You go home," Hazard insisted as they drove off the university campus. "Drop me back at Our Lady of Angels so I can get my car, and I'll check out the last two names myself."

"That doesn't seem right."

"You're not a real cop, anyway," Hazard said. "You gave that all up for fortune and the chance to kiss celebrity ass. Remember?"

"You're only in this on account of me."

"Wrong. I'm in this because of these," Hazard said, and rang the set of three silvery bells.

The sound resonated in the fluid of Ethan's spine.

"Damn if I'm gonna have spooky shit like this in my life," said Hazard, "or guys walking into mirrors. I'm gonna explain it somehow, blow all these hoodoo thoughts out of my head, and get back to being who I was, such as I was."

The remaining two names were those of professors of American literature at yet another university. They had been put at the bottom of the list because Reynerd's partial screenplay suggested that his co-conspirator would prove to be an acting teacher or an academic associated in some other way with the entertainment business. Stuffy professors of literature, lounging about in tweed coats with leather patches on the elbows, smoking pipes and discussing participles, did not seem likely to be celebrity stalkers or murderers.

"Anyway," Hazard said, "I think maybe these two won't pan out any better than the others."

He read from notes made during phone calls that he had placed en route between Professor Fitzmartin at Cedars-Sinai and Dr. Bob.

Responding to Mr. Hachette with a shrug, Ethan went in search of Fric.

Mrs. McBee disliked whole-house paging on the intercom. She considered it an offense against the stately atmosphere of the great house, an affront to the family, and a distraction to the staff. "We are not at work in an office building or a discount warehouse," she had explained.

Senior staff members carried personal pagers on which they could be summoned from anywhere on the sprawling estate. Squawking at them through the intercom system was seldom necessary.

If you needed to track down a junior staff member or if your position included the authority to seek out a member of the family at your discretion—which among the household staff was true only of Mrs. McBee, Mr. McBee, and Ethan—then you must proceed on the intercom one room at a time. You began with the three places where you most expected to find the wanted individual.

As five o'clock approached, only a minimal staff remained on duty to be distracted, all of them scheduled to leave within minutes. Fric was the sole member of the Manheim family in residence. The McBees were in Santa Barbara. Nevertheless, Ethan felt obliged to follow standard procedures in respect of tradition, in deference to Mrs. McBee, and in the conviction that if he paged Fric in all rooms at once, the dear lady in Santa Barbara would instantly know what had transpired and would have her brief holiday diminished by unnecessary distress.

Using the intercom feature on one of the kitchen phones, Ethan first tried Fric's rooms on the third floor. He sought the boy next in the train room—"Are you there, Fric? This is Mr. Truman"—in the theater, and then in the library. He received no reply.

Although Fric had never been sulky and certainly never rude, he might for whatever reason be choosing not to respond to the intercom even though he heard it.

Ethan elected to walk the house top to bottom, primarily to find the boy, but also to assure himself that, in general, all was as it should be.

He began on the third floor. He didn't visit every room, but at least opened doors to peer into most chambers, and repeatedly called the child's name.

The door to Fric's suite stood open. After twice announcing himself and receiving no answer, Ethan decided that, this evening, security concerns took precedence over household etiquette and family privacy. He walked Fric's rooms but found neither the boy nor anything amiss.

Returning through the east wing to the north hall, heading toward the main stairs, Ethan stopped three times to turn, to listen, halted by a crawling on the back of his neck, by a feeling that all was not as right as it appeared to be.

Quiet. Stillness.

Holding his breath, he heard only his heart.

Tuning out that inner rhythm, he could hear nothing real, only absurdities that he imagined: stealthy movement in the antique mirror above a nearby sideboard; a faint voice like that on the telephone the previous night, but fainter than before, crying out to him not from a third-floor room but from the far side of a blind turn on the highway to eternity.

The mirror revealed no reflection but his own, no blurred form, no boyhood friend.

When he began to breathe again, the distant voice that existed only in his imagination ceased to be heard even there.

He descended the main stairs to the second floor, where he found Fric in the library.

Reading a book, the boy sat in an armchair that he had moved from its intended position. The back of it was tight against the Christmas tree.

When Ethan opened the door and entered, Fric gave a start, which he tried to conceal by pretending that he had merely been adjusting his position in the armchair. Stark fear had widened his eyes and clenched his jaws for an instant, until he realized that Ethan was only Ethan.

"Hello, Fric. You okay? I paged you here on the intercom a few minutes ago."

"Didn't hear it, ummm, no, not the intercom," said the boy, lying so ineptly that had he been hooked up to a polygraph, the machine might have exploded.

"You moved the chair."

"Chair? Ummm, no, I found it like this, here like, you know, just like this."

Ethan perched on the edge of another armchair. "Is something wrong, Fric?"

"Wrong?" the boy asked, as though the meaning of that word eluded him.

"Is there something you'd like to tell me? Are you worried about something? Because you don't seem like yourself."

The kid looked away from Ethan, to the book. He closed the book and lowered it to his lap.

As a cop, Ethan had long ago learned patience.

Making eye contact again, Fric leaned forward in his chair. He seemed about to whisper conspiratorially but hesitated and straightened up. Whatever he'd been about to reveal, he let slide. He shrugged. "I don't know. Maybe I'm tense 'cause my dad's coming home Thursday."

"That's a good thing, isn't it?"

"Sure. But it's pretty tense, too."

"Why tense?"

"Well, he'll have some of his buddies with him, you know. He always does."

"You don't care for his friends?"

"They're okay. They're all golfers and sports fanatics. Dad likes to talk golf and football and stuff. It's how he unwinds. His buddies and him, they're like a club."

A club in which you're not and never will be a member, Ethan thought, surprised by a sympathy that tightened his throat.

He wanted to give the boy a hug, take him to a movie, *out* to a movie, not downstairs to the mini-Pantages here in Palazzo Rospo, but to some ordinary multiplex crawling with kids and their families, where the air was saturated with the fragrance of in ancient Rome, when maybe I was traumatized by watching the stupid lions eat stupid people in the stupid Colosseum."

This cheeky rap would have seemed funnier to Ethan if he hadn't believed that the Face might, in fact, have reacted to his son's drinking in pretty much that fashion.

"Maybe your father would never find out. But you're forgetting about She Who Cannot Be Deceived."

Fric whispered, "McBee."

Ethan nodded. "McBee."

Fric said, "I'll have Pepsi."

"With or without ice?"

"Without."

"Good lad."

CHAPTER 70

Although frightened, bitter, and struggling against despair, Rachel Dalton remained a lovely woman, with lustrous chestnut hair and blue eyes mysterious in their depths.

She was also, in Hazard's experience, uncommonly considerate. Having agreed by phone to an interview, she had prepared coffee by the time he arrived. She served it in the living room with a plate of miniature muffins and butter cookies.

In the line of duty, homicide detectives were rarely offered refreshments, never with damask napkins. Especially not from the wives of missing men for whom the police had done embarrassingly little.

Maxwell Dalton, as it turned out, had vanished three months earlier. Rachel had reported him missing when he had been four hours late from an afternoon class at the university.

The police, of course, had not been interested in an adult who was missing only four hours, nor had they been intrigued when he'd not shown up in a day, two days, or three.

"Apparently," Rachel told Hazard, "we're living in a time when a shocking number of husbands—and wives—go off on drug binges or just suddenly decide to spend a week in Puerto Vallarta with some tart they met at Starbucks ten minutes ago, or walk out on their lives altogether without warning. When I tried to explain Maxwell, they couldn't believe in him—a husband so reliable. They were sure he would turn up in time, with bloodshot eyes, a sheepish look, and a venereal disease."

Eventually, when Maxwell Dalton had been gone long enough for even contemporary authorities to consider the length of his absence unusual, the police had allowed the official filing of a missing-persons report. This had led to little or no activity in search of the man, which had frustrated Rachel, for she had wrongly assumed that a missing-persons case triggered an investigation only a degree less vigorous than a homicide.

"Not when it's an adult," Hazard said, "and not when there are no indications of violence. If they had found his abandoned car . . ."

His car had not been found, however, nor his discarded wallet stripped of cash, nor any item that might have indicated foul play. He had vanished with no more trace than any ship that had sailed into but not out of the Bermuda Triangle.

Hazard said, "I'm sure you've been asked already, but did your husband have any enemies?"

"He's a good man," Rachel said, as he expected

she would. Then she added what he had not expected, "And like all good people in a dark world, of course he has enemies."

"Who?"

"A gang of thugs at that sewer they call a university. Oh, I shouldn't be so harsh. Many good people work there. Unfortunately, the English Department is in the hands of scoundrels and lunatics."

"You think someone in the department might . . ."

"Not likely," Rachel admitted. "They're all talk, those people, and meaningless talk at that." She offered more coffee, and when he declined, she said, "What was the name of the man whose death you're investigating?"

He had told her only enough to get through her door; and he did not intend to elaborate now. He hadn't even mentioned that already he had chased down and shot Reynerd's killer. "Rolf Reynerd. He was shot in West Hollywood yesterday."

"Do you think his case might be related to my husband's? I mean, by more than the fact that he took Max's class in literature?"

"It's possible," he said. "But unlikely. I wouldn't . . ."

Oddly enough, a sad smile rendered her more lovely. "I won't, Detective," she said, responding to what he had been hesitant to say. "I won't get my hopes up. But damn if I'll let them fade, either."

As Hazard rose to leave, the doorbell rang. The caller proved to be an older black woman with white hair and the most elegant hands he had ever seen, slender and long-fingered and as supple as

CHAPTER 71

From the entrance rotunda, at a window beside the front door, Ethan watched as Mr. Hachette's car dwindled along the driveway, into the tintack rain and the riddled darkness. The chef had been the last member of the day staff to leave.

Set flush in one wall of the rotunda, tucked discretely near a corner, a dark display screen brightened when Ethan lightly pressed one finger to it. This was a Crestron touch-control unit by which he could access all the computerized features of the house: the heating and air-conditioning, the music system, the gas heating for swimming pools and spas, both the in-house and landscape lighting, the phone system, and much more.

Crestron panels were positioned throughout the mansion, but the same features could also be controlled from any computer work station, such as the one in Ethan's study.

After Ethan activated the screen with a touch, three columns of icons were presented for his consideration. He tapped the one that represented the exterior surveillance cameras.

Because eighty-six outdoor cameras were positioned across the estate, he was next presented with eighty-six designating numbers. For the most part, to obtain quickly a view of any specific portion of the grounds, you had to have memorized the numbers—at least those that, in your particular staff position, you were most likely to use frequently.

He touched 03, and the Crestron screen at once filled with a view of the main gate as seen from outside the estate wall. This was the same camera that had captured Rolf Reynerd delivering the package that contained the doll's eye in the apple.

The gate rolled open. Mr. Hachette's car drove off the grounds, onto the public street, turned right, and disappeared from the frame.

As the front gate rolled shut, Ethan touched the screen and exited the exterior-camera menu. He pressed the icon for the house alarm system.

Not all staff members were authorized to activate and deactivate the alarm; consequently, the screen requested Ethan's password. He entered it, was granted access, and set the house-perimeter alarm.

All public areas of the mansion—virtually everything except bedrooms, bathrooms, and staff quarters—featured motion detectors that would register the passage of anyone moving along a hallway or through a room. They were activated 24/7, but were actually linked to the alarm only when it was in the "nobody-home mode," when the house was entirely deserted, a rare occurrence.

With Fric and Ethan in residence, if the motion detectors had been linked to the alarm, the breach siren would have gone off every time that they passed through a monitored space or so much as made a gesture with one hand.

All he needed was the assurance that the siren would sound if a door or window were opened. This precaution, along with the team of guards monitoring the additional layers of detection on the grounds beyond the house, ensured that no one could set upon him or Fric by surprise.

Nevertheless, he didn't want Fric to sleep alone on the third floor. Not tonight, not tomorrow night, not anytime soon.

Either they would make arrangements for the kid to camp out on the ground floor or Ethan would spend the night in the living room of Fric's third-floor suite. He intended to discuss the matter with the boy after dinner.

Meanwhile, for the first time since returning home, he went to his apartment, to his study, to the desk where he had left the three silvery bells. They were gone.

In the deepest garage at Our Lady of Angels, when he had found only a single set of bells missing from the ambulance, he'd suspected that the set currently in Hazard's possession was the same one that he had found in his hand outside Forever Roses.

The phantom that he had seen in the bathroom mirror at Dunny's apartment, the phantom that had vanished into a mirror in Hazard's bedroom, had somehow come here during the night, as Ethan slept, had taken the bells, and had transferred them to Hazard, for reasons that were mysterious if not forever beyond understanding. And the phantom, more likely than not, was Dunny Whistler, dead but risen.

Ethan marveled that he could stand here, entertaining such bizarre thoughts, and still be sane. At least he believed himself to be sane. He might be wrong about that.

Although the bells were gone, the items from the black boxes remained on display. He sat at the desk and studied the six parts of the riddle, hoping for enlightenment.

Ladybugs, snails, a jar containing ten foreskins, the cookie jar full of Scrabble tiles—OWE, WOE—a book about guide dogs, the eye in the apple . . .

On better days, in a better mood, he'd been unable to make sense of these messages. He hoped that in his current state of wound-tight tension and mental exhaustion, his intellectual fences might fall away, allowing him suddenly to see everything from a new perspective and to understand what before had seemed indecipherable.

No luck.

He phoned the guards in the security office at the back of the estate, in the groundskeeper's building. On duty from four until midnight, they were already aware that he had set the house-perimeter as to be comical. He answered, therefore, only with his hate-filled stare.

Corky pressed the muzzle of the weapon against Dalton's cracked lips.

Instead of turning his head away, the lover of Dickens and Twain and Dickinson boldly opened his mouth and bit the barrel, though this act had the flair of Hemingway. His eyes were fiery with defiance.

Behind the wheel of the sedan, parked across the street from the Laputa house, trying to get a grip on himself, Hazard thought of his Granny Rose, his dad's mother, who believed in mojo though she didn't practice it, believed in poltergeists though none had ever dared to trash her well-kept home, believed in ghosts though she'd never seen one, who could recite the details of a thousand famous hauntings that had involved spirits benign, malign, and Elvis. Now eighty years old, Granny Rose—Hoodoo Rose, as Hazard's mom called her with affection—was respected and much loved, but she remained a figure of amusement in the family because of her conviction that the world was not merely what science and the five senses said it was.

In spite of what he had just seen in the street, Hazard couldn't get his mind entirely around the idea that Granny Rose might have a better grasp of reality than anyone he knew.

He had never been a man who harbored much doubt about what to do next, either in daily life or in a moment of high peril, but sitting in the car, in the rain, in the dark, shivering, he needed time just to realize that he should turn on the engine, the heater. Whether or not he should ring the bell at the Laputa house, however, seemed to be the most difficult decision of his life.

If you *die, I can't bring you back,* Dunny had said, with the emphasis on *you.*

A cop couldn't back off just because he feared dying. Might as well turn in the badge, get a job in phone sales, learn a craft to fill up the empty hours.

I'm not your *guardian,* Dunny had said, with the emphasis on *your,* which was a warning, of course, but which also had implications that made Hazard dizzy.

He wanted to pay a visit to Granny Rose and lie with his head on her lap, let her soothe his brow with cool compresses. Maybe she had homemade lemondrop cookies. She could brew hot chocolate for him.

Across the street, through the screen of rain, the Laputa house didn't look the same as it had when he'd first seen it. Then it had been a handsome Victorian on a large lot, warm and welcoming, the kind of home that protected families in which all the kids became doctors and lawyers and astro-nauts, and everyone loved one another forever. Now he looked at it and figured that in one of the bedrooms there had to be a young girl strapped to a levitating bed, vomiting violently, cursing Jesus, and speaking in the voices of demons.

As a cop, he must never allow fear to inhibit him, but also as a friend, he couldn't walk away from this and leave Ethan with no one to guard his back.

Information. In Hazard's experience, doubt came from having too little information to make an intelligent decision. He needed someone to chase down the answers to a couple questions.

The problem was that officially he had no reason to be pursuing these leads. If this cheese-eater were related to any active case, it was Mina Reynerd's murder, which was on Kesselman's desk, not on Hazard's. He couldn't seek information through the usual department channels.

He phoned Laura Moonves in the Detective Support Division. She had dated Ethan, she still cared for him, and she had helped him track down Rolf Reynerd from the plates on the Honda that had been filmed by one of the estate's video cameras.

Hazard worried that she would have left for the day, but she took his call, and with relief he said, "You're still there."

"Am I? I thought I'd left. I thought I was halfway home, already stopped for a bucket of takeout fried chicken, double slaw. No, son of a bitch, here I still am, but what does it matter, since I don't have a social life."

"I tell him he's an idiot for letting you slip away."

"I tell him he's an idiot, too," she said.

"Everyone tells him he's an idiot."

"Yeah? So maybe we all ought to get together and come up with a new strategy, because this telling-him-he's-an-idiot thing isn't working. I like him *so much,* Hazard."

"He's still getting over Hannah."

"Five years, man."

"When he lost her, he lost more than her. He lost his sense of purpose. He couldn't anymore see a bigger meaning to things. He needs to see it again, 'cause that's him."

"The world's full of sexy, smart, successful guys who wouldn't recognize a bigger meaning to life if God punched them in the face wearing a ring that left His initials in their foreheads."

"That would be your pissed-off Old Testament version of God."

"Why do I have to fall for a guy who needs meaning?"

"Maybe because you need it, too." That thought silenced Laura, and into the silence, Hazard said, "Remember that guy you helped him track down yesterday morning—Rolf Reynerd?"

"Famous wolf," she said. "Rolf means 'famous wolf.' "

"Rolf means *dead.* Don't you watch the news?"

"I'm not a masochist, am I?"

"So check the homicide overnights. But not now. Right now I need you to do something for me, for Ethan, but off the record."

"What do you need?"

Hazard glanced at the house. The place still radiated that dual atmosphere: as if the Brady Bunch had built their home over the gate to Hell.

"Vladimir Laputa," Hazard said. He spelled it for

"I'm sure the boy will be thrilled when, in his first starring role, he fascinates the masses in greater numbers than his father ever has."

&

The storm lost its strength, became a windless drizzle. Fog plumed through the street, like cold breath come down out of the hidden moon.

Alerted now to the nature of the individual with whom he was dealing, Hazard sat in the car, mulling over how best to approach Vladimir Laputa.

His cell phone rang. When he answered it, he recognized the voice that he had heard a short time ago, in the street, issuing from the apparition.

Dunny Whistler said, "I'm Ethan's guardian, not yours, not Aelfric's. But if I save him—if I *can*—there'll be no point to it if either you or the boy dies."

Usually able to draw upon a rich account of words, Hazard found himself bankrupt in this case. He had never talked to a ghost before. He didn't want to start.

"He'll blame himself for the loss of either of you," Whistler continued. "And then the shadow on his heart will become a darkness deep within it. Don't go in that house."

Hazard found a voice not too much thinner and shakier than the one he usually could rely upon: "Are you dead or alive?"

"I'm dead *and* alive. Don't go in that house. The Kevlar vest won't matter. You'll be head shot. Two

bullets in the brain. And I have no authority to res-
urrect you."

Dunny hung up.

Corky in the kitchen, stylishly outfitted to storm
the castle of Hollywood's reigning king, glanced at
the wall clock and saw that he had less than an
hour until his rendezvous with Jack Trotter in Bel
Air.

Murder and mayhem sharpened the appetite. On
his feet, roaming back and forth from refrigerator
to pantry, he made a makeshift meal of cheese,
dried fruit, half a doughnut, a spoonful of butter-
scotch pudding, a taste of this, a bite of that.

Such a chaotic dinner was well suited to a man
who had brought so much disorder into the world
in one day, and who still had much work to do before lying down to sleep.

The Glock, with sound suppressor attached, lay
on the kitchen table. It would just fit in the deepest
pocket of his storm suit.

In other pockets, he had spare magazines, far
more ammunition than he ought to need, considering that he didn't expect to have to kill anyone
else today except Ethan Truman.

If Hazard had been nothing more than a man
who wanted to live, he would have driven away
without crossing the street to ring that doorbell.

He was, however, also a good cop and Ethan's

friend. He believed that police work was not just a job, that it was a calling, and that friendship required commitment exactly when commitment was hardest to give.

He opened the door. He got out of the car.

CHAPTER 73

Upon receiving the call, Dunny at once responds to it not by automobile this time but by highways of fog and water, and by the *idea* of San Francisco.

In a Los Angeles park, he pulls about him a cloak of earthbound cloud, and hundreds of miles to the north, he arrives through the soft folds of another fog, having traded the footpath in the park for the planking of a wharf.

Because he is dead but has not yet moved on from this world to the next, he inhabits his own corpse, a strange condition. After he died in a coma, his spirit had resided briefly in a place that had felt like a doctor's waiting room with neither tattered magazines nor hope. Then he was readmitted to the world, to his familiar mortal shell. He is no mere ghost, nor is he a traditional guardian angel. He is one of the walking dead, but his flesh is now capable of whatever amazing feat his spirit demands of it.

In this more northern and colder city, no rain falls. Water laps at the pilings of the wharf, an unpleasremain on the case, for fear that he already knows the answer.

After Typhon tastes his martini again, he says, "My, but you are a firecracker, Dunny. You're headstrong, impetuous, frustrating—but you're also a hoot. You tickle me. You do."

Uncertain how to interpret those statements, Dunny waits, still and silent.

"I don't mean to be rude," Typhon says, "but my dinner guests will shortly be arriving. Your lean and hungry look—to quote the Bard—and your rough edges might alarm them. They are a wary group, and skittish. One politician and two of his handlers."

Dunny dares to ask, "May I continue to protect Ethan?"

"After your repeated breaches, I'd be justified in removing you now. There must be standards for guardian angels, don't you think? Something more than good intentions. The position ought to require greater ethics than those of United States senators and cardsharps."

Typhon rises from his chair, and Dunny gets quickly to his feet, as well.

"Nevertheless, dear boy, I'm inclined to cut you some slack this one last time."

Dunny accepts his mentor's offered handshake. "Thank you, sir."

"But understand that you're on a minute-by-minute reprieve. If you can't operate within the terms of agreement, then your authority and powers will be at once revoked, and you will instantly be sent home for eternity."

"I'll abide by our deal."

"And when you're sent home, Ethan will be fending for himself."

"I'll walk the line."

Putting one hand on Dunny's shoulder, squeezing affectionately, like a father counseling a son, Typhon says, "Dear boy, you've walked a crooked line so long that keeping to a straight one isn't easy. But now, minute by minute, you must watch your step."

By foot, Dunny leaves the restaurant and follows the wharf into mists reverberant with the low, hollow notes of boat horns. Traveling by fog, by the moonlight above the fog, and by the *idea* of Palazzo Rospo in Bel Air, he departs and makes his journey and arrives all at the same time.

CHAPTER 74

Two bullets in the brain.

Wearing his Kevlar chest protector and conscious of what an easy target his lionesque head would make, Hazard closed the car door and crossed the street.

The house of the mother-killer seemed to attract the incoming fog, which moved not in a monolithic bank but in curious eddies and lithe plumes: one quick-footed vaporous slinkiness after another, tail following tail of Angora mist, as though here were a thousand cats drawn home by the scent of tuna fresh from the can.

The aura of the house so entranced Hazard that he had crossed the street and followed the private walkway while remaining oblivious of the rain. Only when he reached the foot of the front-porch steps did he realize that he had approached with such deliberation that he had gotten wet to the skin.

Ascending the porch steps, he felt something in his hand—and discovered the cell phone on which he had spoken to Dunny Whistler.

I'm dead and *alive,* Dunny had said, and Hazard at the moment was of much that same sentiment.

At the top of the steps, instead of proceeding straight to the door and ringing the bell, he paused, realizing that he had neglected to do a standard bit of follow-up to Dunny's call that he would have done had he received a menacing message from anyone else who should not have had his mobile number. He pressed *69.

The call was answered on the second ring, but the person at the far end of the line said nothing.

"Somebody there?" Hazard asked.

A hard voice came back at him: "Oh, somebody here. Somebody here, sure enough, you hook nigger."

Gang talk: *hook* meaning phony, imitation.

"I be here, got lit up by you, punched twice, and still taste pencil."

Pencil meaning lead, meaning bullets.

Hazard had never heard this voice before, but he knew to whom it might belong. He could not speak.

"When you come across after me, you wannabe ofay, better get ready for a million nightmares of eastlies. You know eastly, man?"

"Yeah. An ugly person," Hazard said, surprised that he had spoken, sensing at once that responding was a bad idea, that it was an *invitation.*

"Worse than ugly, man. Extreme butt-ugly. This crib ain't got nothin' *but* eastlies. I be here when you come across, ofay. I be first in line."

her, the longer she would be his, and his alone. As soon as he found out who she was, she could no longer be his make-believe mom.

Something rapped against a window.

Fric sprang from the chair, dropping the photo.

The face at the window was hooded and hideous, but the hood was rain gear, and the face belonged to one of the security guards, Mr. Roma. Because he had a long upper lip and a small nose, Mr. Roma could pull his lip over his nose, and it would stay that way, so his face looked deformed and his teeth appeared to be huge. Held at his chin and aimed upward, the beam of a flashlight enhanced this effect.

"Ooga-ooga," said Mr. Roma, because without the use of his upper lip, he couldn't pronounce the b in booga.

When Fric went to the window, Mr. Roma allowed his face to pop back into shape. The guard said, "How you doin', Fric?"

"I'm fine now," Fric replied, raising his voice to be heard through the glass. "For a second there, I thought you were Ming."

"Ming's in Florida with your dad."

"He came back early," Fric said. "He's out there walking in the rain somewhere."

Mr. Roma's smile froze.

"He wanted me to walk with him," Fric said, "so he could teach me all about how rain washes the planet's spirit or something."

The frozen smile cracked, crumbled. Mr. Roma

lowered the light from his face and turned his back to Fric, sweeping the night with the beam.

"You'll probably run into him," Fric said.

Realizing that the flashlight pinpointed his position, Mr. Roma switched it off. "See you, Fric," he said, and dashed away into the foggy gloom.

Although Fric was a lousy liar and had not sounded convincing even to himself, Mr. Roma didn't dare call his bluff if there was a one in a thousand chance that Ming, in a talkative mood and in full guru mode, might be in the vicinity.

CHAPTER 76

In the car, out of the rain, shivering in the warm blast from the heater, still sought by the dead Hector X, Hazard listened to the ring, ring, ring until he wanted to roll down the window and throw the cell phone into the street.

The ringing stopped just as he noticed activity at the Laputa residence. A man came out of the house, paused to lock the front door, and descended the porch steps.

Even in the rain and steadily clotting fog, Hazard recognized the guy who had earlier entered the house by way of the garage. All but certainly, this was Vladimir Laputa.

At the junction of private walkway and public sidewalk, Laputa turned right and retraced the route by which he had arrived. He still swaggered, but he didn't seem to be either talking to himself or singing.

He had changed into an entirely black outfit that appeared to be weatherproof, as if he would soon be driving north to Mammoth or to some other ski resort in the Sierras.

Like a premonition of snow, white masses of fog drifted around him, nearly obscuring him, before he turned right at the corner and moved out of sight.

Having already released the hand brake and put the car in gear, Hazard switched on the headlights and drove to the corner, where traffic splashed past on the cross street. He looked to the right and saw Laputa walking northward. When the professor was almost out of sight, Hazard turned the corner and followed him.

Whenever he drew within half a block of Laputa, he pulled to the curb and waited, letting his quarry proceed toward the limits of fog-diminished visibility. Then he drove after him again.

In these fits and starts, Hazard tracked the professor two and a half blocks. There, never having glanced back, Laputa got into a black Land Rover.

Remaining too far behind to read the license plate, letting other traffic intervene from time to time to mask his continuous presence, Hazard shadowed the Land Rover along a direct route to the Beverly Center, at Beverly Boulevard and La Cienega. Although somewhat oddly dressed for a trip to the mall, Laputa apparently intended to go shopping.

Conducting on-the-roll surveillance in a parking garage was a lot trickier than doing the same thing on public streets. Hazard followed the Land Rover up ramp after ramp, floor by floor, past ranks of

Fric asked what it was like to be a homicide de-tective, and sought especially to hear about the most grotesque murders, hideously mangled bod-ies, and bugshit-crazy killers that Mr. Truman had ever encountered. Mr. Truman said much of that stuff wasn't suitable for table talk and that some of it wasn't fit for the ears of a ten-year-old kid. He did tell cop stories, however, most of them funny; a few were gross, although not so gross that you wanted to puke up your lemon-butter chicken, but gross enough to make this by far the best dinner chat that Fric had ever experienced.

When Mr. Truman noted that Mr. Hachette had prepared a coconut-cherry cake for dessert, Fric tapped his knowledge about the island nation of Tuvalu, exporter of coconuts, to make a contribu-tion to their conversation.

Tuvalu led him to lots of other things he knew about, like the biggest pair of shoes ever made. They were size forty-two, cobbled for a Florida gi-ant by the name of Harley Davidson, who had nothing to do with the motorcycle company. Size forty-two shoes are twenty-two inches long! Mr. Truman was properly amazed.

Giant shoes led eventually to Yoo-hoo, civet, and sneezing, and as they were finishing dessert—as yet showing no signs of arsenic ingestion—Fric said, "Did you know my mother was in a booby hatch?"

"Oh, don't pay attention to ugly stuff like that, Fric. It's an unfair exaggeration."

"Well, my mother didn't sue anyone who said that stuff."

"In this country, celebrities can't sue for slander or libel just because people tell lies about them. They have to prove the lies were told with malice. Which is hard. Your mom just didn't want to spend years in a courtroom. You understand?"

"I guess so. But you know what people might think."

"I'm not sure I follow you. What might people think?"

"Like mother, like son."

Mr. Truman appeared to be amused. "Fric, no one who knows you could believe you've ever been in a booby hatch or ever will be."

Pushing aside his empty cake plate, Fric said, "Well, say like someday I see a flying saucer. I mean, *really* see one, and a bunch of big greasy extraterrestrials. You know?"

"Big and greasy," Mr. Truman said, nodding and attentive.

"So then if I tell anyone, the first thing they'll think is *Oh, yeah, his mother was in a booby hatch.*"

"Well, whether or not they remembered those stories about your mom, some people in this world wouldn't believe you if you had one of those big greasy extraterrestrials on a leash."

"I wish I did," Fric murmured.

"They wouldn't believe me, either, if I had one on a leash."

"But you were a *cop*."

"Lots of people are unable to see all kinds of truths

right in front of their eyes. You can't worry about them for a minute. They're hopeless."

"Hopeless," Fric agreed, but he was thinking less about other people than about his own circumstances.

"If you came to me or Mrs. McBee, however, we'd drop anything we were doing to run and see those big greasy freaks because we know you can be taken at your word."

This statement immensely heartened Fric, and he sat up straight in his chair. Into his mind crowded all the things about which he wanted to tell Mr. Truman—Mysterious Caller stepping out of a mirror and flying through the attic rafters, spirits trying to come through the telephone cord and into your ear when you pressed *69, guardian angels with strange rules, child-eating Moloch, the *Los Angeles Times* with the story of his kidnapping—but he hesitated too long, trying to put all this stuff in order, so it wouldn't gush out of him in one hysterical torrent.

Mr. Truman spoke first: "Fric, until I can troubleshoot it and figure out what needs to be repaired, this voltage-flow problem in the alarm system has me concerned."

The security chief's words might as well have been the three-pronged hook on a fisherman's well-cast fly, so firmly did they snare Fric's full attention. The phony voltage-flow story again.

"Nothing's going to happen, but I'm a worrier. Your dad pays me to worry, after all. So until this is fixed, I'd rather you didn't sleep alone on the third floor."

An edgy quality in Mr. Truman's eyes suggested that he himself had seen big greasy ETs, or expected to see them shortly.

"I'd like to set up camp for the night in the living room of your suite," he continued. "Or you could come down to my apartment, sleep in my bed, and I'd move to the sofa in my study. What do you think of that?"

"Or I could sleep on your sofa, and you wouldn't have to give up your bed."

"That's thoughtful of you, Fric. But I've already changed the sheets on my bed in case that was the option you chose. Now if it turns out I changed them for no reason and used up an unscheduled set of linens, I'll have to answer to Mrs. McBee. Don't put me in that position, I beg of you."

Fric knew that Mr. Truman wanted the sofa for one reason and one only: He intended to be stationed between the entrance door to his apartment and the bedroom in which Fric would be sleeping, not because Fric might fall down a set of stairs while sleepwalking, but because maybe some thugs would break down the apartment door and try to get to Fric, in which case they'd have to go through Mr. Truman.

Something was going on, for sure.

"All right," Fric said, worried but also pleasantly excited. "I'll come to your place, and you can have the sofa. This'll be great. I've never stayed overnight away from home."

know what he could do next. He didn't like being at a loss for action.

Every time he tried to puzzle out his next move, however, into his memory came the image of Dunny Whistler sorcerously transformed from flesh into a cascade of water, in an instant becoming one with the puddle in which he had stood, performing a splashless vanishment.

In the wake of that sight, in the cold continuing echo of the conversation with the dead Hector X, logical reasoning failed Hazard. He found his thoughts spiraling again and again through the same disturbing chambers, down into a nautilus shell of dread.

Although he had missed lunch, he wasn't hungry. Although he had no appetite, he stopped at a drive-in fast-food palace for a king's plate of cheeseburgers and French fries.

The king's plate proved to be a bag, of course, and the chalice of coffee was a Styrofoam cup full of a bitter swill that had been brewed with tree bark. Probably hemlock.

He remained too agitated to sit in the restaurant parking lot to have dinner. He drove while he ate.

He needed to keep moving. Like a shark, he felt that he would die if ever he stopped.

Eventually he returned to the tony neighborhood in which the professor lived. He parked across the street from the house.

Sitting there, he heard in his mind the warning voice of Dunny—*Two bullets in the brain*—and he knew beyond doubt that he would have suffered precisely that end if he had rung Laputa's doorbell.

For now the hyena, as Rachel Dalton had called him, was out on an Acura adventure. Without its resident demon, the house was just a house, not a killing ground.

Hazard phoned Robbery/Homicide and obtained Sam Kesselman's home telephone number.

In possession of the number, he considered what he was about to do. He knew that with this move he might be handing his enemies all the weapons they would need to destroy him.

His Granny Rose had once told him that woven throughout the very fabric of the world is an invisible web of evil, and that across this vast construction, deadly spiders quiver to the same secret seductive music, and do the same dark work, each in its own way. If you don't resist this sticky web when you feel it plucking at you, as often it does, then you will become one of the twisted eight-legged souls that dance upon it. And if the poisonous spiders are not crushed at every opportunity, there will sooner than later be spiders uncountable, but no humanity at all.

Hazard keyed in the number.

Sam Kesselman himself answered, first with a cough and a sneeze and a curse, but then in a voice so cracked and rough that he sounded like the product of a genetic-engineering lab working on human-frog crossbreeds.

"Man, you sound bad. You seen a doctor?"

"Yeah. Flu's a virus. Antibiotics don't work. Doctor gave me some cough medicine. Said get lots of rest, drink lots of fluid. Been drinkin' ten beers a day, but I think I'm gonna die anyway."

"Go to twelve."

Kesselman knew about Rolf Reynerd's murder by Hector X, and he knew that Hazard had in turn shot the shooter. "How are you with the OIS team?"

"I'll come through with a clean report. Sounds like they're ready to give it to me now. Listen, Sam, there's a connection with the murder of Reynerd's mother, and that's your case."

"You're gonna tell me Reynerd was involved with it."

"You've smelled something wrong with him all along, huh?"

"His alibi was just *too* airtight."

"There's a lot of that going around."

Hazard told Kesselman about the partial screenplay, but he edited the story line. He recounted the part about the swap of a killing for a killing, as in Hitchcock's *Strangers on a Train,* but not the part about the scheme to murder a movie star.

"So you think . . . Reynerd had . . . a kill buddy," Kesselman said between explosive coughs.

"I know he did. I'm pretty sure it's this guy named Vladimir Laputa. I know Vamp and the Lamp is your case, Sam, but I'd like to develop this further, nail this Laputa if I can."

Maybe Kesselman really did need to hack up a Guinness-record weight of phlegm, or maybe all the throat clearing was a delaying tactic to give him time to think. Finally he said, "Why? I mean, you have your own caseload."

"Well, I think this one is on both our desks as of last night." He hadn't directly lied to Kesselman yet. Now he started: "Because I think Laputa didn't just murder Mina Reynerd, he also hired the hit man, Hector X, who dropped Rolf."

"Then even though the file's on my desk, it's de facto your case, too. The way I feel now, I'm gonna have to stay at all times less than twenty steps from a bathroom until at least next week, so you might as well go for it."

"Thanks, Sam. Just one more thing. If you're ever asked about you and me and this, could I have stopped by your house instead of phoning you, and could we have had this conversation earlier today, like twelve hours ago?"

Kesselman was silent. Then he said, "What kind of hellacious destruction are you bringing down on us?"

"When I'm done," Hazard said, "they'll kick your ass out of the department, strip away your pension, and clean a public toilet with your reputation, but they'll probably let you go on being a Jew."

Kesselman laughed, and the laugh turned into a cough, but when the coughing finally ended, he finished the laugh. "As long as we wind up in the same gutter, at least it'll be entertaining."

After he concluded the call, Hazard sat in the car for a while, staring at the Laputa house, thinking through his approach. He was committed to bold action, but he didn't want to act rashly.

Getting into the place was the easy—even if not legal—part. He still had the Lockaid lock-release gun that he had used to spring the deadbolt at Reynerd's apartment.

Conducting a search without leaving evidence that he had been there, then getting out again, all as smooth as an apparition first manifesting and then fading back to the spirit world: *that* was the hard part.

Throughout his career, he'd largely gone by the book, no matter how incoherent the text sometimes might be. Now he had to convince himself that the justification for rogue action was overwhelming.

From a jacket pocket, he removed the set of silvery bells. He turned them over and over in his hand.

At ten minutes past eight o'clock, he got out of the car.

CHAPTER 79

Following a brief stop in the kitchen, Ethan returned to his apartment, intending to put away the six items that had come in the black gift boxes. If Fric saw them, he would inevitably ask questions that couldn't be answered without making him worry unnecessarily about his father's safety.

In the study, the computer screen glowed. Ethan had not switched it on since coming home.

He quickly searched the apartment but found no intruder. Someone must have been here, however. Perhaps someone who had come and gone by mirrors.

Returning to the desk, taking a closer look at the screen, Ethan saw that a message had been left for him: HAVE YOU CHECKED YOUR NETWORK E-MAIL?

Network e-mail—netmail for short—originated from computers on the estate, those in Channing Manheim's offices on the studio lot, and those in the hands of the security detail on location with the actor in Florida. Netmail was sorted into a different box from the one containing e-mail sent by all other correspondents.

Ethan had just three messages in the netmail box. The first was from Archie Devonshire, one of the porters.

MR. TRUMAN, AS YOU KNOW, I AM NOT ONE WHO FINDS IT INCUMBENT UPON HIMSELF TO MONITOR AELFRIC AND TATTLE ON HIS BEHAVIOR. IN ANY EVENT, HE'S AS WELL BEHAVED AS ANY CHILD CAN BE AND USUALLY ALL BUT INVISIBLE. THIS AFTERNOON, HOWEVER, HE WAS ENGAGED IN SOME CURIOUS BITS OF BUSINESS THAT I MIGHT HAVE DISCUSSED WITH MRS. MCBEE HAD SHE BEEN IN-HOUSE. YOUR VISITING FRIEND, MR. WHISTLER, BROUGHT TO MY ATTENTION THAT AELFRIC—

Ethan read the startling revelation without fully comprehending it, and had to back up to read it again.

YOUR VISITING FRIEND, MR. WHISTLER, BROUGHT TO MY ATTENTION—

The ghost or walking dead man, whichever he might be, if either, had ceased to perform his mysterious work at the edges of perception, and had boldly walked the halls of the mansion, talking to staff.

—BROUGHT TO MY ATTENTION THAT AELFRIC WAS UNPLUGGING QUAKE LIGHTS FROM ODD PLACES IN THE HOUSE, GATHERING THEM IN A PICNIC HAMPER. MRS. MCBEE WOULD SURELY DISAPPROVE OF THIS BECAUSE OF THE RISK THAT, IN A NIGHT EMERGENCY, SOME MEMBER OF STAFF OR FAMILY MIGHT FIND HIS ESCAPE FROM THE HOUSE HINDERED OR ENTIRELY THWARTED BY THE ABSENCE OF THE VERY QUAKE LIGHT CRUCIAL TO HIS EXIT.

Up in Santa Barbara, Mrs. McBee was no doubt uneasily aware that *something* had changed.

Archie Devonshire's netmail continued:

LATER, WHEN I ENCOUNTERED AELFRIC WITH THE HAMPER, HE TOLD ME IT CONTAINED HAM SANDWICHES, WHICH HE CLAIMED TO HAVE MADE HIMSELF, AND THAT HE INTENDED TO HAVE A PICNIC IN THE ROSE ROOM. LATER I FOUND THE HAMPER EMPTY IN THAT VERY ROOM, WITH NO EVIDENCE OF BREADCRUMBS OR SANDWICH WRAPPINGS. THIS SEEMS ALL VERY ODD TO ME, AS AELFRIC IS GENERALLY A TRUTHFUL BOY. MR. YORN HAS LIKEWISE HAD AN UNUSUAL ENCOUNTER AND INTENDS TO WRITE YOU ABOUT THAT SEPARATELY. YOURS IN SERVICE TO THE FAMILY, A. F. DEVONSHIRE.

The netmail from William Yorn, the groundskeeper, proved to be in a tone different from Devonshire's.

FRIC IS MAKING HIMSELF A HIDEY-HOLE IN THE CONSERVATORY, STOCKED WITH FOOD, DRINK, AND QUAKE LIGHTS. YOUR FRIEND WHISTLER BROUGHT IT TO MY ATTENTION. IT'S NONE OF MY BUSINESS. OR WHISTLER'S. BOYS PLAY AT ROBINSON CRUSOE. THAT'S NORMAL. FRANKLY, YOUR FRIEND WHISTLER SCRAPES MY NERVES. IF HE TELLS YOU I WAS ABRUPT WITH HIM, PLEASE UNDERSTAND I MEANT TO BE. LATER, I SAW FRIC AT THE ROSE-ROOM WINDOWS. HE SEEMED TO BE IN A TRANCE. THEN HE SHOUTED SOMETHING AT ME ABOUT HAM SANDWICHES. LATER, IN RAIN GEAR, HE WENT OUT TO THE LITTLE WOODS PAST THE ROSE GARDEN. HAD BINOCULARS. SAID HE WAS BIRD WATCHING. IN THE RAIN. HE WAS OUT THERE TEN MINUTES. HE HAS A RIGHT TO BE ECCENTRIC. HELL, IF I WAS IN HIS SHOES, I'D BE FULL CRAZY. I'M WRITING YOU ABOUT THIS ONLY BE-

CAUSE ARCHIE DEVONSHIRE INSISTED. ARCHIE GETS ON MY NERVES, TOO. I'M GLAD I WORK OUTSIDE. YORN.

The thought of Duncan Whistler, dead or alive, prowling Palazzo Rospo, secretly watching Fric, brought a chill to the nape of Ethan's neck.

He suspected that the mind of a detective was inadequate to solve this increasingly Byzantine puzzle. Deductive and inductive reasoning are poor tools for dealing with things that go bump in the night.

CHAPTER 80

Before committing an illegal entry, Hazard rang the doorbell. When no one responded, he rang it again.

Darkness in the Laputa house didn't mean that the place was deserted.

Rather than slinking around to the back of the residence, where his furtive behavior might catch the attention of a neighbor, Hazard entered boldly by the front. With the Lockaid, he popped both locks.

Pushing the door inward, he called out, "Anyone home or is it just us chickens?"

This was prudence, not comedy. Even when silence greeted his question, he crossed the threshold cautiously.

Immediately upon entering, however, he located the wall switch and flicked on the foyer-ceiling fixture. In spite of the rain and fog, some passing motorist or pedestrian might have seen him enter. The unhesitating use of lights would establish his legitimacy in suspicious minds.

Besides, if Laputa came home unexpectedly, he would be alarmed to see one lamp lit that had not been on when he'd left, or the beam of an inquiring flashlight in the darkness, but he would be disarmed to find the house blazing with light. The success of an operation like this depended upon boldness and quickness.

Hazard closed the door but didn't lock it. He wanted easy exit in the event of an unexpected confrontation.

The ground floor most likely did not contain the incriminating evidence that he sought. Murderers tended to keep mementos of their crimes, gruesome and otherwise, in their bedrooms.

The second-favorite repository for their treasures was the basement, often in concealed or locked rooms where they were able to visit their collections without fear of discovery. There, in an atmosphere of calculated dementia, they could dreamily relive the bloody past without fear of discovery.

In respect of land prone to earthquakes and mud slides, houses in southern California seldom had basements. This one, as well, had been built on a slab, with no door that opened to a lower darkness.

Hazard toured the ground floor, not bothering to search cabinets and drawers. If he found nothing upstairs, he would take a second pass at these rooms, probing them with greater care.

Right now he cared only about establishing that no one lurked in any of these chambers. He left lights on everywhere behind him. Darkness was not his friend.

In the kitchen, he unlocked the back door and left it standing ajar, providing himself with a second unobstructed exit.

Tentacles of fog wove through the open door, drawn by the warmth but dissipating in it.

Everything in the house appeared to have been scoured, scrubbed, vacuumed, polished, and buffed to a degree that approached obsession. Collections of decorative items—Lalique glass, ceramic boxes, small bronze figures—were arranged not with an artful eye but with a rigid sense of order reminiscent of a chess set. Every book on every shelf stood precisely half an inch from the edge.

The house seemed to be a refuge against the messiness of the world beyond its walls. However, in spite of conveniences aplenty, in spite of comfortable furnishings, in spite of cleanness and order, the place was not welcoming, with none of the warmth of hearth and home. Instead, entirely apart from the tension that Hazard felt due to being here illegally, an air of edgy expectation was endemic to the place, and a desperation not quite nameable.

The only clutter on the ground floor lay on the dining-room table. Five sets of charts or blueprints, rolled and fastened with rubber bands. A long-handled magnifying glass. A yellow, lined tablet. Rolling Writer pens—one red, one black. Although these items had not been put away, they had been arranged neatly side by side.

backpack that he had taken from the trunk of the Acura, he had greeted Jack Trotter and his two-man prep crew, who arrived in a thirty-eight-foot truck. Corky directed them along the curved drive-way, where they parked close to the house.

"This is madness," Trotter had declared as he climbed out of the truck.

"Not at all," Corky disagreed. "The wind has died completely."

"It's still raining."

"Not furiously. And a little rain provides some covering noise, just what we need."

In full Queeg von Hindenburg mode, Trotter wore pessimism with the grim authority of Nostradamus in his darkest mood. His bloated face sagged like a deflating balloon, and his protuberant eyes were wild with visions of doom. "We're screwed in this fog."

"It's not that thick yet. Just enough to give us ex-tra cover. It's perfect. The trip is short, the target easily identifiable even in a medium fog."

"We'll be seen before we're half ready to go."

"This property's on a knoll. No houses have a view down on it. We're surrounded by trees, can't be seen from the street."

Trotter insisted on disaster: "We're damn sure to be seen by someone between here and there."

"Maybe," Corky acknowledged. "But what will they make of what they've seen between pal-isades of fog?"

"Palisades?"

"I have an interest in literature, the beauty of the

language," Corky said. "Anyway, your entire mission time is probably seven or eight minutes. You'll be back here, out of here, on the road before anyone can figure where your staging area was. Besides, I've got agents all over these hills, and they won't let cops get near you."

"And when I split from Malibu, I disappear from all government records. Me and all the names I've used."

"That's the deal. But you'd better get your ass in gear. The clock is ticking."

Grimacing like a man in an advertisement for a diarrhea remedy, Trotter looked Corky up and down, then said, "What the hell do you call that getup you're wearing?"

"Weatherproof," Corky said.

Now, more than an hour later, Trotter and his two-man crew had nearly completed preparations.

During that time, Corky had entertained himself by studying the ruins of the half-demolished chateau from numerous angles.

He had not, of course, worked with Trotter and his men. As Robin Goodfellow, he was a highly trained human weapon, a valued government agent. Robin had signed up to pursue truth, justice, and adventure, but had never agreed to perform menial labor of any kind. James Bond does not dust furniture or do windows.

Without his assistance, however, the blimp had been fully inflated.

CHAPTER 82

The third netmail was from Mr. Hachette. INSPECTOR TRUMAN: I MYSELF BITTERLY EXPRESS HEREWITH EXTREME DISPLEASURE AT BEING EXPECTED TO CREATE THE MOST SUPERIOR OF HAUTE CUISINE THAT I AM CAPABLE ON A MOMENT'S NOTICE FOR THE BOTTOMLESS STOMACH OF A GUEST WHOSE PRESENCE IN THE HOUSE ISN'T REVEALED UNTIL HE APPEARS IN MY KITCHEN, SURPRISING ME LIKE A WEEVIL IN THE FLOUR SUPPLY. MR. WHISTLER'S MAGNIFICENT TASTE IN FOOD AND HIS PRAISE FOR MY UNIQUE COQUILLES ST. JACQUES, AS FOR EVERY REFINED DISH OF MY DIFFICULT PREPARATION, IS PLEASING BUT DOES NOT GLUE TOGETHER MY SHATTERED NERVES, WHICH I WARN YOU ARE DEVASTATED AND FRAYED. IF THIS IS DONE TO ME AGAIN, BY YOU, I MUST RESIGN WITH CONSEQUENCES OF UNSPEAKABLE EXTREMITY. I AM ALSO DISPLEASED TO ANNOUNCE THAT THE BOY CLAIMS TO HAVE MADE HAM SANDWICHES IN MY KITCHEN WITHOUT PERMISSION, AND THAT I AM SHARPLY INVENTORYING THE PANTRY AT THIS TIME TO LEARN THE EXTENT OF HIS DESTRUCTION. HOPING THAT THESE OUTRAGES MUST NEVER BE REPEATED, I REMAIN, CHEF HACHETTE.

Dead Dunny had moved right in. And with an appetite.

This was crazy. Ethan wanted to laugh, but he couldn't work up as much as a smile. His mouth had gone dry. His palms were damp.

He went back to Yorn's message: FRIC IS MAKING HIMSELF A HIDEY-HOLE IN THE CONSERVATORY . . . YOUR FRIEND WHISTLER BROUGHT IT TO MY ATTENTION . . . BOYS PLAY AT ROBINSON CRUSOE . . . WHISTLER SCRAPES MY NERVES. . . .

During Hannah's battle with cancer, Ethan had felt helpless as never before. He had always been able to take care of the people who mattered to him, to do everything for them that needed to be done. But he couldn't save Hannah, she who had been the dearest to him.

Once more, he felt control slipping out of his hands. With a state-of-the-art security system, on-site guards, and well-conceived security protocols, with full diligence, he could not keep Dunny off the estate, out of the house. Man or ghost, or a force to which no easy label applied, Dunny somehow had a connection with Reynerd and probably with the professor about whom Reynerd had written in his screenplay. Dunny must be part of the threat, and he mocked Ethan by his every intrusion, proving that no one here was safe.

If Ethan failed Channing Manheim, if someone got at the star in spite of all precautions, he would be failing not only his boss but also the special boy who'd be left fatherless. Fric would be remanded to the mercy of his self-absorbed mother, set fur-air, traveling with the wind. As long as he remained aloft, the agents of evil could not seize him and cast him down into a dank cell with no light other than the red glow of rats' eyes.

He owned a traditional rig—the colorfully striped envelope, the inflation fan, the propane-fueled burner, the basket for pilot and passengers— which he sometimes took up alone, the sole balloonist on a sweet spring morning or on a golden summer evening. He also joined rallies of celestial navigators, when twenty or thirty or more bright balloons launched in rough synchronization and drifted in a school through the heavens.

A hot-air balloon was all but entirely at the mercy of the wind. The pilot could neither plan a pinpoint destination nor provide an estimated time of arrival to the minute or even to the quarter hour.

The assault on Palazzo Rospo required a highly maneuverable craft that could travel at cross purposes to at least a light wind. As well, it must be able to ascend without the ungodly roar of a propane burner, which always set dogs barking within a quarter-mile radius. Furthermore, it must be able to descend as smoothly as a dove glides from cloud to bower, if more slowly than a dove, and must also be able to hover like a hummingbird.

Trotter enjoyed the astonishment and excitement with which fellow sky sailors regarded his custom-made craft on those occasions when he left his hot-air balloon at home and brought the little blimp instead. Not garrulous by nature, lacking many social graces,

Trotter nonetheless could expect to be the hit of the rally in his miniature airship.

Corky suspected that in his perpetually fevered mind, Trotter also regarded the blimp as a last-ditch escape vehicle in the event that an abruptly declared dictatorship tried for any reason to seal off highway traffic in and out of major metropolitan areas like Los Angeles and surrounding communities. He probably envisioned himself foiling the totalitarians on a night of a crescent moon, with enough light to navigate but not enough to be easily seen, sailing high above roadblocks and concentration camps, north into farm country and toward the Sierra foothills, where he could eventually set down and proceed on foot, overland, to one of his well-prepared bolt-holes.

After drawing Corky away from the ruins of the chateau, Trotter said, "We'll be out of here in less than five minutes."

The two-man prep crew was conducting final checks of the airship systems and gear.

They were rent-a-thugs involved in Ecstasy distribution with Trotter. After he delivered Corky to Palazzo Rospo and returned to the chateau in the blimp, when these men had snared the nose line and anchored him by three tethers, Trotter would kill them.

"I haven't heard you charging the batteries," Corky said.

"They were fully charged before we came here."

"Airborne, we can't use the engine, not for a minute."

"I know, I know. Man, haven't you busted my ass about it enough already? We won't need the engine for this short a trip, with the air this calm."

The blimp's twin can-mounted propeller fans, slung from the back of the gondola, were usually driven by a riding-lawnmower engine. The turning blades produced an acceptably soft sound, but the engine racket made stealthy travel impossible.

"With little or no headwind," Trotter said, "I can run two hours on batteries, maybe longer. But I hate this rain."

"It's just a light drizzle now."

"Lightning," Trotter said. "The thought of lightning makes my bowels loose, and it ought to do the same to yours."

"It's inflated with helium, isn't it?" Corky asked, indicating three discarded cylinders of compressed gas, each the size of a hospital oxygen tank. "The Hindenburg was hydrogen. I thought helium didn't explode."

"I'm not worried about an explosion. *I'm worried about being struck by lightning!* Even if lightning doesn't rupture the bag and set it afire, it could fry us in the gondola."

"The storm's winding down. No lightning," Corky observed.

"There was lightning earlier today."

"Only a little. I told you, Trotter, we in government *control* the storm. When we want lightning, it strikes where we need it, and when we *don't* want lightning, not one bolt leaves the quiver."

In addition to being inflated with nonflammable

helium instead of hydrogen, the blimp was different from a zeppelin in that it had no rigid internal structure. The skin of the *Hindenburg*—a vessel as long as the Eiffel Tower is tall, nearly as long as four Boeing 747s standing nose to tail—had been stretched around an elaborate steel frame that contained sixteen giant gas cells, great cotton sacks made airtight by a coating of plastic, as well as an entire luxury hotel. Trotter's blimp, any blimp, was just a flat bag when deflated.

With no missing strawberries to obsess about and with no roller bearings to manipulate obsessively in one hand, a la Bogart in *The Caine Mutiny,* Captain Queeg von Hindenburg studied the slowly seething fog overhead, squinting to catch a glimpse of the clouds above the fog. He looked worried. He looked angry. With his orange hair pasted to his head by rain, his protuberant eyes, and his walrus mustache, he looked like a cartoon. "I don't like this at all," he muttered.

ment. The computerized audio analyzer filtered out static, identified patterned sounds that fit the profile of speech, clarified and enhanced that speech, and finally eliminated gaps in order to condense the call to its essence before storing it.

Caller 56 still sounded as though she cried out from a great distance, across an abyss. Her fragile voice made him lean forward in his chair, afraid that he would lose it. Nevertheless, because of the computer enhancement, he could hear every word spoken, though the message puzzled him.

The voice was Hannah's.

CHAPTER 85

In his mind's ear, Corky Laputa listened to Richard Wagner's *Die Walküre*, particularly to the music meant to portray the flight of the Valkyries.

Through the drizzle and fog, through the windless Bel Air, the mad Queeg's miniblimp sailed as smoothly as one dream melting into another.

The swish and sizzle of the rain entirely masked what noise the battery-powered propellers made, so that it seemed as though Corky and his sour-faced pilot journeyed in utter silence, without sough or bated billow. Neither the sun nor the moon could claim a quieter ascent and transit of the sky.

Suspended under the airship, the open gondola was similar to a rowboat, but with rounded stern and prow. The two bench-style seats were capable of accommodating four.

Facing forward, Trotter sat at the yoke on the bench nearer the stern. He was immediately in front of the engine, the helium feed, and the other controls.

At first Corky faced Trotter, looking back the way they had come. Then he turned to look forward, frequently leaning out to one side or the other to spot landmarks through the misty murk.

Treetops slid by only a few feet below them. Casting no faintest shadow in the absence of the moon and stars, they progressed with such stealth and with such minimal disturbance to the air that birds in the highest branches, sheltering from the rain, were not once frightened into flight.

This wealthy community had been built in a forest of oak and ficus and evergreen, of metrosideros and podocarpus and California pepper. More accurately, a forest had been imported to dress these hills, glens, and canyons, which long ago had been only semiarid pastures of wild grass and bleak ravines cluttered with scrub.

To pass all but invisibly above unsuspecting Bel Air, they were required to stay at the lowest prudent altitude. In these hills, most streets were serpentine and quite narrow, flanked and often overhung by huge trees, providing motorists with tightly circumscribed views of the sky. As long as the blimp seldom crossed above streets and thereby took full advantage of the forests that would screen it from all eyes except those directly below, it might slip all the way to Palazzo Rospo and back again without being noticed, for few if any residents would be afoot on their properties—and in a position to look up—in this weather.

A direct route as the blimp flies, from the ruined chateau on the knoll to Palazzo Rospo, downslope, measured less than half a mile. In windless conditions like these, running on batteries, the airship could make a top speed of fifteen miles per hour. To disturb the fog as little as possible and thus shroud themselves in its welcome veils, they were making just ten miles per hour, which would get them from door to door in approximately three minutes.

Through the Internet, Corky had accessed not only maps and city-planning charts but also a trove of aerial photography produced by the state of California, offering a bird's view of these exclusive and secluded enclaves. A majority of the homes in this community were true estates, particularly in that portion over which they now flew; and Corky had memorized the roof lines and the salient features of each palatial structure that lay along their route.

Trotter had done his homework, too. He consulted landmarks less often than Corky, however, for he relied more on compass readings.

The only light associated with the airship was the soft glow of the compass, the altimeter, and the few other gauges on the control panel. They were swivel-mounted on a stanchion, allowing Trotter to position them as needed. The combined radiance of these instruments was insufficient to paint the faintest glimmer on the curve of the helium bag immediately overhead.

Indeed, more light rose from the great houses over which they glided than from the craft controls. Gold and silver reflections of this rising incandes-

Ethan's breath caught in his throat. He slid to the edge of the chair.

"Tuesday's child is full of grace. . . ."

He knew this. A children's rhyme. He mouthed the words of the third line along with her.

"Wednesday's child is full of woe. . . ."

The Cookie Kitten was filled with Scrabble tiles that spelled WOE ninety times.

A kitten was a young cat. A kitten was a *child*. Like Fric.

Why ninety? Maybe it didn't matter. Ninety of each letter, two hundred and seventy tiles in total, were the number needed to fill the jar. Wednesday's child is *full* of woe.

Call 53. Hannah.

Even with the static filtered out and the speech enhanced, her message could not be understood, as if on this occasion, the river between life and death had widened until the far shore lay at the other side of an ocean.

Call 52. Also unclear.

Call 51. Hannah with another nursery rhyme.

"Ladybug, ladybug, fly away home. . . ."

As he shot to his feet, Ethan knocked over his chair.

"Your house is on fire, and your children will burn."

Channing Manheim would not arrive home until the afternoon of December 24. The operative theory had been that the Face wouldn't be in danger until that time, at the earliest.

Maybe the Face himself had never been in danger. Maybe the target had always been Fric.

Twenty-two ladybugs in a small glass jar. Why not twenty-three or twenty-four? Unlike the cookie jar, the beetle container had been less than half full. So why not fifty ladybugs packed to the lid?

This was Tuesday, December 22.

CHAPTER 87

As Corky slid from the center of his bench toward the port side of the gondola, Trotter said, "Easy, easy."

The sudden shift of Corky's 170 pounds could cause the miniblimp to wallow, perhaps even bobble, which was a risk they couldn't take this close to the roof.

While Corky moved slowly, balancing breast-down on the gunwale, one leg in and one leg out of the gondola, Trotter employed his own body as a counterweight, shifting starboard on his bench, and he used the controls to fine-tune the attitude of the vessel.

The blimp wallowed but not dangerously.

At a signal from Trotter, Corky slid the rest of the way out of the gondola, though he did not at once drop free of it. First he hung by both hands from the gunwale, while the pilot compensated for this further shift of weight.

As the airship steadied, Corky lowered his left hand from the gunwale to a ballast-tank bracket, then his right. The metal was cold and wet, but with his leather-and-nylon gloves, he got a firm grip.

Peering down, he saw that his dangling feet were still eighteen or twenty inches from the roof.

He dared not drop that far. Though he would most likely keep his balance, he would land with too much noise, alerting the two guards who were in the security office that occupied half the second floor of the groundskeeper's building.

Evidently, Trotter recognized the problem. He vented a whisper of helium, and the vessel sank until Corky felt the roof under him.

Straddling the ridge line, one foot on the south slope of the roof, one foot on the north slope, he let go of the ballast-tank bracket. He had touched down almost as softly as Peter Pan.

Freed of his weight, the blimp at once soared ten feet, fifteen. The tail began to rise, which wasn't good, but with an adjustment of the rudders, Trotter raised the nose and recovered even as he brought the vessel around for the return trip to the knoll, which he would be making alone.

With the boy in his control, Corky would leave Palazzo Rospo in style, using one of the automobiles in Manheim's first-rate collection.

Back at the ruined chateau, once the three tethering lines were well anchored to truck and trees, Trotter would shoot the two men who served as ground crew. Although the abandonment of the airship would be a wound to his heart, he would activated, into the security-office bathroom, and from there into the entire building.

Closed doors would not inhibit dispersal. The sleep-inducing vapors would rush between door and threshold, between door and jamb, through any tiniest crack and crevice, through heating vents and plumbing chases.

Prior to the scheduled nine o'clock foot patrol of the grounds, both guards were in the office below Corky. The sedative was so fast-acting that in ten seconds from the time the ADU emptied, the two men would have collapsed unconscious.

He waited more than half a minute before departing the ridge line for the north slope of slate. The roof was not steeply pitched, and he descended it with ease.

At the front of the building, which was as large as an upscale suburban house, a loggia was covered by a sturdy redwood trellis entwined for decades by a trumpet vine. He jumped from the roof onto the trellis.

From the trellis, he leaped to the lawn, allowed his knees to buckle as would a parachutist, fell, rolled, and sprang to his feet.

He felt like Vin Diesel.

After shrugging out of his backpack, he withdrew from it a gas mask. He tossed the pack aside and put on the mask.

The central entrance to the groundskeeper's building was not locked. He stepped into a service foyer.

Just like the blueprints.

To his right: a door into a gardening-supplies storeroom large enough also to garage the three riding lawnmowers as well as the two electric carts with which Yorn and his day crew moved fertilizer and other materials around the immense grounds.

To his left: a door to Yorn's spacious office, another door to the bathroom used by gardeners.

Directly ahead were stairs to the second floor.

Upstairs, Corky found the two evening-shift guards unconscious in the main monitoring room. One sprawled on the floor, and the other slumped in a chair in front of a bank of video monitors.

They would be profoundly unconscious for between sixty to eighty minutes. That was plenty of time for Corky to do his job and be gone.

He pulled up a chair in front of a computer. Neither the power supply nor the estate-specific networking arrangements had been affected by the careful severance of outgoing and incoming phone service.

In his gas mask, his breathing sounded like that of Darth Vader.

At the start of the shift, as always, one of the guards had earlier accessed the security system with a personal password. To Corky, the elaborate status display on the screen revealed, among many other things, that the house-perimeter alarm had been activated, making it impossible to enter Palazzo Rospo by window or door without triggering sirens.

According to Ned Hokenberry, the three-eyed freak—now the two-eyed freak, now the *dead* two-eyed freak—the perimeter alarm usually wasn't engaged until eleven o'clock or even midnight. This evening they had closed up early.

Corky wondered why.

Perhaps they had been spooked by certain black boxes and the contents thereof.

Delighted to have made them uneasy and yet still have slipped this far past their defenses, Corky began to sing the Grinch's theme from *The Grinch Who Stole Christmas.* The gas mask lent the tune a wonderfully spooky, even savage quality.

Mick Sachatone, poor dead Mick in his Bart Simpson pajamas, had hacked the Manheim security system by linking to it via the computer of the off-site armed-response company that maintained a 24/7 line to this room. He'd given Corky some rudimentary instruction in its operation.

First, Corky checked the status of the two panic rooms in the mansion. Neither was in use.

Using the computer, he put the two panic rooms in siege mode, engaging their locks by remote. They could no longer be opened using their hidden on-site lock releases. No one could take refuge in them.

The house-perimeter alarm could be armed or disarmed simply by selecting from a YES-NO option. Currently the YES was lit on the screen. Corky used the mouse to click the NO.

Now, with a door key, he could enter Palazzo Rospo as though it were his own sweet home. Keys dangled from the belt of each sleeping guard. He unclipped one set, jingled them, and smiled.

When he picked up a phone, he heard no dial tone. He tried one of the guard's cell phones. It didn't function. Reliable Mick.

Leaving the guards to their dreams, Corky descended the stairs and returned to the loggia under the trellis and the trumpet vine. He stripped off the gas mask and threw it away.

Through a screen of trees and darkling rain, the great house could be seen perhaps two hundred yards to the north. With only Ethan Truman and the boy in residence, not many windows were lighted, yet the mansion nonetheless reminded Corky of an enormous luxury liner making way on a night sea. And he was the iceberg.

He unzipped the deepest pocket on his storm suit and withdrew the Glock that previously he had fitted with a sound suppressor.

CHAPTER 88

"Ladybug, ladybug, fly away home. . . . Your house is on fire, and your children will burn. . . ."

After listening to Call 51, Ethan had no doubt that some of the first fifty recordings also contained messages of value to him, but he did not think he dared take time to review them, and he *knew* that he didn't need to hear them in order to solve the riddle.

Twenty-two ladybugs. The twenty-second of December.

Today. And only a little more than three hours remained until the calender turned to December 23. If something terrible were going to happen, it would occur soon.

His pistol was in his apartment.

By now Fric must be waiting there, as well.

He fled the white room, leaving the blue door open behind him.

No need to panic. The perimeter alarm would shriek at the first breach of door or window. Between wails of the siren, a voice module would announce, in a clear computerized voice, the room in which the break-in had occurred.

Besides, the men in the security office would know the moment anyone crossed the estate wall, long before an intruder could reach the house. At the first evidence that the property had been violated, they would call 911 and the private armed-response security firm.

Nevertheless, with no time for the elevator, first to the back stairs in a sprint, then down six flights, down and around he went in a thunder, slamming through the door at the bottom of the stairs, into the ground-floor west wing.

He threw open the door to his apartment, called to Fric, and got no answer.

Evidently the boy was still in the library. Not good. He had gotten through ten years of life alone more often than not, but he wouldn't make it through this night by himself.

Ethan hurried to the desk in the study. He had left the pistol in the top right-hand drawer.

Pulling open the drawer, he expected to find that the gun had been taken. But there it was. A beautiful thing.

As Ethan slipped into the shoulder holster, he surveyed the items on top of the desk, between the computer and the telephone.

Nursery rhymes.

Your house is on fire, and your children will burn. . . .

Wednesday's child is full of woe. . . .

Nursery rhymes.

Foreskins circumcised from ten men. Ten because Fric was ten years old. What are foreskins? Rags of tissue. Scraps. *Snips.*

And snails are *snails.*

The book of dog stories, *Paws for Reflection,* a collection of puppy-dog *tales.* Different spelling, same word to the ear. *Tails.*

What are little boys made of?

Snips and snails, and puppy dogs' tails.

That's what little boys are made of.

The note that had come with the apple lay on the desk: THE EYE IN THE APPLE? THE WATCHFUL WORM? THE WORM OF ORIGINAL SIN? DO WORDS HAVE ANY PURPOSE OTHER THAN CONFUSION?

In this case, confusion was their sole purpose. The sixth object had been the easiest to interpret, so the professor, whoever the hell he was, had confused the issue with distracting—and mocking—words.

The eye in the apple is blue, the same color as the famous eyes of Channing Manheim. Not the eye in the apple. *The apple of his eye.*

Not that good Fric was ever the apple of his father's eye. He was the *blind spot* in his father's eye, too often overlooked, never seen in the fullness of his character. In this instance, the sender of the black boxes had made an incorrect assumption. The Face himself was the apple of his own eye, and there could be no other.

If you knew the true relationship between this father and this son, you might be forgiven for not making the connection between the doll's eye nestled in the black-sutured apple and the wonderful boy. Yet Ethan cursed himself for missing the clue.

He pressed INTERCOM on the telephone keypad and then the line number for the security office at the back of the estate. "Pete? Ken? We might have a situation brewing."

No one answered.

"Pete? Ken? Are you there?"

Nothing.

Ethan snatched up the handset. No dial tone.

CHAPTER 89

The hyena slept in a clean den, unsoiled by mementos of his killings. No articles of clothing stained with the victims' blood that he could press to his face to savor the scent of death. No items of women's jewelry that he could fondle. No Polaroid photos of Justine Laputa or Mina Reynerd after he tested their mortality with a fireplace poker and a bronze-encrusted marble lamp. Nothing.

After a quick but meticulous search of the walk-in closet, the bureau drawers, the nightstands, and every place else in the bedroom where Laputa might have hidden the kind of pornography that appealed not to prurient interest but to an obsession with violence, Hazard turned up no evidence of either a crime or psychopathy.

As before, the most notable thing about the Laputa house was the scrupulous cleanliness, which rivaled that in any hermetically sealed and frequently sanitized biochemical-weapons lab, and the fetishistic alignment and geometry of every object large and small. Not only the items on open display but also the contents of drawers were placed as though with the aid of micrometer, protractor, and straightedge. The socks and sweaters appeared to have been folded and stowed away by a precision-programmed robot.

Again, Hazard sensed that, for Vladimir Laputa, this house was a desperate refuge from the messiness of the world beyond its walls.

He retreated from the bedroom, into the upstairs hall, where he stood for a moment, listening intently, hearing only the tepid tattoo of the diminishing rain on the roof. He glanced at his watch, wondering how much time, if any, he had to pore through the other second-floor chambers.

Instinct seldom failed Hazard, but it told him nothing now. The professor might return at any moment or not for hours, days.

He tried the first door past the master bedroom, on that same side of the hall, snapped on the light.

Judging by appearances, this was a storeroom. Plain cardboard cartons emblazoned only with red stenciled numbers were stacked three high, in well-ordered rows.

A quiver of interest drew Hazard a few steps past the threshold. Then he realized that the boxes were sealed with precisely applied strips of strapping tape. If he tore open a few, he would not be able to restore them to the degree necessary to conceal the fact of his unauthorized explorations.

Approaching the last room on that side of the hall, he detected an unpleasant odor. By the time he reached the open door, the malodor had become a stench.

Central to the stink, Hazard recognized the smell of corrupted flesh, of which he'd had more than a little experience in his career with Robbery/ Homicide. He suspected that here he would find at least one of Laputa's mementos that would make him wish he had not stopped earlier for cheeseburgers and fries.

The glow from the hall sconces spilled only a short distance into the room. Hazard couldn't see much.

When he stepped across the threshold and flipped up the wall switch, a nightstand lamp came on. For a moment he thought the man in the bed, less than half concealed by a sheet, must be a corpse.

Then the bloodshot eyes, which were fixed on him in pitiful appeal, blinked.

Hazard had never before seen firsthand a living human being in such wretched condition as this. Here was what the starved slave laborers in concentration camps looked like when, at last worked to death, they were tumbled into raw graves.

In spite of the IV rack and catheter-fed urine jar, Hazard knew at once that in this situation Professor Laputa was not a caregiver tending to a family member. The man in the bed had been afforded none of the tenderness due a patient but all the brutality that could be rained upon a prisoner by a demented jailer.

Both windows had been boarded over and

sealed with caulking to keep out daylight and to hold in all sound.

On the floor in one corner were tumbled chains and handcuffs and ankle shackles. Surely these bonds were from the early days of the imprisonment, when the man in the bed had been strong enough to require restraints.

Hazard had been speaking aloud for a while before he quite heard himself. He had been reduced to the childhood prayers that Granny Rose had taught him long ago.

Here was evil as pure as he had ever seen it, forever beyond the understanding of a simple sinner like himself. This way a wicked thing had come and gone, and would come again, a demon on sabbatical from Hell.

The uncommon neatness and order elsewhere in the house didn't represent Laputa's need for a refuge from the disorder of the world outside. It was instead a desperate denial of just how apocalyptic was the chaos that churned within him.

By the time that Hazard reached the side of the bed, each breath he drew further sickened him. Weeks' worth of dried sweats, rancid body oils, and festering bedsores raised a nauseating stench.

Nevertheless, Hazard gently took hold of the nearer of the stranger's fragile hands. The man had insufficient strength to lift his arm, and he could barely squeeze his rescuer's hand in return.

"It's all right now. I'm a cop."

looked as if he could do nothing more than blink his eyes.

"The can smashed through the window and rolled down the porch roof as I was coming up the front walk. I heard you feebly calling for help, so I forced entry."

The story sucked. The first officers on the scene would know that it was bogus, but in light of Dalton's ordeal, this would be a flavor of bogus that they could swallow.

By the time Laputa found himself in a courtroom, Dalton would have largely recovered, and the jury would not know just how horribly weak he had been on the night of his rescue. Time could give this shabby story enough luster to make it look attractive.

Shifting his eyes from the open doorway to Hazard, Dalton said anxiously, "Hurry," as if he feared Laputa's imminent return.

Hazard threw the can of disinfectant at the window. The glass shattered with a satisfying crash.

CHAPTER 90

Having further seared the roots of the potted palm with his mighty Manheim urine, which he could probably have bottled and sold to his father's craziest fans, Fric shopped the library shelves for a book, mindful that Mr. Truman had said not to dawdle.

In case they didn't make s'mores and sit on the floor telling scary stories, he took the trouble of finding a book that he might actually enjoy reading. He figured that he would be awake most of this long night, and not because he was excited about Christmas Eve coming in just two days. If he didn't have a book to pass the time, he would go as crazy as Barbra Streisand's two-headed cat.

He had just found a novel that looked good when he heard noise overhead: a shimmering, bright music much like the soft ringing of a hundred tiny wind chimes all agitated at once.

When he looked up at the stained-glass dome, he saw hundreds of pieces of glass break out of the leading and fall toward him.

No. Not glass. The stained-glass mosaic remained in place across the entire arc of the thirty-foot dome. Shards of color and shadow fell out of the glass without breaking it, fell *through* it from the night above or maybe from somewhere immeasurably stranger than the night.

The shards fell slowly, not to the demand of gravity, and as they drifted down they changed color. As they changed color, they tumbled upon one another and fused together. As they fused together, they acquired greater dimension and a form.

The gathered shards became Mysterious Caller, whom Fric had most recently seen pictured in the *Los Angeles Times* in the rose room this afternoon, whom he had last encountered life-size in the memorabilia maze the previous night. As the guardian angel had on that occasion glided without benefit of wings from rafters to attic floor, so now he descended with soundless grace to the carpet only a few feet from Fric.

"You have this knack for entrances," Fric said, but his shaky voice belied his cocky Hollywood-kid attitude.

"Moloch is here," the guardian declared in a tone of voice so dire that it would have made Fric's heart clench and then punch his ribs even if the message had been a fraction as terrifying as this. "Run to your deep and special place, Fric. Run *now*."

Pointing to the stained-glass dome, Fric said, "Why don't you just take me up there, out of here, where you came from, where I'll be safe?"

"I told you, boy, you must make your own choices, exercise your free will, and save yourself."

"But I—"

"Besides, you can't go to the places I go or travel by the means I do, not until you're dead." The guardian stepped closer, leaned forward, thrusting his pallid face within an inch of Fric's. "Do you want to *die horribly* just to be able to travel more conveniently?"

Fric's hammering heart knocked all the words out of his throat before he could speak them, and as he struggled to sputter through his silence, he was lifted off his feet and held high by his weird guardian.

"Moloch is in the house. Hide, boy, for God's sake, *hide*."

With that, Mysterious Caller threw Fric as though he were only a bundle of rags, but threw him with a magical knack that prevented him from crashing hard into furniture. Instead, he tumbled in slow motion across the library, over the club chairs and tables, past the islands of bookshelves.

As he rotated on a curious axis, head over heels, Fric saw the photograph of the pretty lady, his make-believe mom, which had slipped out of his pocket and now drifted lazily beside him through the air, in his sphere of influence. Like an astronaut reaching for a floating tube of food in the gravity-free environment of a space shuttle high in orbit, he grasped for the picture but could not quite close his hand on it.

Corky wondered what exquisite holiday cookies people of this wealth enjoyed. Once he had killed Truman and secured the boy, maybe he would dare to take a few minutes to investigate the stock of baked goods in the kitchen. He might pack a tin of homemade treats to enjoy later at home.

He turned right and followed the north hall past the tea room, the intimate dining room, the grand dining room, toward the kitchen and ultimately toward the west hall where Truman waited to be killed in his apartment.

CHAPTER 92

On the desk in Ethan's study, the telephone produced no dial tone, and when he tried to use his cell phone, he discovered that he had no service.

Land lines might on rare occasion experience disruption after a two-day downpour. Not cell phones.

In the bedroom, when he tried the telephone on his nightstand, he heard only a dead line. No surprise.

From the nightstand drawer, he extracted a second magazine of ammunition for his pistol.

He had prepared this spare on the evening of his first day in Palazzo Rospo, ten months ago. At the time, he'd seemed to be taking an unnecessary precaution. An extended shootout requiring more than ten rounds, within these well-protected walls, had been a possibility so slim as to be beyond calculation.

Dropping the magazine in a pants pocket, Ethan hurried back into his study.

The apple of his eye.

Fric. Fric must still be on the second floor, in the library, selecting a book to get him through the night.

Okay. The thing to do was go to the library. Hustle the boy into the nearest panic room. Tuck him away safely in that comfy, armored, self-contained vault. Then chase this situation to its source, find out what the hell was happening.

He stepped out of his apartment, turned left in the west hall, and ran to the back stairs that earlier he had taken to the third floor and the white room.

Goofing, having more fun than the law allowed, proceeding at times with exaggerated stealth, in a crouch like a commando slipping through an enemy fortress, at other times strutting like Vin Diesel when he knows the script specifies that all bullets will miss him, Corky followed the north hall past the breakfast room, the butler's pantry, the kitchen.

He wished that it would have been practical to wear his yellow slicker and his droopy yellow hat. He would have enormously enjoyed seeing Truman's amazed expression when confronted by a banana-bright assassin spitting death.

In the west hall, the door to the security chief's apartment stood open.

At the sight of this, Corky at once grew more serious. With caution he approached the apartment. He stood with his back to the hallway wall, beside the open door, listening.

When he crossed the threshold, he went in low and fast, holding the Glock in two hands, sweeping left to right, right to left.

The study was deserted.

Quickly but prudently, he searched the rest of the apartment and found no sign of his quarry.

Returning to the front room, he noticed the contents of the six black boxes on the desk. Evidently, Truman was still trying to solve the riddle. Amusing.

Lines of text on the computer screen drew his attention. Truman appeared to have stepped out in the middle of reading e-mail.

Indulging the curiosity that was such a fundamental part of him and that had served him remarkably well over the years, Corky spotted YORN at the end of the e-mail. William Yorn, the groundskeeper.

He read the message from the top: FRIC IS MAKING HIMSELF A HIDEY-HOLE IN THE CONSERVATORY. . . . Much of Yorn's complaint meant nothing to Corky, but the stuff about the hidey-hole definitely interested him.

With his two targets roving beyond Corky's ken, he needed to get to another Crestron panel, and fast. One was inlaid in the bedroom wall here in the security chief's apartment, but Truman might return at any moment, while Corky was distracted in the other room.

He saw something on the floor, near the sofa. A cell phone. As if it had been not dropped but flung aside.

volving a perp who starved and tortured a victim while keeping him alive on an IV drip.

Some days you thought you had seen everything. This wasn't one of them.

Having concluded the 911 call, he darted across the street in the rain, to his department sedan. He stowed the Lockaid lock-release gun under the driver's seat.

By the time he returned to the front porch, he heard approaching sirens.

Coming through the library door, Ethan saw the creased and tattered photograph on the floor. Hannah. The same picture that had once stood on the desk in Dunny's apartment, that had been torn out of the silver frame.

The disappearance of the string of little bells from Ethan's desk suggested that Dunny had been in Palazzo Rospo. The e-mails from Devonshire, Yorn, and Hachette had supported what the missing bells suggested. As far as Ethan was concerned, this photo qualified as hard proof.

Dead, stone-solid-perfect dead, according to Dr. O'Brien at Our Lady of Angels, Dunny remained at large in the world, but with powers that defied reason and that *defined* a supernatural entity.

He had been in Palazzo Rospo.

He was here now.

Ethan wouldn't have believed in a walking dead man if he hadn't been shot point-blank in the gut, hadn't died and been resurrected, if he hadn't been trashed by a PT Cruiser and a truck, hadn't been on his feet again an instant after his second death. He himself wasn't a ghost, but after the events of the past two days, he could believe in a ghost, all right, and in lots of things to which previously he had given no credence.

Maybe Dunny wasn't a ghost, either. He might be something else for which Ethan had no name.

Whatever Dunny proved to be, he was no longer merely a man. His motives, therefore, couldn't be identified either by the process of deduction or by the intuition on which a cop relied.

Nevertheless, Ethan sensed now that his childhood friend, so long estranged, wasn't the source of the threat to Fric, that Dunny's role in these bizarre events was more benign than not. A man who had loved Hannah, who had kept her picture five years after her death, must have within him at least the potential for good and surely could not harbor the purity of evil required to harm a blameless child.

Folding the photo away into a pocket, Ethan called out, "Fric! Fric, where are you?"

When he received no answer, he hurried through the library, along the canyons of books, from Aesop and Conrad Aiken to Alexandre Dumas, from Gustave Flaubert to Victor Hugo, from Somerset Maugham to Shakespeare, all the way to Emile Zola, afraid of finding the boy dead and of not finding him at all.

No Fric.

The reading nook farthest from the library entrance included not only armchairs but also a worktable with a telephone and a computer.

Although the outgoing lines were no longer working, the in-house intercom was a function of the system separate from phone service. Only a power failure could disable it.

Ethan pressed the button labeled INTERCOM, then pressed HOUSE, and broke one of Mrs. McBee's cardinal rules by paging the boy from the third floor to the lower garage. His summons issued from the speaker in every phone in the mansion: "Fric? Where are you, Fric? Wherever you are, speak to me."

He waited. Five seconds was an excruciatingly long time. Ten equaled eternity.

"Fric? Talk to me, Fric!"

Beside the telephone, the computer switched on. Ethan hadn't touched it.

The ghost operating the computer accessed the house-control program. Instead of presenting him with the usual three columns of icons, the screen immediately revealed the floor plan of the ground level of the mansion, the eastern half.

Before him, unbidden, was the motion-detector display. A blip, signifying movement and body heat, blinked in the conservatory.

❧

Seventy-four feet in diameter, forty-eight feet from floor to ceiling, the conservatory was a jungle with windows, tall panels of leaded glass, salvaged from a palace in France that had been mostly destroyed in World War One.

Here Mr. Yorn and his men maintained and continually refreshed a collection of exotic palm trees, tulip trees, frangipanis, mimosas, many species of ferns, spaths, smithianthas, orchids, and a shitload of other plants that Fric was not able to identify. Narrow pathways of decomposed granite wound through the curbed planters.

A few steps after you entered the green maze, the illusion of tropical wilderness was complete. You could pretend to be lost in Africa, on the trail of the rare albino gorilla or in search of the lost diamond mines of King Solomon.

Fric called it Giungla Rospo, which was Italian for "Toad Jungle," and felt that it had all the cool stuff of a real tropical forest but none of the bad. No humongous insects, no snakes, no monkeys in the trees, shrieking and throwing their crap at your head.

At the center of its carefully orchestrated wildness, Giungla Rospo offered a gazebo built of bamboo and bubinga wood. There you could have dinner or get puking drunk if you were old enough, or just pretend to be Tarzan before the nuisance of Jane.

Fourteen feet in diameter, raised five feet above the floor of the conservatory, reached by eight wooden steps, the gazebo held a round table and four chairs. A secret panel in the floor, when slid aside, revealed the door to a small refrigerator stocked with Coke, beer, and bottles of natural

He didn't like the shadows, either. Shadows, shadows everywhere in layered complexity, calculated for dramatic effect, unnatural and therefore double deceiving.

Nearing the center of the jungle, Ethan heard a strange sound, *thhhup,* and then again, *thhhup,* and heard greenery click-rustle-snap, but he didn't realize that he was being shot at until the bole of a palm tree took a bullet inches in front of his face, spraying him with flecks of its green tissue.

He dropped fast and flat. He rolled off the path and crawled through ferns and pittosporum, through mimulus drenched with red-purple flowers, into sheltering gloom where he was grateful for all shadows, natural and not.

The jakes arrived before the ambulance, and after Hazard briefed them and told them where to send the paramedics, he went upstairs to look after Maxwell Dalton.

The withered man, more hideously emaciated on third sight than he had appeared to be on first and second, rolled his sunken eyes and grimaced, greatly agitated, struggling to cough up barbed words from his no doubt cracked and bleeding throat.

"Easy, easy now," Hazard said. "Calm down. Everything's going to be all right now. You're safe now, Professor."

The hooked edges of the words pained Dalton as

he spat them out, but he insisted on saying, "He's . . . coming . . . back."

"Good," Hazard said, grateful to hear the ambulance siren rising in the night beyond the broken window. "We know just what to do with the sick son of a bitch when he shows up."

Greatly distressed, Dalton managed to roll his head side to side and produce an anguished mewling.

Thinking Dalton might be worried about his wife and daughter, Hazard revealed that he had just sent a pair of uniformed officers to their house not only to inform Rachel that her husband had been found alive but also to give her and Emily protection until Laputa could be located and arrested.

In a hiss-and-hack voice, Dalton said, "Coming back with," and winced in pain as his throat seized up.

"Don't stress yourself," Hazard advised. "You're pretty fragile right now."

At the end of the block, the shrieking ambulance turned the corner. The rainy night licked away and swallowed the last shrill note of the siren as the brakes barked on the blacktop in front of the house.

"Bringing back . . . a boy," Dalton said.

"A boy?" Hazard asked. "You mean Laputa?"

Dalton managed a nod.

"He told you?"

Another nod.

"Said he was bringing a boy back here tonight?"

"Yes."

As he heard the paramedics thundering up the steps, Hazard leaned closer to the withered man and said, "What boy?"

❧

Crouching among mimulus and Mauna Loa spaths and ferns, Ethan heard a second burst of fire, three or four shots, from a weapon fitted with a sound suppressor, and after half a minute of silence, a third burst.

None of these rounds seemed to come near him. The gunman must have lost track of him. Or maybe the guy had never known where Ethan was, had fired blindly through the jungle, and had come close with the first spray of bullets solely by chance.

Gunman—singular. Guy—one.

Common sense argued that an assault against this estate required teamwork, that one man couldn't jump the wall, deceive the electronic security measures, disable the guards, and breach the house. That was Bruce Willis on the big screen. That was Tom Cruise in makeup. That was Channing Manheim playing a role from the dark side. That wasn't anyone real.

If a coordinated team of kidnappers had gotten inside Palazzo Rospo, however, there would be more than one gunman squeezing off short bursts of suppressing fire. They would have chopped at Ethan with one, two, three fully automatic carbines. Uzis or worse. By now he would be down, dead, and dancing in paradise.

When silence persisted after the third brief volley, he rose from cover and eased warily through the ferns, between the palms, to the edge of the pathway.

In any jungle movie, stillness like this always signaled the wilderness-savvy characters that villainy in one form or another had stepped into the natural world, silencing cricket and crocodile alike.

Green-juice smell of crushed vegetation rising from underfoot.

Muffled voice of a heating-system fan purring in the walls.

A gnat, a midge, hovering in the air before him, hovering.

Taste of blood in his mouth, the discovery that he'd pinched tongue with teeth when he dropped to the ground, the throb just now arising in the bite.

A flutter of foliage spun him around, and he brought the pistol toward the sound.

Not foliage. Wings. Through the jungle, high above the pathway, flew a flock of brightly colored parrots, blue and red and yellow and the iridescent green of certain strange sunsets.

No birds made their home in the conservatory. Neither a flock of parrots nor a single sparrow.

Plummeting in front of Ethan but then swooping high again, the colorful birds passed without one screech or squawk, and became white doves on the rise.

This was the phantom in the steam-clouded mirror. This was the impossible set of bells in his hand outside the flower shop. This was the heavy fragrance of Broadway roses in his study when no roses had been there, the precious voice of his lost wife speaking of ladybugs in the white room. This was the hand of some supernatural force held out to him and eager to lead.

After spiraling high in a frenzied flapping, down again came the swarming doves, feathering the air, toward him, past him, with a *thrum* that both exhilarated and frightened him, that plucked notes of wonder from his heart but also struck hard the jungle-drum terror of the primitive within.

They flew. He ran. They led. He followed.

"Wait," Hazard told the paramedics as they came quickly to the bed in spite of the vile stink, as they stood wide-eyed and gaping in spite of all the horrors that they had seen day after day in the conduct of their vital work.

"Boy," Dalton croaked.

"What boy?" Hazard asked, having taken the withered man's hand once more, holding it in both of his.

"Ten," said Dalton.

"Ten boys?"

"Ten . . . years."

"A ten-year-old boy," Hazard said, failing to understand why Dalton thought Laputa meant to return here with a boy, not sure that he was correctly interpreting what the wracked man meant to tell him.

Dalton strained to speak in spite of throat pain

that threatened to convulse him: "Said . . . famous."

"Famous?"

"Said . . . famous *boy.*"

And Hazard *knew.*

In the elevator, Moloch dropped Fric, and Fric
tumbled in a loose heap on the floor, not sure what
had happened to him. No mere pepper in that
pepper spray. He could see but could not turn his
eyes with the usual quickness, could blink but only
slowly. He was able to move his arms and legs, but
as though straining against the pressure of deep
water, like a weary swimmer being pulled down by
a relentless undertow. He couldn't strike a blow in
self-defense, couldn't even fully close his hand
into a fist.

As they descended toward the garage, Moloch
grinned at Fric and brandished the little aerosol
can at him. "Short-acting semiparalytic inhalant
developed by a colleague with the help of a generous grant from the Iranian secret police. I wanted
you docile but *alert.*"

Fric heard himself breathing. Not an asthmatic
wheeze.

"That gazebo didn't appear on the architectural
plans," said Moloch. "But the moment I saw it, I
knew. I'm still in touch with the child in me, the wild
spirit that we are when we're born, and I *knew.*"

Fric didn't hear the sound of healthy breathing,

either. Clear but shallow, a faint whistle in his throat.

With scary face-twitching spasms of glee that would have caused Fric's bladder to empty in a rush if he had not such a short time ago relieved himself on the potted palm, Moloch said, "I wanted you alert to experience all the terror of being snatched out of your posh digs, knowing that your big-shot daddy can't swoop down in cape and tights or on a flying motorcycle like you once thought he could. Not all the muscled movie stars in the world, certainly not all the supermodels, not even all the beefed-up bodyguards in Bel Air can save your pampered ass."

Fric knew then that he was going to die. No chance to sneak off to Goose Crotch, Montana. No hope of someday leading a real life. But maybe at last some peace.

As the shepherd to the sheep, as the hound to the posse, as the scout to the cavalry, the doves showed Ethan the way, bird by bird, out of the conservatory, into the east hall, past the indoor pool, to the north hall and then westward toward the rotunda.

Such a sight: thirty or forty luminous-white birds flowing along the corridor, a feathered river in this canyon of sumptuous decor, as might a party of freed spirits soar toward Valhalla.

Into the entry rotunda they flew, and circled there as if caught in the whirlpool currents of a forming cyclone, until Ethan caught up with them, where-upon the many birds swarmed closer to one an-other, closer, until they knitted together in one tur-bulent entity. They flowed down from the three-story heights to the floor, changing color as they came, changing form again, becoming that friend of childhood who had lost his way.

Standing but ten feet from Ethan, the apparition that was Dunny Whistler said, "If you die this time, I can't bring you back. I am at the limits of my au-thority. He's taking Fric down to the garage. He's almost out of here."

Before Ethan could speak, dead Dunny was not Dunny anymore, but doves again, exploding in a glory of radiant wings, knifing straight at the enor-mous Christmas tree. They fled not into the nee-dled boughs but into the silvery and scarlet shine of the ornaments, no longer birds but only the shadows of birds, darkening across the glimmer-ing curves, then gone.

By a fistful of his shirt, semiparalytic Fric was dragged across the garage floor, facing away from his captor, watching the elevator alcove recede into the distance.

Moloch had snared car keys from the pegboard, where every set hung under a label citing the make, model, and year. The kidnapper seemed to know his way around as well as if he had lived in Palazzo Rospo.

Also receding from Fric was his medicinal inhaler, his precious asthma drug. The device had come unclipped from his belt. He tried to grab the inhaler when first it rattled loose, but his limbs were jelly.

Moloch might be insane or just evil. But Fric couldn't imagine what the Iranian secret police had against him.

In his ten years, he had known fear. In fact it had been nearly a constant. The fear familiar to him for so long, however, had been of the quiet variety, a nagging rather than threatening force, more like the persistent pecking of small birds than like the rending ferocity of a pterodactyl. Worry that his father's absences would grow ever longer, until they stretched into years, like those of his mother. A gnawing concern that he would forever be the geek that he was now, that he would never figure out what to do with life or with himself, that he would grow old and still be more than anything else the son of Channing Manheim, the Face. During every second of the journey between the conservatory and the garage, however, a great dark terror thrashed its leathery wings in the cage of his heart, swooped through the hollows of body and soul, shivered flesh and blood, and bone.

For his getaway, Moloch could have chosen from the collection any of the older classic cars worth hundreds of thousands of dollars. Instead he selected a more recent model, a favorite of Fric's: the cherry-red 1951 Buick Super 8, with chromed fins and fender wings.

He heaved Fric into the front passenger's seat,

slammed the door, hurried around the Buick, and got in behind the wheel. The engine started at once because every vehicle in the collection was maintained in perfect condition.

Guardian angels apparently could not be relied on in a pinch. Mysterious Caller had never seemed much like an angel, anyway: too spooky looking, his style too ominous, and such sorrow in his eyes.

As Moloch backed out of the parking stall, Fric wondered what had happened to Mr. Truman. He must be dead. When he focused on the thought of Mr. Truman dead, Fric discovered that the semi-paralytic inhalant didn't prevent him from crying.

Entering the upper garage by way of the stairs, Ethan heard the growl of an engine, smelled exhaust fumes.

The Buick was poised for flight at the foot of the exit ramp, where the garage door had almost finished rolling up and out of its way.

A man behind the wheel. One man. No accomplices in the backseat. No gunmen elsewhere in the garage.

The passenger's side of the car was nearest to Ethan as he ran toward it. Against the side window at the front, Fric's tousled head was tipped against the glass. He couldn't see the boy's face, but the head seemed to loll, as if Fric were unconscious.

Ethan almost reached the Buick before the rising door provided clearance. Then the car jumped toward the door and the ramp beyond at such acceleration that a man on foot couldn't catch it.

Stepping from a run into an isosceles shooting stance, squarely facing the target, right leg quartering back for balance, left knee flexed, both hands on the weapon, Ethan risked three quick shots, aiming low in fear of hitting Fric with a ricochet, targeting the rear tire on the passenger's side.

The fender skirt shielded almost half the wheel, giving him a narrow window in which to place the shot. One round pocked metal, one went wide, but one popped the tire.

The car sagged back and to one side. Kept going. Still too fast to be chased down. The *slap-slap-slap* of loose rubber marked its ascent along the lower half of the ramp.

The quartzite paving provided good traction, dry or wet, but the Buick's rear tires spun briefly, churning up a spray of dirty water and blue smoke, maybe because of the cant to the right.

As Ethan closed the gap once more, the Buick found its footing, lunged forward, upward. Spin-shredded rubber flapped louder than before, and the exposed wheel rim bit at the quartzite with a sound like a stone saw cutting cobbles.

When Ethan reached the top of the ramp, he saw the car following the driveway along the side of the mansion. Heading toward the front. Forty feet away. Making speed in spite of being crippled. Nothing to stop it from grinding all the way to the distant gate, which opened automatically from the inside when sensors buried in the pavement of the exit lane detected traffic.

Ethan gave chase. He couldn't catch the car. No hope.

He pursued anyway because he could do nothing else. Too late to go back, get keys, another car. By the time he was driving out of the garage, the Buick would have cleared the main gate and vanished. He ran, ran, splashing through cold puddles, ran, pumping his arms and trying to compensate for the weight, the bulk, of the pistol in his right hand, because running well was a matter of balance, ran, ran, because if Fric were killed, then Ethan Truman would be a dead man, too, dead inside, and would spend the rest of his time in this world looking for a grave, a walking corpse as sure as Dunny Whistler ever had been.

splashed into shapeless sprays, flowed away, were gone.

A full turn didn't drain the Buick's momentum, and they spun another ninety degrees, colliding with one of the trees that lined the driveway, thereby brought to an abrupt stop as the passenger's door sprung open and the windshield dissolved.

Laughing in the face of chaos, Corky reached down past the steering wheel, feeling for the Glock on the floor between his feet. He touched the handgrip of the gun, grasped it, brought the weapon up to shoot the boy.

The driver's door opened with a shrill protest of buckled metal, and Ethan Truman reached in for Corky, so instead of shooting the boy, he shot the man.

Arriving at the Buick in the moment that it crashed to a stop, Ethan slammed his pistol down on the roof and left it there because he didn't want to shoot into the car, not with Fric in the line of fire. Heedless of the risk, he yanked open the tweaked door and reached inside. The driver thrust a handgun at him—*thhhup*—and he not only saw the muzzle flash but also *smelled* it.

He felt no consequence in the instant of the shot, too focused on the struggle for the gun to be able to assess whether he'd been hit or not. He swore he felt the second shot part his hair, and then he had the pistol.

At once flinging the weapon away into the dark, he would have dragged the driver out of the Buick, but the bastard came without coaxing, barreling into him. They both went down harder than gravity required, Ethan on the bottom, rapping the back of his head against the quartzite cobblestones.

On impact, when the door flew open, Fric found himself sliding off the seat, out of the Buick, onto the puddled pavement. Flat on his back, the worst of all positions when he couldn't breathe.

Rain falling in his eyes blurred his vision, but he worried less about the blurring than about a crimson tint that seeped across the night, making rubies of the raindrops.

His thoughts clouded to match his vision—too little oxygen to the brain—but he was clearheaded enough to realize that the effect of the crap he had inhaled might be wearing off. He tried to move, and could, but not with any grace or control, rather like a hooked fish flopping on a shore.

On his side, he had more ability to clench and relax his neck, chest, and abdominal muscles, which he must do in order to force out the stale air condensed like syrup in his lungs. More ability, but not enough. If paper were a sound, it would not be as thin as his wheeze had become, nor a human hair as thin, nor a film of dust.

He needed to sit up. He couldn't.

He needed his inhaler. Gone.

Although the world was crimson to him, he knew

that he must look blue to the world, for this was one of the really bad attacks, worse than any he'd known before, an occasion for the emergency room, for the doctors and nurses with their talk of Manheim movies.

No breath. No breath. Thirty-five thousand dollars to refurnish his rooms, but no breath.

Funny thoughts crowded his head. Not funny ha-ha. Funny scary. Red thoughts. So dark red at the edges that the red was really black.

Currently not in a mood to teach the deconstructionist theory of literature, but in a mood to deconstruct anything in his way, with a wolfish fury howling in his skull, Corky *needed* to gouge eyes, to chew at the face below him, to tear with teeth, to claw and rip.

Cracking his jaws for the first bite, he realized that Truman had been stunned when he rapped his head on the pavement, that his resistance was not as strong as expected. In his savage frenzy, Corky dimly realized, too, that if he succumbed to the animalistic urge to finish this by tooth and nail, something would snap in him, some last organizing restraint, and he would be found hours hence, still bent to the savaged body of his victim, his snout and jowls in the fleshy ruins, searching for grisly morsels as a pig for truffles.

As Robin Goodfellow, who had not actually received training to be a lethal weapon but who had read his share of spy novels, he knew that a sharp blow with the heel of his hand to an enemy's nose would shatter nasal bones and drive the wicked splinters into the brain, bringing instant death, and so he did this, and cried with delight as Truman's blood answered the blow with a bright spray.

He rolled off the useless cop, rose, turned toward the Buick, and went looking for the boy. Corky leaned down at the driver's door to peer inside, but Fric had apparently gotten out through the sprung door on the passenger's side.

The semiparalytic inhalant would not yet have worn off entirely. The brat couldn't have crawled far.

Straightening up from the driver's door, Corky saw a handgun on the roof of the Buick, in front of his eyes.

Rain gleaming like diamond inlays on the checking of the grip.

Truman's weapon.

Find the boy. Shoot him but only in the leg. To keep him from going anywhere. Then hustle back to the garage for another set of keys, another getaway car.

Corky could still salvage the plan, for he was the son of chaos as surely as Fric was the son of the biggest movie star in the world, and chaos would not fail its child as the actor had failed his.

He rounded the car and saw the boy on his side, kicking at the sodden ground, hitching forward like a crippled crab.

Corky went after him.

Although Fric proceeded by the strangest form

ached and the taut chain, having scored the fingers of his right hand, finally broke like cheap
string.

The teeth stopped snapping. The eyes fixed on
something beyond Ethan, beyond the night itself.
Limp fingers released twisted locks of hair.

Gasping, rising from the dead man, Ethan looked
at the chain in his hand. A locket. A glass sphere in
which floated a watchful eye.

Moloch seemed to be dead, but he had seemed
to be dead before. Fric watched the fight from an
art-film angle and through a crimson haze, wondering why the director of photography had chosen to shoot an action scene with a distorting lens
and a red filter.

All this he wondered and worried about not with
full attention but dreamily, as if he were asleep and
having two nightmares at the same time, one involving two men in mortal combat and the other
about suffocation. He was back in the old suffacatorium, wheezing like a geezer of a coal miner with
black-lung disease, like in that movie Ghost Dad
had been wise to turn down, and the mother of the
original owner of Palazzo Rospo was trying to
smother him with a fur coat.

Mr. Truman lifted him and carried him to the garden bench. Mr. Truman understood that during an
attack Fric needed to be sitting up to better use his
neck, chest, and abdominal muscles to force air
out of his lungs. Mr. Truman knew the drill.

Mr. Truman propped him on the bench. Held him upright. Checked Fric's belt for the medicinal inhaler.

Mr. Truman spewed out a string of vulgar and obscene words, all of which Fric had heard before in his years among the entertainment world's elite, but he'd never heard them from Mr. Truman until now.

More red everywhere and more of it darkening to black, and so little air getting through the mink, the sable, the fox, whatever fur it might be.

Breathing through his mouth because his nose had clogged with wacked cartilage and clotting blood, Ethan didn't know if he had enough wind left to carry the boy back to the house at a run, all the way to Mrs. McBee's office where spare inhalers were stored.

A bullet had nicked his left ear, too, and though the wound was superficial, blood followed the folds of the ear, into the resonant depths, half deafening him but also oozing down his eustachian tube and into his throat, causing him to cough in fits.

After a hesitation, realizing that Fric was experiencing worse than an asthma attack, that this was something life-threatening, he scooped the boy off the bench, into his arms, turned toward the house—and confronted Dunny.

"Sit down with him," Dunny said.

"Get out of my way, for God's sake!"

"It'll be all right. Just sit down, Ethan."

"He's bad, I've never seen him this bad." Ethan heard in the hoarseness of his voice an emotion deeper and better than fear and anger: the raw and wrenching love for another human being that he'd not been sure he still had the capacity to feel. "There's no strength in him to fight this time, he's so weak."

"That's the paralytic spray, but the effect is wearing off."

"Spray? What're you talking about?"

With one hand and with a gentle force greater than mere mortal strength, Dunny Whistler pressed Ethan backward with the boy in his arms, and guided him down onto the wet garden bench.

Standing over them, a pale and somewhat haggard man in a fine suit, Dunny appeared to be nothing special, yet he walked through mirrors, transformed himself into parrots that flew themselves into doves, vanished into the ornaments of a Christmas tree.

Ethan realized that his old friend's suit remained dry in the rain, as did Dunny himself. The drizzle appeared to strike him but with no effect. No matter how intently Ethan stared, he could not see what happened to any drop that met Dunny's suit and face, could not puzzle out the secret to the trick.

When Dunny placed one hand on Fric's head, the trapped breath exploded from the suffering boy's lungs. Fric shuddered in Ethan's arms, tipped his head back, and *breathed,* sucked cold air without inhibition, exhaled a pale plume of air with no asthmatic wheeze.

Gazing up at Dunny—coma-thinned, waxy-looking Dunny—Ethan felt no less bewilderment than when, after being killed in traffic, he had found himself alive outside the door of Forever Roses. "What? How?"

"Do you believe in angels, Ethan?"

"Angels?"

"The last night of my life," Dunny said, "as I lay dying in the coma, I received a visitation. This spirit who calls himself Typhon."

Ethan thought of Dr. O'Brien at Our Lady of Angels, earlier this same day. The DVD recording of Dunny's brain waves. The inexplicable beta waves of a conscious, alert, and agitated person spiking across the screen when Dunny had been in a deep coma.

"In the hours before my death," Dunny continued, "Typhon came to me to reveal the fate of my best friend. That's you, Ethan. In spite of the lost years between us and all the ways I went wrong, that's still you. My friend . . . and Hannah's husband. Typhon showed me when and where and how you would be murdered by Rolf Reynerd, in that black-and-white room with all the birds, and I was so afraid for you . . . and grieved for you."

At several points, the EEG had recorded a wildly spiking beta tracery that according to Dr. O'Brien represented the brain waves of a terrified individual. Subsets of beta had indicated conversation.

Dunny said, "I was made an offer . . . was given

the chance to . . . to be the guardian you needed these past two days. With the power granted to me for this short mission, I could among other things fold back time."

When a guy stands before you, saying he can turn back time, and you at once believe him, and you also accept with rapidly diminishing amazement that he remains dry in the rain, you have changed forever—and probably for the better, even though you feel as if the earth itself has been pulled out from under you, as if you have fallen into a rabbit hole deeper and stranger than Alice ever dreamed.

"I decided to let you experience your death in Reynerd's apartment, your scheduled destiny, then take you back to the moment before it happened. I figured to scare the shit out of you and give you the extra edge you were going to need to get through the rest of what was coming—and to get this boy through it."

Dunny smiled at Fric, and arched an eyebrow as though to suggest that he knew there was something the boy would want to say.

Still weak of body but once more quick of mind, Fric said to Ethan, "You're probably surprised angels can say 'shit.' I was, too. But then, you know, it's in the dictionary."

Ethan remembered a moment in the library with Fric, earlier this evening, when he had told the troubled boy that everyone liked him. Disbelieving, disconcerted, Fric in his enduring humility had been at a loss for words.

On the library Christmas tree behind Fric, the angel ornaments had turned, nodded, and danced in the absence of a draft. A strange expectation had overcome Ethan, a sense that a door of understanding might be about to open in his heart. It had not opened then, but now it had been flung wide.

Dunny sees his friend holding the boy in his lap, in his arms, and he sees the boy holding as tightly as he is able to Ethan, but he sees far more than their wonder at his supernatural presence and more than their relief to be alive. He sees a surrogate father and the son whom he will unofficially adopt, sees two lives raised from despair by the complete commitment of each to the other, sees the years ahead of them, filled with the joy that is born of selfless love but marked also by the anguishes of life that in the end only love can heal. And Dunny knows that what he has done here is the best and cleanest thing that he has ever done or, ironically, ever will.

"The PT Cruiser, the truck," Ethan wonders.

"You died a second time," Dunny says, "because destiny struggles to reassert the pattern that was meant to be. Your death in Reynerd's apartment came by your own free will, because of choices you made. In setting time back, I thwarted your self-made destiny. You don't need to fully understand. You can't. Just know that now . . . destiny won't reassert that pattern. By your choices and by your acts, you've now made another destiny for yourself."

"The bells from the ambulance," Ethan asks, "all the games with them . . . ?"

Dunny smiles at Fric. "What are the rules? How must we angels work?"

"By indirection," the boy says. "Encourage, inspire, terrify, cajole, advise. You influence events by every means that is sly, slippery, and seductive."

"See, there's a thing you now know that most other people don't," Dunny says. "More important perhaps than knowing that civet is squeezed from the anal glands of cats into perfume bottles."

The boy has a smile to make his model mother's fade from memory, and he has an inner light that shines without the help of spiritual advisers.

"Those people that . . . that rose up out of the driveway and threw themselves at the car," Ethan says with lingering bewilderment.

"Images of Moloch's victims, which I conjured out of water and sent running at his car to frighten him," Dunny explains.

"Damn, I missed that!" Fric says.

"Furthermore, we guardian angels don't pull our white robes around us and just harp-strum ourselves from here to there the way movies would have you believe. How do we travel, Fric?"

The boy starts well but falters: "You travel by mirrors, by mist, by smoke, by doorways . . ."

"Doorways in water, by stairways made of shadows, on roads of moonlight," Dunny prompts.

Fric picks up the thread of memory: "By wish and hope and simple expectation."

"Would you like one last exhibition of an angel flying in this way that angels *really* fly?"

"Cool," the boy says.

"Wait," Ethan says.

"There is no waiting," Dunny says, for now he receives the call and must answer. "I'm done here forever."

"My friend," Ethan says.

Grateful for those two words, grateful beyond expression, Dunny transforms his body by the power granted in his contract, becoming hundreds of luminous golden butterflies that rise gracefully into the rain and one by one, with flutter of wings, fold themselves into the night, away from the sight of mortal eyes.

CHAPTER 95

When Dunny materializes on the third floor of the great house, in answer to the call, Typhon steps through the double doors from Channing Manheim's private suite, into the north hall, shaking his head in amazement. "Dear boy, have you taken a tour of these rooms?"

"No, sir."

"Even I myself have not enjoyed quite such luxury. But then again, with all my traveling, I stay mostly in hotels, and even the finest of them offer no suites comparable to this."

Sirens arise in the night outside.

"Mr. Hazard Yancy," Typhon says, "has sent the cavalry a tad too late, but I'm sure they'll be welcome."

Together they walk to the main elevator, which opens as they approach.

With his usual grace, Typhon indicates that Dunny should enter ahead of him.

As the doors close behind them and they begin to descend, Typhon says, "Splendid work. Magnificent, really. I believe you achieved all you hoped and much more."

"Much more," Dunny admits, for between them he is required to speak only the truth.

Merry eyes twinkling, Typhon says, "You must acknowledge that I honored all the terms to which we agreed, and in fact I interpreted them with considerable elasticity."

"I'm deeply grateful, sir, for the opportunity you gave me."

Typhon pats Dunny's shoulder affectionately. "For a few years there, dear boy, we thought we'd lost you."

"Not even close."

"Oh, much closer than you think," Typhon assures him. "You were almost a goner. I'm so glad it worked out this way."

Typhon pats his shoulder one more time, and Dunny's body drops to the floor of the elevator, while still his spirit stands here in suit and tie, the very image of the corpse at its feet, but far less solid in appearance than the lifeless flesh.

After a moment, the body vanishes.

"Where?" Dunny wonders.

With a pleasant chuckle of delight, Typhon says, "There's going to be some shocked and confounded people in the garden room back at Our Lady of Angels. The naked cadaver they lost is suddenly found well-dressed, with folding money in its pockets."

They have reached the ground floor. The garages wait below.

With that note of sweet concern that is so characteristic of him, Typhon asks, "Dear boy, are you afraid?"

"Yes."

Afraid but not terrified. At this moment, in his immortal heart, Dunny has no room for terror.

Minutes ago, looking at Ethan and the boy on the stone bench, aware of the love between them and of the future they would share as father and son in everything but name, Dunny had been pierced by a regret sharper than any he had known before. The night that Hannah died, a sorrow flooded through him, almost swept him away, sorrow not only for her, not only at the loss of her, but sorrow for the mess he had made of his life. Sorrow had changed him but had not changed him enough, for it brought him no further than to the point of regret.

This anguish that now comes upon him on the way from ground floor to garage is not, in fact, merely a keener regret, but is instead remorse so powerful that he feels sharply bitten and torn by guilt, which is the mother of remorse, feels a terrible gnawing in the bones of his spirit. He trembles, shakes, shakes violently with the first true realization of the hideous impact that his misled life has had on others.

Faces rise in memory, the faces of men he has broken, of women he has treated with unspeakable cruelty, of children who have found their way to a life of drugs and crime and ruin along the path that he has led them, and though these are faces painfully familiar, he sees them as if for the first time because he sees in each face now, as never he had seen before, an individual with hopes and dreams and the potential for good. In his life, all these people had been but the means with which he satisfied his desires and needs, not people at all to him, but merely sources of pleasure and tools to be used.

What had seemed to him to be a fundamental transformation of the heart following the death of Hannah had been more sentimental self-pity than meaningful change. He had known sorrow, yes, and a degree of regret, but he had not known this fierce remorse and the wracking humility that comes with it.

"Dear boy, I understand what you're going through," Typhon says as they pass the upper garage. He means the terror that he believes now consumes Dunny, but for Dunny terror is the least of it.

Mere remorse is an inadequate description, as well, for this is such devastating remorse, such a grinding anguish, that he knows no word for it. As the faces plague him, faces from a life squandered, Dunny asks forgiveness of them, one by one, *begs* forgiveness with a profound humility that is also new to him, cries out to them though he is dead and cannot make amends, though many of them died before him and cannot hear how desperately he wishes he could undo the past.

The elevator has passed the lower of the two garages, and still they descend. They are not in the elevator any longer, merely in the *idea* of an elevator, and a strange one. The walls are mottled with mold, filth. The air reeks. The floor looks like . . . compacted bones.

Dunny is aware that changes are occurring in Typhon's face, that the sweet androgynous features and the merry eyes are giving way to something that better reflects the spirit within the grandfatherly form that he has heretofore assumed. Dunny is aware of this only from the corner of his eye, for he dares not look directly. Dares not.

Floor after floor they descend, though the numbers on the panel above the door run only from one to five.

"I am developing quite an appetite," Typhon informs him. "As far as I am able to recall—and I've got a fine memory—I've never been as famished as this. I'm positively ravenous."

Dunny refuses to think about what this might mean, and in fact he is beyond caring. "I have earned whatever comes," he says, as the faces from his life still haunt his memory, faces in legions.

"Soon," Typhon says.

Dunny stands in spirit bowed, looking at the floor from which his body had disappeared, ready to accept whatever suffering comes if it will mean an end to this unbearable anguish, this gnawing remorse.

"As terrible as this will be," Typhon says, "perhaps it would have been as bad for you if you had rejected my offer and chosen to wait a thousand years in purgatory before moving . . . up. You weren't ready to go directly to the light. The sweet deal I gave you has spared you from so much *tedious* waiting."

The elevator slows, stops. A *ping* signifies arrival, as if they are going nowhere more exotic than to work in an office building.

When the doors slide open, someone enters, but Dunny will not look up at this new arrival. There is room in him for terror now, but still he is not dominated by it.

At the sight of the person who has entered the elevator, Typhon curses explosively, with a rage inhuman, voice still recognizable but with none of its former humor or charm. He thrusts himself in front of Dunny and says with bitter condemnation, "We have a bargain. You sold your soul to me, boy, and I gave you more than you asked for."

By the exertion of his greater will, by the awesome power at his command, Typhon makes Dunny look at him.

This face.

Oh, this *face.* This face of ten thousand nightmares distilled. This face that the mind of no mortal ever could imagine. Had Dunny been alive, the sight of this face would have killed him, and here it withered his spirit.

"You asked to save Truman, and you did," Typhon reminds him in a voice that by the word grows more guttural and more saturated with hatred. "Guardian angel, you told him. *Dark* angel was nearer the truth. Truman is all you asked, but I gave you the brat and Yancy, too. You're like those Hollywood pooh-bahs in that hotel bar, like the politician and her handlers that I snared in San Francisco. You all think you're clever enough to slip out of the deals you make with me when the time comes to fulfill the terms, but all pay in the end. *Bargains are not broken here!*"

"Leave," says the new arrival.

Dunny has chosen not to look at this person. If there are worse sights than what Typhon has here become—and surely there will be an infinite progression of far worse sights—he will not look at them by choice but only as he is forced to look, as Typhon forced him.

More insistently this time: *"Leave."*

Typhon steps out of the elevator, and as Dunny starts to follow him, going to the fate that he has earned and accepted, the doors slide shut, barring his exit, and he is alone with the new arrival.

The elevator begins to move once more, and Dunny trembles at the realization that there may be even deeper realms than the abyss into which Typhon has gone.

"I understand what you're going through," the new arrival says, echoing the statement Typhon had made earlier as they had descended out of Palazzo Rospo to places stranger still.

When she'd spoken the single word, *leave,* he had not recognized her voice. Now he does. He knows this must be a trick, a torment, and he will not look up.

She says, "You're right that the word *remorse*

can't describe the anguish that's come over you, that tears so painfully at your spirit. Neither can *sorrow* or *regret* or *grief*. But you're wrong to think you don't know the word, Dunny. You learned it once, and you still know it, although until now it's been an emotion beyond your experience."

He loves that voice so much that he can't forever avert his gaze from she who speaks with it. Steeling himself for the discovery that the gentle voice issues from a face as hideous as Typhon's, he raises his eyes and finds that Hannah looks as beautiful as she did in life.

This surprise is followed by an astonishment: He has misjudged the motion of the elevator. They are not going down to a darkness even deeper than the darkness visible. They are ascending.

The walls are no longer encrusted with mold and filth. The air no longer reeks.

With wonder, not yet daring to hope, Dunny says, "How can this be?"

"Words are the world, Dunny. They have meaning, and by virtue of the fact that they have meaning, they have power. When you open your heart to sorrow," Hannah says, "when after sorrow you learn regret, and when after regret you achieve remorse, then beyond remorse lies contrition, which is the word that describes your anguish now. This is a word of awesome power, Dunny. With this word sincerely in your heart, no hour is too late, no darkness eternal, no stupid bargain binding on a man as changed as you."

She smiles. Her smile is radiant.

The Face.

Her face is lovely, but within it, he sees another Face, as within Typhon had been another, though this visage is not poured from a distillery of nightmares. Impossibly, this Face—*the* Face—within her face is yet more beautiful than hers, the source of her radiance, so profoundly beautiful that he would be stunned breathless if he were not a spirit who had given up breathing when his body had been shorn from him.

The Face of infinite and beautiful complexity is also the Face of a mercy that—even now, in his ascendant state—he can't fully comprehend but for which he is inexpressibly grateful.

And yet another amazement: He realizes from Hannah's expression that she recognizes within his countenance the same shining awesome Face that he sees within hers, that in her eyes, he is as radiant as she to him.

"Life is a long road, Dunny, even when it's cut short. A long road and often hard. But that's behind you." She grinned. "Get ready for the next and better ride. Man, you ain't seen nothin' yet."

Ping!

CHAPTER 96

Ethan and Fric stood side by side at a window in the second-floor drawing room, which was known as the green room for reasons obvious to all but the color-blind.

Ming du Lac believed that no great house of this size could be a place of spiritual harmony without one room furnished and decorated entirely in shades of green. Their feng-shui consultant agreed with this green decree, perhaps because his own philosophy included such a notion, but more likely because he knew better than to cross Ming.

All the shades of green that had been applied herein to walls, upholstery, carpet, and wood finishes were seen by Ming in dreams. You had to wonder what he'd been eating before bed.

Mrs. McBee called this room "the horrid moss pit," though not within Ming's hearing.

Beyond the window, the sprawling estate presented better shades of green, and above it all hung a glorious blue sky rinsed clean of even the memory of rain.

From where they stood, they could see the front gate, and the mob of media in the public street beyond. Sunlight flared off cars, news vans, and larger network-television trucks with satellite-uplink dishes on their roofs.

"Gonna be a circus," Fric said.

"Gonna be a carnival," Ethan agreed.

"Gonna be a freak show."

"Gonna be a zoo."

"Gonna be Halloween on Christmas Eve," Fric said, "if you look at how they'll use us on the TV news."

"Then don't look," Ethan suggested. "To hell with the TV news. Anyway, it'll all blow over soon enough."

"Fat chance," said Fric. "It'll go on for weeks, big story about the little prince of Hollywood and the nut case who almost got me."

"So you see yourself as the little prince of Hollywood?"

Fric grimaced with disgust. "That's what *they'll* call me. I can hear it now. I won't be able to go out in public until I'm fifty, and even then they'll pinch my cheeks and tell me how *worried* they were about me."

"I don't know," Ethan said. "I think you're overestimating how interesting you are to the general population."

Fric dared to look hopeful. "You think so?"

"Yeah. I mean, you aren't one of those Holly-

wood kids who wants to go into the family business."

"I'd rather eat worms."

"You don't take bit parts in your dad's movies.
You don't sing or dance. You don't do imitations,
do you?"

"No."

"Do you juggle or keep a dozen plates spinning
at the top of a dozen bamboo poles all at the same
time?"

"Not all at the same time, no," said Fric.

"Magic tricks?"

"No."

"Ventriloquism?"

"Not me."

"See, I'm bored with you already. You know what
I think's got them all excited about this story, that's
really the focus of it?"

"What?" Fric asked.

"The blimp."

"The blimp," Fric agreed, "is totally cool."

"No offense, but a kid your age, with your lack of
experience . . . I'm sorry, but you just can't com-
pete with a blimp in Bel Air."

Out at the north end of the property, the gates
began to open.

"Here comes the gang," Fric said as the first
black limousine glided in from the street. "You
think he'll stop out there and give the reporters
face time?"

"I've asked him not to," Ethan said. "We don't
have anywhere near enough manpower to police a

media mob like that, and they don't like being po-
liced."

"He'll stop," Fric predicted. "Bet you a million
bucks to a pile of cow flop. What limousine is he
in?"

"Number five out of seven."

The second limo cruised through the gate.

"He'll have a new girlfriend," Fric worried.

"You'll do fine with her."

"Maybe."

"You've got the perfect ice breaker."

"What's that?"

"The blimp."

Fric brightened. "Yeah."

The third limousine appeared.

"Just remember what we agreed. We're not going to tell anyone about . . . the stranger parts of it
all."

"I sure won't," Fric said. "I don't want to be
booby-hatched."

The fourth limousine entered, but the fifth
paused outside the gates. From this distance,
without binoculars, Ethan could not see that
Channing Manheim had in fact gotten out of the
limo to meet the cameras and charm the press,
but he was nevertheless morally certain that he
owed Fric a pile of cow flop.

"Doesn't seem like Christmas Eve," Fric said quietly.

"It will," Ethan promised.

Christmas morning, in his study, Ethan listened yet again to all fifty-six messages that had been recorded on Line 24.

Before Manheim and Ming du Lac had returned to Palazzo Rospo, Ethan had loaded the enhanced recordings onto a CD. Then he erased them from the computer in the white room and removed them from the phone logs. Only he would ever know that they had been received.

These messages were his, and his alone, one heart speaking to another across eternity.

In some of them, Hannah solved every element of the maniac's riddles. In others, she only repeated Ethan's name, sometimes with yearning, sometimes with gentle affection.

He played Call 31 more times than he could remember. In that one, she reminded him that she loved him, and when he listened to her, five years seemed no time at all, and even cancer had no power, or the grave.

He was opening a box of cookies left by Mrs. McBee when his phone rang.

Fric always set the alarm clock early on Christmas morning, not because he was eager to discover what had been left under the tree for him but because he wanted to open the stupid gifts and be done with it.

He *knew* what the fancy wrappings concealed: everything on the list that he had been required to give to Mrs. McBee on the fifth of December. He had never been denied the things for which he'd asked, and each time that he asked for less, he had been required to amend his list until it was at least as long as the list from the previous year. Downstairs, under the drawing-room tree would be a shitload of fabulous stuff, and no surprises.

On this Christmas morning, however, he woke to a sight that he had never seen before. While he had slept, someone had crept into his room and left a gift on his nightstand, beside the clock.

A small box wrapped in white with a white bow.

The card was bigger than the box. No one had signed it, but the sender had written these words: *This be magic. If there be no blink, you will have great adventures. If there be no tear shed, you will have a long and happy life. If there be no sleeping of it, you will grow up to be the man you want to be.*

This was such an amazing note, so mysterious and so rich in possibilities, that Fric read it several times, puzzling over its meaning.

He hesitated to open the white box, for he did not believe that anything it contained could equal the promise of this note.

When at last he peeled away the glossy paper, lifted the lid, and folded aside the tissue paper, he found that—*oh!*—the contents were the equal of the note.

On a new gold chain hung a glass pendant, a sphere, and in the sphere floated an eye! He had seen nothing like this in his life and knew that he never would again. A souvenir from the lost continent of Atlantis, perhaps, the jewelry of a sorcerer, or the protective amulet worn by knights of the Round Table fighting for justice under the protection of Merlin.

If there be no blink, you will have great adventures.

No blink, no blink ever, for this eye had no lid.

If there be no tear shed, you will have a long and happy life.

No tear, no tear from now until time immemorial, for this eye could not cry.

If there be no sleeping of it, you will grow up to be the man you want to be.

No sleep, no shortest nap, for this eye was always open wide with magical meaning, and needed no rest.

Fric examined the pendant by sunlight, by lamplight, by the glow of a penlight in his otherwise dark closet.

He studied the orb under a powerful magnifying glass and then by indirection through an arrangement of mirrors.

He put it in the shirt pocket of his pajamas and knew that it was not blinded.

He held it in his closed right hand and felt its wise gaze on the pads of his cupped fingers, and knew that if he kept his heart pure and dedicated his mind to the defense of what is good, just as knights were supposed to do, then one day this eye would show him the future if he wished to see it and would guide him in the path of Camelot.

After Fric had thought of a thousand things that

he might say and had rejected nine hundred ninety-nine of them, he returned the pendant to the box and, while meeting its patch-eyed-pirate gaze, placed his phone call.

He grinned, hearing in his mind the first nine notes of the *Dragnet* theme song.

When the call was answered, Fric said, "Merry Christmas, Mr. Truman."

"Merry Christmas, Fric."

With only those words, they hung up by mutual unspoken consent, for at this moment in time, no more needed to be said.

NOTE

In Chapter 32, Mr. Typhon counsels Dunny Whistler that he should take inspiration from Saint Duncan, for whom he was named. No Saint Duncan has ever been canonized. We can only speculate on Mr. Typhon's motives for this seemingly minor deception.

—DK

ABOUT THE AUTHOR

DEAN KOONTZ, the author of many #1 *New York Times* bestsellers, lives with his wife, Gerda, and their dog, Trixie, in southern California.

Correspondence for the author should be addressed to:
  Dean Koontz
  P.O. Box 9529
  Newport Beach, California 92658